THE
SECOND
COMING

HOWARD
BOOKS

JOHN D. HEUBUSCH

THE SECOND COMING

A THRILLER

HOWARD BOOKS

New York London Toronto Sydney New Delhi

HOWARD
BOOKS

An Imprint of Simon & Schuster, Inc.
1230 Avenue of the Americas
New York, NY 10020

First Howard Books hardcover edition August 2018

HOWARD and colophon are trademarks of Simon & Schuster, Inc.

For information about special discounts for bulk purchases, please contact Simon & Schuster Special Sales at 1-866-506-1949 or business@simonandschuster.com.

The Simon & Schuster Speakers Bureau can bring authors to your live event. For more information, or to book an event, contact the Simon & Schuster Speakers Bureau at 1-866-248-3049 or visit our website at www.simonspeakers.com.

Manufactured in the United States of America

10 9 8 7 6 5 4 3 2 1

Library of Congress Cataloging-in-Publication Data
Names: Heubusch, John, author.
Title: The second coming : a thriller / by John D. Heubusch.
Description: First Howard Books hardcover edition. | New York, NY : Howard Books, 2018. | Series: The shroud series ; 2
Identifiers: LCCN 2018005859 (print) | LCCN 2018007874 (ebook) | ISBN 9781501155765 (eBook) | ISBN 9781501155727 (hardback)
Subjects: LCSH: Religious fiction. | BISAC: FICTION / Suspense. | FICTION / Religious. | GSAFD: Suspense fiction.
Classification: LCC PS3608.E928 (ebook) | LCC PS3608.E928 S43 2018 (print) | DDC 813/.6—dc23
LC record available at https://lccn.loc.gov/2018005859

ISBN 978-1-5011-5572-7
ISBN 978-1-5011-5576-5 (ebook)

To my reasons for living—
Marcella, Brock, Max, and Jordana

Then war broke out in heaven. Michael and his angels fought against the dragon, and the dragon and his angels fought back. But he was not strong enough, and they lost their place in heaven. The great dragon was hurled down—that ancient serpent called the devil, or Satan, who leads the whole world astray. He was hurled to the earth, and his angels with him.

REVELATION 12:7–9

PART 1

CHAPTER 1

Kolkata

I t was an hour after sunset when the bright orange van carrying Dr. Shakira Khan arrived in front of the India Institute of Hygiene and Public Health in downtown Kolkata.

Khan was displeased.

The travel assistant on loan from the U.S. National Institutes of Health had not counted on the ride from the airport being so choked with traffic, and as a result, Khan and her dream team of scientists flown in from across the globe had suited up too early. They had baked for half an hour inside their biohazard suits as the van inched its way down Chittaranjan Avenue in the sweltering heat of an Indian summer evening. Lumbering in front of their van for the entire trip was a decrepit sewer sump truck that billowed large black clouds of diesel exhaust into their open windows.

Khan sat completely stiff and alert in the front row, eyes moving from side to side as if scanning the scene for danger. She stood up before the van came to a halt at its destination and turned toward the anxious team assembled in their neon-yellow coveralls, arranged two by two in their seats like eggs. The mood was tense.

"Can everyone hear me clearly?" Khan asked.

Heads nodded in the dim light of dusk all the way to the back of the long van.

"Excellent." She turned to the travel assistant seated in the front of the vehicle. "What is your name?" she asked the young woman, loudly enough for even those in the back to hear.

"Jennifer," she replied, with a broad, toothy smile.

"Jennifer, you're fired," Khan said. "Out of the van now!" She pointed to another young assistant near the front whose name she did not know. "You. Congratulations. You are our new logistics co-ordinator. This won't happen again. Anyone else in this bus capable of doing their job, follow me."

The best public-health-crisis team the Global Outbreak Alert and Response Network could field—at least on such short notice—shuffled through the narrow front door of the van without a word, passing by the former travel aide, who stood in tears. Made up of experts gathered by the World Health Organization and including scientists from seven member countries hosted by the India Health Ministry, the GOARN rapid-response team had been hurriedly assembled to investigate one of the deadliest and fastest-spreading epidemics reported in years.

Leading the effort was Khan, widely acknowledged as the foremost immunologist and contagious-disease specialist in the world. A swashbuckling but brilliant scientist, she was a veteran of high-risk public health investigations involving disease outbreaks of international importance. Her work had taken her to Bangladesh, Sudan, Afghanistan, Kosovo, Ethiopia, Yemen, and beyond. Her knowledge of the field, combined with leading-edge practices she pioneered for WHO, had helped to prevent pandemics of bird flu, SARS, Ebola, and West Nile virus. Over the years, she had saved an untold number of lives and earned numerous international public-health and safety awards.

But her challenge in Kolkata was immense, and she knew it. While the morbidity rates—the percentage of the population affected—for the unnamed disease were similar in scale to those of the Ebola virus, the fatality rates for those infected were not. One-third of those stricken by a recent outbreak of Ebola in the Republic of the Congo had survived. This unidentified disease, which had slowly slithered its way like a snake through both posh and poor neighborhoods in India's seventh-largest city, had killed *every soul* infected in its path.

"Dr. Khan, we're ready for you in the theater just upstairs," the director of the institute announced as he greeted her in the lobby and grasped her hand warmly in appreciation that she'd arrived. Khan was revered in public-health circles, and her presence meant both expertise and welcome relief. "It will be a comfortable place to brief you and your team. We have tea for you as well."

"I'm not interested in a briefing, and I'm not interested in your tea," Khan said. She tugged a well-worn biohazard hood over her head and completely covered her face except for the small glass window that revealed her intense eyes. The nearly twenty scientists and assistants on her team knew the drill and followed suit, pulling on their hoods as well. "Get me to your lab, or get out of my way," Khan said flatly.

For those detailed to the project who'd gathered from around the world, a few of whom had worked with Khan before, her utter lack of social graces—indeed, her trademark rudeness—came as no surprise. Khan's team had simply joined a long line of predecessors on previous assignments who had been humiliated, humbled, degraded, demeaned, or debased in her service. Those not around to tell war stories about their treatment by Khan had either quit in fear or, more likely, been caught in her firing line before. Nicknamed "Genghis," after the bloody warlord of the twelfth century, by those who'd had the displeasure to work with her on previous assignments, Khan was insufferable to nearly every person she met. Blunt to a fault and intellectually overpowering to most, she took no particular pleasure in degrading those in her presence. She simply had no use for most people. She found them to be impediments to progress she could likely achieve more readily on her own.

She was born to a Mongolian father descended from an ancient line of itinerant cattle breeders and an illiterate Hungarian mother who'd fled life on a failing wheat farm. Her most striking feature, beyond her impossibly caustic manner, was her devastating beauty. Like the attractive delphinium that graced the slopes of her mother's homeland, she was pleasing to the eye but poisonous to the touch. Her hair was thick and jet-black. It surrounded her sun-washed face in jagged edges she trimmed herself, most often arranged to conceal her expressions or block others from her view when she wished. Her wide blue eyes, framed by nomad cheekbones common to the rangelands of Central Asia, were a stark contrast to the rustic desert tan of her face. At thirty-eight years of age, she was as exotic as she was outlandish, and every aspect of her attitude and presence seemed designed to prove it.

When Khan and her team burst into the institute's laboratory, they came upon a haphazard area filled with tired incubators, refrigerators, centrifuges, and microscopes on a half dozen tables hurriedly arranged in the center of the room.

"Who is in charge of this room?" Khan asked as she strode forward. Her voice was slightly muffled under her thick hood.

"I am," a young Indian scientist said as he approached to meet her. His tired eyes greeted Khan through his dingy blue mask. It was plain he'd gone without sleep for days. He held out his hand to shake hers but was ignored. "I'm sorry the lab looks a mess, but as you can imagine, we've been through a great deal," he said.

"It's not a lab," Khan said, "it's a disaster. But that's India for you, is it not?" She looked directly into his eyes and didn't wait for an answer. "I want to see the specimens you've collected, presuming you haven't lost or destroyed them. Are you capable of that?"

"Dr. Khan," the lab director replied, exhausted and clearly offended, "we are honored to have you here. But I don't know that insults are necessary. I'm more than happy to get you what you want without them. If I could first give you an overview—"

"What is your name, sir?" Khan said.

"I am Raj Sen. Dr. Raj Sen. I am the director of this lab." He rose onto the balls of his feet.

"You are Hindi? Sikh? Whom do you pray to when the proverbial stuff hits the fan?"

"Actually, I am Christian."

"I have single-handedly saved more people on this earth than your Jesus Christ. If I am to do that here, in this godforsaken place, I need answers—and now. Stop wasting my time and tell me where the specimens are."

Sen gave her an odd stare and backed away. "They're here," he said. He pointed toward a large glass enclosure with several shelves and two six-inch-wide holes spaced closely together. The openings, covered with neoprene seals, allowed safe access to what sat inside. On the shelves in the glass box's interior sat several dozen petri dishes, each carefully labeled with its contents.

Khan pressed her hood against the glass enclosure and reached her gloved arms through the holes for one of the several specimens inside. She pulled one close to the glass in front of her to examine it.

"You have doctors on staff who have attempted aggressive antibiotic regimens for those afflicted?" she asked.

"That's correct."

"Streptomycin, chloramphenicol, tetracycline, gentamicin, doxycycline, and the like?"

"We've tried them all."

"All patients deceased? Regardless of dosage?"

"Yes."

"Yesterday I was told the number had reached three hundred or so," Khan said.

"Almost a thousand more since then, Dr. Khan."

"Accelerating. I will want to examine several of the most recent dead myself. I want only those who've succumbed in the past twenty-four hours. I'll need you to arrange that. No briefings. No tea. Just arrange it."

"Of course."

"I see by the samples that there is not a single incidence of flea vomit discovered in any of these."

"None."

"This is not garden-variety black plague," Khan said. "What are you finding?"

Though Dr. Sen's face was hidden by his mask, Khan could see the fear in his eyes. "From the interviews we've been able to conduct in the last twenty-four hours, we're getting a clearer picture. It appears the disease . . . the disease—"

"The disease what, Dr. Sen? Spit it out."

"It appears to be running free."

Khan paused for a moment. "Airborne? Are you suggesting airborne contagion?" Even she appeared rattled.

Sen's voice began to quaver. "The evidence suggests transmission of all types. Bodily contact, blood, coughing, sneezing, fecal-oral, and, yes, airborne."

Khan slowly removed her arms from the sterile incubator. "Let me see your slides. I want to see this beast under a microscope myself," she said.

Sen carefully reached into the glass enclosure, pulled out a small steel box, and led Khan to a large microscope two tables away. He carried the box gingerly. Khan's entire entourage shuffled forward and leaned in when they reached the table. Sen delicately pulled a single glass slide from among several in the box and stooped over the instrument. He gently slid it into the microscope stage above its diaphragm and turned on the light. He leaned forward, rotated the objective lens to 100X, and adjusted the coarse-focus knob.

"Your eyes might be better than mine," Sen said. "If you'd like, I can . . ."

Khan could tell he was having difficulty getting a clear view of the slide through his worn biohazard mask. She stepped forward and nudged him slightly away with her hip. Then she leaned in and placed the glass of her own mask directly against the eyepiece of the microscope to examine what she had traveled five thousand miles to see.

"This is absurd," Khan said. "I'm unable to get a fix on this."

A trace amount of fog inside her mask from her breathing obscured the target slide. Frustrated, she tore away her biohazard hood and tossed it toward Sen, who caught it with both hands. She set her naked eye against the eyepiece. Gasps came from some in her entourage. The slide she was about to examine contained live bacteria with airborne potential.

She held up one hand in the group's direction as if to stiff-arm their concern, and with the other hand she adjusted the fine-focus knob of the microscope to her satisfaction.

"I've been exposed to more life-threatening viruses than any other living human and survived," Khan said. She stared through the lens carefully for more than a minute, not saying a word. The room was silent.

As she continued to look into the eyepiece, the cell phone in her pocket rang. Without removing her eye from its focus on the slide, she reached her arm inside her biosuit for its tiny interior pocket, pulled out her phone, and put it to her ear.

"I'm busy," Khan said. She continued to hold her eye steady on the microscopic scene that unfolded before her. "This is different . . . No. Not one I've seen before . . . Way past blood-borne . . . I'm being told it's airborne . . . You heard me . . . It's very strange . . . That's my feeling too . . . Hah! . . . I would try prayer, Mantas."

With that, she hung up, returned the phone to her pocket, and continued to stare intently at the slide below. Finally, she looked up at the sea of concerned faces in her group, which she seemed to have forgotten. Their looks were locked in apprehension; a few showed signs of dread.

"Come along, now, children," Khan said. "Let's examine the dead."

CHAPTER 2

Kolkata

As soon as Hans Meyer arrived inside the musty library of the guarded compound where the child clone was hidden, he was determined to either fire Ria Kapoor on the spot or choke her to death with his bare hands. He was so furious that he hadn't yet made up his mind which of the two she deserved.

Meyer, supreme elder of the Demanian Church, had seen incompetence in the senior ranks of his clergy before, but none that equaled the ineptitude Kapoor had displayed in Kolkata over the past two months.

"I left you in charge here for good reason, you damn wog!" Meyer yelled, his synthesized voice rising in anger with the insult. He spoke through a pad held to his throat and attached by a short cable to an electrolarynx speaker, having lost his vocal cords to throat cancer several years before. His pockmarked face was a mess, covered in the adult acne that had plagued him for many years and that became worse during times of stress. "But it's obvious from what I've been told that you've abused the special privilege afforded you."

Meyer watched as Kapoor, homely and overweight, sank farther into the recesses of the sofa from the sheer weight of the slur he'd hurled. She avoided his eyes, stared down at her hands in her lap, and began to shake.

"A thousand pardons, a thousand pardons," was all Kapoor could say as she nodded her head low with each apology. "God forgive me."

"For God's sake, Ria, forget *God*," Meyer said, his voice tinny and staccato from the speaker. "Right now, your problem is with *me*."

He yanked the padded mic from his throat, set it aside, and flipped hurriedly again through the report prepared by his staff for his interrogation of Kapoor. He tossed it onto the table and fumed. The report was clear: While Kapoor had wholeheartedly adopted Demanian beliefs during her initiation years before, the Demanian intelligence officials' investigation since her mishaps in Kolkata had revealed something new. Contrary to Demanian practice, she'd nominally remained one of India's few Catholics, apparently for outward appearances with friends and relatives with whom she'd shared the faith since birth.

Her original interview had revealed that Demanianism spoke more directly to her deep interest in the concept of resurrection than Catholicism ever had, since no faith in an afterlife was necessary. Demanianism's most fantastic scientific and spiritual precept—that mankind was destined to achieve rebirth through the miracle of human cloning for all those who adopted the faith—offered real and concrete hope to Kapoor. She could improve in the next life what had been a lonely state of affairs throughout her miserable existence in this one. She looked forward to the next, better world she was certain waited for her after the promised resurrection. Her aggressive recruitment of acolytes to the secretive sect and ten years of rapid ascent through Demanian Church hierarchy had provided evidence for Meyer and others that she could be fully trusted.

Meyer reached for a bottle of water on the table. He slowly poured the water into two glasses and offered one to Kapoor. Her hands trembled as she reached for the glass.

"You are EDN-008012," Meyer said, the pad now back at his throat. He leaned back in his chair as though to give Kapoor permission to relax. He needed to get his anger in check if he was to secure the information he sought from her.

"I am," Kapoor said. Meyer watched as she tried in vain to force a smile at the supreme elder's recognition of her special status.

"An honor, Ria. You were singularly chosen."

Kapoor continued to nod her head but said nothing. She was unmarried and childless, with no prospects of a relationship on the horizon, but God had miraculously smiled upon her. Almost three years earlier, it was her precious donated ovum, Egg #8012, that was the only one among thousands to be successfully enucleated by Dr. François Laurent, chief Demanian scientist. Laurent had perfected the process whereby stem cells could be reprogrammed and fused to form the special embryo, one that had thrived as a fetus and been given life as a human clone the year before. The secret child was the Demanian Church's—and the unknowing world's—second cloned infant and single most divine piece of property. Second in that Dr. Laurent had used Demanian resources in a previous experiment to bring his own dead son back to life. Divine in that the child's DNA was derived from a drop of blood that stemmed from a particularly rare and important historical source, the burial cloth of Jesus Christ, known as the Holy Shroud of Turin.

Meyer rose from his chair, grabbed his voice box by the handle, and moved toward the large window that faced the chaotic street scene below. Antique vending carts of every size, shape, and color were crammed side by side as far as the eye could see. Overflowing from them all was every manner of spice and garment and fresh vegetable to be found. The shouts of the proprietors hawking their wares could barely be heard above the traffic noise. The bustling location—an obscure structure in downtown Kolkata that sat among countless similar low-rise buildings on Kabiraj Row in the heart of the city—had been a perfect hiding place for the child clone, he felt.

"The child is what? Eighteen months old now?" Meyer asked as he stared at a merchant in a brightly colored madras Nehru, selling fried fish and kati rolls from a cart on the corner and arguing heatedly with another man.

"Eighteen months, eleven days," Kapoor said. She nervously took small sips from the glass in her hand.

Hidden from sight since he had been secreted from Mumbai as a newborn more than a year before, the cloned child slept quietly on the second floor directly below them. He had spent nearly every minute of his life isolated inside the ash-colored building, under the watchful eyes of Kapoor and two nurses who had faithfully served the Demanian Church for years. Knowledge of the child's presence at the compound had been limited to only a trusted few. Kapoor, instructed to supervise the center, its caregivers, and the child's well-being, was to report to Meyer at Demanian Church headquarters in Geneva once daily. Rules laid down by Laurent were to be strictly enforced. The infant was not to leave the compound; visitors were prohibited on the second floor; and any unusual activities of the child were to be recorded and transmitted in timely, coded messages according to the protocols established by Meyer, Laurent, and the elders on the sect's executive committee.

While the child, nearly flawless in features and disposition, had by all accounts developed normally, a series of unusual incidents involving Kapoor's care of him had gone unreported for weeks. When rumors of the strange events eventually leaked to Meyer and Demanian Church elders, an investigative team was sent to India to assess the damage. The stories they brought back were severely troubling. Meyer had journeyed to Kolkata to verify the incredible reports with his own eyes. And given the disastrous health crisis that had begun to swallow the nervous city, he was also intent on making preparations to move the boy. The child required a safer hiding place in a different country altogether, a place where Meyer could keep him under his own watch.

Meyer turned away from the loud and colorful distractions of the street scene below and stared at Kapoor.

"Tell me about your complaint, this supposed 'mother's right of instinct,'" he said. The psychological workup on Kapoor was succinct. Meyer knew she'd fallen into the trap of treating the child as though he were her own. He eyed Kapoor as she slowly summoned the strength to respond.

"He was born of my egg. *My* egg," Kapoor said flatly, as though she had rehearsed the explanation.

"An *empty* egg, Ria," Meyer said. "Enucleated. You understand that, with the nucleus removed, there is not a trace of your genetic code in the boy?"

"Yes, but I—"

"Nor were you the surrogate mother who actually carried the child to term," Meyer said.

"Yes, but where is *she* now?" Kapoor asked. A quiet disdain was evident in her voice.

"I would give a fortune to know," Meyer said. He balled his fingers into a fist.

His people had scoured the world to find Domenika Jozef, the surrogate mother of the child clone. She'd been daringly rescued from the Demanian compound in Mumbai by her lover, Jon Bondurant, following the child's birth. They both knew too much about Meyer's cloned boy, and Meyer was desperate to hunt them down before they talked.

"Forget the mother. When did they start?" Meyer said.

"When did what start?" Kapoor asked.

"These incidents. The reason I'm here," Meyer said with all the patience he could muster. He returned to his chair and stared directly across at Kapoor.

"In my experience," Kapoor said, "children should take their nap alone. But I—but I—"

"But you what?"

"I guess I was wrong," Kapoor said as she set her glass down on the table and clasped her hands together. "At least with this child."

"Tell me exactly what happened," Meyer said.

"Our vigilance over the boy since he arrived has been constant, including his hours of sleep. We recorded every minute of activity in our logs, as you requested," Kapoor said. "However, a few months ago, I began to feel that this constant monitoring of my—forgive me—*the* child, particularly while he slept, was unnecessary. It was plainly intrusive. And it has been a terrible burden on the nurses who must spend long shifts watching him at cribside while he simply sleeps. I thought it a waste of time."

"Not entirely unreasonable," Meyer said, coaxing her forward. "Then what?"

"Within about a week of being left to nap on his own, and absent our monitoring, certain, well, certain things began to happen," Kapoor said. "We were not aware of them at first, but then they were brought to our attention from the outside."

"Outside? What do you mean?" Meyer asked.

"Each morning, an assortment of birds, mostly crows, often a half dozen or more, could be found lying dead and crushed on the sidewalk outside the child's nursery window," Kapoor said. "Mr. Murali, the building supervisor, became very upset. He told us tales of watching these poor birds fly at full speed into the window as though they were intent on breaking the glass. Then, well, there were the dogs."

"What dogs?"

"Stray dogs. They roam the city in packs like wolves," she said. "Many come. They hold vigil each night on the street below the nursery window, howling and pacing. Mr. Murali is forced to chase them away quite often."

"Birds and dogs? That's it?" Meyer asked. He had been told that she knew more but had refused to discuss it with anyone.

Kapoor hesitated. "The child's naps during the day, while alone, caused a larger problem," she said.

"What kind of problem?"

"Several people, well, many passersby—and I know this is difficult to believe—reported spotting the boy . . . levitating inside his crib. Floating above his mattress," Kapoor said. She looked up at Meyer and locked her eyes with his for the first time.

Meyer leaned forward in his chair. He had expected to eventually hear of supernatural-like signs from the child. "Impossible," he said as casually as he could in a synthesized monotone.

"Actually, quite possible," Kapoor said. "His crib sits directly in front of the nursery window, just above street level. If he were levitating, he could be seen easily from the outside."

"That's not what I mean," Meyer said, growing exasperated. "Exactly what is it these people saw?"

"We had not made it a practice to draw the blinds, and many people apparently witnessed his levitation over the course of several days. Larger and larger groups had begun to assemble on the street before we were even made aware. They spoke of the 'flying child.' Mr. Meyer, I swear to you, I observed it once myself."

Meyer closed his eyes and cupped his hands over his face as he envisioned the commotion on the street outside the compound. He was delighted with the reported miraculous capability of the child, but Kapoor's lack of attention to secrecy and security was unforgivable.

"And then?" he asked.

"The police and a local newspaper were called to investigate. I assure you, Supreme Elder, we acted quickly," Kapoor said apologetically. "I appealed to their reason. It's a simple illusion, that's all, I said. Light from the sun that played tricks on their eyes through the glass. They had to believe me. What else could they do? Since then, we've nailed the blinds shut. We've moved the crib. The child is monitored during sleep again. We have not seen the levitation since."

Meyer shook his head. Then he picked up the report and skimmed through it until he found the spot he'd marked. "What is this I hear about the child and his relationship to the death of your nephew?" Meyer asked.

Kapoor appeared stunned that Meyer knew so much. "The nurses have spoken?" she asked.

"We have a number of details from others, not all of them clear," Meyer said. "I want to hear it from you."

Kapoor clasped her hands together again, this time as though in confession. She spoke rapidly, as if to rid her mind of the tale as quickly as possible. "I took the child to my brother's home," she said.

"You did what?" Meyer shouted.

"It was a special occasion. I—"

Meyer's face turned redder than usual. "You *what?*"

"It was a Saturday morning. He had been sheltered indoors for so long that I—"

"You are telling me you ignored the strictest rule, that the boy remain in the compound?"

"It was only a small family gathering," Kapoor said. "A party in honor of my nephew's confirmation in the Catholic faith. But it was a mistake, one I will forever regret."

"Tell me exactly what happened," Meyer said.

"When we arrived at my brother's home, we were greeted warmly," she said. "It was a surprise to many that I had care of the boy. I suppose that some were under the mistaken impression that the child was my own."

"Yes," Meyer said. He watched as Kapoor turned her gaze toward the window to avoid his eyes.

"Supreme Elder, everyone at the party who saw the child found him radiant. There were many photos and a great deal of fuss. I suppose . . ."

"You suppose what?"

"I suppose it angered my sister-in-law very much when so much attention was paid to the child. She took me aside as I held the child in my arms. She was furious. The boy had ruined her son's special day, she said. She ordered me to leave and to take the 'bastard child' with me. It was only moments after that when the accident happened."

The term for the child unsettled Meyer. He wanted to upbraid Kapoor for its use, but he was pressed for time. "The accident?"

"There were terrible screams from the backyard," Kapoor said. "It's all such a blur to me now. My brother rushed into the home with my nephew in his arms. He lay there lifeless, bleeding from his skull." Kapoor stared out the window now.

"What happened?" Meyer said.

"He dove headlong into the empty swimming pool," she said, shaking her head. "It had been drained of water in the winter several months before. His parents are certain he knew this. My nephew's friends followed behind my brother in shock. They were screaming. One of them shouted out, and then the others joined in, 'The water came! The water went! The water came! The water went!' as though an illusion in the pool had occurred to them all. I don't know what to say beyond that."

"And your nephew?"

"He died in his mother's arms before the sun could set," Kapoor said. Tears had begun to run down her cheeks.

Meyer shifted uncomfortably in his chair and sat in silence for more than a minute as he considered Kapoor's story. He took a deep breath. "Now, before I look in on the boy, I'm going to ask you about this ridiculous baptism incident, and I want you to be very specific about what occurred," Meyer said.

Kapoor took a deep breath of her own. "I realize we do not baptize until age twelve," she said. "My fear—" Kapoor stopped herself. "My fear was that the boy was vulnerable. That if it was to be ten years before his baptism, it would not be safe. What if something were to happen to the child? So I made arrangements."

Meyer kicked the coffee table in front of him so hard it toppled the large bottle of water and the half-empty glasses beside it. His speaker tumbled onto the floor. Kapoor sat half-drenched from the explosion before her.

"Arrangements?" Meyer cried out as he righted his machine.

"Yes, yes, yes," Kapoor responded as her entire body shook with fear. "I made arrangements. Arrangements with a local Catholic priest to perform the baptismal rite. Something to hold him over until the age of twelve, you see?"

Meyer reached for the toppled bottle and heaved it hard, just over Kapoor's head. It missed her by only inches. When the bottle hit the wall behind her, it shattered and littered the rug with shards of glass. He had tried to retain his composure, but hearing the story directly from Kapoor, whom he had once trusted implicitly, was just too much.

Kapoor stared down at her lap again and pressed forward with her story as though to quickly bury it behind her. "I met the priest with the child along the banks of the Hooghly River not far from here. It was a Sunday morning. There was a problem with the child that morning. I don't know why, but he was inconsolable. He kicked and resisted every step of the way. The farther we waded into the river toward the priest, the louder he cried. I asked the priest to perform the rites as quickly as possible so that we could return to the center unnoticed. But the baptism was difficult."

"What exactly do you mean?" Meyer asked.

"When he, the priest, reached the part of the ceremony . . . you know the part I mean. The necessary part," Kapoor said.

"The necessary part?"

"'Do you reject Satan and all his works?' he asked. 'Yes, I do. Of course, I do,' I said on behalf of the child. But by then, the boy had begun to wail," Kapoor said. "He turned blood-red. He tried to hide his head under the blanket wrapped about him. Then, as soon as the priest poured water from the river over his head, he writhed in my arms. His breathing stopped for a moment, and he turned a pale shade of blue. His eyes rolled toward the back of his head and showed only their whites. That's when I knew something had gone terribly wrong."

Meyer sat stunned. He began to feel sick to his stomach. Something *was* terribly wrong. The child's reaction to the sacrament was exactly the opposite of what he'd expected to hear. When he broke the silence, he asked only one last question. "This was on Sunday the twenty-first, about six weeks ago?"

"Yes, it was. Sunday the twenty-first," she confirmed.

Meyer turned to the back of the report. On the last page was a copy of a frayed newspaper clipping. He quietly read portions of it again. It was a story, dated the day following the extraordinary baptism Kapoor had described, about several mysterious events that had occurred in the city. A Catholic priest had been found dead in his sacristy only three blocks from the Hooghly River, horribly disfigured, cause of death unknown. Found dead in their homes that same evening were the two paramedics who had attended to the withered priest. Yet another person was found dead a day later, this one the coroner who'd reluctantly performed an autopsy on the cleric.

Meyer sat in silence across from Kapoor for five minutes and scratched away at the side of his pockmarked face. Why these incidents had happened after the simple baptism of a child he hadn't a clue. But he was certain of two things. One was an imperative, the other a mystery.

As to imperatives, it was more critical than ever that he find Bondurant and Jozef. They had to be eliminated, given all they knew, no matter the cost. No one could be privy to the power of the strange child clone until Meyer understood exactly whom his scientists had created and what powers the child might possess. The very future of his church was at stake.

As to mysteries, the stories that Kapoor related about the child clone and what they might mean were terrifying, even to Meyer. Since the ill-conceived sacrament had been performed and the unsolved events of that day had been reported, Kolkata's Hooghly River had been named by the World Health Organization as ground zero for the spread of the deadliest virus known to man.

Chapter 3

St. Michaels, Maryland

D r. Jon Bondurant stood on the top step of his shiny aluminum-clad Airstream trailer and looked down. His lean but muscular swimmer's frame and broad shoulders filled the doorway. He glanced at the delivery boy, who extended two large pizza boxes in Bondurant's direction. Bondurant lifted the white cardboard lid of the box on top. He felt no rush of heat as he opened the lid, and he looked at the teen in disappointment.

"It's cold," Bondurant said.

The delivery boy looked confused as his wide eyes darted about the welcome scene of spring that surrounded them. It was only a week before that winter had shown no sign of letting go.

"I mean the pizza," Bondurant said as he smiled. He reached into his faded jeans to pay for the pies.

"You know this place isn't even on the map, mister?" the boy said unapologetically. "I spent twenty-five minutes trying to find you."

Bondurant's trailer sat on an abandoned dirt lot at the end of a shady lane by the river outside St. Michaels. It was nestled in a grove of oaks and evergreens, and neither the driveway nor the trailer was marked by an address, for good reason. But Bondurant knew it wasn't the pizza boy's problem as to why. At forty-two and wealthy beyond his dreams from the royalties on his bestselling books and the sale of the television rights, he could afford a permanent retreat and a lifestyle filled with so much more than the lot he presently called home. He'd been rushed into retirement a couple of decades earlier than most, a retirement he could thankfully afford. It was true that living on the run and on the road had turned out to be more expensive than Bondurant had figured. He'd done the simple math. Money had never meant much to him before. But at the current burn rate, the millions in his investment portfolio combined with the royalty payments to come could support him and his little family for a hundred years or more. For that he was grateful.

Bondurant warily scanned the lot around them for other signs of life under the canopy of fresh green leaves that had seemed to sprout overnight. He gave the boy two twenties to cover the pizza and a generous tip for his trouble in finding the hideaway. Then he turned and stepped back inside his cozy six-wheeled home. As much as Bondurant wanted to settle in somewhere more permanently someday, a house that could be hitched to a trailer ball and towed at a moment's notice was unfortunately a real and potentially lifesaving necessity.

"Finally," Domenika said. She angled gracefully from the tiny kitchen only a few feet away from the trailer entry and reached for the pizzas they'd anticipated for more than an hour. "I'm famished."

She pressed a warm kiss on Bondurant's lips and pulled him in close after placing the boxes on the counter. Her green eyes, set in the most angelic face Bondurant had ever seen, captivated him as much as they had the day they'd been thrown together in Italy a few years before. Bondurant playfully reached with his free hand for her long auburn ponytail and pulled it gently downward. The tug on her hair forced her chin up so that her lips interlocked perfectly with his own. He kissed her with considerably more warmth than the occasion deserved.

"Must you?" Father Parenti shouted from the little wooden booth, a small seating area beyond the kitchen. He spied the newlyweds in their warm embrace. "Get a room. Yes, that's what they say. Get a room!" he protested as he set down the television remote.

Domenika smiled but turned toward the little priest to scold him. "Get a room? This *is* our room," she said. She looked out the trailer window and pointed to the miniature mobile home parked just outside that served as Parenti's own modest home. It sat like a shiny, misshapen drop of dew on the grass, hidden a few yards behind Bondurant's larger rig. Inside one of its tiny rectangular windows, Domenika could see Parenti's miniature dog and sidekick, Aldo, mesmerized in front of small TV. "I haven't seen you in your own room all day," Domenika said.

"I didn't want to miss the pizza," Parenti said. Even at sixty-five years old and balding, he was still strong and spry. He leaped up from the booth and quickly ensconced himself on one side of the small wooden table that served as the Bondurants' dining room. He was only five feet tall—even after the miraculous healing of his severely deformed hunchback a few years earlier—and Parenti's feet dangled from the bench where he sat, the floor beneath him just inches out of reach. Bondurant watched as the priest's eyes grew wide in anticipation when Domenika gently set the pizza boxes before him.

Parenti quickly reached for a large slice where a school of anchovies seemed to swim atop a sea of red tomato sauce. Anchovies were his favorite, to be sure, but he paused to examine the slice warily before he took his first bite.

"Cold. Cold again," Parenti muttered as he set the slice down disappointedly and looked up at Bondurant. "Just like this godforsaken place."

Bondurant reached inside the small refrigerator for three bottles of beer and settled into the worn bench across the table from the little priest.

"Don't start in on me again about the weather here," Bondurant warned. It was early afternoon on Easter Sunday, a day that had settled on warm. His tan and chiseled handsome face glowed in the light from the sun. "I've found most hiding places by their nature tend to be cold, but you get used to them."

"I still say if Meyer was really after us, he'd have found us by now," Parenti said. He took his first bite of pizza and started to chew quickly. Bondurant knew the little priest well enough to know a weightier conversation was on the way. "I think it's something else you're hiding from," Parenti said.

Domenika slid onto the bench and sat beside Bondurant. Bondurant watched as she shook her head pointedly at Parenti. It meant she wanted to steer the priest away from the conversational collision he was headed toward, one he knew she wanted to avoid.

"Go ahead, say it, Father," Bondurant said. He raised his bottle of beer in a toast and then brought it to his mouth. He gulped more than half of it down before he looked at Parenti again.

Bondurant watched as Parenti reached for his own beer. The priest pressed his back against the wall behind him as if to strengthen his resolve for the argument to come. He knew the difficult issue was about to be as squarely on the table as the pizza before them.

"The truth!" Parenti said. "The truth. About the Shroud of Turin! The fact that it's truly real, and that you *know* it is."

"Father Parenti," Bondurant said, "how many times—"

"It is the burial cloth of Jesus Christ himself," Parenti said quickly. He'd already finished his first slice. "Your own investigation proved it. You know it. I know it. Domenika knows it. The Church knows it."

"I've said it's an authentic burial cloth from the *time* of Jesus Christ. I didn't say it was—"

The little priest could not help but cut Bondurant off again. "You have the clear evidence, and now the world deserves to hear it from you. But you refuse to budge."

"I—"

"You refuse to tell them the truth. It's . . . it's—"

"It's what?" Bondurant demanded. He'd developed a sense of patience for the feisty little priest over the years but was wary of being interrupted. He finished the rest of his beer in another single gulp and slowly set his bottle on the table. Then he gritted his teeth as he did every time they'd had this argument before.

"It's your damn pride, that's what it is," Parenti blurted out. "And pride's a big sin. A B-I-G one," the priest said, as if spelling it out would somehow strengthen his point. "In fact, it's a big *deadly* sin."

Bondurant tried to ignore his theatrics. He was no longer the avowed atheist he once had been, but he'd refused to accept the common trappings of man-made religions, including the concept of sin.

"You mean I should go public and admit I was wrong about the relic all along?" Bondurant said. He pushed his half-eaten piece of pizza away. They had only begun to get into his least favorite subject, and his appetite for lunch was already gone. He threw his empty beer bottle into the trash can behind him and relished the effect when it exploded against another bottle inside. It seemed to add force to his point of view. Bondurant could feel Domenika reach her arm around his shoulder to soothe him, but he playfully shrugged it off.

"Yes, that's right. People make mistakes," Parenti said. The priest squirmed his way into the corner of the kitchen's booth as far as he could go. "Dr. Bondurant, even world-famous scientists—even Galileo—made mistakes. So what if you have too?"

"Galileo was never a laughingstock, at least not outside the Church," Bondurant said. "But that's exactly what I'd be in the entire scientific community, maybe even the world."

"I think you're exaggerating, Jon," Domenika said.

"Admit that the Shroud of Turin is no fake after I've spent a lifetime proving it so? Excuse the comparison, hon, but I'll be crucified," Bondurant said. "And I'll deserve it."

"Oh, Jon, stop it," Domenika said. "The world is forgiving. Yes, you were wrong. But you were deceived. It's not your fault. You're a scientist. The truth is the truth, and you can't hide the truth from the world forever—especially from people of faith who need to know what you now know to be true."

"It's not the truth we're hiding from, Domenika, and you know it," Bondurant said, exasperated.

"I meant that—"

"I know what you meant. I'm sorry. But what exactly *is* the truth,

Domenika?" Bondurant closed his eyes in anticipation of her an-swer. He loved her deeply but knew from experience that her re-sponse would sound as if it came straight from a passage in the Bible—not, in his view, the most reliable of books.

"That you, one of the best forensic anthropologists in the world, have authenticated the Shroud," Domenika said. "And in doing so, you have proved beyond a shadow of a doubt that our savior Jesus Christ died, was buried, and rose again in fulfillment of the scrip-tures. You have given hope to—"

"The Shroud is real! I admit it! Okay?" Bondurant cried out. He banged both fists on the table hard enough to nearly split it in two. Then he quickly checked his temper, something that, with Dome-nika's help, he had only recently learned to do. "Yes, I admit it dates from the time of the purported life of Jesus Christ. But it—"

"Purported?" Domenika said, now clearly exasperated as well.

"Domenika, the Shroud of Turin is a burial cloth, stained with blood, that was once wrapped around a crucified man," Bondurant said. He'd reached a reasonable calm. "Of that there is no doubt. And Father Parenti is right. Our investigation proved it. The Shroud dates from the time of a man you know and believe to be Jesus Christ. I admit that."

Bondurant watched Domenika fix her eyes on the serene scene outside the window in what looked to be an effort to tune him out. He smiled. Marriage was among the most imperfect of institutions, Bondurant felt. They'd had this same dispute over and over since he'd rescued her from Meyer's compound in India. He knew it was not an argument he'd ever win with her, most especially on Easter Sunday afternoon.

Bondurant looked up, surprised, to see Parenti, who now towered over both of them from across the table. The priest had climbed up on his side of the bench and stood erect as a statue. His speckled head nearly touched the trailer's wood-paneled ceiling.

"You see this perfect specimen of a man standing here before you now, do you?" Parenti asked. His dog, Aldo, had left his pillowed perch next door and bounded up the steps of Bondurant's trailer, as though anxious to catch the present scene. He began to bark.

"Perfect, I don't know," Bondurant said. He'd sometimes detested the priest for his high-minded stubbornness but genuinely adored him. He picked up Aldo and began to scratch Parenti's companion behind the ears. "But I admit to seeing you standing there now."

"Well, you see before you a man who may not rise tall in stature," Parenti said. "But let there be no doubt, I was once a decrepit hunchback who now strides as straight as any other man, completely healed. You were there to witness that miraculous transformation."

"Your healing, Father, is unexplainable," Bondurant said. "I admit that as well. The cloth you brought forth, what you believe is the Veil of Veronica—"

"What I *know* is the Veil of Veronica," Parenti said.

"What you *know* is the Veil of Veronica performed a miracle right in front of my eyes, the likes of which I have never seen nor will I ever be able to explain. It has had me question everything, it seems. But your healing by that remarkable cloth has no relationship to the Shroud of Turin."

"Jon," Domenika said, "how is it that you can bring yourself to admit that miracles like Father Parenti's can happen but the miracle of Christ's resurrection is nothing but a fairy tale, when the evidence has been right there before you all along? Your own studies revealed a perfect match between the wounds of our Christ and savior and those found on the Shroud. I don't understand you."

"I've never said it was a fairy tale," Bondurant said. "I've said it's something I don't yet understand."

A long pause ensued as all three merely stared down at their pizza in silence. A warm and welcome breeze blew through the screen of the large window beside them.

"Listen to me, both of you," Bondurant said as he broke the calm. "I've thought about this a lot. There are some real problems if I come forward and tell the world what I know about the Shroud, regardless of who once lay wrapped inside it. Not the least of which is your safety," he said as he pointed at each of them.

"First, there's Meyer," Bondurant said. "If any of us raise our heads above the waterline, he'll find us. Believe me, a major event with the media to admit the truth—that my findings about the Shroud were wrong—will get worldwide attention. And that's going to spell trouble. I'll be painting a target on all of our backs the moment I come forward to reveal what I know. I'm worried about your safety. Meyer will find us, and he will kill us. We all know too much."

"You can choose a very public place," Parenti said. "A place where no one, particularly Meyer, will be able to get to you while you're in front of so many others."

"We could hire security to be there with us," Domenika said. "There are ways to protect us."

"Us? Us?" Bondurant said. He cringed. "If I step in front of the cameras and stand scientific opinion on its head by revealing that the Shroud is authentic to the time of Christ, and there's even the slightest chance Meyer or his people will be there, you will not be within a thousand miles of me. I won't risk it."

"But I—"

Bondurant cut Domenika short. "But there is the other little matter that the three of us—and Meyer—know about. The bigger can of worms."

"Yes, they still squirm, do they not?" Parenti said, as if fascinated, not frightened, by the mystery to which Bondurant had referred. Aldo, as if eager to join the conversation, jumped into Parenti's lap.

"How I found *two* different sources of blood on the Shroud, not one. How one source of that blood has been used by some crazed French geneticist—that fool François Laurent—to clone a living human being. Who will believe that?"

"You have a point," Parenti said. He massaged his balding head as if in search of the answer. "Not many will believe that."

"And who *is* he? Who is the source of the child Laurent has cloned? Any guesses? We don't know. That's the question I lose sleep over every night. How am I to possibly explain it all?"

"Well, you might have to leave *some* parts out," Parenti said. His hangdog look now replaced any previous hint of fascination.

"You think?" Bondurant asked.

Bondurant hadn't a clue about just who the child he'd had to leave behind in India during his rescue of Domenika from Meyer really was, but he'd long ago taken responsibility for his existence. Given that the secret cloning had its very roots in Bondurant's investigation into the Shroud of Turin, he'd vowed to answer the question. What he'd do if and when he found the clone-child's true identity was another issue entirely. And now disjointed news stories about a terrifying epidemic exploding in India had begun to trouble him more each day. He suspected it was more than a coincidence the child-clone had been born there.

"Look, discredit myself because I was wrong to believe the Church's most holy relic has been a fake for years? Fine. That's one thing," Bondurant said. "I could explain how I was deceived by Sehgal. And I can swallow my pride, my seventh sin." He looked straight at his friend. "But then explain to the world that Laurent helped Meyer clone a human being from blood on the Shroud? And that you," Bondurant said, nodding toward Domenika, "were tricked by Laurent into believing the cloned child of the Shroud you carried was mine?"

"It's a bit much when you think about it," Parenti said.

"But it's all true," Domenika whispered, as if to soften a blow.

Bondurant watched as tears welled up in her eyes. He felt terrible that he'd stirred memories of those incredible and difficult times.

"Yes, it is," Bondurant said. He reached for her hand when he saw the familiar pained look on Domenika's face. He knew she had relived the nightmare of her captivity by Meyer's geneticist Laurent nearly every night when he too tossed and turned in search of sleep. Laurent had cleverly induced her to believe the child she carried to term was Bondurant's and not a clone. It wasn't until her rescue that she learned the truth. Bondurant knew she'd put on a brave face, but all she'd wanted from that terrible moment of discovery was to hide with him from what had become a strange and threatening world.

Bondurant stood up from the table, frustrated with their dilemma. There was no easy way out of their predicament, and he knew it. He stood in silence for a moment and thought about their year of hiding and how it had to come to an end in order for them to live normal lives again.

He got up, reached for his handgun on the counter, and made his way to the front door. The gun was anathema to him, but for the sake of their safety, he hadn't left home without it in more than a year.

Domenika got up from the table and reached for him. "Where are you going?" she asked. Bondurant watched as she tried to dry her tears.

"For a swim," he said, unable to look into her troubled eyes. "I just have to think."

"But it's Easter Sunday, Jon," she said. "It would be so special for you to join us."

Bondurant's tolerance of religion had moved a little. He no longer criticized those who professed to be of faith. But he personally saw no real value in religious services and felt it would be hypocritical for him to attend Mass with them. He carefully wiped away the rest of Domenika's tears with his shirtsleeve and pulled her in close. They embraced again as they had done only minutes before, this time with a tinge of sadness between them.

"I think I need some time alone, Domenika. I need to clear my mind," he said.

"Come with us, Jon," Domenika said. "It will do you good."

"I'm not right with myself. I don't feel right hiding. I don't feel right not telling the truth about what I know. I don't feel right about a lot of things. And right now, I know I wouldn't feel right sitting beside you in a church."

Domenika wrapped her arms around Bondurant's neck, and his tone quickly warmed.

"You're headed to St. Parenti's, right?" he asked. A grin broke across his face.

"Of course," Domenika said. They both turned toward the little priest of that name and laughed.

Parenti had received permission to marry the two in a private ceremony at a nearby church several months before. To the local community, it was known as St. Peter's, but since Parenti had presided over their wedding there, the nickname for the little church had stuck for the three.

"We'll be careful, like always. We sit in the back," Domenika said.

Bondurant paused. He wondered if he should go along for protection as he had before, in the event that trouble might follow them there. He shook his head to lose the thought. Domenika and Parenti had made it safely to this same church on a few special occasions previously. He kissed Domenika once more. Then he turned and made his way down the narrow path that led through the deep woods to the dock on the cold river below.

Chapter 4

Queenstown, Maryland

omenika and Father Parenti barely arrived in time for the start of Mass at St. Peter's, the quaint clapboard church in Queenstown, a half-hour drive from their hideout in St. Michaels. It was a faded white wooden Victorian-style church with a crooked, timeworn steeple. It sat just off Rural Route 50, a lonely road that wound its way through verdant cornfields stitched together like thick green and yellow carpet rolling for miles all the way to the Chesapeake Bay.

The pair quietly slid unnoticed into a tattered wooden pew in the rear of the church and bowed their heads as the priest gave the welcome benediction. Parenti's ever-present companion, Aldo, remained snug and sheltered inside his jacket pocket. He peered out from his tiny perch at the sparse congregation assembled for the last Easter service of the day.

As Parenti settled in for the Mass, his thoughts began to wander like the tiny wisps of incense smoke that wafted through the church. It was a good time to take stock of how far he and his beloved friends Domenika and Bondurant had come in the past few years. He couldn't help but worry that the troubles that threw the three of them together long ago in their quest to solve the mystery of the Shroud now threatened to tear them apart.

The seemingly endless search Bondurant had undertaken to find Domenika for more than a year had taken its toll on the once bold and driven anthropologist. Parenti could tell Bondurant was exhausted. It was as evident as the new lines on his face. He'd also watched his friend reluctantly walk away from the professional life he'd built, including the successful Enlightenment Institute he'd founded several years before. Bondurant had shuttered the organization, afraid that it only invited risk for him to be there and probable trouble for his colleagues and grad students, without whom the institute could not thrive.

Parenti knew that Domenika's life had changed immeasurably as well. Once a senior adviser to the pope, tasked with minding Bondurant on his quest to study the Shroud, she had a story that was impossible to imagine. She'd lost an infant son. What greater loss might there be for a mother? Parenti wondered. The priest would often watch her sit silently in solitude overlooking the wide river beside their makeshift camp. She'd stare out at the horizon long past sunset, as though the vast distance had something to tell her.

Parenti also knew that a terrible secret had bothered Domenika for too long. It seemed a lifetime ago that Domenika had first met Bondurant and learned from obscure Vatican files that he and his younger brother had been childhood victims of sexual abuse at the hands of a priest. Neither she nor Parenti had ever shared with Bondurant a word of what they knew. Was it their business anyway?

Parenti often wondered. But every day that went by as the two fell further in love had made it more difficult for Domenika to reveal to Bondurant what she'd come to learn while getting to know him.

And, of course, there was the memo, the infamous "Jozef Memo." Parenti reasoned it was the underlying reason for her silence. It was a dossier that had come to be known by her name that she had written about Bondurant only a week after they'd met in Turin. It was replete with her analysis of why Dr. Jon Bondurant, the world's most famous critic of the Catholic Church, had likely raged against the faith his entire professional life. Her memo surmised that Bondurant's hatred toward the Church was not driven, as many had thought, by scientific reasoning and an extraordinary IQ. Rather, it was probably personal after all.

The dossier on Bondurant was written for her boss, the Holy Father, and *only* the Holy Father. But in the course of storing it on the Vatican's vast network, Domenika had accidentally made the memo available for the entire Holy See to view. Dozens of Vatican officials, from cardinals on high to librarians down low, had been made privy to her confidential psychological assessment of the man she'd despised at the time. The memo's existence was a secret kept from Bondurant, but it was widely available for a time to those in the clergy who had come to loathe the charismatic scientist and author who'd spent a lifetime debunking their faith.

Terrible secrets aside, Parenti had watched the couple find life-giving solace in each other, so much so that his friend Bondurant had amazingly embraced something he'd never imagined before: marriage. It was the ultimate commitment for the elusive, relation-less soul that Bondurant had once been. Previously an inconceivable vow for Bondurant, who had nurtured an aloof persona over the years, marriage was obviously a pledge his friend now intended to keep for life.

Parenti also found himself a restless soul. Beyond their present troubles, he wondered where his own life was headed next. While his bond to the priesthood and commitment to service to others remained, he couldn't help but daydream about starting his life all over again. He was certain he would never return to work in the Vatican Library, where he'd toiled as a cripple for years, and his eyes had been opened to the world. A miracle had saved him. He relished the thought of learning new things, meeting fascinating people, and traveling to the exotic lands that were the stuff of his dreams.

Before Parenti's thoughts could wander further, his daydream lifted like the incense above him. He realized that the first and second biblical readings of the Mass had already been said. He leaned back and squared his shoulders against the pew in anticipation of what he knew would be a reading of the traditional Easter Gospel. It was a favorite—he could recite it by heart. He watched the priest leave his seat near the altar to approach the lectern.

"The Lord be with you," the priest said to the faithful, who numbered only several dozen. His deep voice resonated through the rough-hewn wooden rafters that formed the arch of the cathedral ceiling overhead.

"And also with you," the congregation said in unison.

"A reading from the Holy Gospel according to Matthew."

"Glory to you, O Lord," came the refrain.

As the pastor looked out across the humble but festive candlelit church, he began the Gospel reading: "'Joseph took the body, wrapped it in a clean linen cloth, and placed it in his own new tomb that he had cut out of the rock. He rolled a big stone in front of the entrance to the tomb and went away. Mary Magdalene and the other Mary were sitting there opposite the tomb.'"

The pastor paused, looked about him briefly, and continued. "'The next day, the one after Preparation Day, the chief priests and the Pharisees went to Pilate. "Sir," they said, "we remember that while he was still alive that deceiver said, 'After three days I will rise again.' So give the order for the tomb to be made secure until the third day. Otherwise, his disciples may come and steal the body and tell the people that he has been raised from the dead. This last deception will be worse than the first."'"

The pastor paused again. This time, Parenti could see the celebrant had begun to scan the congregation, as though his eyes were in search of someone in particular. Strangely enough, when the pastor looked up from his text again and spotted Parenti in the very last pew in the rear, it appeared as though the priest momentarily stared only at him. Parenti was unnerved.

He watched the priest continue, his eyes on him, and without a glance toward the text before him: "'"Take a guard," Pilate answered. "Go, make the tomb as secure as you know how." So they went and made the tomb secure by putting a seal on the stone and posting the guard.'"

Suddenly, Parenti felt a cold sweat of sorts, and his head began to spin as though he might faint. He felt himself involuntarily rock from side to side. When he closed his eyes to avoid the intense gaze of the priest, his back-and-forth swaying grew severe enough that he clumsily collided with Domenika's shoulder several times. Domenika threw him an annoyed look and shifted several inches away from his side. Parenti then attempted to steady himself as he grasped the side of the pew. He strained to open his eyes, but try as he might, they felt sewn shut to the world around him.

"'After the Sabbath, at dawn on the first day of the week, Mary Magdalene and the other Mary went to look at the tomb.'"

With the pastor's mention of the tomb, Parenti's body abruptly ceased to sway, and he instantly froze in place. Frightened at his sudden paralysis, Parenti tried to cry out. He reached his hand toward Domenika's for comfort but found it impossible to move or speak. It was then that Parenti—the seventh son of a seventh son—realized for the first time ever the promised gift of the power of premonition. What had been foretold to him as a child long ago was now actually proving to be true. In a tiny church on an Easter Sunday afternoon, he had strangely become a vessel for a vision, one only *he* was meant to see.

"'There was a violent earthquake, for an angel of the Lord came down from heaven and, going to the tomb, rolled back the stone and sat on it.'"

At these words, Parenti felt as though his body were being pulled in a spiral through a dark and endless tunnel. He fell into a deep, trancelike state. Time appeared as a dimension that slowed to an unnatural crawl. He could envision the pastor's words falling to the ground in the shapes of letters that appeared like drops of bright, silver rain. Soon he felt his whole body lifted by an invisible force that propelled him toward a vision that slowly materialized before him. It began with a brilliant flash of light.

"'His appearance was like lightning, and his clothes were white as snow. The guards were so afraid of him that they shook and became like dead men.'"

Soon Parenti found himself in a full dreamlike state on the slope of a rocky hillside surrounded by a small grove of mature olive trees framed by a cloudless sky. The air and every element of life in the seeming dream froze in perfect stillness as though time had found a stopping point. Before him was a figure, a semitranslucent being from a world not his own. Its face appeared to alternate between indescribable beauty and a mask of grotesque horror.

The giant being's entire form glimmered in a light so intense that it mimicked the brightness of the sun. It held what appeared to be a sword of light, and it possessed a single bleeding wound on its brow. Three slain Roman sentries lay scattered before it, several feet from a shallow cave. Beside the cave was a large capstone swept from its entry.

As the vision further unfolded, Parenti shielded his eyes from the brightness of the light. He peered cautiously inside a grave the spirit had breached. Inside the tomb, now radiantly lit, he watched the glowing specter bend slightly over a crude shelf hewn into the rock. It had been carved for a corpse to lie on in repose. No other trace of life or death could be found within the cave save a large white linen cloth left on the shelf, suggesting a spot where a body had once been.

Parenti watched as the spirit, too late in its search and angry that it had found an empty tomb, let forth an agonizing roar that shook the ground beneath him. Before the being turned to leave the tomb, Parenti watched as it reached for the burial cloth that remained. The beast picked it up and examined it carefully from end to end. Parenti looked on as the ghoul slowly, and with seemingly prescient purpose, dabbed the cloth on its wounded brow. It let out a howl and hastily discarded the sheet, leaving it on the floor of the tomb. When the being emerged from the cave, it looked about. In an incredible turn, it transformed itself into a pleasing humanlike form. Then it strode toward a pathway that led down a hill. Parenti watched as a small crowd began to make its way up the narrow trail toward the tomb to greet the being.

"'The angel said to the women, "Do not be afraid, for I know that you are looking for Jesus, who was crucified. He is not here; he has risen, just as he said. Come and see the place where he lay."'"

The pastor raised the Bible in his hands and proclaimed to the congregation: "This is the Gospel of the Lord."

"Praise to you, Lord Jesus Christ," the congregation replied.

Parenti was dumbstruck. He opened his eyes and bolted upright in his pew, enough so that Aldo let out a tiny squeal. Terrified of what he'd seen, he sat quietly, minded only himself, and said nothing to Domenika. After the Mass had concluded, he dropped to his knees in his pew for a moment and tried to steady himself and his thoughts. His entire body shivered as if he were cold, yet around him was only incense and warm spring air.

He was certain he'd experienced for the first time in his life a frightening power, one that had been foretold. But there was no doubt in Parenti's mind just what he'd seen and what it meant. He'd been privy to a true revelation from the scriptures, not a simple dream. It was a terrible thing that not a soul would believe. He would have to tell Bondurant—and quickly. For he was certain the mystery of the child born from the Shroud had been solved.

Chapter 5

Isle of Man

Khan did not consider herself immortal. Far from it. She'd seen more death by plague by the time she was thirty years old than anyone she'd ever met. Mortality was inevitable. Even she had to admit it. But she deeply resented the prospect of death, the great equalizer. It placed her destiny on the same footing as everyone else in the world, inviting a comparison she'd prefer to avoid.

She didn't know just how she would one day perish, but from the time she was a young child raised on the wide-open green steppes of Central Asia, she lived with a strange conviction. It was a certainty as firm as the ground on which she was raised, earth that was flat as far as the eye could possibly see. And just like a wild Mongol horse approaching from a distance in her native land, she had an absolute certainty that she would see her own end coming long before it arrived. Death would be such an important event in her life that it deserved, indeed dictated, a warning. A premonition, to be exact. Khan's adherence to this belief had worn an unusual path for her in life and a way of living it day-to-day unlike anyone else. This was, of course, fine with her.

Whether it involved the simple task of waking in the morning and commuting to work each day or determining whether to leap out of an airplane in a free fall, opening her chute dangerously close to the ground, she practiced a simple routine. First, she visualized in her mind whether the experience she was about to undertake would be her last. If she could not clearly conjure up a forewarning of her demise in the act, she pressed on. "Always do what you are afraid to do," her father said. She followed his guidance without limit.

Khan had grown up an only child and a lonely child. With few souls close enough to compare or connect to on the wide and wind-swept plains of her birth, her role model and father—Ganzorig Khan—was a solitary figure himself. A stout, powerful man as strong as the horses he bred, his name meant "steel courage" and defined the essence of the man. Every task, chore, and challenge he presented to his daughter as she grew was strictly designed to ensure that she would far more than survive what life might throw her way. He wanted her to *rise*. He knew that when he died, he would likely die hard, perhaps thrown by a stallion over a cliff. He was determined to mold a woman who would thrive long after his death and win in what he knew was a man's world.

Khan's faith in this approach toward living, winning, and dying gave her clear license to test the boundaries of risk and the invis-ible edge where life sometimes met the unknown. The few who got close to her and survived with their wits and well-being intact embraced a life of reckless abandon with her or, for their own sake, quickly moved on. Her belief in this attitude toward life defined her. She put herself in harm's way as a matter of routine. But it was the world outside her career that was every bit as riveting to Khan, a life she shared with precious few.

Now, as the ocean mist began to burn off the black pavement from the late-morning sun, the hiatus of a week away from the troubles in Kolkata offered a thrill of a different kind for Khan. It was one she coveted, having practiced it for many years. A "Superbike" enthusiast, Khan hadn't missed the famous Isle of Man Tourist Trophy Race in five years. Once the most prestigious motorcycle event in the world, it was now considered the world's most dangerous race.

Beginning in the small village of Douglas on the windswept southeast coast of the island, the course was a small and winding rural road closed to the public on race day. The winning bike that wound its way around the thirty-eight-mile course reached an average speed of more than 130 miles an hour, often becoming airborne while it exceeded speeds of more than 200. Men dominated the course. Very few women qualified to challenge it, but Khan was one. She had run the race enough to memorize every single one of the two hundred bends in the road from sea level to hilltop. Almost two hundred forty riders had lost their lives in the more than one hundred years the race had been run.

Khan knew that if ever there was an event that threatened death for her, this was it. She sat alone in a lotus position before the race near its starting point, helmet in her lap, with her eyes fixed on the horizon of the sea. Not a single premonition of death was in sight before she set out on the course aboard her black-and-yellow-checkered Honda CBR 1000 RR. If she had imagined herself splayed out across the side of a stone farmhouse, having hit it head-on at 150 miles an hour, she might have readily packed it in and gone home.

But she hadn't. She was vibrantly alive and, ten minutes into her time trial, absolutely pouring it on. The world record for a female rider around the course was just over an average of 116 miles an hour. In the previous year's trials, Khan had averaged 114.

She knew the exact turn that had prevented her from capturing the course record. It was just outside the tiny town of Ramsey on the bare northeast coast of the island. Not quite a hairpin turn, it was one of the most difficult elements of the course to master. The road, which narrowed toward the apex of the turn, dove a quarter of a mile straight down toward a ravine protected by a stone wall five feet high. Beyond the wall was a farmer's field. The steepness of the decline dictated that the bike should get nothing but brake, several downshifts, and a hard lean to the right as the rider approached. Anything less would mean a velocity of more than eighty-five miles an hour, a speed far too dangerous to make the curve. The turn was the exact spot where Khan knew she had lost too much valuable time the year before. She was determined it wouldn't happen again. Her ride had gone well. She'd taken her bike and her ability to the limit and was on track to achieve a personal best.

Just before she entered the turn, every instinct in her body told her to brake hard as she flew down the hill. Her engine was in an absolute roar. It strained at nearly eight thousand rpm in second gear, close to the red danger line. She knew she needed to slow further, but her competitive nature and the absence of a premonition before she took off urged her on. Tempted to let loose on the gas and sail safely through the turn, she checked herself. Then, in one swift motion, she jerked the throttle back hard to accelerate through the next two hundred feet of the impossibly narrow corner, which looked like it yearned to reach out and grab her. When she leaned in, she dipped her bike dramatically steep to clear the last few feet of the treacherous turn. As she did, the metal foot peg of the bike dragged along the road bed in a fury of flying sparks, until it unfortunately found a hole in the pavement several inches deep.

Khan grimaced. She knew the physics. Metal foot peg attached to motorcycle inserted into hole at eighty-five miles an hour equals large flying object. In an instant, she was airborne. She did exactly what her instincts dictated. She let go of the bike's handlebar, curled into a ball with her hands gripping her knees, stayed loose, and prepared to do a body roll. Her Honda, in an unforgiving explosion of metal, plastic, rock, and debris, took out a large section of the stone wall. Khan sailed over the same unyielding rocks, missing them by six inches, and somersaulted her way forty yards deep into a farmer's field. She came to rest, still conscious, within a few feet of a Guernsey cow that feigned complete disinterest in her sudden landing.

Khan, bruised but with pride intact, slowly pushed herself off the ground with both arms, and in doing so pressed her right hand deep into a fresh pile of warm cow dung. She stared out at the broken wall and what was once her prized bike. It now lay in a thousand pieces along the road. She glanced down once more at her filthy hand.

"Crap!" was all she could think to say.

Chapter 6

St. Michaels, Maryland

Jon Bondurant dove headlong into the Miles River. As he pierced the water's surface with only a minimum of splash, every graceful movement of his muscular body was geared for speed. He hadn't swum competitively for twenty years, but given that he'd been in the water several days a week since his college days at Stanford, he'd lost very few precious seconds off his personal best. Halfway across the wide and fast-moving stream within seconds, he entered his usual and comfortable stride.

Suddenly, the water exploded around him, with sharp sounds like a woodpecker knocking on wood. The black-and-yellow helicopter gunship that hovered menacingly overhead like a giant wasp had come from out of nowhere. When he realized that he was under fire, he immediately dove beneath the surface. From then on, only ten feet of murky water concealed his form and separated life from death. As hundreds of bullets continued to trace a lethal path around him, Bondurant stayed safely submerged. He knew that the rounds pierced the water at 2,800 feet per second, certain to shatter on impact. Their fragments slowed as they penetrated the water and sank harmlessly past him to the river bottom below.

But he couldn't stay submerged forever. He knew his time was about to run out. He held his breath for more than two minutes while he swam swiftly below the surface toward the dilapidated dock he'd leaped from only seconds before. He knew his only chance was to make it to his .44 Auto Mag where he'd left it on the pier at least fifty yards away. His lungs began to burn. The faster he swam, the more oxygen he used. He knew he had about twenty strokes left before he'd be forced to the surface to breathe. He pressed forward, counted each stroke methodically, and squeezed his lungs for every ounce of air that remained.

As he made his final surge underwater toward the dock, the pilings that moored it to the river bottom came into view. When he finally emerged, hidden beneath the slats of the ancient wooden pier, Bondurant lifted his mouth barely above the waterline and gasped for air. Out of sight for the moment, he crept his way beneath the shadows of the dock toward the spot where he'd left his gun. He spied the towel it lay beneath. He knew he had five seconds, maybe less, to reach over the top of the pier, grab his semiautomatic, and fire back. Hopefully, he'd hit something fragile like a fuel line, or even the pilot. Barring that, he'd be exposed and dramatically outgunned.

Bondurant looked up and saw the helicopter firing a hail of bullets into the water forty yards from the dock where he hid. He leaped straight out of the water beside the pier, tossed aside his towel, grabbed for his gun, and, with both arms extended, fired directly at the cockpit of the helo that hovered a hundred feet above. For a moment, the gunship swerved wildly to the east and gained altitude in an attempt to avoid his fire. Then, unfazed by the handful of bullets that had passed, the aircraft turned toward him and sent a rain of fire swiftly across the river in a straight line toward the dock.

He took a last, giant gasp of air and dove headlong into the river's depth for cover again. He spun reluctantly from the dock and the inviting light that reflected off the water's surface above. Given the circumstances, he was likely going to die. He was sure of it, and he was certain the gunner relentlessly firing on him from above now knew it, too. He kicked hard with his powerful legs and dove toward the dark river bottom below, determined to spend his last few seconds of life where he could make peace with himself quietly, alone.

As he reached a depth of twenty feet, his mind raced along with a disjointed string of thoughts, some trivial, some profound, until the dim world around him began to slow to a crawl. As he thrust himself farther into the darkness toward the shadows that began to come into view on the river floor, he settled on the few things he wanted to remember as he left the world.

There was Domenika, of course. He'd kissed her good-bye only minutes before on the steps of the trailer hidden in the grove upstream. He'd known many women, but it was her and her alone that he'd loved. She was beautiful and brilliant and everything he'd ever wanted but had been too clumsy and distant to find until they'd met. Devout and his polar opposite in so many ways, she'd found a way to reach his soul and taught him to love. It was a miracle.

There was Father Parenti too. He'd dearly miss him. He was the one who had forced Bondurant to open his eyes to the mystery of life, to admit the unknown. Once a brazen scientist with an overinflated ego tough to tame, Bondurant had learned much from the tiny priest. Parenti had helped him gain a measure of humility and even a sense of compassion for others that he'd never possessed before.

There was the secret, too—his secret—the very dark one he'd locked away as a child. Bondurant had succeeded in life. He was wealthy. And as a scientist, he was world-renowned. But he'd never dealt with *it*. It was a secret terrible enough that he'd rather it die that day inside him than revisit it once more.

But of all the thoughts Bondurant had as he surged toward the river bottom below, it was the changes that churned inside him that intrigued him the most. By no stretch was he now a believer in God. Religion, the product of man-made belief, was still alien to him. But, remarkably, he now harbored doubts about his doubts. Who or what was the creator of the created? How could miracles like the kind he'd seen in Parenti actually occur? Was it really possible for life to follow death? Ironically, with death now imminent, it anguished him that the journey of self-discovery he'd only just begun would end so soon.

Bondurant reached a depth of thirty feet, and his lungs, now completely starved for air, began to spasm in pain. He felt as if his chest was on fire from within. Water began to flood into his mouth and the back of his throat as if to douse the flame. It pushed past his nostrils, intent on filling every cavity it could find. He knew his time was close. Only a few feet from the river's bottom, he looked around frantically in the silt for something, anything he might grab to anchor himself in the depth. Without such a hold, his survival instincts would send him speeding toward the surface and the deadly gunfire that waited above.

As he peered into the darkness across the river floor, a large, hazy object about fifty feet away came into view. At first, he thought his mind and eyes deceived him, driven by the panic that had overtaken his brain. It was an odd sight, clearly out of place. But as he scuttled toward it and agonizingly inhaled a mouthful of water deep into his lungs, he knew the sight was for real. It rested upside down on its cabin, with its V-shaped hull still fully intact. It was a forty-foot-long skipjack, an oyster dredger once common in the nearby Chesapeake Bay.

A fitting resting place, he thought. As he called on his last ounce of strength, he reached into the hole on the side of the hull and pulled himself into the blackness. He began to choke violently from the water that filled his lungs and rose to slam his head against anything solid he might find. He wanted to knock himself unconscious to kill the misery that rushed to overtake him. But when he bolted upward to strike a heavy beam and end the torture, he found something else instead.

Air.

From bow to stern, a pocket of oxygen about eight inches wide was trapped between the briny water inside the boat and the narrow V of the hull. In one great heave, Bondurant vomited into the open space and expunged from his lungs most of the water he'd swallowed. For a full minute, he coughed and wheezed forth every droplet he could.

It took a few more moments in the complete darkness that surrounded him for Bondurant to fully comprehend what had occurred. When he did, an enormous sense of exhilaration consumed him, so overwhelming that he began to sob. He realized then, more than at any other moment in his life, that he was alive. The air pocket he'd discovered in the pitch black was small. He craned his neck painfully to gasp the stale oxygen inside the tiny space. But he knew one thing for sure. There was plenty of air for him to stay submerged inside the sloop for a while, at least enough to outlast the fuel tanks in the helicopter that hovered above.

I'm going to make it, he thought.

Bondurant was determined to swim his way out of the river and make it to St. Parenti's as fast as he could. There he hoped to find Domenika still alive. They would make plans. They would flee once more. And now that they'd been found, there was no choice about what to do next. He knew he had to act—and soon. If he didn't, many more were going to die.

Chapter 7

Barcelona

Father Giancarlo De Santis stared at himself in the ornate full-length mirror and admired the view.

He marveled at how well the vestments of Bishop Santiago Alvarado so perfectly fit his own physique. Alvarado, on an assignment from Rome, was not expected to return until the following day. In the meantime, De Santis, a favorite of the pope yet just a priest, had been seconded to Alvarado's diocese for several days. He'd taken advantage of the present private moment and borrowed the ceremonial dress of the bishop to . . . to . . .

Strive as he might to invent a legitimate reason for donning the robes of a bishop, De Santis knew he had no other purpose in mind than to dream big. For a few unexpected minutes, the priest had the grand sacristy of the Cathedral of the Holy Cross all to himself. He intended to take full advantage of the glorious moment to look the part.

De Santis, Italian by birth, descended from a family renowned for its strong Catholic roots. His surname, De Santis, meant "holy" or "devout." Every generation before his, reaching back to the Middle Ages, bore at least one or two sons who had risen through the ranks of the Catholic Church. Numerous priests, several bishops, and even a cardinal who reigned in the eighteenth century before a scandalous defrocking had contributed to the hierarchy and history of the Church.

Naturally, De Santis had always viewed his family as having a rightful role in the Church's ruling class. He was an intellectual, well versed in catechism and lore. He knew that when Rome had come full circle, from persecution to praise of Christians in the fourth and fifth centuries, it was the Church that often provided legal authority to settle disputes in vast regions of the Holy Roman Empire where there was no rule of law. As a result, a Church official, particularly one in the more senior position of bishop, often took on the role, likeness, and accoutrements of a Roman judge.

Beneath Alvarado's extraordinary but expropriated robes, De Santis wore the typical black cassock and a clerical shirt and white collar, the uniform for all Catholic priests. What he had borrowed for the time being were the numerous ornate vestments, layer upon layer, typically worn by a bishop for special events. His outermost wear included a deep violet–colored *cappa magna*—great cape—that flowed behind him. He admired the long train of the robe as he sashayed in front of the looking glass. There was also a stole, a sash that extended from the back of his neck across his shoulders to his chest, which hung down and almost touched the ground.

He held in his hand a crosier, the bishop's staff. He briefly set down the staff and reached for the bishop's gold embroidered mitre, the white canonical hat. He placed it on his head. Then, cautiously so as not to disturb the crown, he reached for the staff again.

De Santis closed his eyes. For just a moment, he savored the thought of the procession before him. He imagined himself gliding like a swan down the long central aisle of a grand and glorious cathedral. He was preceded by countless assistants swinging their censers of incense. This assemblage was accompanied by a choir of young men and boys, all dressed in their black cassocks and white lace surplices. They sang in perfect harmony and marched in perfectly straight rows out ahead.

This would be a day of magnificence, De Santis thought. This would be a day of love. This would be a day for all mankind to give praise to God's glory and his kingdom here on earth.

This would also be the wrong day for Bishop Alvarado to come home early. But he did. So when he unexpectedly stopped into *his* sacristy upon his return to find Father Giancarlo De Santis in front of *his* dressing mirror bedecked in *his* robes, there was going to be a very big problem in Rome on De Santis's return.

Chapter 8

Washington, D.C.

W hen Bondurant slammed on the brakes of his Audi in front of St. Peter's Church in Queenstown, he left a decent-sized skid mark and a billow of white smoke behind him. He leaned on his horn.

"Get in!" he shouted to Domenika and his little priest friend. "Get in!"

The small crowd of worshippers who had left the early-afternoon Easter Mass were startled at the scene. It wasn't often that their services were met with a crazed man in a car on the run. Bondurant was amazed that Domenika and Parenti were still alive. They got into the car, and Bondurant drove as fast as he could away from the hideout near the river that they once called home and toward Washington, D.C.

It was late at night by the time they pulled into the parking lot at the Key Bridge Marriott that overlooked the rain-soaked city. Bondurant's joints ached. The city of monuments, now shrouded in a spring thunderstorm just across the Potomac River, was still slightly aglow from the street lamps that ran from the cobblestone alleys of George-town all the way to Capitol Hill. Other than the distant rumble of thunder that rolled in from Maryland to the north, the town, like Domenika curled up in the backseat, was sound asleep. A handful of cars headed into the city slowly made their way in the rain across Key Bridge just below their parking-lot perch. Parenti sat with Bondurant and watched in awe as a lone airliner dropped from the impossibly low clouds and banked southward, hugging the outline of the river on its final approach toward Reagan National Airport upstream.

"What an invention," Parenti said. His voice was filled with mar-vel as the airplane that seemed to fill the car's windshield streaked across the night sky.

"Yeah," Bondurant said. "The pilot of that thing probably didn't see the ground until—"

"No, no, I mean these french fries," Parenti said.

Bondurant watched as Parenti stared at the large pack of Mc-Donald's fries in his lap. He ate them slowly, one by one, as if to savor every moment of the experience. Aldo sat inside the priest's vestment pocket and emerged every so often to snatch one of the treats held forth.

Bondurant turned toward Domenika in the backseat. "I can't believe she's able to sleep through all this."

"She's exhausted. It's been a long day," Parenti said.

"I need to tell you something that I'm sure would upset her," Bondurant said, lowering his voice to a near whisper. "I might be wrong about it. But it's tied to some ancient biblical stories—just stories, mind you."

They had been through enough adventures together that

Bondurant was comfortable thinking out loud when his friend was at hand. So he was surprised to see Parenti's stunned look in return.

"I need to tell you something as well," Parenti said. "I know you had quite a day. People shooting at you from the sky and all that." Parenti dug deeper into his pack of fries. The patter of rain on the roof of the car began to grow louder as the intensity of the storm gathered around them.

"So what's wrong? Did anyone recognize you in the church?" Bondurant asked.

"Not as far as I know." He looked about them in the dark, but the rain on the windshield now completely obscured his view. "It's what happened during the service that concerns me."

Bondurant watched Parenti hesitate. Something troubled him deeply.

"Then you *were* seen," Bondurant said.

"It's not who saw me," Parenti said, "but who I saw."

"What do you mean?" Bondurant asked.

"When I was a child," Parenti said, as he fed the last remaining french fry to Aldo, "only six years old at the time—"

"Father, you're kidding me," Bondurant interrupted. "Can we pick up your story where it starts at church this afternoon?"

Bondurant watched Parenti scowl. It meant his request would be duly ignored, and he would be in for a longer night than he'd planned. He leaned against the headrest and closed his eyes, resigned.

"All right, then, you were saying you were six years old."

Parenti continued. "Thank you. I was told when I was a young boy, very young, that there would be moments like this. But these admonitions were many years ago. I'd nearly forgotten them. And now, well, this is the first of such revelations I've ever seen."

A lightning bolt in the distance filled the night sky with light, and Bondurant could see in the brief flash that Parenti's face was filled with genuine concern.

"I don't know if I've told you this before, but I was born the seventh son of a seventh son," Parenti said. "You know what that means?"

"You're Catholic. No birth control."

"Seventh sons of seventh sons are extremely rare. Particularly those with no sisters in between. It is said such sons are often blessed—or cursed—with powers to see things, to know things, that others may not. Events from the past or the future are sometimes revealed to them for reasons beyond their understanding or control."

"And you're saying you're blessed with such a gift?" Bondurant asked. The skepticism in his voice was clear.

"I've also been skeptical my entire life that this gift of revelation existed. It had never appeared before. But today . . ." Bondurant watched as the priest struggled to find the words to recount what had happened. "Today I was privy to a true revelation. I saw something in my mind's eye as I sat in God's presence in that humble church. It revealed something very important."

Bondurant watched as Parenti began to fidget nervously with the buttons on his cassock. "Father," Bondurant said, "exactly what was it you saw?"

In the next several minutes, as the rain from the storm grew heavier and the wind began to howl around them, Bondurant listened as Parenti recounted his revelation.

Bondurant was speechless. In Parenti's mind, the riddle of the clone-child had been answered. The priest was certain he knew whose DNA could be found in the second, unknown source of blood taken from the Shroud of the savior, and that this was terrifying beyond belief. The priest started to tremble and looked around as though it might be too dangerous to go on.

"You're absolutely certain this dream, this vision that came to you, was seen only by you? Not Domenika or anyone else?" Bondurant checked behind him to see if Domenika was still asleep.

"There is 'general revelation,' made available by God to us all. God, whom you see manifested in nature, in this storm itself and all that we are. Even you, ever the skeptic, can see it."

Another massive lightning bolt from the storm split the sky of Georgetown directly across the river from them. It was accompanied by a clap of deafening thunder. Aldo dove deep into Parenti's pocket and yelped. Domenika stirred but didn't wake.

"And there is 'particular revelation,'" Parenti continued. He nearly shouted to be heard over the din of the rain on the roof and the howl of the wind. "It is where God has chosen to reveal himself to some for a special purpose. Some are chosen and receive it through dreams and visions, or even physical manifestations."

"Like Abraham and Moses," Bondurant said.

"That's high company, Doctor," Parenti said. "We're in Virginia in a Marriott parking lot. I don't know that I would go that far."

Bondurant felt the priest take his forearm.

Parenti continued. "But I believe this revelation concerning the Shroud provides a clue that no man, no scientist—not even you—could ever hope to learn without God's help. And I believe I have been made to see this revelation so that I might pass this news to you for a reason."

Bondurant turned away from Parenti and cast his eyes toward

the sheets of rain coming down in front of the hotel. He was now certain his own suspicions might be true. Then he felt Parenti's grip on his arm again as he squeezed hard to get his attention.

"The second source of blood on the most holy Shroud," Parenti said, "the blood other than Christ's, is that of . . ."

Bondurant watched the priest stop himself one last time. Parenti looked at Domenika, still sound asleep, and then looked about them again. It was as if revealing the truth out loud would bring another deadly lightning bolt, this one aimed directly at them.

"A supernatural being? An angel of some kind? Believe it or not, Father, that's been my hunch. It's why I need to get to Yale. There's an expert there who I know will have some answers."

Bondurant turned toward Parenti, who looked dumbfounded. He watched as Parenti reached for the button to make sure his car door was locked. The moment he did, the wail of the wind and the rain from the storm that had pelted the car came to a sudden halt. There was only dead quiet and absolute stillness around them.

"You know much, my son. And you've come far," the priest whispered. "But it was no angel that Domenika nurtured to life. I believe it was a *Watcher*. And that, God help us, is a very different thing."

Chapter 9

Geneva

Meyer sat in his office in Geneva and stared across his massive black marble desk at Vitaly Galerkin in absolute fear for his life. Galerkin had worked for him on contract for years and had been paid handsomely for his services, but Meyer knew that would not be enough to save him if their conversation took even the smallest turn for the worse. While the distance that separated them was almost five feet, he was certain that if he didn't find a way to keep Galerkin calm while he got to the truth, it was possible the Russian monster would do something rash. Galerkin might reach for the letter opener Meyer had left so carelessly on top of the desk and in an instant plunge it deep into the middle of his brain. He'd seen Galerkin do it before with a pair of scissors when the Russian had lost his temper with someone else.

"You're *sure* Bondurant is dead."

The sound of the synthesized, monotone voice generated by the little machine was enough to grate on even the most patient listener. Meyer had also dispensed with his usual turtleneck that day. The stoma where his larynx had once been was fully exposed, a permanent, mouthlike slit in the center of Meyer's throat where doctors had attached his windpipe in order for him to breathe—and smoke. Even after the loss of his larynx to cancer from cigarettes, Meyer had continued his smoking habit against his doctor's orders. Only now he used the hole in the center of his throat. He wedged a filterless Camel cigarette into the slit in his windpipe and, while he contorted and contracted the muscles in his neck, inhaled smoke through the grotesque hole.

"Bondurant's dead," Galerkin responded. There wasn't a trace of emotion in his voice.

"Absolutely sure?" Meyer asked. He eyed the letter opener on the desk once more and slowly leaned farther back in his leather chair to put several more inches between himself and the blade.

"Dead is dead," Galerkin said. He placed one of his giant, weathered hands on the desk. Meyer eyed it warily.

"Then how is it possible, Vitaly, my friend—and we are friends," Meyer said guardedly, "that I have word from an associate that Bondurant was seen in the lobby of a hotel outside Washington, D.C.? It was just a few hours ago. He was with the girl." Meyer turned up the volume on his voice machine slightly to ensure that Galerkin could hear him.

"Not possible," Galerkin said. The Russian leaned over and reached toward the tiny knobs of the voice machine. He lowered the volume a notch and grunted. Meyer took it as a sign that he wasn't pleased. Galerkin's huge head, absent a neck to support it, was affixed like a stump to massive shoulders as wide as a freezer locker. Six feet eight inches tall and just over three hundred pounds, he was a thick man in every sense of the word.

"You said Bondurant drowned. Floating facedown in the water and all that?" Meyer asked.

"I take the shots from one hundred feet above the river. I unload two, maybe three thousand rounds on top of him," Galerkin said. "Then we sit. We sit in the helicopter in a hover above him for maybe half hour, maybe more. Until we have to go. You must understand this. No man stays underwater for half an hour. He's dead. Bottom of the river."

"I see," Meyer said, concerned that the Russian might be wrong but unsure what to do about it. It had taken Meyer a year to track them down. "And the girl?"

"Not at mobile home when I finish the game of hide-and-seek with boyfriend. But I'll find her," he said. He looked Meyer directly in the eyes. "Then you will pay me."

While Meyer's orders to kill them hadn't yet been realized, he knew that they eventually would be. It was nearly impossible to live off the grid nowadays. Public records Galerkin had found online revealed that the couple had obtained a license to be married months earlier in a rural Maryland church. There was time. And there was Galerkin. He was the best. He might have screwed up this time, but it wouldn't happen again. In Meyer's mind, now that they were hot on their trail, the odds were that both Bondurant and Domenika would be dead within days, or weeks at the most. And not just normal dead. Not regular dead. But "bad dead," as Galerkin liked to put it: "The way it's to be done."

Vitaly Anatoly Galerkin was born in Oymyakon, Russia, considered to be the coldest, most remote place on earth, located along the Indigirka River in the northeastern Sakha Republic between two permanently frozen mountain ranges. The town's population of five hundred unfortunate souls routinely weathered temperatures colder than ninety degrees below zero. In Galerkin's place of birth, there were only three things to do: drink, ice-fish, and live miserably. His family was highly accomplished at all three.

Raised as an only child, Galerkin had lost his mother when he was twelve to a shovel cracked across her forehead by his father in a drunken rage. The father confessed to the neighbors that he could take the misery of Oymyakon but had heard quite enough from her. Before the *politsiya* could travel the thirty kilometers from the nearby town of Tomtor to arrest his father, Galerkin used a hand auger to corkscrew cleanly through his father's chest as he slept in a drunken stupor. Once the boy had dragged him outside in the cold, the remaining two feet of steel bit had pinned his father to the frozen ground like a fish on a spit. The bit had entered the chest cavity, broken through the ice, and created a nice hole, where the boy sat and calmly fished while he waited for the police to arrive.

Galerkin had grown up in prisons in eastern Russia. He grew to love the confines of an isolation cell. The psychiatrists who paid him visits once a year until he was released at the age of thirty termed him a misanthrope.

In Galerkin's mind, there were simply too many people populating the earth. There was not one soul alive that Galerkin felt did anything more than occupy his precious space. Excess people stood endlessly in lines in front of him to purchase things, wasting his valuable time. They ate the bread from the shelves, taking more than their share. They filled the seats on trains and buses, requiring him to stand. They created interminable lines of traffic to prevent him from being on time. They chattered about the smallest, most insignificant things until his head would ache. He had no use for them.

When he was released from prison, he was ordered to relocate for parole to Vladivostok. Each day after breakfast, he walked to the street corner from his decrepit apartment to retrieve the daily newspaper. He only glanced at the headlines but always read the obituaries, delighted by the notion that people he might have seen on the streets only yesterday were to be buried underground tomorrow. There he could see them no more. Another item he looked for in the paper was word of a major tragedy of any kind to be found in the world. He relished such news. The more loss of life to a war or a disaster, man-made or natural, the better. He saw these incidents of earthquakes, floods, and famine as God-sent, sweeping people efficiently away from an overcrowded planet.

He did his own part for the cause of population reduction in spectacular fashion. To Galerkin, killing was an art form, and the manner of death chosen for every victim was critical. Each was an important moment to be savored. The more unique the kill, the better. He locked an entire family in a warehouse meat locker and watched them freeze to death for hours. He spent three days without sleep hunting a man like a deer using only a bow and arrow to kill him. He forced a woman to eat herself to death with an overabundance of food, crammed two brothers inside a refrigerator and buried them alive, and drowned someone in a bucket of beer.

So Meyer gave the benefit of the doubt to Galerkin's boast that Bondurant was dead. Galerkin had spotted Bondurant on his swimming dock the day before he launched his attack. An easy kill with a shot to the back of his head from ten feet would have sufficed. But once the idea for target practice with a .50-caliber machine gun mounted on a swift-moving helicopter had crept into Galerkin's head, there was no other way. Meyer was in no position to object.

Now Galerkin said to Meyer, "The other girl, the fat one in Kolkata. The woman, Kaput. You said ten thousand dollars for her."

"Kaput?" Meyer said. "Who is Kaput? Oh, you mean Kapoor. Ms. Ria Kapoor. My egg donor."

"Kaput, Kapoor," Galerkin said dryly. "She is kaput by this week."

Galerkin stood and stared out the massive floor-to-ceiling windows of Meyer's modern office building. It overlooked the emerald-green Rue du Rhone, which wound its way through the tree-lined parks of picturesque Geneva below. Off in the distance, he spied St. Peter's Cathedral. An architectural treasure, it towered over the heart of Geneva's Old Town. All who came to the fabled city admired it, but to Meyer, it was nothing but an eyesore.

"There's no longer a need, Vitaly," Meyer said. "She has contracted the same plague that's killing everyone else in Kolkata. It's why I had to move the child from there so quickly."

Meyer figured his assassin was not pleased by the prospect of losing out on a contract to the strange, unknown virus that had made its way through India. He watched as Galerkin's face suddenly broke into a broad, unexpected smile.

"I love this plague," Galerkin said. He rubbed his beefy hands together. "Whole villages wiped out. The papers this morning are reporting ten thousand dead. I think they are lying. I think it is more."

"Why do you think that?"

Galerkin couldn't help himself. "These people, they bring in Lady Khan. You know Lady Khan?"

"I'm afraid I don't, Vitaly."

"Lady Khan only comes when it's very, very, very big," Galerkin said. "Maybe this could be the big one."

"Vitaly, the elimination of Bondurant and Jozef. It means a great deal to me," he said. "They're in the way of a bigger plan. The beginning of the end."

"End of what?" Galerkin asked.

"Of Christianity."

"I don't know about the beginnings and the endings. I just know—"

"Never mind, Vitaly," Meyer said. He'd nearly reached the limit of his patience. "Just know that their very existence threatens exposure, something I can't afford. Bondurant may be dead, as you say. But I'll not rest while Domenika Jozef remains alive. Sehgal and Laurent tricked her quite well. She—"

"Sehgal, the famous scientist who shoots himself. This one?" Galerkin said. "How he shoot himself? In mouth? In temple?"

"What *matters* is that he tricked her into birthing my Christ child. But then she got away. She's undoubtedly angry. Who wouldn't be? But I don't need her or anyone else summoning the courage to come after the child or, God help me, getting the authorities involved. That's something my nascent little church can't afford."

"You tell me this six times now," Galerkin said, clearly irritated.

"Well, I want you to know I mean it," Meyer said. He got up from his desk as a signal for Galerkin to leave. "I want her head on a platter."

Meyer could see Galerkin smile broadly again as he considered the image in his mind. He wondered whether he had given the assassin a fabulous idea.

"I get my million dollars," Galerkin said as he ambled toward the door. He turned around a final time before he departed and grunted. "And you, Salome? You get head on plate."

Chapter 10

Washington, D.C.

Domenika arrived for lunch at the secluded Hotel Suisse in Washington, D.C., twenty minutes early. She took a moment to relax while she waited for her sister, Joanna, to arrive in the small formal dining room facing the green lawn of Lafayette Square. It was a glorious spring day that brought beams of bright morning sun through the Palladian windows that lined the hotel along the black and gray cobblestones of H Street. Small sprays of violets that matched a massive floral display in the restaurant's foyer sat on the white linen-topped tables that dotted the room.

Domenika was excited to see her sister. They hadn't been together in many months. Between Joanna's chaotic schedule as a fashion model and Domenika's unpredictable life as a seeming fugitive, the two had spoken only a handful of times on the phone. Their lunch was on the spur of the moment as they were both unexpectedly in town.

Domenika knew it was important to leave a good impression

with her only sister. Every word of their conversation would likely find its way home to Krakow. There, her parents, often mystified from afar by Domenika's topsy-turvy life, would eagerly await any news of their eldest daughter. She was too often out of touch. The sisters, just two years apart in age, looked nearly like identical twins. But beyond the fortune of their *Vogue*-cover looks and affection for each other, that was as far as their similarities went.

Try as she might, Domenika had not been able to shake the mood she'd found herself in that morning, which stemmed from what she'd overheard between Bondurant and Parenti as she lay half-awake during the thunderstorm the night before. Domenika had lived a life of mourning and confusion since the day she'd awoken disoriented in a hospital room in Rome a year before. She'd been told the child she'd nurtured in pregnancy and in near solitary confinement at a convent in India was not that of Jon Bondurant, the only man she'd ever loved. She was heartbroken and shaken beyond belief at the news. She'd merely been a vessel for Meyer and Dr. Laurent's plans. But to have this "fatherless" child taken from her after birth the way a thief steals a purse had proved too much. A child for whom she once harbored such high hopes had been lost.

For the sake of her marriage, she most often forced a smile for Bondurant and lived life as positively as she could. But in moments of solitude, when she had time to reflect, Domenika would often withdraw inside a shell of her former self. Counseling didn't help. Antidepressant prescriptions didn't work. And daily acts of kindness and understanding from her husband went only so far toward healing the wound of a lost child. In the end, she knew it was only the passage of time and the strength of her faith that might bring her peace.

But now, like the fleeting storm of the night before, her life was only more unsettled. She'd learned that the story of the child she'd lost was even worse. She knew very little about the fabled Watchers, the kind of beings Parenti had apparently conjured up in his Easter Sunday vision. The priest's tiny stature often belied his giant imagination, which was something Domenika might normally discount. But hearing her often skeptical husband's suspicion, even fear, of a dark being that might now walk the earth in the form of a child was a total shock. And to be reminded that she may have given birth to such a monstrosity was for Domenika a nightmare beyond the pale.

"Nika!" Joanna cried out.

Domenika, lost in thought while her sister approached, was so startled that she nearly dropped her cup of tea. "Nika" was Joanna's pet name for her. Domenika recovered quickly, rose from her chair, and hugged her sister long and close. Joanna was dressed exquisitely, as usual, in a bright red Giambattista Valli suit that struck a perfect contrast with her shoulder-length brunette hair. Once they had sat and exchanged their usual but genuine pleasantries, Domenika wasn't surprised when Joanna got right to the heart of what was on her mind.

"You look terrible, Nika," Joanna said. "What's wrong?"

"Well, it's great to see you too," Domenika said. She thought she'd pulled herself together well given that she'd had so little sleep since she and Jon had arrived at their hotel across the river late the night before. Her sister always had high expectations when it came to how she looked.

"Worry lines," Joanna explained. "They come and go. Me too. Look. Here. And here too."

After her sister had pointed out the spots on her own forehead and brow where the tiniest trace of apprehension might be found, they were interrupted by their waiter.

"I'm so sorry; if I may?" the waiter said. He set two tall champagne flutes on the table before them. They brimmed to the top with sparkling white bubbles.

"On the house?" Joanna asked, as if she expected the courtesy.

"No, madam," the waiter responded. He nodded toward a table across the small dining room occupied by two graying gentlemen, perhaps in their seventies, impeccably dressed.

Joanna, undoubtedly used to such come-ons, completely ignored the men and their gesture as she took a small sip from her glass.

"You asked what's wrong?" Domenika said. "I don't even know where to start."

She wondered how she might possibly explain how she felt. How was it that the child she had protected in her womb for nine months, the one she would have given her own life to protect, might actually be an awful being who deserved to be wiped from the face of the earth?

"What about . . . India? Have they been caught or punished?" Joanna asked.

"One is dead," Domenika said. She looked around to be sure no one could hear. "Sehgal, the scientist? He shot himself, right in front of Jon. The other doctor, Laurent, the one from France, is on the run. I'm afraid the ringleader, Meyer, the one who founded that crazy cult and organized it all, is another story altogether."

"Have the police found him? He deserves to die."

"No," Domenika said. She looked around the room again for any sign of trouble, as she had so many times since Bondurant had rescued her in India the year before. "If fact, Jon and I have been on the run from *him*."

"You can't be serious, Nika," her sister said.

"These people," Domenika said. "They're powerful. It's just insane even to think what they may have in mind. Imagine a cult that believes science can resurrect Jesus, that they can bring him back from the dead."

"I told you, Nika," Joanna said. "I told you. Go to church. That's fine. But must *everything* in your life have to do with God?"

Domenika and her sister had disagreed over religion years before. They'd both been raised as devout Catholics. Domenika's faith was steady, but Joanna had left Catholicism and Poland behind. She'd dabbled in various faiths for several years but had never settled on a firm set of beliefs. In the time she'd been in America, she'd veered from Catholicism to Buddhism to kabbalah, and for the time being had left them all behind. She was now an atheist.

"Joanna, something terrible has happened," Domenika said. "I've just learned of it. And I don't know what to do."

Joanna reached across the table and took Domenika's hands in her own. "Tell me how I can help," she said.

"I've done something wrong. Maybe it's not my fault," Domenika said. She hesitated to go any further, as there was no way her sister could even begin to understand her predicament. "But I'm all mixed up in it, and there just has to be something I can do."

"What is it, Nika?" Domenika could feel her sister's concern as she gripped her hands tightly.

"It's about the child. The one I was forced to have."

"Have they found him? The last time we talked, you hadn't a clue where he might be."

"I still don't, but he's—he's—" Domenika didn't know what to say next, particularly if there was any chance that word of her incredible dilemma might find its way back to her parents at home. That was out of the question. Another interruption from their waiter spared her for the moment.

"I'm so sorry to disturb you again, I really am," the waiter said. He set a sterling-silver bucket beside their table, filled with ice and a bottle of Dom Pérignon champagne. Domenika recognized the label but not the vintage. She knew her sister would.

"Wow," Joanna said as she reached over and turned the bottle slowly in its ice. "Their best year in decades, 2002."

Joanna looked toward the two elderly men who had sent the previous round. They stared back, glad to be recognized, but both had looks of concern.

The waiter shook his head. "I'm sorry, no," he said.

He nodded once more, only this time in the opposite direction, toward another table across the room, this one occupied by two other handsome middle-aged businessmen. The waiter set two business cards on the table next to the champagne, smiled uncomfortably, and retreated swiftly toward the kitchen. Joanna glanced at the cards for a moment, turned them over dismissively, and turned toward her sister.

"Where were we?" Joanna asked.

"Does this happen everywhere you go?" Domenika asked. "I mean, what's next? A vineyard?"

Joanna laughed.

"Joanna, I—" It was no use, she thought. There wasn't a soul on earth other than Bondurant and Parenti who might believe or understand her plight. If she couldn't confide in Bondurant and she couldn't trust her family with her predicament, who was there? In some ways, she was all alone, and she knew it.

She paused, reached for her glass of champagne, and raised it to eye level, ready to give a toast. She thought for another moment about better times and her idyllic life with Joanna as a child. Those days seemed a lifetime ago. There was an old Polish saying their father often used with the two sisters when they were young that came to mind. It was apropos for the troubling time, and one her sister might recall.

"*Niech będziesz w niebie pół godziny,*" Domenika recited.

"May you be in heaven a full half hour," Joanna said. She held her own glass high and laughed as her memory served her.

"*Zanim diabeł zna umarły,*" Domenika said.

"Before the devil knows you're dead."

Chapter 11

New Haven, Connecticut

Nothing had changed, Bondurant thought.

Although he hadn't visited the faculty offices of Yale's Religious Studies Department in years, he could close his eyes and still find his way to Professor Tom Harrington's disheveled basement office. He simply followed his nose. The faint smell of marijuana grew stronger as he approached Harrington's doorway, just like it had during the days under his advisement as a doctoral candidate almost two decades before. Harrington, an aging hippie from the sixties who claimed he held the record for Vietnam draft deferments at six, was a campus radical caught in a time warp.

An avowed socialist, he lived on a five-acre farm outside New Haven, Connecticut, where he raised llamas and chickens for reasons even he couldn't fully explain, given that he was allergic to both. His long, graying ponytail, thick black-rimmed glasses, and wardrobe straight off the racks of a Salvation Army thrift store created the impression of a professor one step away from home-lessness and life on the street. But he had two key things going for him: sheer brilliance, and the blunt truth emblazoned on the large button pinned to the lapel of his lone corduroy sport coat. It read "TBIT," short for "Too Bad, I'm Tenured."

Holding doctorates in religious studies, divinity, and theology, Harrington was considered a leading authority on "angelology," the obscure study of angels found in biblical texts. Angels were referenced in the Old and New Testaments almost two hundred times, but academic investigation into the nature of angels, their origin and purpose, and their role in the context of the scriptures was strangely sparse. Harrington had found this odd, given that the authors of biblical texts made mention of angels in thirty-four separate books of the Bible, from the first book, Genesis, to the last, Revelation. He also reasoned that angels merited study because if Jesus Christ found their legion deserving of mention, they had to be worth a look. As a result, he had written the greatest number of definitive academic works in existence on the study of angels and their worlds.

"Tell me, Jon," Harrington began now, as he took one last drag on the tiny remnant of his joint before extinguishing it by rolling it between his forefinger and thumb. "You've become famous. And famous people write famous reports. Now that you've publicly slain the Shroud with that book of yours, I figure it's my angels you're coming after next. You know I can't let you do that."

"No intention, Tom," Bondurant said as he sank into the com-fortable leather sofa in Harrington's office. All four walls were lined from floor to ceiling with disordered shelves of ancient books. Scat-tered among the many rows of religious texts were framed photos that documented the professor's numerous travels, to the Taj Mahal, Machu Picchu, and a dozen other exotic or mysterious sites.

Bondurant had bridled at the mention of the Shroud. He'd tried to put out of his mind the high-risk press conference in New York that he'd scheduled for the following week. He knew coming out of hiding even for just the moment would place him in grave danger. But he also knew it was finally time to admit error and come clean about the partial authenticity of the relic.

"I'm actually here to learn more of what you know about the power of certain angels," Bondurant said.

"Two questions: Are you an alien, and what have you done with Jon Bondurant?" Harrington asked. "The Jon Bondurant I know would have said what I *believe* about the power of angels, not what I *know*. Out with it. Make my day. Tell me you've left the dark side."

"Maybe I've seen a little light, let's put it that way," Bondurant said. "You could say I have a more open mind now, depending."

"Okay, then. Good or bad?"

"Good or bad what?" Bondurant asked.

Harrington cocked his head sideways and wheeled his squeaky antique office chair across the worn tile floor to get within whispering distance of Bondurant. He slid his glasses down to the tip of his nose and stroked his ponytail several times as if to soothe himself while he pondered the question.

"Good angel or bad angel, Jon?" he said.

"A Watcher, I'm told. Tell me everything you know about Watchers," Bondurant said.

"Bad."

"Bad?"

"Really bad."

"That's it? You're the leading authority on angels, and that's all you have to say?"

"I mean, a Watcher is a type of fallen angel," Harrington said as he reached toward the bookcase behind him. He pulled down an oversize text bound in old leather. "You used to laugh at me when I would try to interest you in this stuff. You sure you want to hear this?"

"Very sure, Tom."

"Okay, here's the short course. As you know, the Bible is a little vague on the history of angels. Before God created man, he created spirits a great deal more powerful than man could ever hope to be. More intelligence. More power."

"Superior to man. Inferior to God," Bondurant said.

"That's right. An entire army of them. Soldiers, born before man, who exist to carry out his will. God's will. There are several 'super' angels—archangels—like the famous Michael, a general of sorts in God's army. Then there's Satan," he said as he mimicked horns on either side of his head with both forefingers. "Satan was once an angel who became enraptured with his own beauty, and in trying to place himself above God led a rebellion. He and a great many of the angels fell out of grace with God. It's the stuff of Revelation twelve. Some were banished from heaven to remain in the abyss until a thousand years after the Second Coming. They'll be judged again. See here?" Harrington pointed toward a vivid medieval painting of deformed creatures writhing in the fires of hell. "Here they are, bound by chains, awaiting final judgment, just as depicted in the passage from Revelation."

"You said 'some,' Tom."

"Yes, well, this first group is essentially locked away to live forever in a painful lake of fire." Harrington pointed to another hideous illustration in the book on his lap. "Think Dante's *Inferno*. We need not worry about them. Out of sight, out of mind."

Harrington reached for another book on the shelf behind his visitor and held it so that Bondurant could get a good look at its cover.

"Now we turn to the pseudepigrapha. Stories left out of the Old Testament and deemed by the Church to be false. The books of Enoch, Daniel, and some others. Stories about Abraham, Moses, Noah, and the like. They were mostly left off the hit parade because of the angel stories. The early Church founders believed the stories these writings told about angels—how they came to be, how they ended up on earth, and how some were the source of evil in our world—were too far-out and too contradictory to be included in the Bible as we know it today. But here they are, as credible as Genesis and the beginning of the world, if you ask me," Harrington said.

Bondurant looked on as Harrington ran his thumb across the tome he held and stopped at a section in the middle.

"The book of Enoch?" Bondurant asked. Harrington had clearly marked every book with a tab.

"That's right. Enoch. The son of Cain. They say he lived for three hundred sixty-five years."

Bondurant began to chuckle.

"Be polite," Harrington said. "This is *my* house."

"I remember the story now," Bondurant said. "Enoch's tale of how angels fell is a lot different from what Christianity believes today."

"That's right." Harrington gently set the ornately bound collection of writings on the coffee table between them.

"There's the traditional biblical story about Lucifer and the fall of the angels, the one everyone knows," Bondurant said. "The great Battle of Heaven. Satan's loss. The casting down of hundreds of other 'fallen' angels who inhabited the earth. The source of all evil in this world. Have I got that right?"

"On the nose," Harrington said. "But not according to Enoch. His version is a wild one—a lot sexier, as far as I'm concerned. One that's more revealing about the Watchers you have in mind. And while you haven't explained your interest, you would do well to avoid them."

"Avoid?" Bondurant said as he folded his arms.

"Watchers are a special breed, Jon. They're also called the Grigori. I suppose if one wasn't a believer in fallen angels but did believe in good and evil in the abstract sense, then here is where there's common ground. They're the personification of evil. They've lived here on earth among us at times, and even intermingled among the human race. They've been left with the power and freedom to carry out the will of Satan himself on mankind."

"Where did they come from?" Bondurant asked.

"There's the rub," Harrington said. "And that's why few have heard much about them before. The way Enoch tells it—Daniel too—angels didn't fall from grace when they lost the great war of heaven. Rather, hundreds of them were placed on earth by God as 'shepherds.'"

"To watch over mankind?"

"Right. The earliest humans. Watchers are defined as 'those who are awake, those who do not sleep.' Part of God's plan to mind us. But the plan went awry," Harrington said.

"How so?"

"These Watchers were only supposed to watch over mankind. Look but don't touch, God said. He posted signs everywhere. But, as the story goes, these Watchers couldn't resist the temptation of mankind, especially beautiful women. You have some experience in that department."

Bondurant stared up at the ceiling for a moment and tried not to squirm. This was a reference to Bondurant's ousting in disgrace years before as a professor at Princeton; he'd slept with one of his undergrads, who, as bad luck would have it, also happened to be the daughter of one of the university's deans.

"I jest, Jon," Harrington said. He slapped Bondurant's knee to lighten the mood. "And I digress. These Watchers began to lust for earthly women. They married. They intermingled their blood."

"Blood?" Bondurant asked.

"That's right. Their angel juice. Their heavenly hemoglobin. Their blood. Why the look?" Harrington asked.

"No reason," Bondurant said.

"So, as I was saying, they created new races with this blood. And against God's instructions, they became teachers and revealed the secrets of the universe—science, the arts, technologies—all things that humans were meant to learn, but gradually, over time, on their own."

"I feel a fall coming on," Bondurant said.

"A big one. Genesis six. Once the Watchers started to procreate, creating giant half-beast, half-men called Nephilim, God had seen enough. Time for a flood."

"*The* flood?" Bondurant asked. "You mean the Great Flood?"

"That would be the one. Noah, build me an ark! A big ark! Fifty cubits long, thirty cubits wide! Fast as you can!" Harrington shouted as he spread his arms wide to portray the size of a giant ship. "It was the Nephilim that God wanted destroyed in the Great Flood, not mankind."

"So what happened to the Watchers? Swept away at sea?"

"We could only wish, Jon. The Nephilim, they're gone forever. But the Watchers, they were bound to what the book of Daniel calls 'the valleys of the earth' until Judgment Day. They were unable to be drowned or killed."

"You're saying they still exist?"

"They are said to still roam the earth, and they're what's left of Satan's power here. It's why there is evil in the world. Sometimes appearing in human form—what we call angelophanies—and sometimes in spirit form. They're wicked smart. Truly world-class deceivers."

"So, the opposite of guardian angels?"

"There you have it, Jon. Most people today believe in the concept of guardian angels that look out for them in times of trouble. These Watchers are their counterparts, guardian angels for Satan's use, as it were. When we see great acts of evil by mankind in this world today, it's Satan's work. And some, myself included, believe that behind man's greatest tragedies is the work of a Watcher who seeks to destroy God's creation. They're the proverbial devil on your shoulder, whether tempting you to cheat on your wife or to push the button to start a nuclear war."

"The devil made me do it," Bondurant said.

"Yes. They seek to control and ruin, but it's not that simple. There has been a great deal of speculation, from the interpretation of several biblical passages, that they incarnate. They can take on human bodies and possess powers that go beyond evil persuasion. They can wreak havoc in many ways—through the creation of illusion, the stirring of confusion, acts that lead to horrific, truly tragic events."

"Exactly what do you mean, Tom?" Bondurant stirred uncomfortably in his seat.

Harrington looked up toward the ceiling and thought for a moment. "This is the part where you're going to tell me I'm simply high."

"Try me."

"It's the unexplainable, Jon. They're not acts of God. They're the opposite. An airliner full of people goes down over the ocean in the dead of night for no good reason. No call for help. A perfectly healthy child of loving parents goes to bed one evening and doesn't wake in the morning. Reason unknown. A killer virus without a cause or cure mysteriously explodes from no apparent source, inexplicably vanishing when it's had its fill of human loss. Do you remember the Spanish flu?"

"Not personally. It struck a long time ago," Bondurant said.

"In 1918, to be exact. It came right out of nowhere and lasted for several years. Nearly one hundred million people died, about six percent of the world's population at the time. It spread all the way from the tropics to the Arctic. A hundred years later, scientists are still baffled by its origin. There are some credible immunologists who are starting to make comparisons to this mystery virus that's indiscriminately killing its way across the Indian subcontinent. A half million dead so far is what I've heard. There are similarities."

Bondurant leaned in, highly interested. It was what he'd come for. "In what respect?"

"Unknown origin. No scientific explanation. Highly lethal. Symptoms similar to the bubonic plague. Bad angel blood," Harrington said. "And here's the tricky part: I've heard that the stronger your immune system, the quicker you die. It apparently creates a 'cytokine storm' effect, where your body overreacts to the virus. You essentially kill yourself. If that's not the devil's work, I don't know what is."

Bondurant sat in still silence for a moment. When he closed his eyes for several seconds, as if to escape the moment, a sinking feeling in his stomach signaled that he couldn't avoid his responsibility and the journey he knew likely lay ahead.

"Now, Jon," Harrington said while he slapped Bondurant's shoulder as if to snap him from a spell. "Fill me in. Why the sudden interest in Watchers? Why all this blood on your mind?"

"It's a long story, Tom." Bondurant said. He leaned back and sank deeper into the couch as if seeking a place to hide. "I don't think even you would believe me if I tried."

Bondurant watched as Harrington fumbled through the pocket of his sport coat behind him. He appeared delighted to find another joint. He placed his feet up on his desk beside him, lit the joint, and looked at Bondurant with raised eyebrows.

"Okay, then, Tom," Bondurant said, staring intently back at him through the haze. "The story begins with blood on the Shroud— the *authentic* Shroud of Turin."

Chapter 12

The Vatican

Father De Santis bent over slightly and kissed the massive gold ring of Pope Augustine for what must have been the hundredth time in his life. He noticed that the pontiff's aged hands trembled more than usual. It was rumored that Augustine, who'd recently attended to a grueling schedule of duties, had been quietly ailing. The pope's special assistant hadn't seen the Holy Father in a month.

De Santis had been summoned to the *appartamento nobile*, the pontiff's residence on the top floor of the Apostolic Palace overlooking the splendor of Vatican City. Just a few floors below them sat some of the greatest artistic treasures the world had ever known. A few steps from the Sistine Chapel, the site where Michelangelo had painted his glorious ceiling and *The Last Judgment*, was the *Pietà*. Michelangelo's sculpture was commissioned during the Renaissance and was the only work of art ever signed by the artist. It depicted the body of Jesus Christ in the lap of the Virgin Mary following his crucifixion.

While De Santis customarily sat during his visits in the small living room adjacent to the pope's corner bedroom, today he was escorted by the pope down the hallway to Augustine's private library, a more formal room where they had never sat together before. It was an unusual place for them to meet. The library, comfortably arranged with deep-red velvet furniture on massive marble-slab floors intricately inlaid with stone, contained more than twenty thousand rare books, the pontiff's private collection. Centered on the wall behind them was an enormous painting in a bright gold frame of the serene, iconic face of the Black Madonna.

He was invited by the pontiff to take a seat. De Santis paused briefly to take a look out the famous window from which Augustine greeted pilgrims in St. Peter's Square each Sunday morning. Through this window, many who had traveled great distances got a once-in-a-lifetime glimpse of the man believed by Catholics the world over to be Christ's messenger on earth. While De Santis had more than a clue to why he, one of the pope's most trusted advisers, had been summoned on this warm summer afternoon, he knew the change of venue from their usual meeting place meant their conversation would carry special importance.

After an exchange of pleasantries, the pope stared silently toward the many bookcases across the room. He said nothing for nearly a minute, as if reflecting on a thought he had considered for a long while.

De Santis, nervous, began to tremble. He could bear the silence no more. "Holy Father. About Barcelona," De Santis began. "I—"

"Your ambitions are no secret to me," the pope said. "And they are not the reason I have asked you to come today."

De Santis was surprised and relieved.

Augustine continued. "You are aware of the Vatican's participation in the news conference being held in America next week, are you not?" He nervously spun the ring on his left hand around his finger several times as he spoke.

"I am, Holy Father," De Santis replied. "It is a day for which we have all prayed for some time. I'm thankful to see it come."

"Yes; this American scientist, this Dr. Bondurant, has provided us with his draft statement. We've reviewed it, and it appears quite satisfactory to us. Here," the pope said as he pulled a piece of paper from a leather valise that sat on a small coffee table between them. "Have a look for yourself."

De Santis scanned the document quickly and looked at the pontiff. "A sufficient admission, even an apology, I would say," De Santis said. He turned away from the pope and shook his head.

"What is the matter, Giancarlo?" the pope asked.

"I still can't believe that my Domenika, my star student at the Gregorian University, could fall in with this man. You no doubt remember the Jozef Memo, the document Domenika wrote that summarized his abuse as a child by one of our own?" De Santis said.

"I do." Augustine nodded his head in sympathy.

"If Domenika's analysis is to be believed, this Bondurant is a hollow man. I can understand his lashing out at the Church for what happened to him. I can't understand his lack of candor as to why."

"Domenika has since disavowed that dossier, the one she wrote," the pope said.

"Yes, well, she did the inexcusable: She fell in love with her subject. I suppose stranger things have happened. At least now something's been salvaged."

The pope slowly rubbed his temples with his forefingers as if he were in unusual pain. "Well, we have lit upon the subject for which I've summoned you," he said. "There is much to discuss, but when I conclude, I am going to seek your help."

"Of course, Your Holiness. You will have it, as always."

De Santis was anxious to hear of his charge. Any assignment successfully achieved for the pontiff would only further redound to his credit and the possibility of bishophood someday.

The pope nodded silently. Over the next twenty minutes, he relayed a story to De Santis that the priest was stunned he'd never heard before. The Vatican could be a compartmentalized palace, where secrets hidden within secrets passed down by only a few were kept for centuries. De Santis thought his long-standing friendship with the pope and his chair at the Gregorian University, created for him by Augustine himself, had made him privy to even the most confidential of subjects.

He learned of the discovery of the "Revelation of the Sindon," an ancient codex buried deep within the Vatican's archives for centuries. The information it contained proved beyond all doubt the authenticity of the Church's most revered relic, the Shroud of Turin. Notwithstanding the Church's knowledge of such an important piece of history, it had been the pontiff's personal decision to agree with the counsel of his Commission of Bishops, who had recommended withholding the information revealed in the codex—a veritable ancient autopsy report on Christ himself—from the Church's flock and the world. Instead, a plan had been hatched to allow for an unprecedented scientific examination of the Shroud, the burial cloth of Jesus Christ. The Vatican aimed not only to prove the validity of the artifact to a skeptical public but also to embarrass its longtime critics, Dr. Bondurant chief among them. His best-selling books criticizing Christian doctrine had been a sore spot with the Vatican for years. The pope explained to De Santis that his bishops' advice and his own decision to embarrass Bondurant through such a plan had turned out to be a grave mistake, one he had come to regret.

"You remember Father Parenti, don't you?" the pope asked De Santis. "One of our more obscure librarians for several years?"

"I do, Your Holiness," De Santis said. "The little one with the terrible affliction in his spine."

Just as De Santis spoke, a tall but crooked figure slowly crossed the library entrance. He had a pronounced limp in his walk and balanced a delicate white china tea set on a tray in both hands that looked to be in peril of tilting over with every step. With his neck bent and his head seemingly fixed permanently toward the floor, the sullen figure arrived at the coffee table between them, unable to look up. De Santis noticed a slow stream of drool at the corner of the mouth of the disfigured servant-priest with unnaturally bulging eyes. He watched with pity as the tea service clanked noisily and nearly crashed onto the table before them. As hot tea splashed and cookies tumbled, De Santis looked away out of deference to the decrepit waiter.

"That will be all, Father Barsanti," the pope said. He slowly shook his head in pity. When the twisted priest had shuffled silently away and was clear of the room, the pontiff spoke again.

"It's a long story about Father Barsanti, Giancarlo," Augustine said. "And an even more interesting one involving little Father Parenti and the miracle of his healing. It's as if they've traded places, he and Barsanti. There is difficult history between them, but that is for some other time. For now, let me continue."

"Of course, Your Holiness," De Santis said.

"I had the chance to sit with our Father Parenti for hours some time ago," the pope said. "You'll recall he was assigned to the Vatican's council when it looked over Dr. Bondurant's shoulder during his examination of the Shroud."

"Yes," De Santis said. "I know he was with Domenika in Turin when the investigation took place."

"He sat in the same chair as you do now," Augustine said. "And he came to reveal a great many things, none of which have gone further than this room."

De Santis's eyes grew wide.

The pope continued. "Apparently, Dr. Bondurant's study team, a renowned group of scientists, had been infiltrated."

"I'm not sure what you mean," De Santis said.

"Infiltrated by someone in league with a cult. I've no doubt you know their name. They are the Demanians."

"The cloning sect?" De Santis asked.

"One and the same," the pope said. "They pretend to be concerned with mankind's resurrection, but the deplorable science they practice is free of any human value whatsoever."

"Indeed."

"This scientist in question," Augustine said, "the one in league with the cult, a Dr. Sehgal, came to betray Bondurant. According to Father Parenti, he not only provided the basis of false evidence to discredit our most holy Shroud but he engaged in another, graver act of treachery that is cause for even greater concern."

The pope looked about him. He pulled his chair close enough to De Santis to ensure that his words held the import of a secret. De

Santis leaned to within inches of the pontiff's lips, so close he could smell his breath.

"What is it, Holy Father?"

"This scientist, the famous Dr. Ravi Sehgal, a biologist and geneticist, was on a quest, as it were," the pope said. "His intent was to steal specks of blood from the Shroud in order to retrieve DNA."

De Santis closed his eyes. "You mean to—"

The pontiff would not let him finish. "Yes, an attempt to clone from this blood our savior Jesus Christ himself," Augustine said. He shook his head.

De Santis tapped his foot on the marble floor. "Your Holiness, I know this crazed sect. I have studied them. Jesus Christ is but a prophet to them, not the risen Lord."

"Yes."

"They hold the view that Christ Jesus was sent by the Severin— extraterrestrial gods, as it were—along with Moses, Buddha, and others, to instruct mankind, to guide us toward an everlasting life through—"

"Cloning," the pontiff whispered.

"Surely you're not telling me this scientist was successful," De Santis said as he stared directly into the pope's eyes.

"Yes and no," Augustine said as he looked away and stared toward the floor.

"I don't understand," De Santis said.

"It's impossible for the spiritual soul to be cloned. This we know," the pope said. "But these Demanians, they have apparently succeeded in cloning a physical specimen from remains taken from the Shroud. But according to Parenti, the blood they used is not that of Christ our savior. There are apparently two different sources of blood to be found on the sacred Shroud. They have secretly given birth to a child from a second source with no relation to the savior at all."

De Santis was incredulous. "And these Demanians, they know this? They know they have cloned the wrong being?"

"Not to our knowledge. You have heard of Hans Meyer?" the pope asked.

"The head of the sect?"

"Yes. Bondurant's discovery of two different sources of DNA has remained a secret from him. As far as we know, Mr. Meyer, the sworn enemy of our Christian faith, believes he is the ward of the clone of Jesus himself."

De Santis shook his head again.

"There is more, I'm afraid," Augustine said. "Your Domenika— *our* Domenika—has been caught up in all of this. She was of the mind that she had conceived a child by Bondurant. She had not. This sect found a way to trick her, to drug her, to inseminate her and fool her into carrying to term a child she thought to be Bondurant's."

De Santis checked himself. He'd let out a groan so loud he thought he might have been heard across St. Peter's Square. He could read in the pope's aged eyes how concerned he was for Domenika, someone De Santis had mentored as his favorite student for years. "Domenika was right from the start," the pope said as he cupped his hands to his face in sorrow. "I assigned her to watch over Dr. Bondurant and his investigation. She warned us away from the path we chose, our effort to embarrass those like Bondurant whom we called our enemies. All of this has led to real trouble for her and, perhaps, the world." Augustine paused again. He pressed his palms hard against his temples as though to relieve pressure.

"Your Holiness, I have to ask," De Santis said. "Are you all right? You seem to be in considerable pain. Shall I call your physician?"

"There is no need. He's run tests," the pope said. "I hear ringing, but he finds nothing. I'm afraid it's a different kind of trouble that plagues me."

"What is it, Your Holiness? What trouble are you referring to, then?"

"It's what I must ask you to investigate, Giancarlo," the pope said. "The child I've spoken of, the one Father Parenti claims came from the Shroud, is said to be in Kolkata, of all places."

"Kolkata? Are you certain?" De Santis said. "If you're correct, the child is in certain danger. I'm sure you've heard the news from there. It's very dangerous. I've heard reports that there are now a million dead. Some believe it is the beginning of the end of the world."

"Yes, that is the problem. You see, my friend," the pope said as he lowered his voice to a whisper again, "if what Father Parenti relays is true, and I believe it quite possibly is, this child clone may be the cause of this terror."

"What are you saying, Your Holiness?"

"I'm saying the Church—indeed, the world—has not seen something like this in a very long time. I'm saying we're getting word that this child born of the Shroud is possibly a Watcher."

The term nearly made De Santis ill. He couldn't believe the pontiff's words. The last time he'd heard mention of a Watcher was in relation to studies done by noted Vatican scholars more than half a century before. They had carefully researched the suspected relationship between Adolf Hitler and the occult. It was suspected that the depth of Hitler's evil and his near success in achieving his unthinkable goals stemmed from a pact between the heinous dictator and a supernatural force that had befriended him in the form of a Watcher. There had even been rumors of a document, an agreement signed in blood, between the two. He knew the Vatican's deep archives held secret files that some had said provided definitive proof.

De Santis was a confident man, but he looked down at the floor as though a great weight had been placed directly on his shoulders. Perhaps his assignment was not a gift after all, he thought.

"What is it you would like me to do in your service, Your Holiness?" he asked. He had never imagined such a story was possible, nor had he expected an assignment so large. On the other hand, success might mean extraordinary things, perhaps even a mitre, a bishop's cap.

"I'm deeply sorry to say this," the pope said. "But in some way, we are responsible. The Church is responsible. *I* am responsible. We have put Christianity at risk. If what I've learned is true, we helped to bring about this godforsaken resurrection of evil through our ill-conceived plans to humiliate Dr. Bondurant. And now we have a responsibility here. You must find the child. We must learn for ourselves what we have done."

"I suppose I should start with our Domenika," De Santis said. "I know that she and Bondurant have wed. Forgive me, Holy Father, but I still despise the man."

"I beg you to remember the Church's sin against him when he was a child," Augustine said.

De Santis turned his head from the pope as if to avoid the charge. "However, perhaps he can be of use to us by providing a clue," De Santis said.

"Yes; reach them quickly, Giancarlo. We've no time to lose."

The pain now evident on the pope's face looked as if it stemmed from the blade of a knife twisting into the back of his neck.

"And if I do track down a monster, a Grigori, Your Holiness," De Santis said, worried about the misery on the pontiff's face. "If there is indeed a Watcher reborn, then what?"

"Then God forgive us, my son. Our souls are at risk, for we have opened a doorway to hell," the pope said. "We are but his servants, and as his son proclaimed, we know not what we've done."

Chapter 13

Kolkata

It was two o'clock in the morning, and Khan made her way across the living room of her massive suite at the Oberoi Grand, the finest hotel in Kolkata. Her assistant, Juliet Armistice, had just rung the doorbell to Khan's suite. Khan, bleary-eyed and in search of the front door, had to navigate her way through the dark to find it. An obstacle course of paper mounds and towers of research reports reached for the ceiling at almost every turn. They were poised to topple at the slightest touch.

"These are the very last of them," Armistice said as she breathlessly unloaded the heavy stack of documents into Khan's waiting arms at the door. "WHO says this is it. It's everything they have left on the flu."

As a foremost authority on the Spanish flu, a devastating disease that had appeared out of nowhere exactly one hundred years before, Khan had begun zeroing in on some grave similarities between that flu and the plague that had swept the Indian subcontinent during the past year.

Armistice, a lovely brunette almost six feet tall, had the figure of a runway model. But her looks betrayed her. She had worked on post-doctoral studies in immunology at Duke for the past year, and had been invited up from several floors below to confer with the "Great Khan" for a few reasons. For starters, she was one of the few on Khan's investigative team who had knowledge of the science behind the evolution of certain plagues, including the Spanish flu.

The Spanish flu—or the "Great Flu of 1918"—was the largest medical catastrophe in history. It had likely killed more people than the infamous "black death" of the Middle Ages or even World War I. Five hundred million people around the world had suffered from the Spanish flu. One hundred million had died. Life expectancy around the world had declined by twelve years. The flu had killed more than seventeen million people in India alone. While the new "Devil's Sweat" in India had claimed just more than one million lives since Khan had been asked to intervene, most of her highly confidential computer models showed at least twenty million dead in India *alone* before a cure might be found.

Khan invited Armistice into the suite and turned on a single lamp in what was once an opulent sitting room. The light revealed some-what of a catastrophe, a space that resembled a dormitory study lounge more than a presidential suite. Khan had not allowed the housekeep-ing staff to touch the room for several days, for fear they might shift a single document out of place. She had even threatened to horsewhip one of the waitstaff who had attempted to collect the scores of take-out cartons and water bottles strewn about the floor. A few piles of trash overtook a coffee table that had disappeared from sight.

"Let's talk about shapeshifters, shall we?" Khan said as she cleared several pizza boxes from a white linen sofa to find a seat.

"We can talk all night," Armistice said.

Khan watched as Armistice sorted through the pizza boxes. To her delight, she found one box half-full of slices that looked relatively fresh. She reached for a piece.

"Okay, then," Khan said. "We've been running tests for a week now on frozen remnants from the 1918 flu virus."

"Yes," said Armistice. "I was on the team that ran the compares on the Devil's Sweat today. We detected H1N1 in the mix."

"Which means, for starters, we have a known quantity on our hands. A highly known virus containing subsets of eight commonly recognized genes."

"I can name the genes if you'd like," Armistice said. "But while we haven't fully confirmed it, we may have a shapeshifter in our midst. With sixteen possible H types, mankind has only ever seen and identified three: H1N1, H2N2, and H3N2. We wouldn't know what to do if the genetic structure of a virus such as H4 or H5 appeared. We'd be . . . well, we'd be—"

"Screwed," Khan said as she helped herself to Armistice's pizza find. She took a slice in one hand and with the other picked up a document that had been lying on the coffee table. She flipped to its executive summary and handed it to Armistice to read. Khan stretched her legs on the coffee table before them while Armistice spent several minutes carefully studying the summary of the report.

"In the last century," Armistice said, "we . . ."

"Go ahead and say it," Khan said.

"We've never seen shapeshifting like this before," Armistice said.

Her voice quavered a little. "Call it what you want: H4, H5, H6. Call it faerie blood. The genetic substructure of our Devil's Sweat is truly different from anything we've seen before."

"It carries an extra gene," Khan said.

"This explains why everyone who encounters the virus is dying regardless of what we try."

"Yes, it does," Khan said. "There's not even partial immunity to a virus mankind has never seen before. There's no 'herd' immunity present. It's what I thought. Everyone dies."

"What do you mean, everyone dies?" Armistice asked.

"Well, it takes time for *everyone* to die, Juliet," Khan said. She spied a thermos on the table and hoped it held the slightest bit of warm coffee inside. Mercifully, two cups were left. Khan poured the coffee into some Styrofoam cups she found stuck together on the floor. "Do you recall what they said about the Spanish flu when it had run its course?" Khan asked.

"Somewhat," Armistice said.

"Before the virus burned itself out, it circled the world three times," Khan said.

"What does that mean?"

"It means you and I are just going to have to find a way to save everyone."

Armistice took a seat on the couch beside Khan, crossed her legs, and stared forward.

"What's wrong?" Khan asked. She knew she'd struck a real nerve.

"I had the opportunity, if that's what you want to call it, of talking with some of the dying today," Armistice said. "It's for that report I promised to Dr. Ryan. I can't help but envision the likes of me, the likes of you, in these terrible circumstances sooner than we might know, and I—"

"Cyanosis? The bluing of the skin?" Khan asked. "Edema of the lung? The suffocation?"

"For God's sake, stop it, Dr. Khan," Armistice said. She looked sick. She pulled away from Khan and retreated into a ball in the corner of the couch.

"If we're to do any good in this great big mess we find ourselves in, it means it's likely we may find the answer outside the bounds of science. Something strange is happening here, and I'm worried but hopeful that we're going to stumble upon a solution. You know about Albert Mitchell, don't you?"

"I used to laugh when I heard the stories about him when I was an undergrad. You don't mean to say you believe any of those tales?"

"What did you hear?" Khan asked.

"He was the devil's agent or something who started the Spanish flu, and he was the only one capable of stopping it."

"On the morning of March 4, 1918, a company cook by the name of Albert Mitchell reported sick to the infirmary. He was stationed in Fort Riley, Kansas, at the time."

"Here he was in Kansas, but they called it the Spanish flu. I never understood that," Armistice said.

"Just about every country in the world censored its press over how devastating the flu had become so as not to cause a panic," Khan said. "The only exception was Spain. They censored nothing, and as a result, the world looked at Spain as the likely source of the plague. But it wasn't."

"So it all starts with this Mitchell?"

"Toward the end of his shift, he reported to the infirmary with a simple fever," Khan said. "By noon that day, more than one hundred soldiers had checked themselves into the same hospital. They literally melted in their beds. Within a week, more than five hundred men reported in sick, but just as many had been sent around the world to fight the war with their flu intact."

"I know the symptoms were horrid," Armistice said. "Unspeakable."

"Here's the thing, Juliet," Khan said. "The Army researched this over and over and over. They're world-class record keepers. But they have no record of a company cook by the name of Albert Mitchell at Fort Riley, Kansas. There is no record of his ever being stationed there. No record of his having spent even a day in the infirmary. Yet somehow he became the cause of the greatest pandemic in the history of the world."

"But how could he possibly matter today?" Armistice asked. "I don't see the relevance."

"Juliet, I can't explain it. But I believe that for the first time in our lives, we're facing a completely unknown threat, something not of this world," Khan said. For a very rare moment, she felt what it was like to be truly afraid. Her father had taught her to meet every fear, every challenge, with eyes wide open and head-on. Those who couldn't were weak.

"I saw your notes, Dr. Khan," Armistice said. "You believe our odds of defeating the plague in the time we have are slim."

"I know it sounds strange, but I *know* when the long odds are right. My gut is telling me that just like a hundred years ago, there's an Albert Mitchell out there somewhere," Khan said. "We need to find him, or he needs to find us. Otherwise, it really could be the end of it all."

Chapter 14

Amtrak Acela, Washington, D.C., to New York

As soon as Domenika's photo popped up on his phone, Bondurant smiled and tapped the screen to answer her call.

The picture he had chosen to identify her when she called from her cell was a classic, one of Bondurant's favorites. Her mother had taken it when Domenika was only about eight years old. In the photo, she posed playfully, holding her first violin in one arm and striking a classic "muscleman" pose with the other. For Bondurant, the photo captured the essence of both the child and the woman he had come to love. Beautiful, strong, artistic. He was fascinated by the determination in her eyes.

"Where are you?" Domenika asked. The urgency in her voice was clear. "Do you have Wi-Fi?"

"We're on the Acela to New York. The press conference is at ten a.m.," Bondurant said. He took his phone away from his ear for a moment to look at its screen. "I'm fine. Plenty of signal here."

"I need to send you a video. I have something incredibly important for you to see."

Bondurant looked past Parenti to catch the swift-moving scenery as it passed by in the large window beside them. The train was moving at top speed halfway between its two main stops along the Northeast Corridor.

"Padre Parenti says hello, by the way," Bondurant said.

The little priest nodded. Bondurant could see he was preoccupied, positively captivated by the coffee, juice, and Danish the first-class car offered for free.

"Did you get it yet? Did you get it?" Domenika asked.

"Get what?"

"The link! The link I sent you from Fox!"

"What link?" Bondurant asked. He hadn't a clue what she was talking about.

"The link about Laurent!" Domenika shouted. "I just texted you."

Bondurant looked down at his cell phone's screen again. As he did, a new text message from Domenika popped up. She'd spared any words in her haste. It was simply a link to a video. Bondurant tapped it with his thumb. "Okay, stand by," Bondurant said. "I'll call you right back."

He hadn't heard news of Laurent in a long while. He'd wondered whether Meyer had eliminated him after the cloning when he was no longer of use. He stared at the screen. Suddenly, he saw the face of the man he had seen only in news photographs before: Dr. François Laurent.

Parenti set down his treats. He too fixed his eyes on the small screen, incredulous at what was before them. As the two looked on, video of an anchor at Fox News appeared.

The anchor said, "Speaking of science and mystery, we have a strange story to report to you today, this one from France. An infamous French obstetrician—Dr. François Laurent—who had gone missing and was once tied to a strange religious sect, has turned up claiming success for something he has purported to be attempting for years: the cloning of a human being. Michelle DuMont has our story from Paris. Michelle?"

"David," the correspondent said, "I'm standing outside the apartment building of Dr. François Laurent, who, just days ago, apparently returned to Paris and has informed medical authorities here that he has accomplished what few scientists believed was possible—that is, the cloning of a human being; indeed, his own son."

Bondurant paused the video. "I can't believe this," he said.

Parenti sat stunned.

Bondurant hit play again. "While he has not yet provided specific proof of his effort, he is promising to deliver remarks before the French Academy of Sciences next month detailing what he claims is an unprecedented scientific feat. If his claims prove to be true, he will have succeeded in making history, history that most in the scientific and religious communities around the world have feared for several decades. We've been down this road before, though, with bogus claims from one group or another suggesting success in human cloning, only to find hoax after hoax. Before Laurent went underground a few years back, he was known to be affiliated with the Demanian sect, the same sect that previously claimed success in this area only to have their assertions proved false. Laurent is not talking for now, so we'll have to stay tuned. I'm Michelle DuMont, Fox News, Paris."

Chapter 15

Kolkata

They called them "Heaven's Steps."

Ria Kapoor plodded her way steadily upward along the mountainous trail in the same unbearable pain that had wracked her body for days. She wore her finest dress. She stopped to catch her breath and looked around her. The blood that pooled in her mouth from the open sores in her gums was now a familiar taste. She spat onto a mound of rocks beside her. Kapoor was only twenty yards from the crest of the barren hilltop, but she didn't believe the summit ahead was possible to reach. Exhausted, her breathing severely labored, she tried once again to put one foot in front of the other. She reckoned it would be another ten minutes before the edge of the cliff was hers.

The spot she chose to leap from was carefully selected. Not far from the home where she was born, the hillside was steep and rose like a protective sentry above the neighborhoods and playgrounds she had known so well as a child. She wanted to ascend into heaven from ground that was familiar.

Her symptoms had worsened. Flulike headaches, fever, nausea, and aching joints a week before had quickly graduated to attacks on her lymph nodes. Massive sores and pustules in her armpits, neck, and groin had spread to her limbs. Her blackened hands and fingers showed the first signs of gangrene. She had seen the terrible disease take the life of many neighbors in Kolkata. She knew from the onset of her respiratory problems and the vomiting of blood that the end was near. The lucky ones had passed in two days. Her only consolation for lasting a few weeks was the chance it provided to make good-bye calls to friends and family and set her affairs in order.

She was sure God had shown his vengeance for what she'd done. It was anger from the heavens above so great the world was to suffer forever. Unlike the others, she knew she was partly to blame for the curse. She knew she deserved to die. Her only hope was that God would have mercy on her soul and lead her to another, everlasting life.

Many thousands of others across her homeland had ascended Heaven's Steps of their own accord and leaped to their deaths in recent weeks to avoid the dreadful scourge. Some had chosen to leap from bridges that, in turn, created open mass graves below. Spans across the country were now guarded by police and forced to close. But alternatives abounded. Building rooftops, cliffsides, treetops, radio and water towers—even airplanes chartered for the sole purpose of suicidal jumps had become commonplace.

Others who had contracted the unforgiving illness and could not suffer the days of agony they had witnessed all around them chose to end their lives in less "romantic" ways. They stepped in front of fast-moving cars on the freeway or trains on their tracks to bring a quick end to their misery. In the process, they created havoc across the continent as those vital modes of transportation nearly ground to a halt, struggling to deal with the bloody calamity.

Entire families chose to die together. They held hands and chewed on morphine tablets until the end mercifully came. The government, helpless to aid the overwhelming number of afflicted, had no choice but to resort to dispensing cyanide pills to those who begged for relief.

Many believed they were seeing the "end of days" and participated in celebrations or acts of mass euphoria. Reports of robberies, murders, and rapes across the country had more than tripled in the span of several months. Police were called upon to quell spontaneous riots that broke out in a dozen major cities. Acts of violence, many involving religious rivalries in an effort to cast blame for the scourge, were commonplace.

Having finally reached the top of the hill, Kapoor stood motionless and out of breath at the cliff's edge as she looked out over the idyllic village where she was born. Modest, pristine, and orderly homes with manicured gardens and verdant slopes dotted the familiar countryside. As the setting sun dipped below the horizon, she could see the house where she was raised far off in the distance. She wondered if a young woman lived there now and whether the world would ever hold promise for such a girl as it once did for her. She wondered where in the world the deep and meaningful thoughts she expected at this moment could have possibly gone. She considered her last few weeks of life and remembered only the common things. Walking her cherished dog. A favorite show on TV. A phone call with her mother, who had passed just days before.

She wondered if she had remembered to lock her home. And there was laundry still to do.

Bowing her head at the cliff's edge, Kapoor made the sign of the cross. Then she bent at the knees and, with the last bit of strength she had, leaped bravely from Heaven's Steps.

Chapter 16

Mechanicsburg, Pennsylvania

Bondurant grimaced slightly as he set his empty plastic cup on the table and poured his third shot of Macallan. He looked on as Father Parenti pulled the plastic floral-print curtains across the only window in the room, their temporary lodging on the second floor of the Motel 6, now allowing only a few slivers of dull light inside.

The gray afternoon haze had swept southwest along Interstate 78. Mechanicsburg was the picture of a nonpicturesque town in which to lie low on their way to meet Domenika at Dulles Airport. They had put François Laurent and Paris in their sights.

Four hours had passed since Bondurant's media event in New York City that morning. His plan had worked. He'd been safe from all that had come, including a couple of Meyer's helpless goons, able to hide in plain sight among the crush of reporters who had packed the room to catch his every word. A quick escape backstage from anyone who wanted a piece of him had worked well. A fast private elevator to the basement of the Waldorf Astoria hotel did the trick. Two sleek black Cadillac Escalades had waited there underground to whisk them away. That and some high-speed evasive driving in the Lincoln Tunnel had ensured they hadn't been tailed.

For now, they were safe from the threat from Meyer. Outside, near the motel's office, an art deco sign cut through the haze: "Color TV/Air Conditioning." At the moment, of the motel's premier offerings, Bondurant's only interest was the color TV.

"That's three, Doctor," Parenti implored. "And it's not even noon."

Bondurant knew the priest's goal was to slow his frenetic mind. Domenika had insisted he go along.

Parenti stole another look at the device Bondurant wore on his wrist. The dial read 18:06. He could tell by the look on the priest's face that the blue digital numerals had confounded him once again. He still wore the "silly contraption," as Domenika called it, the band on his wrist routinely mistaken for a watch. It was his "life meter." Patented by Bondurant years before, it was the only one in the world. It summarized in actuarial fashion every conceivable genetic trait and risk factor he could input, as well as the present state of his physical health and lifestyle. It then estimated to the year and month the amount of time he had left on earth. That is, if it were natural causes that led to his demise.

Bondurant recalled that at least a year had been subtracted off his dial in just the past few weeks. No doubt they were under great stress. There'd been the need for the temporary security detail he'd hired for the day to protect himself and the priest when they were so out in the open and exposed. While Bondurant was proud of the genius that went into his invention, he also knew it was the paltry amount of time the device computed he had left that often worried Parenti and Domenika much more.

He knew that Parenti, like Domenika, was frustrated with his little vices. He pictured the priest, on this trip as a spy for his wife, sweeping his pack of cigarettes and the glass of Scotch in front of him off the table in a desperate gesture to buy him more time. It was what Domenika would have asked him to do. But he was also certain Parenti would hold his fire for the moment. It had been a tough morning, and today he could tell Parenti was resigned to looking the other way.

Bondurant sat alone at a small table as he channel-surfed for news programs that might cover the headlines of the day, one in particular that involved him. Parenti, relaxing across the bed, was delighted to find a cheap mint candy atop a pillow behind him. Aldo rested safely beside the little priest in the crook of his arm and enjoyed his tiny share of the sweet surprise. Parenti rose from the bed and leaned in toward Bondurant as if to confide in him.

"What did you think of the pompous fool?" Parenti said in a low voice. "He arrives from out of nowhere at dinner last night, and now it's like old home week around here."

"Which pompous fool are you talking about?" Bondurant asked. Dozens of Church officials had flown in from Rome to attend his press conference. "The restaurant was full of them. I felt like the whole Catholic Church was there to celebrate my demise."

"How could you miss him?" the priest said. The disgust in Parenti's voice was clear. "I'm talking about Father De Santis, the one in love with Domenika."

Bondurant was midway through a large gulp of Scotch and nearly choked getting it down. He turned his head toward Parenti in an instant. "In love with Domenika? You have to be kidding me."

"Oh, I know the type," Parenti said.

"The last thing I'm worried about is her running away with a man who wears the collar."

"Then you're naive, my friend," Parenti said. The priest placed a hand on his hip and imitated Domenika in a moment of sheer delight as she described her longtime friend. "'Giancarlo is divine! Giancarlo was my mentor! Giancarlo! Giancarlo!' I've never seen her so animated over someone. I tell you, I don't like the smell of it."

Bondurant laughed for the first time that day. Aldo joined in with a sudden bark.

"If I didn't know you so well, Father, I'd say you were jealous. Is that it?"

Parenti turned as red as the burgundy bedspread beside him and sat back down on the bed. He focused on the TV as if to avoid Bondurant's knowing stare.

"I'm just saying, of all the Vatican representatives who professed to know her, the way he described their relationship was a little too close for comfort to me," the priest said. "And the Cary Grant looks? He's trouble. I don't trust him."

Before their conversation could continue, news footage played across the screen that caught Bondurant's eye. He used the remote control to turn up the volume of the TV.

The top news story of the hour, one that Bondurant had followed with an intense interest for months, was about the Devil's Sweat pandemic, which had ravaged its way across southern Asia from India all the way to the Philippines. The virulence of the unknown microorganism that spread the disease and the lethality of its effects on the population were so powerful that they had earned the nickname from the top epidemiologists at WHO.

The news story entranced Bondurant for good reason. What was once a hunch in his mind about the origin of the plague had now become a well-formed theory: the source of the virus was otherworldly, and the world might be powerless to stop it.

In what was a foreboding sign, the CNN anchor interrupted his exchange with the network's top health correspondent to cut to a press conference under way in New Delhi. Bondurant leaned in to listen to the story and remembered everything Harrington had told him at Yale only days before.

"Excuse me, could you state your name for the record one more time and for those viewers just joining us?" a correspondent off camera shouted toward the podium.

The striking woman at a lectern that strained under the weight of a mountain of microphones looked perturbed that she would have to repeat herself.

"My name is Dr. Shakira Khan. I am on special assignment with the World Health Organization. I have no formal statement for you at this time. I will take a few questions, and then you will have to let me get back to work."

Bondurant had heard of Khan before, but this was the first time he had actually gotten a glimpse of her.

Parenti sat transfixed as well by the scene that unfolded before them.

Another reporter's voice shouted from off camera. "Dr. Khan, is WHO continuing to insist on an indefinite ban on international travel of all kinds in the affected regions in southern Asia? There have been many complaints that these restrictions are harming the ability of families to reunite during this crisis."

"I would warn anyone considering a defiance of the travel ban to and from the affected areas that they would not only be putting their own lives at risk," Khan said, "but they would be risking the spread of this disease to their relatives on all seven continents. The path of the disease has widened by a thousand miles in recent weeks because of the wanton actions of many who have defied the ban. Twenty thousand are now dead in Bangkok because of a single air traveler who skirted the rules."

"But the *New York Times* is reporting this morning that your travel ban is threatening to bring commerce in one of the world's largest economies to a halt," another reporter shouted. "What do you say to that?"

"I say screw the *Times*," Khan said. Her penetrating eyes looked to be on fire. "Tomorrow they will be reporting that more than one of every fifty living persons on this planet is likely to succumb to this disease."

"On what basis do you say that?" another quickly asked.

"On the basis that I just said it, sir," Khan said. "Look. I'm making news here. N-E-W-S. Here's your headline. I'll wait while you jot it down. One in fifty will die. Or would you like me to *write* the story for you too?"

There was a distinct pause and a stunned silence before another question was cautiously thrown by a reporter in the first row. "How does WHO arrive at those calculations?"

"This presumes the development and rapid fielding of a vaccine in the affected regions within six months, worldwide in one year," Khan said. "For every year's delay in finding a cure, our projections are that an additional one percent of the world's population will perish."

Bondurant grimaced. Parenti lowered his head.

Another reporter shouted a question. "How does the outbreak of Devil's Sweat compare to the spread of viruses you've seen in the past?"

"If we aren't able to locate the source of the virus and from it derive a compound to test and then treat the disease," Khan said, "this one has the potential to easily outdo similar events of historic proportions."

"Can you be more definitive?" another asked.

Bondurant watched as Khan leaned forward and stared directly into the cameras, as if for effect. He was fascinated by her detached demeanor regarding the numbers and the terrible news.

"We have a runner here. It's a very fast runner. Meanwhile, we have no way to stop it. No cure. This monster may only run its course once it's begun to kill off its hosts at a faster rate than they can transmit it."

Bondurant watched as the room packed with journalists became dead silent.

"Without a vaccine, it's like a fire that must burn itself out, you see?" Khan said.

Bondurant shook his head. He turned to talk to Parenti, but as he did, the CNN anchor interrupted Khan's press conference with the story Bondurant had waited the last few hours to hear.

"Sasha, I'm sorry to interrupt, but we have some other breaking news coming out of New York this afternoon. It's the story we've been anticipating for a week. We'll return to you in just a moment."

"Okay, here it comes," Bondurant said as he prepared to take his public beating.

"Apparently, the chief scientist responsible for the famous investigation of the Shroud of Turin that took place two years ago has produced a startling revelation likely to turn both the religious and scientific communities on their heads. Let's go to Sam Weist in New York, who has that story for us. Sam?"

Bondurant stared grimly at the TV screen. He knew what came next.

"That's right, Craig. This one's a head turner, and the Catholic Church and millions of Christians throughout the world have greeted it as welcome news. More than two years ago, we were led to believe that irrefutable scientific evidence existed disproving the authenticity of one of Christianity's most sacred relics, the burial cloth of Jesus Christ, popularly known as the Shroud of Turin. We all recall the extraordinary news events at the time stemming from the unprecedented scientific investigation sponsored by the Catholic Church meant to validate the relic after so many years of controversy. That investigation backfired terribly when new evidence uncovered by the group of scientists hired by the Church proved the Shroud to be a hoax."

The anchor commented, "I know the Church vehemently disputed the results of the investigation, but my understanding is that they have never come forward with any evidence to contradict it. The whole affair was a real embarrassment for the Church and a disappointment to Christians worldwide."

"That's right," the correspondent said. "Well, in an extraordinary turnabout, the chief scientist of that investigation, an atheist and the author of a bestselling book on the subject, Dr. Jon Bondurant, has come forward today to disclaim the results of the investigation he led. He even went so far as to claim foul play by one of the scientists on his team, remarkably pointing a finger at Nobel Prize winner Ravi Sehgal, who you'll remember was found shot dead in his native India more than a year ago."

"What exactly is this Dr. Bondurant saying?" the anchor asked. "That there's now a chance the Shroud is real?"

"Here's Bondurant from his news conference this morning."

Bondurant suddenly appeared on the TV screen. He looked confident but contrite as he said, "What I'm saying is that our findings disputing the authenticity of the Shroud of Turin should be discounted. It's as plain as that. Unfortunately, our evidence was compromised by one of our scientists intent on biasing the investigation. The burial cloth we examined is not the work of some artist experimenting with animal blood, as we first reported. The relic is actually A.D. first century, and all aspects of its nature—including the blood samples gathered from its surface—are not of animal origin. Our findings now are consistent with the alleged story of the crucifixion of one who went by the name of Jesus Christ."

As he watched himself on the screen, Bondurant flinched at the incompleteness of his statement, but he had no interest in being held up to further ridicule or, worse yet, branded a lunatic as he tried to explain the entire story involving Hans Meyer and the Demanian plot to clone a child from the Shroud.

A flood of questions from the ballroom packed with reporters poured forth. Only the carefully crafted half-truths Bondurant had rehearsed would suffice to prevent further sensationalism or even panic as he tried to explain the unexplainable.

"How could such a fundamental deception occur?" a reporter asked.

"You would have to ask Dr. Sehgal about that, but obviously now that's impossible," Bondurant watched himself say.

"What do you know about the circumstances of his death?"

"He shot himself. I'm afraid there isn't anything more I can add."

"How did you come to learn of his efforts to compromise the study? Do you believe it's connected to his suicide?"

"I received evidence from someone I presume worked as one of his assistants. I've never heard from him again. As for Sehgal, I presume his reasons for doing what he did died with him."

"You were the lead scientist in the effort. You oversaw the development of the report. You made a lot of money selling your story. Do you feel the Church is owed an apology?"

On the screen, Bondurant opened his eyes wide and looked straight into the cameras stacked three rows deep. "Yes, I do," he said. "I failed in my responsibility to deliver findings with true scientific integrity, and I deeply regret the pain this has brought upon the Catholic Church. It sowed confusion for people of faith worldwide. It was my fault we got this wrong, and I am truly sorry we did."

Chapter 17

alerkin leaned uncomfortably far over the large steering wheel and craned his massive body as best he could to get a better view through the dirty windshield of his 1983 Winnebago. He cursed his luck.

Wedged between the horizontal slats of his RV's imitation-chrome grille as he traveled eighty-five miles an hour on I-95 North was a bright-red Chuck Taylor high-top tennis shoe. It looked ridiculous stuck there, and Galerkin was embarrassed. He was in a hurry, but he vowed to pull over at the nearest truck stop to remove the sneaker before too many others passing in the southbound lanes had the chance to see it.

Galerkin's now-shoeless victim was a man who lay crushed to death fifty feet beyond a culvert near a Motel 6 on the interstate ten miles behind him. He'd hitchhiked in the wrong place at the wrong time. On a good day, Galerkin would have let him be. But it had not been a good day—or a good week. Galerkin felt it was completely within his rights to clip the man who'd stuck out his thumb when he saw the Winnebago approach. After all, he wasn't entirely off the shoulder of the road as he should have been, and Galerkin was certain hitchhiking was illegal on the interstate anyway. In Galerkin's mind, the man's profile presented an inviting target in the dusk, he was in a bad mood, and that was all there was to say about it.

On the road somewhere between Philadelphia and New York, Galerkin felt like his head was ready to explode. The day before had not started off well. He had received a call from Meyer in his hotel room, one that had lasted all of five seconds.

"Are you watching this?" Meyer had said through his hideous voice machine. "Turn on CNN." Then he'd hung up the phone.

Galerkin had sat up, slid to the edge of his bed in his boxers, grabbed the remote, and turned on the TV. When he'd found the right channel, he turned up the volume. While he hadn't recognized the voice, he knew the face. It was Dr. Jon Bondurant, speaking calmly in front of a nest of microphones on a brightly lit stage. The logo of the Waldorf Astoria hotel in New York City was emblazoned across the podium. This was not the image of the dead Dr. Jon Bondurant that Galerkin had happily stowed away in his memory. That Dr. Jon Bondurant could be found riddled with bullets, rotting somewhere on the banks of the Miles River. This was a living Dr. Jon Bondurant, who had now obviously succeeded in making a complete fool out of Vitaly Anatoly Galerkin.

Galerkin's immediate reaction at the time was completely defensible in his own mind. He had gone for his Smith & Wesson Model 500 double-action revolver on the nightstand, clicked the safety off, and fired the gun point-blank at the visage of Bondurant on the TV screen. Hitting his target, a forty-six-inch Sony flat-screen, dead center was to be expected. He was, after all, only four feet away from the TV. But what Galerkin had not had the time to consider in his moment of rage between the instant he spotted Bondurant on TV and the moment he fired his weapon was that his revolver was rated the most powerful handgun on the planet.

Beyond the 350-gram bullet that exploded the TV in front of him, as it most spectacularly did, its 3,030 foot-pounds of force required a great distance to stop. Traveling at 1,975 feet per second, the bullet blew through an inch of drywall, two inches of plaster, yet another TV, three more inches of drywall and bathroom tile, the rear end of an unfortunate woman showering in the room next door, more tile and drywall, and the thigh of a housekeeper changing the sheets on a queen-sized bed two rooms farther down the hall. There his bullet finally had come to a bloody rest.

Galerkin, slightly concerned over the ruckus that ensued, had determined that rather than remain in the hotel one more night as planned, it was the better part of valor to leave as quietly as possible down the back stairs. And so he had. He'd climbed into his Winnebago and headed north. There Dr. Jon Bondurant would be found, and Dr. Jon Bondurant would die.

Galerkin had more paying customers beyond Meyer, more than he cared to count. And he had at least that many victims in waiting identified by those same clients. Their names were scrawled on a list that never left his wallet. Yes, there had been some distractions with other work. And yes, Galerkin had gotten a little older and a little slower. But Meyer's target, Jon Bondurant, while only one of many on his list, had made this personal. He'd been smart—too smart. Galerkin had chased him, the woman, their tagalong priest, and his silly dog for more than a year now with no luck. Each time he thought he'd gotten close, he found he'd missed by inches. An empty hotel room, a changed address, a different car, and assumed names had all come into play. They'd kept moving and moving, staying a step ahead, as if to taunt him along the way.

Galerkin had not been humiliated in front of an important customer like this before. Never. It was no way to do business, and Bondurant and the girl were going to pay. He hadn't yet figured out just how Bondurant in particular was going to be eliminated when he actually caught up with him, but the hit was sure to be of a nature the assassin would relish for years.

As he spied signs for a truck stop three miles ahead, Galerkin checked his watch. He wanted to make the city by nightfall. But there was still the shoe in the grille. It was embarrassing. It had to be removed. He knew no self-respecting assassin would leave it be.

Chapter 18

Over the Atlantic

There were only two things Domenika knew had the power to take her mind off the terrifying turbulence they were experiencing on their flight to Paris: one was prayer, and the other was her seat companion, Jon Bondurant. Domenika's pleading to the heavens hadn't calmed their jarring ride. Now it was Bondurant's turn to distract her from the thought of dying. She thought it was also likely her only chance to discover what he had in mind for her nemesis, Dr. François Laurent.

"Jon, there's something I want to ask you about," Domenika said. She grabbed his forearm and clung to it once again as she felt the airplane's giant aluminum wings shudder so hard that they vibrated the entire plane. She pictured the aircraft's ailerons snapping off like wooden toothpicks in the storm that surrounded them.

"Our last will and testament?" Bondurant joked as he turned toward her and produced a smile.

Domenika envied him for how he seemed to rest at ease during the bumpy ride. He'd probably already calculated the odds of the plane disintegrating over the ocean at thirty-five thousand feet. She hoped they were infinitesimally small.

"Well, besides that," Domenika said. "You said in the taxi you had an idea in mind for Laurent. That he might be good for something instead of turning him over to the police."

"I did. It's based on a theory I have," Bondurant said. "It's not scientific, by any means. If I'm wrong, well, we've got nothing to lose. But if I'm right, we may have a chance to use him to help a lot of people."

"Use him how?" she asked. She wanted justice.

"You have to trust me on this one. I need you to go along."

"You said it could help a lot of people," Domenika said. "Is it about this plague that's had you so worked up?"

"It is. But I think it's also bigger than that."

"I don't know how we can possibly help, but if you think we can lend a hand to these poor people falling ill, then I'm in."

"Good, because, knowing you, you're going to believe there's some risk involved," Bondurant said. "No risk in my view, mind you, but I'm sure there are a whole lot of people, your friends in the Vatican included, who would want to stop something I think we need to try."

Domenika dug her nails into Bondurant's arm and left several marks. Her concern came half from fright over another lurch in the plane and half from fear of what Bondurant might have up his sleeve.

"Exactly what is it you want to do?" she asked.

"First, tell me what you know about rapture in the Bible," Bondurant said.

"That's a trick question," Domenika said.

"What do you mean?"

"The word *rapture* never appears in the Bible."

"All right, then," Bondurant said, "let me put it another way. What do you know about the prophecies in the book of Revelation?"

"I know them by heart." Domenika said. Bondurant had a genius IQ, and she delighted in reminding him that she was often his peer.

"Okay, then, tell me about the part when Jesus Christ comes riding like a superhero through the clouds on a white horse with a giant army behind him. He has an iron staff clenched between his teeth or something like that."

"You're talking about a description of the Second Coming, Jon," Domenika said. "It's been misunderstood by many. So while I know you're making sport of biblical prophecy, you're playing with fire."

"I know, I know. I figured you'd say that."

Domenika closed her eyes to concentrate. She was a classically educated theologian who knew countless biblical passages by heart. "Revelation, nineteen," she said. "'I saw heaven standing open and there before me was a white horse, whose rider is called Faithful and True. With justice he judges and wages war. His eyes are like blazing fire, and on his head are many crowns. He has a name written on him that no one knows but he himself. He is dressed in a robe dipped in blood, and his name is the Word of God.'"

"Very good," Bondurant said. "And then? Get to the part about the sword."

Domenika closed her eyes again. "'The armies of heaven are following him, riding on white horses and dressed in fine linen, white and clean. Coming out of his mouth is a sharp sword with which to strike down the nations. He will rule them with an iron scepter. He treads the winepress of the fury of the wrath of God Almighty. On his robe and on his thigh he has this name written: KING OF KINGS AND LORD OF LORDS.'"

"That's it!" Bondurant said. "Exactly. When Jesus Christ returns, he will strike down nations with his sharp sword. Millions, maybe billions, will die. That's the risk I'm talking about."

"Forgive me, Jon," Domenika said, "but I'm not following you at all."

"What if, Domenika," Bondurant said, "just what if it were possible to use Laurent, only this time for good? Use him to resurrect DNA we have from the Shroud, only now from blood we *know* to be that of Jesus Christ?"

Domenika sat stunned. Meanwhile, the turbulence that had engulfed all four hundred passengers aboard Air France Flight 23 came to a complete halt as she considered Bondurant's absurd idea. She wondered if the sudden stillness that surrounded them, like the eye of a storm, presaged a disaster.

"To do *what*?" Domenika asked. Bondurant had suggested outlandish ideas before, but this was too much. She couldn't believe her ears.

"Domenika, I know, I know. You're going to tell me two wrongs don't make a right."

"Two wrongs *don't* make a right, Jon. This is Demanian logic. It's what got us into this mess in the first place."

"Fine. But I have a notion this plague that started in India and now threatens the whole world is somehow connected to the child we had to leave behind there."

Domenika stiffened. Even though she knew just what he was

likely to finally reveal about the child, for some reason, she wanted to hear him say it.

"I don't think the child's of this world, Domenika."

"I know."

"You do?"

"I do. Go on."

"And I'm betting this plague isn't either."

"So then what?"

"I have a hunch the only way to stop the carnage and maybe even to stop the child from doing worse is to, like you said, play with fire. Biblical fire."

"Fight fire with fire? Is that it?"

"Well, yes. Sort of."

Domenika released Bondurant's forearm and folded her own arms as if to dismiss him. She was upset that he hadn't confided in her before about the origin of the clone-child. Now she could tell he didn't have a clue to the drastic consequences that might come with the kind of "artificial" Second Coming he'd proposed. Either that, or his complete lack of belief in biblical prophecy and the true Second Coming meant that he was denigrating the beliefs of Christians the world over. Prophecy of the Second Coming came not just from the book of Revelation. It came from the mouth of Jesus, himself. To doubt the Second Coming was to doubt the words of Jesus, and therefore the word of God. Either way, she felt Bondurant had to be set straight.

"Jon," Domenika said. "First, like many others, you're confusing the Rapture with the Second Coming. They're two separate events."

"I've read that Christians like you see them tied together as one."

"Well, there's the Catholic faith's view of 'end times,' Jon, one that has stood for thousands of years. And then there's everybody else's version, that of many modern-day Christians. They have a very different vision for the Second Coming. It comes from the nineteenth century. They believe something else altogether will happen before the world's end."

Domenika knew the dispute between Catholics like herself and the many "born-again" Christians who believed much of biblical prophecy in the literal sense was a sensitive one. It was fraught with differences of opinion and interpretation over many years. She knew she needed to tread carefully, as Bondurant had proved adept at exploiting cracks and contradictions in religious dogma his entire life. If he could dismiss the consequences of the Second Coming as foretold in the Bible and Christ's certain return to earth, she felt his half-baked experiment to bring about a scientific resurrection of Jesus Christ through DNA might look harmless, even reasonable.

"So you'll admit that—"

Domenika wouldn't let him finish. "All right," she said. "Make light of prophecy if you will. There are honest disagreements over more biblical passages than you can count. There's a real divide among those of faith when it comes to what happens at the end the world. You may not believe this, but I'm just as skeptical of the premillennial dispensationalists as you."

"The premillennial who?"

"The Left Behinders, Jon," Domenika said. "My gosh, don't you read anyone's books but your own?"

The bumpy ride resumed as the plane encountered more turbulence, although not nearly as violent as before.

"Your Christian 'cousins.' The ones who believe in the Rapture that occurs *before* the Second Coming. Jesus comes, and there's real hell to pay. All the righteous who believe or have believed rise up to heaven, and all those with sin, the nonbelievers—"

"Like you," Domenika said. .

"Yes, like me. Well, it's hell on earth for us for a thousand years of tribulation until he comes again."

"What I believe—what we of faith believe—presages the end of the world and the Second Coming—the literal return of Jesus Christ to earth—is something that *ought* to bother you, because some of it might have already happened."

"What do you mean?"

"Catholic doctrine states that terrible things—just like the plague you want to stop—will be part of the great tribulation just before he returns. And then, like you've said, there's the child I bore . . ."

Domenika had to stop for a moment as horrendous thoughts tied to her captivity in India the year before raced through her mind.

"You should know I've had premonitions of my own," she continued. "The child in the hands of Meyer, the one Laurent brought to life through me? Like you, I've asked myself, who might he be?"

She paused again. The "Fasten Seat Belt" light illuminated as the chaos of their flight returned. She was prepared to shock Bondurant into a possibility not even he might have considered. Her hope was that he might take the prophecy of the Second Coming in the serious light it deserved.

"Go on," Bondurant said.

"I don't know for sure. But I do know we've been warned of a day like this, Jon." Domenika said. "Jesus himself foretold that 'false messiahs and false prophets will appear and perform great signs and wonders to deceive.'"

Bondurant sat up in his seat and gripped the armrests to steady himself in the chop. His eyes were now more intense. "Domenika, what do you believe would happen if we successfully cloned a being from the DNA of your Christ?" he asked. "Do you really mean to tell me you think it would lead to the end of the world? Really? Truly?"

"I can't answer that, Jon," Domenika said. "What I know is what I believe. It's in the book of Matthew."

"What's it say?"

Domenika closed her eyes again. "Matthew twenty-four, verse thirty-seven. 'As it was in the days of Noah, so it will be at the coming of the Son of Man. For in the days before the flood, people were eating and drinking, marrying and giving in marriage, up to the day Noah entered the ark; and they knew nothing about what would happen until the flood came and took them all away. That is how it will be at the coming of the Son of Man. Two men will be in the field; one will be taken and the other left.'"

Domenika watched Bondurant close his own eyes when she finished, as if to avoid the consequences of what she'd said. Meanwhile, their giant aircraft had slowed as if to prepare for more of a wild ride ahead.

"So if it's possible to clone Jesus . . ." Bondurant said. He opened his eyes once more.

"So that he truly comes before us?" Domenika asked.

"Yes, and he's the Son of Man, as you've said."

"Then according to biblical prophecy—" Domenika stopped herself short, unable to imagine the thought.

"It's possible the world could be *saved*, Domenika," Bondurant mused.

"Yes, or half the world will be dead."

Chapter 19

Paris

D r. François Laurent's face grew red. He knew it had been a mistake to agree to see an unknown emergency patient with no referral who'd called him on the phone on a weekend. He'd been trying to slowly rebuild his failing obstetrician's practice in Paris amid the controversy surrounding his claims about human cloning. He'd taken on cases he would never have considered before. And now, despite his good intentions, he had a large and powerful hand gripped brutally tight around his throat.

Laurent had no idea who the intruder was or why he found himself in the man's choke hold. He'd been shoved from the waiting area of his office all the way to the very end of the hall, where he was slammed onto the examination table in the last open room. At first, Laurent assumed it was one of Meyer's stooges. Some had been sent before to intimidate him and ensure his continued silence over his work to birth the child of the Shroud. But once he caught a glimpse of Domenika standing behind the man, he knew whom he was dealing with. The day he'd feared had finally come.

"Up on the table and feet in the stirrups, *Dr. Lawrence*," Domenika flatly demanded. It was the false name he had used with her in India the year before.

"You have to be joking," Laurent protested as he gasped for breath. Bondurant had driven him into a prone position against the inclined table. All that was left to obey Domenika's command was for Laurent to elevate his legs a few more inches toward the footrests raised high.

"You heard her," Bondurant commanded. "In the stirrups."

Laurent knew he was completely overpowered. He gave up any notion of escape. He slowly spread his legs and rested both ankles in the horseshoe-shaped leather pads stretched out before him.

"L-L-Look," he stammered as he glanced toward Domenika. "I know why you're angry. I can explain. I—"

"Do it, Jon! Castrate him," Domenika said as she pulled a large kitchen knife from her purse and pressed the handle into Bondurant's hand.

"Wait, wait, wait! Let's talk this out," Laurent pleaded. Several beads of sweat had begun to rise on his forehead. "At least hear me out before you do something insane."

"Insane?" Domenika said. "You mean as insane as what you did to me?"

"I owed a debt to Meyer. I know it was wrong. But it's Sehgal you have to blame for choosing you. I gave you a living miracle, madame," Laurent protested.

"I was unconscious, and not by choice!" Domenika screamed.

"You raped me! The child wasn't mine. And then you deceived me for eight full months to carry it to term? Cut them off, Jon!"

Laurent watched as she reached down and gripped Bondurant's wrist in both her hands. She shoved the knife to within an inch of Laurent's crotch.

"I wasn't aware at the start that you were unwilling, Domenika. You have to believe me," Laurent pleaded as he watched the blade begin to slice easily through the thin fabric of his pants. He watched in terror as she leaned against the blade handle with all her weight. "It was only later that Ravi let on that you were involuntary. It was too late. By then I had no choice."

"Too late?" Domenika cried.

She struggled repeatedly to plunge the knife forward against the resistance of Bondurant's powerful arm.

"I sat trapped in that bed for months carrying that child to term, and all the while you knew. You *knew*! You had me in a prison, you monster."

Laurent cringed again as Domenika shoved Bondurant's wrist farther forward with all her might. As he began to feel the knife blade puncture the flesh of his upper thigh, he cried out in pain. He closed his eyes and struggled to inch backward away from the blade but had precious little room to move.

"Domenika, I know this is of no solace to you now, but you have given the world a gift," Laurent pleaded as he squirmed sideways to buy an inch of space. He tried to reason with her. "You nurtured the living Christ. We have made history! And the world may never be the same."

"I'm afraid you're right about one thing, Doctor," Bondurant said as he wrested his hand free from Domenika's grip. "The world *may* never be the same."

Laurent watched in relief as Bondurant withdrew the blade from his pant leg and tossed the knife onto the counter beside him. He could tell Domenika was disappointed that Bondurant had found a way to keep his cool. She took a seat in a chair next to the exam table but continued to eye the knife. Laurent pressed his back against the apparatus and looked on as Bondurant turned, locked the door behind him, and took a seat on the stool directly opposite his outstretched legs. Bondurant reached for the knife he'd just discarded and held it aloft to examine it closely. Laurent braced himself once more.

"Whose DNA do you think we might find on this?" Bondurant asked as he watched a tiny droplet of Laurent's blood work its way down the sharp edge of the blade.

"Mine, of course," Laurent said. He gripped his groin area in pain.

"And whose DNA do you believe you cloned from the Shroud with Ravi Sehgal?" Bondurant asked.

"That of Christ," Laurent responded. "I watched your announcement myself on the news just yesterday."

"The trouble with that theory," Bondurant replied as he buried the knife with a loud thud an inch into the exam table, "is that while the Shroud *may* have belonged to someone named Jesus Christ, the DNA from the blood you used to clone the child did not."

"That's impossible," Laurent replied.

"The child, the one Domenika gave birth to—do you know where he is?"

"That's not something I can reveal. I'm on call in the event there's an emergency with the clone. But I have no interest in giving Meyer and his cult another reason to hunt me down until I'm dead."

Laurent watched anxiously as Bondurant yanked the knife from the table and turned the handle over and over in his palm. The tip of the blade pointed in his direction again.

"Let us spare you the trouble, Doctor," Domenika interrupted. "Would it be Kolkata?"

Laurent stared at her. "I've been told the child's been moved because—because of, you know, the deaths," he said.

"Do you believe in hell?" Bondurant asked.

"Of a sort, yes," Laurent replied.

"Hell is what you and Meyer and Sehgal have unleashed on this earth," Bondurant said. "The countless who have died so far, from Kolkata to Saigon? They're just the beginning. This plague is now creeping across four continents. And there's no force in this world that can possibly stop what you've done."

In what little time remained of the morning, Bondurant recounted for Laurent what he knew to be the true source of Laurent's child of the Shroud. He described for him the extraordinary powers that the cloned offspring—a Watcher—even in a childlike state, could possess as prophesied in the Bible and other religious texts.

Laurent sat in stunned disbelief. "This is why you believed the child could be found in Kolkata?" he asked. "Because it's the birthplace of this plague they say has no earthly origin?"

"Yes," Domenika responded. "And no earthly cure."

Laurent gathered himself and bowed his head. His body went limp. "Spare me, please. What can I do to help you?" he asked.

"Plenty," Bondurant said. "Domenika and I talked it over on our way here." Bondurant turned to look at Domenika, but she only turned away. "There's something we need from you urgently that, as fate and science would have it, only you apparently have the power to perform."

"And what is that?" Laurent asked.

"I possess the DNA of the man purported to be Jesus Christ, Doctor," Bondurant said. "I've pulled it from another relic, a piece of fabric from almost two thousand years ago found in the Basilica of the Holy Blood in Bruges," Bondurant said. "This DNA matches with the blood of Jesus Christ on the Shroud. And Sehgal's techniques to rescue a usable amount of that DNA from ancient blood are now nearly commonplace for those insane enough to attempt cloning. So I'm asking you, how many eggs are required, and how long will this take?"

"Required for what?" Laurent said. He was incredulous. "For cloning? To perform it again?"

"How many?" Bondurant pressed.

"At least a thousand."

"How many do you have access to?"

"Twice that in frozen storage," Laurent replied. "They've not yet been returned to Meyer."

"Then ready them, Doctor," Bondurant said. "Ready them as though your life depends on it."

"What could you possibly mean?" Laurent said.

"There is a beast, in the form of a child you've delivered, that has somehow let loose a virus on this earth. It's supernatural. It's going to devour millions. My hunch is we're going to need miracle blood to stop it."

"And it's a child savior as well who will slay this Watcher, rescue Christianity, and save us all?" Laurent asked.

"A savior shed his blood to save us all once before," Domenika said. "It may be there is no other way."

"And this savior's blood. You're certain it will stop this plague?"

"No, but we have no choice but to try. It may be that a child's blood is all we have," Bondurant said. "Like it or not, I share some responsibility for all this. I'm not taking no for an answer."

"And who will serve as surrogate this time, Doctor? Who shall be the mother of God?" Laurent asked. His mock piousness was clear.

Bondurant had no response. He looked at Laurent with dread for the predicament they were in.

Domenika got up from her chair and unlocked the door as she readied to leave. "I was chosen before without my knowledge," she said. She turned toward Laurent with a cold stare. "I nurtured this Watcher, this beast, and gave it life. If I am ever to see redemption, it must be me."

Chapter 20

East of New Delhi

K han did a double take.

Very few things in her world came as a shock, but the sight before her was definitely one. A petite and pretty young girl with large brown eyes and a white bow in her hair pushed a rickety shopping cart directly into the path of Khan's truck. The cart she pushed held a young boy, one Khan figured to be about eight years old. At first glance, he looked to be asleep, half-naked, dressed in only a T-shirt and underwear. He lay comfortably curled up in a ball as the girl, about ten years old, shoved him forward on half-broken wheels. On second look, however, Khan could tell the boy had likely been dead for a day.

For almost a week, Khan's solo fact-finding quest in the relentless heat of India had taken its toll. She'd been on the move from one deserted or lifeless village to the next east of New Delhi, the once-bustling capital city. She'd seen countless other dead bodies along the way on her nightmarish journey. The corpses spilled forth from every space imaginable—windows, balconies, shop doorways, or cars strewn along the roadside from Dasna to Masuri to Hapur. Why Khan would take notice of the plight of this single lost soul and the dead boy in her derelict cart she didn't know.

She gripped the steering wheel hard as she screeched to a halt in the road in front of the girl. Her mind wandered in the swelter of the blazing sun. Perhaps the girl's predicament was symbolic of Khan's own life journey. The girl pressed forward, expressionless but with steely determination.

No doubt, seeing death by plague on massive scales had hardened Khan over the years. Her job as a disease hunter came with a strange gift, it seemed. Death had forged an ironlike resolve inside, one that allowed her to take on any sight, any circumstance, in a calm and collected way, detached from the ordinary emotions that afflicted so many. Feelings and sentiments were fine for others but useless, even dangerous, to Khan. They served only to sabotage her ability to quickly and efficiently determine where an answer might lie or a cure might be found, one critical to the saving of lives.

Khan kept her foot on the brake as she watched the girl, eyes vacant but now fixed searingly on her own. She had come to a full halt with the boy to block Khan's path. The girl, probably the dead boy's sister, was a living miracle in Khan's mind. She was the only sign of life Khan had seen in more than a day. She had traveled from one ghost town to the next in search of where rumors, some of them wild, had placed the plague's first but hopefully most revealing deaths.

Khan had seen the destruction wrought by plagues many times before. But this was different. When morbidity *and* mortality rates for a disease reached 100 percent, as pandemics rarely did, life simply stopped. With millions of lives now spent near the epicenter of the plague's very birth, the world around her was apocalyptic. Khan had never seen anything like it before. She had read scientific texts on the aftermath of the explosion of a neutron bomb. There was no picture of the imagination any closer in her own mind to describe what she'd seen. Designed to maximize death by radiation while minimizing physical destruction, such weapons would leave in their wake a surreal world, one that Khan had come to know as the terrible reality of the Devil's Sweat.

"'Now I am become Death, the destroyer of worlds,'" Khan quoted like a mantra.

They were words from the Bhagavad Gita, spoken by Krishna, the eighth avatar of Vishnu. They'd been famously evoked by Robert Oppenheimer when describing his experience at Trinity, the site of the first successful test of an atomic bomb. And nothing could come closer to describing what Khan had seen. A world at halt, not at rest or peace. A world of black and white. Color, like life, had been wrung from the world. Buildings, now only skeletons, still stood in place but everywhere were barren. Stores and shops were long ago looted or burned. They littered the background as wasteland, dark and empty. Abandoned cars and cycles and carts of every kind sat discarded and deserted where they'd stalled or fallen. They formed massive piles and clogged streets one intersection to the next. Incessantly blinking or shattered, broken lights were everywhere, as far as the eye could see.

And there was the silence. Never before had Khan experienced anything like it. She would sometimes clap her hands together to produce a sound, any sound, to assure herself she hadn't gone deaf. Beyond the hum of her Land Rover's motor when she was on the move, noise had vanished.

Khan reached for the handle to open her driver's-side door. Millions had died, and many millions more would pass. Why this one young life had come to matter she didn't know.

She knew of a medical college that operated a girls' hostel in Hapur, thirty miles to the south behind her. It was completely overwhelmed with orphans of the plague. But she would befriend the young girl. She would attend to her immediate needs. She would have the boy cremated, as was the custom and need. She would backtrack to the hostel in Hapur as quickly as she could. *This* little girl was not going to die. This little girl was going to live.

Chapter 21

St. Moritz, Switzerland

Galerkin sweated profusely from the midday heat. He trudged down the marble steps that led from the mansion toward the pool house of Hans Meyer's summer residence. He walked right past Meyer and didn't even recognize him.

Meyer couldn't blame him. Gone was his electrolarynx machine, once his constant companion and the eerie replacement for his larynx that allowed him to speak. Gone was the grotesque stoma, the hole in the center of his windpipe that allowed him to breathe and smoke. His throat was now smooth and perfectly healed. Gone were the horrendous acne and the resultant pockmarks that had once riddled Meyer's face. His complexion was clear. And gone were the thin wisps of hair protruding from the back of his head that had futilely attempted to hide his massive bald spot for years. Now he sported a thick mane of sandy-blond hair. Hans Meyer had been transformed.

Once Meyer had persuaded Galerkin to sit down in the lounge

chair beside him, it took nearly five minutes more to convince the hulking Russian that he was the man he claimed to be. Meyer was amused at Galerkin's astonishment over his makeover, one that also made him look at least ten years younger.

"What you do? Super vitamins? Growth hormone?" Galerkin asked. "You used to look like head of dead fish."

Meyer blanched at the backhanded compliment, but let it pass.

"I'll tell you how it happened in just in a minute. Soon it will be obvious," Meyer said as he filled a glass with iced tea. He offered one to Galerkin, who gulped it down quickly and held his glass out for more. "But first, some business."

As Meyer and Galerkin talked, they looked over an Olympic-sized pool adorned by a dozen massive Roman sculptures that stood sentry at the water's edge. A light breeze that blew in from the west stole the sky's reflection off the water as countless ripples shimmered on the pool in the reflection of the sun. Beyond the pool was a wide, verdant lawn that stretched down a hillside that afforded a magnificent view of Lake St. Moritz and the Piz Bernina, the highest summit in the Eastern Alps. At the far end of the pool in the distance was a small child pedaling a red tricycle in a wide circle as he enjoyed the glorious day.

"Your baby Jesus," Galerkin said. "This is him on the bike?"

"Yes, it is," Meyer said as he beamed. He watched the child intently, since the two-year-old had navigated his way uncomfortably close to the edge of the pool. "You're one of the very few living outside the compound who have gotten this close."

"You should charge people money to see him," Galerkin said. "This is what I would do."

Though the child was more than fifty meters away across the

pool, his striking features were evident. With curly auburn hair that touched his shoulders and a fair complexion lightly freckled by the sun, he looked the picture of playfulness. He squealed in delight. Strewn across the lawn behind the boy were every manner of toy and gadget, several play sets, and a half dozen miniature carnival rides fit for a toddler. Off in the distance behind a small grove of trees were stables. Several ponies, perfectly groomed, grazed on the lawn in front.

"So, when was the last sighting?" Meyer asked.

"You mean Bondurant and the girl? I have someone tell me they go to Dulles. Where? I don't know. But they have the munchkin with them, that little priest."

"Dulles? Are you sure about that?" Meyer asked.

"I'm not there to see. I don't know. This is what I am told."

"I see."

"Look," Galerkin said. "You can go many places from Dulles. The whole world you can go. This man, Bondurant, he is smart. The world is a big place, you see? One time I track a man four, five years. No kidding. Five years." He reached beside him and picked up a small teddy bear that lay on a chair. He wrapped his fat fingers around its throat.

"Bondurant, the girl, they're less worrisome to me now," Meyer said. "They haven't made a peep to the authorities. They're running scared."

Galerkin looked directly at Meyer and began to twist the bear's neck into a knot.

"What you mean no peep? Who is peep? We have a deal. One million dollars," Galerkin said. He rose from his seat quickly. The shadow he presented was large enough to shade Meyer entirely from the sun. Meyer knew better than to stray an inch from a deal with Galerkin.

"Of course, of course, we still have our deal," Meyer said. It was time to quickly change the subject. "Tell me about this Father De Santis," he said. "I'm told he's been dispatched in my direction."

"Sent by the pope," Galerkin said. He sat back down.

"I know that. What else do you know?"

"I hear they have interest in your baby Jesus. That's all I know," Galerkin said. "You want De Santis on the list? I charge extra for priests." Meyer watched Galerkin reach for his wallet on the presumption that he had another name to add to his hit list.

"Not yet," Meyer said. "I need to learn more about him first." He was ecstatic to confirm that he'd gotten the Church's attention already—and at the highest level. This before he'd even lifted a finger to reveal the child and demonstrate to the world the powers the boy had begun to display.

They watched the child closely as he made a wide arc and spun the bike in their direction. Having spotted Meyer's guest, the boy began to pedal cautiously toward them from the far side of the pool.

"Look closely, Vitaly," Meyer said. "The little boy on that bike will one day have the pope on his knees, bowing to me. It will be a Demanian world. Wait and see."

"I don't know. I don't like religions," Galerkin said.

"You've said that before."

"I don't like these Christians most of all. Doing favors. Feed the world. Keeping so many alive."

"Yes, I know," Meyer said, exasperated. He'd heard this speech from Galerkin before.

While Meyer sometimes felt his executioner possessed the

intellect of a child, when it came to the assassin's opinion of Christianity, he enthusiastically supported Galerkin's point of view, although Meyer had important and personal reasons of his own.

He'd always believed the Catholic Church was responsible for the death of his mother. She'd been spurned by the faith for her marriage outside the Church when denied an annulment from her physically abusive first husband. Her very public excommunication in such a small and close-knit town had been bitter. His family, once in the center of a strong circle of faith, had been destroyed and ostracized, and in the aftermath, his mother had taken her own life, thereby committing a mortal sin. As though his mother's death was not enough, according to Church "law," Meyer had been branded a "bastard" son from the age of ten. It was an insult he'd carried into adulthood, one he'd sworn he would eventually avenge.

Now he watched as the child safely made the turn at the corner of the pool. He was headed straight for them.

"I don't like your big plan," Galerkin said. "Silly. Too many people already in this world. Why you need to clone more?"

Meyer let out a quiet sigh. He figured Galerkin had maybe a fifth-grade education at best. It was no use trying to reason with a giant who seemingly possessed the brain of a child.

As the boy sped forward on the tricycle to within a few feet of where they sat, he backed off the pedals, put his feet on the ground to stop, and came to a halt with a broad grin.

"He's little Gorbachev!" Galerkin blurted out. "Where did boy get such god-awful spot on his head?"

Meyer grimaced as he watched the assassin press his fleshy finger directly against the deep purple mark on the child's forehead. The mark Galerkin referred to was a port wine stain that ran halfway across the child's forehead. It was a permanent disfiguration and his only imperfection. The boy, obviously sensitive to the flaw, pushed Galerkin's hand away and cupped his own hand over the spot to hide it. He pushed his bike forward and ran his front wheel on top of Galerkin's pricey Italian leather shoe, over and over.

"That mark's been there since Kapoor had him baptized in the river. It left a stain. I haven't a clue why."

"Little Gorby, that's what he is," Galerkin said. He pointed to the mark again as he chuckled. "Looks the same as him. Too bad for you."

The boy stepped off his bike and said nothing. Instead, he reached for the teddy bear Galerkin held in his hand and seized it. Then he stared at Galerkin purposefully. He held the teddy bear close and plucked out the stuffed animal's eyes.

"Does not look like Jesus Christ to me," Galerkin muttered. He turned away from the child as though to dismiss him.

Meyer could see the boy was upset. Galerkin was being an idiot. Meyer was worried it might prompt one of the child's tantrums, something he wanted to avoid at all costs. People had been severely hurt. He thought of a way to soothe him.

"You see this face?" Meyer said. "You see this throat? Gifts from the child. Several caresses each day, and I was healed within a month." He ran his hand through the child's locks and smiled, but the boy, still offended by Galerkin, resisted and pulled away. "He is pleasant and giving to those he likes. Not so for those he doesn't," Meyer said as he stared at the assassin. "You should choose your words more wisely."

"He's fake child Jesus," Galerkin said. "I don't believe."

Meyer had heard enough, and he could tell Galerkin had too.

His face had turned red with rage over the scolding. Meyer had seen the look before. He was certain Galerkin didn't take well to criticism and probably felt he was being made a fool—to a child, no less.

Meyer got up from his chair. Galerkin rose just as quickly, but instead of turning to depart up the hill, he grabbed the handle of the boy's tricycle. He lifted the bike slowly, stared at it, looked down at the boy, and then pitched it twenty feet away, where it sank into the shallow end of the pool.

"Walk on water, Jesus Christ," Galerkin said. "You go." He let out a loud laugh.

Before Meyer could summon a servant to wade into the water to retrieve the bike, the child bolted in the direction of the pool. When he reached the water's edge, it was clear he could see the bike was fully submerged in the pool almost ten feet from dry land. He stared at it closely and paused as if to consider the difficulty of the feat. Then he stepped forward, one foot after the other, directly on top of the water as if it were a delicate sheet of glass. Having taken several small steps across the top of the water for a full ten feet, he reached down into the pool for the tiny red bike and lifted it into the air by the handle. Then he turned and made his way back, completely dry, with the bike in hand. When he arrived at the pool's edge and stepped onto hard ground again, perfectly dry, he looked up and smiled.

At that, both Meyer's and Galerkin's jaws dropped. Meyer stepped forward, ready to embrace the child for his newfound talent. Galerkin stepped backward, ready to run.

CHAPTER 22

Baltimore
One year later

F ather Parenti sat across from Dr. Terry O'Neil in the living room of the spacious two-story penthouse suite that had been their home for all of two days. It was their third hideout in as many months, and it overlooked the strand of distant lights of the Baltimore skyline. For Bondurant, Domenika, Parenti, and his lovable dog, their life on the run had come to a critical pause.

Nearly swallowed by the massive leather couch that enveloped him, Parenti reverted to his nervous habit. He fidgeted with the buttons on his cassock, one after the other.

"I thought Bondurant said you were considering giving up the priesthood," O'Neil said. "Why the costume?"

O'Neil, a brilliant Oxford scientist, DNA expert, and friend of Bondurant's, had flown in from London the previous evening when he knew the birth was at hand.

"We have a special visitor coming tonight, and it's important I look the part," Parenti said.

"A special visitor?" O'Neil asked. "Bondurant said nothing about such a surprise."

"It was Domenika's idea. He's sworn to secrecy, and I'm not at liberty to say," Parenti responded as he looked about. "And to tell you the truth, I'm not the least bit happy about the setting here."

"I thought the first Christ child was born in a manger, Father. No room at the inn and all that," O'Neill said. "I presume this place will suffice."

Parenti could tell O'Neil was trying to lighten the moment, but it was useless. He was concerned that Domenika and Bondurant had chosen the privacy of their temporary home over the safety of a hospital to bring the child into the world. He was beside himself with anxiety. They all had agreed that the birth should occur with the utmost secrecy, but Parenti was sure a birthing at home was going too far. What if there were problems? Dr. Laurent, who had attended far more complicated births in places much less hospitable than a two-story apartment, had assured Parenti he could relax. He was not the least bit concerned.

Every facet of Domenika's pregnancy, from in vitro fertilization (IVF) a bit more than forty weeks earlier to the full onset of induced labor that day, had gone smoothly. Almost a year had passed since Laurent had found himself at the mercy of the couple who had barged their way into his office in Paris and demanded his help.

Almost two years before, Bondurant and Parenti had obtained a sample from the only other relic beyond the Shroud known to possess what many believed to be the savior's blood—a small cloth in the Basilica of the Holy Blood in Bruges, Belgium. The genetic material on the relic matched that of the Shroud, and, using DNA from the cloth sample spirited away from Bruges, Laurent had successfully created a living embryo from a combination of stem cells and an enucleated egg after more than seven hundred painstaking tries. From there, it left only a routine IVF procedure with Domenika as the surrogate mother for a pregnancy to occur. All that was needed now was the safe delivery of the child, and Laurent's role was complete.

Laurent had induced Domenika into labor six hours earlier. With her pregnancy at full term, she and Bondurant agreed the moment had come. She lay in bed with Bondurant at her side. She was now fully dilated and ready to give birth. Parenti listened closely from the living room. When there was momentary silence, he could tell she was resting between the deep contractions. Then came the inevitable chill of her cries of labor. Aldo sat nervously glued to the couch, his tiny paws covering his ears to muffle the sound.

"Remind me again why this was a good idea?" O'Neil asked as he grew increasingly anxious. "This isn't exactly how I envisioned the Second Coming."

"Nor I. Dr. Bondurant and I debated over this moment and its meaning to no end," Parenti said. "He told me to take swimming lessons if I was so concerned."

"Swimming lessons?"

"I think Domenika filled his mind with prophesies of the Rapture and the great flood that's to come before the savior returns. He's joked about it ever since."

"I see," O'Neil said. He looked about him as though rising water might be a real concern.

"But the devil's agent walks this earth, Doctor," Parenti continued. He reached for Aldo and held him close in the crook of his arm.

"And this Christ child, reborn as it were, is truly our only hope?"

"I have always believed, and still do, that it is Christ's return to this earth that will save mankind. I just never imagined it would happen like this."

"Suppose this *is* the Christ child to be born in this house tonight," O'Neil responded. "Or a clone, that is, from Christ's blood. What is an infant to do in the face of living evil the likes of which you and Bondurant have described?"

Parenti held his ears as Domenika's moaning became loud once again. A worried look grew on his face. "As an infant? Nothing, I'm sure," he replied. "But Bondurant has a theory about the blood you speak of and how it just might halt this plague. But it requires belief. And prayer."

"And after that? Even if the virus were to end, what about the Watcher who remains?"

Parenti paused to think. "He's not much more than a toddler himself. One day, they will meet. And we will need a savior who stops this creature from finding other means to take us all."

O'Neil shifted uncomfortably in his chair. "How old was Jesus when he performed his first miracle, Father?"

"I'm afraid we don't have that long," Parenti replied. "He was thirty years old before he turned water into wine."

"We'll definitely need a bigger feat than that."

Suddenly, the doorbell rang. Aldo leaped excitedly off Parenti's lap and skittered along the marble floor toward the entryway of the apartment. Parenti rose from the couch and bounded as quickly as he could down the hallway after Aldo toward the door. When he returned to the living room a minute later, he was followed by two tall men dressed in black, both carrying sidearms. Behind them marched a priest who carried a small cross of gold held directly in front of him. To Parenti's dismay, the bearer of the cross was followed close behind by Father De Santis, Domenika's mentor and friend. And just behind him, a gray-haired figure slowly appeared. He shuffled forward with age in his step but a look of purpose in his eyes.

O'Neil, stunned at the presence of the two armed men, rose from the couch to greet the visitors behind them. His eyes grew wide.

"Dr. O'Neil," Parenti said as he took a knee and cast his eyes downward, "I would like to introduce you to the Holy Father, Pope Augustine the Second, Successor of the Prince of the Apostles and Vicar of Jesus Christ."

O'Neil, in utter shock, sank to his knees alongside Parenti and his dog and awaited the pope's blessing. Augustine smiled, touched each of their foreheads—including Aldo's—and made the sign of the cross.

"Padre Parenti, I trust you are well?" the pope asked. "You're standing proudly now, I see, and every bit the hero we have come to know."

"I'm fine, Your Holiness," Parenti said, pleased that the pontiff had noticed his straightened stature. "I only hope your secret journey was not too taxing."

"No trouble at all. Now, the mother, Domenika, where is she?" the pope asked.

"Just up the stairs, Your Holiness," Parenti said. "I know that she feels blessed to have you here for the historic birth."

The pope smiled but shook his head. "Padre Parenti, you know that it's only for Domenika that I'm here," he said. "May God bless this child, and may he walk in the light of the Lord. But—"

"I beg your forgiveness, Your Holiness," the little priest said. "You've reminded me of this before."

"I have, good father," Augustine said as he helped Parenti off his knees. "Domenika has every good intention in mind. But I do not believe—the Church does not believe—that the Lord's divinity can be rearranged under a microscope or transferred by what our scientists call DNA."

At that moment, Domenika's cries from the pain grew even louder and began to come in short bursts. The pope made another sign of the cross and went to his own knees in prayer.

Suddenly, Domenika's moans ceased. Sensing something terribly wrong, Parenti leaped to his feet and raced toward the foot of the stairs. Before he could climb them, a faint cry that quickly grew in strength seemed to vibrate the walls of the entire home. It bore the unmistakable sound of a newborn infant, a sound more beautiful than any Parenti had ever heard before. After several minutes in which no one emerged, Parenti could not help himself. He bounded up the steps and was greeted by Bondurant at the top of the landing.

"What has happened, Dr. Bondurant? Is everything all right?" Parenti cried out.

"He's born, Father," Bondurant replied with the broadest smile Parenti had ever seen on his friend. Bondurant then pointed to the window that revealed the cloudless skyline of Baltimore to the east. "And Father, mind you, not a single drop of rain."

The little priest smiled as well and watched Bondurant nod toward the pope as they clasped hands. When they all bowed their heads, Parenti couldn't help but note curiosity in De Santis's eyes. They were fixed on something Bondurant held, a small object, a vial filled with blood, gripped in his free hand. Parenti knew full well what it was. He prayed against all odds that the vial might also be filled with hope for the world.

PART 2

Chapter 23

Coos Bay, Oregon
Four years later

omenika brought her car to a stop and sighed. She knew it would be a minute or more before she could move again. The driver of the log truck with a colossal load of Douglas firs had cut the corner too tight when he tried to make a left turn in front of her. With several cars lined up behind her, there was no way for Domenika to back up and give the truck more leeway to make the turn.

As she waited, Domenika stared up at the slow clouds overhead. They hugged the tall stands of alders that blanketed the steep green hills on either side. It was a Saturday morning, and a gentle rain continued to fall as it had been doing for days. Given that it was her birthday, she'd held on to the false hope that the clouds might somehow miraculously part and make way for the small backyard party they'd planned. But the weather report predicted rain for several more days, and Domenika was resigned to changing plans.

She tapped her fingers lightly on the steering wheel to the

music that played from the radio. It would be easy to move the small celebration indoors, she thought. They hadn't planned a grand affair. Only a half dozen couples had been invited. Domenika and Bondurant had carefully befriended just a handful of people during the few years they'd lived in Oregon. Most of those coming had children who were in Christopher's preschool class. As the truck driver finally cleared the turn on his second try and missed her car by no more than a foot, Domenika glanced in the rearview mirror. She could see that Chris was sound asleep in the car seat behind her.

Coos Bay, a small town on Oregon's central coast, was quiet and as charming as a fishing village could be. It was a perfect place for Bondurant and Domenika to raise a family under an assumed last name, aside from the frequent rainstorms. Most important to Domenika, she felt safe and hidden.

Bondurant was also more loving and relaxed living there. Christopher, albeit shy and somewhat withdrawn from others his age, was happy, healthy, and fine. With the exception of several doctor visits to treat what they thought were minor migraine headaches, he had grown to be a perfectly normal four-year-old boy. Parenti, godfather to young Chris, lived with Aldo in a tiny guest cottage nearby. He too had never been more content. In Domenika's mind, life was good.

It had been four years since they'd made the move from the East Coast and abandoned their life on the run. They remained ever vigilant for Meyer, of course, but as time passed, they'd stopped glancing over their shoulders every day. They weren't completely off the grid and out of danger in tiny Coos Bay, but they had perfected the art of lying low and staying out of sight. Life had finally begun to feel normal, and Domenika had every intention of keeping it that way.

They also followed the news closely and knew full well that their nemesis had his own hands full as he tended to the needs of his growing church. The headlines worldwide told the story. The Demanian Church, with Meyer as its supreme elder, had become the fastest-growing religion in the world. It attracted millions of new faithful each year, all of whom were guaranteed life after death. Not surprisingly, the Demanian Church's growth in new converts showed no signs of slowing. One *Time* magazine cover story on Meyer's new "Wonder Faith" calculated that the Demanian Church would surpass the Catholic faith in number of worshippers within the decade.

There was no doubt what fueled the Demanian Church's phenomenal global growth beyond the promise of everlasting life on this earth. It was the miracle child, Hans Jr., the named heir, who was responsible for the remarkable success of the religion. His first reported miracles, which involved healing a handful of the sick, were initially discounted and widely viewed as hoaxes.

But over time, several families and witnesses had come forward to the media and the medical community with tales of healing. They spoke of uncanny stories involving Hans Jr. While demonstrations of the child's healing powers remained cloaked in secrecy, medical experts at several reputable research hospitals had documented more than one hundred cases of inexplicable cures of church members with various terminal illnesses, from cancer to birth defects.

Meyer, now one of the most famous men on earth, had boasted to many that his son would prove to be none other than the Second Coming of Christ himself. Salvation on earth, according to Meyer, involved conversion to the Demanian faith. For all those who believed, perpetual life through cloning, once legalized, was possible.

Of course, belonging to the Demanian Church involved several mandatory contributions. Female acolytes of childbearing age were accepted only coincident with the donation of at least one of their eggs. Every qualified follower submitted to a cheek swab that provided his or her DNA to the church. In just a few years, these saliva contributions would form the largest DNA repository in the world. It was this collection from which followers, once they had passed away and applicable state laws were changed, would be resurrected at a time of their choosing through the process of human cloning. Lifetime tithing was the rule for all, and church initiation fees were steep. While there had been some credible attempts by news organizations to investigate the Demanian Church's finances, very little had been uncovered. The faith's assets had mounted exponentially and were believed to be in excess of one hundred billion dollars.

Domenika and Bondurant, fascinated by the news of the child's purported healing powers but highly wary of what they knew to be their dark source, had watched the Demanian Church's growth with anxious eyes from afar. Each revelation of Meyer's expanded domain and the reported powers of the child had Bondurant, in particular, more concerned by the day. He knew there would eventually come a time when they would have to act, and he reminded Domenika of it often. She knew that their son, Christopher, might play a vital role along the way. But her family had suffered its share of misery tied to Meyer before, enough to last a lifetime. At present, their little corner of the world in Coos Bay provided all the excitement she desired.

With traffic moving again, Domenika knew she had no time to spare on the way to the store for party supplies. So she decided to take a shortcut onto Montana Avenue on her way to Al Frink's Groceries. In their four years of living in Coos Bay, Domenika had never needed a single item Frink's didn't have in stock. Of course, it involved a few more turns on some roads with steep grades, and the—

Wham!

Before Domenika knew what hit her, it was far more evident *where* it had hit: from the front of the grille of her Jeep wagon all the way back to the now shattered windshield in front of her face. A large and majestic doe had leaped from the woods and jumped directly into the path of her car.

Domenika's instincts were sound. The first thing she did was check on Christopher to ensure he was safe. He was, though the impact of the car on the deer had been enough to jolt him awake. As soon as Domenika had a chance to collect herself, she unhooked Chris from his car seat. She held him in her arms outside the car on the side of the street. There was no other car in sight on the rural road, but one could easily and quickly make its way around the dangerous turn.

Domenika set Chris down and admonished him to stay right at her side as she made two calls, one to 911 and one to Bondurant to let him know it was only the Jeep and the doe that had met their fate.

But in the commotion of the calls, Domenika neglected to see something that Chris had kept his eyes on. A lone fawn stood not more than twenty feet from the Jeep. With an uncanny calm, Chris led Domenika by the hand over to the fawn at the edge of the forest.

Normally, it would be any deer's nature to dash during the shock of such an ordeal. But Chris had demonstrated a way with animals, and they often seemed to approach him with little fear. Within a minute, the tiny fawn stood in perfect calm by Domenika's side, which allowed Chris to wander over to the doe stretched helplessly across the hissing hood of the Jeep. The car's radiator was in pieces, sending white-hot steam skyward.

Domenika looked on in awe as Chris carefully caressed the large deer from her splintered hooves to her bent and broken legs. From there, he stroked across the doe's wide belly. Then he moved his palms upward across the neck and head of the once-powerful animal. Domenika had never seen such healing before, but it was clear that a rapid and transformative effect had begun to take place in the doe. With every stroke of Chris's small hands, a slight trembling took place across the deer. A barely distinguishable aura of white and pale blue light had begun to rise from the animal, and soon the doe's eyes became bright. She scrambled off the Jeep and onto her wobbly legs. Quickly, she rose up straight on all fours and, without a look toward her savior or the minder of her fawn, leaped off into the forest. The small fawn scrambled on the roadway and followed only a few feet behind.

Domenika could not have predicted when Chris would decide to reveal for the first time that he possessed such an extraordinary gift. Bondurant would soon arrive around the bend, and there would be much to tell him. She searched her heart and wondered whether to tell Bondurant only that she had struck a deer, nothing more. The news of the unbelievable powers Christopher had shown was certain to change their lives. It pained her to know how they might put him in peril as well.

As they waited for help and Bondurant to arrive, she could hear the low wail of a siren. She felt the press of Chris's tiny hand in hers. They gazed into the forest where mother and fawn had made their way. Surprisingly, both deer stopped for a brief moment and turned back toward them. Domenika wanted to believe they paused in appreciation for the young boy's gift. Chris only waved as they turned and ran deeper into the woods. Then he laughed lightly as he leaped into his mother's arms.

Chapter 24

Portland, Oregon

As Christopher's frequent headaches increased, Domenika and Bondurant decided they would make the trip to Portland. The boy's doctor in Coos Bay had referred them to a pediatric neurologist at the children's hospital there who had a reputation for being one of the best in the country.

There was no doubt they would be taking the risk of being recognized outside of Coos Bay. Bondurant's fame preceded him somewhat, yet they had no choice. And there was another reason Bondurant felt the journey to Portland with Christopher could be critical. He had tried to carefully draw the boy out about the accident with the deer so that he might describe in his own way what had happened. But it was of little use. Christopher was evasive and seemed uncomfortable talking about the incident. He seemed to treat his very first demonstration of unusual power as though it were as simple as making his bed. But Bondurant, ever the scientist, hadn't slept in days. He'd had a hunch, indeed a hope, about the boy's potential supernatural abilities, but faith and hope weren't enough for Bondurant. It had to be proved. And there was likely no better place than a children's hospital for him to see with his own eyes what power, if any, Christopher might possess when those in need were present. *Then* he could act.

The MRI exam that Christopher underwent at the hospital the morning they arrived showed nothing of concern. Dr. Webb, the neurologist, found no injuries or abnormalities in his brain and spinal cord, and no tumors or cysts of any kind.

The hospital had also run other routine tests on Christopher during his visit that might shed light on the source of his headaches given all they'd ruled out. They were told it would be a short while before those test results were definitive, so Bondurant and Domenika decided to take Christopher to the hospital's playground, a small area in an interior courtyard of the large facility. Most of the young children who'd made it outdoors to enjoy the sunshine were parked in wheelchairs or sat quietly at small tables with their parents. None had the strength to make it to the playground equipment in the center of the tiny yard. It was clear Christopher was concerned that he'd have to play alone. He found a bright red ball under a slide and marched about in search of a playmate. None of the children had the strength or inclination to join him.

Bondurant glanced over as a young boy, about six years old, looked on enviously from his wheelchair while Christopher kicked the ball toward a swing set that served as his imaginary goalie's net. Christopher noticed the boy and walked over to him.

"Can you play goalie?" Christopher asked.

Bondurant was curious to see what might happen but strode

over to prevent an uncomfortable moment, just like any father would.

The child's mother answered for him. "That's very nice of you, young man," she said as she smiled at Christopher. "But I'm afraid Marcus needs to stay here and rest."

"Here, then," Christopher said. He reached out his hand and touched the boy's arm.

As soon as he did, the boy, who'd been sitting listlessly in his pajamas, lit up. Slowly, he pushed himself to the edge of his wheelchair and rose to his feet. Then, without hesitation, he walked toward the swing set. He stood as though ready to tend goal.

The boy's mother clasped her hands to her mouth. "Marcus, how on earth? My boy is walking! My boy is walking!" she cried out. She quickly reached for her phone and fumbled with it to capture video of the moment.

Domenika and Father Parenti, who'd been spying on the scene from several feet away, came to Bondurant's side.

"My Lord," Domenika whispered.

Parenti took a knee.

"I said my boy is walking! Is anyone seeing this?! I said my boy is up and walking!" the mother cried out again.

Bondurant saw Christopher look around him for other promising playmates who might join in. Within several feet, there was a young girl sitting on a bench. A nurse held the weak child's neck in her hand so she could raise her head and look about. Bondurant watched as Christopher approached the little girl. He braced himself, knowing their quiet lives in Coos Bay had likely changed in mere seconds.

"Can she play?" Christopher asked the nurse.

The little girl wore a colorful knit cap; she was likely a cancer patient. She looked pale and weak. The nurse, distracted by the commotion Marcus's mother was making as she hugged and cried over her child, paid Christopher little notice.

"Christopher," Bondurant called out, ready to pull him away. "How about—"

But before Bondurant could finish, Christopher had reached out and taken the girl by the hand. Gradually, as though she had simply been woken from a nap, she yawned, stretched her arms skyward, rose from the bench, and walked over to the swing set. Then she started to swing.

Bondurant's heart began to race. He watched as the nurse looked toward Christopher as though he were a ghost.

"Watch that child!" she cried out. She bolted toward the doors that led from the courtyard back inside the hospital. "Dr. Hastings! Dr. Hastings!" the nurse shouted as she ran.

Bondurant leaped forward to grab Christopher. As he reached for the boy, he felt himself being tugged hard by the back of his shirt. It was Domenika.

"Jon, let him be," Domenika quietly pleaded.

Bondurant had never seen her look so earnest. He'd been in the presence of a miracle before, one that had involved the repair of Parenti's spine, but nothing as meaningful as this. "How are we going to explain this to these parents?"

"There isn't anything we can do, Jon," Domenika said. She held Bondurant's hand and squeezed it tight. "Let it be."

Bondurant felt another hand, this one on his shoulder from below. It was Parenti.

"Amazing," Parenti said, looking on. "Just amazing." It was all the priest could bring himself to say.

Bondurant watched with them as Christopher, Aldo in tow, marched around the circular courtyard and, one by one, reached out to every child he could touch as though he were playing a game of tag.

"You're it, you're it," he said as he laughed and strode along from one to the next.

Before he was finished, almost ten children had been miraculously tapped. Within just a few minutes, the playground was alive with activity, filled with children who stepped forth from their wheelchairs or wrested themselves away from their parents' arms. Everywhere Bondurant turned, he saw only amazement or tears of joy on the faces of the parents or caretakers who looked on. Several had recaptured their children in their arms and rocked them slowly, unable to speak.

A doctor in a white lab coat rushed into the courtyard and looked around him for a moment in complete astonishment. "Is this the boy? Is this him?" the doctor asked the nurse. He pointed to Christopher, who was kicking the ball with another child.

Bondurant stepped in. "We're his parents," he said. "I'm sorry if he's caused a stir. We're just waiting for some test results. But we can be on our way." He knew there was going to be unwanted, maybe even uncontrollable attention.

The physician looked at Bondurant with wide eyes. A half dozen parents now stood behind the doctor and watched. But he had no answers for them.

"I need to know," the doctor said. "Is this the young boy with that church that is said to work miracles? Is this the boy?"

Bondurant shook his head immediately. He understood why the doctor would make such a mistake. "No, no, no," Bondurant said. "We have nothing to do with that church."

"Most of these parents have little money," the doctor said.

Bondurant looked at him, completely confused.

"So there's no charge?" one parent asked. She stood behind the doctor and held her daughter close.

"Charge?" Bondurant asked.

Domenika stepped forward. "Of course not," she said. "Whatever has happened, it's a gift."

"Where are your most severely sick patients?" Parenti said.

"In our long-term care facility, Father," the doctor said, and he pointed to a small, two-story wing beside the courtyard. "They're the children who will not be going home again."

"Christopher," Parenti called out. "Come along for a few moments. There are some other children who'd like to play as well."

Bondurant was certain he knew what Parenti had in mind. It was bound to draw notice that would expose Christopher. He had known the day might come when his son could serve a higher purpose, when he was ready, when *they* were ready. But when confronted with smaller miracles to help just a few, he was at a loss. He stood speechless.

"Let them go," Domenika said. She put her arm around Bondurant's waist and leaned her head on his shoulder.

In the next hour, Bondurant and Domenika followed Christopher, Parenti, and his pup as the hospital administrator guided them from room to room inside the silent hospice for children. Some of the severely ill children Christopher reached out to touch had been in the hospital for months; a few for years, they learned. There were children with cases of congenital heart disease, acute myeloid leukemia, cerebral palsy, and several forms of cancer. All were curious to have such a friendly visitor in Christopher. Some reached out for hugs from the smiling boy as though he were an old friend. Others were cheered with a simple shy wave of hello or a bark from the dog as they passed. Bondurant watched as each of the children Christopher visited sat up in his or her bed, instantly changed. Several children climbed from their beds to race one another down the hall.

With these recent images from their afternoon at the hospital in his mind, Bondurant held Christopher close in his arms as they bounded down the hallway toward the hospital's exit. It had been almost two hours since Christopher had begun to make his "rounds," and news had traveled fast. Twitter feeds and text messages had already alerted the media, and reporters had arrived to report live from the chaotic scene. The small crowd of medical staff, parents, and curious onlookers at the facility's entrance had begun to swell. The uproar as Bondurant tried to clear their way to leave the facility started to make him concerned for Christopher's safety.

As they burst from the hospital entrance into the sunlight of the late afternoon, Bondurant set Christopher down and held his hand as they started to run to their hotel across the street. Domenika and Parenti followed close behind. A dozen or more of the most curious took chase. Fortunately, Bondurant and his group made it to the hotel lobby and into the elevator alone. They were breathless.

When they reached their room, Bondurant went immediately to the outdoor balcony and leaned over the railing to measure the problem. A fast-growing crowd had formed between the hospital and hotel entrances. He estimated around two hundred people had gathered. Among the curious, many who had apparently followed them on foot back to their hotel were families with children who'd come from the hospital to find them. They were joined by a handful of doctors, most still in their gowns and medical garb. As he looked down from the eighth floor, Bondurant could see there were now several TV vans, their satellite dishes extended high, hunkered down at the hotel's entrance.

The noisy crowd that peered upward at the twelve-story building had grown so large that several policemen, their patrol cars double-parked with lights ablaze, attempted to keep the crowd off the busy street that divided the hospital and the hotel. Bondurant watched a man from one of the news crews point his camera directly at him as though he was aiming a gun.

"Domenika, don't unpack," Bondurant said. He stepped away from the balcony railing to edge out of sight of the crowd. "We need to leave right away."

"Jon, what's wrong?" Domenika asked. She stepped out onto the balcony to join him and, startled at the amount of noise from below, looked down on the chaotic scene. "Oh, that's what's wrong."

"Please come down!" a woman shouted from the driveway, having spotted the two of them on the balcony. "There are more children here who need help!"

Bondurant took Domenika's arm and tugged her away from the ledge to get her out of view. He knew it was only a matter of minutes before someone in the crowd would determine their room number based on the location of the balcony where they'd been seen.

"Please! Bring down the child!" another shouted. She held a small boy by the hand. "That's all we ask."

"I'm here to say thank you!" another young woman with a child in her arms cried out.

"Jon," Domenika said, "obviously, they want—"

"I know what they want, but I'm worried about Christopher," Bondurant said. He looked inside for his son and wondered whether they'd made a terrible mistake. Christopher sat on the bed with Aldo, watching a cartoon on TV, unaware of the scene outside. "This could really get out of hand. And put us right back on the grid."

Inside, Parenti had hurriedly arranged their luggage by the door. He turned off the TV and took Christopher by the hand. "Let's make our way to the back stairwell, shall we?" the priest called out.

"Good idea," Bondurant said. "We'll hail a cab a block or two from here."

"But what about our car?" Parenti asked, nearly out of breath.

"Forget it. It's parked too close to the crowd. We'll have to get another one."

Bondurant bolted from the balcony back into the suite, swept Christopher up in his arms, and headed toward the hallway with Domenika, Parenti, and Aldo, who bounded close behind. Bondurant looked Christopher in the eyes and could see that he was worried.

"Daddy, are we in trouble?" Christopher asked. "Why are we running?"

Bondurant smiled at the boy. "Everything's fine, Christopher," Bondurant said. "We just need to leave sooner than we thought."

Bondurant looked down at his son once more. He had bided his time for years. But now he had the certainty he needed. Countless more lives might be saved by a vial that had been half filled with Christopher's blood at his birth. It had been hidden away in the hope that a day like this might come.

Chapter 25

Portland, Oregon

ome on, hop in," Bondurant said. He opened the door to the
cab he'd hailed a block from their hotel. Domenika, Christopher, and Parenti settled into the tattered backseat while Bondurant jumped in front.

"Jesus loves you, mon," the cabbie said as he glanced in the rearview mirror. He adjusted it slightly so he could see all his passengers in the rear. He rested against a sea of large, colorful beads sewn into a seat cover designed to massage his back. Bondurant, who couldn't resist the irony of the cabbie's greeting, let out a nervous laugh.

"He loves you too, my son," Parenti said. The little priest adjusted the flap on his knapsack so that Aldo too had a view. "We need a Hertz rental-car place, pronto, if you please."

Bondurant was certain he smelled weed in the car. He took a good look at the cabbie, a handsome young black man in a yellow T-shirt with dreadlocks flowing from a brightly shaded Rasta cap.

"Hertz!" the cabbie said.

He shoved the car into drive and launched the cab forward. He'd gone only fifty yards down Eleventh Avenue when he hit the brakes hard. It sent the car's tires into a high-pitched squeal. Their driver snapped his head around to get a better look at his passengers. He focused on Christopher's smiling face.

"You that boy," the cabbie said. "And you, mon, are the little priest." He slapped his knee in joy.

Bondurant grimaced.

"My name is Christopher," the boy said. He held out his hand, and the cabbie took it. "Nice to meet you."

"I hear the radio, mon," the cabbie said. He pointed at Chris. "You the miracle boy. The one at the hospital. You save all them children, mon. You have the gift!"

Bondurant watched as a broad grin broke out across Parenti's face. Parenti put his arm around the boy and squeezed him tight.

"Trust me. I told Robaire, I told him it was a trick," the cabbie said. "He say you the boy Jesus, but I say no, no, no. But he was there. His daughter was sick." The cabbie turned his attention to the street in front of him and started the cab down the road again.

When their taxi had reached Gibbs Street, it looped fully around a small and crowded traffic circle and then entered the roundabout once more to go around again. Bondurant stared at the meter and wondered if the cabbie was trying to run up the fare.

"What's your name?" Bondurant asked.

"Jamar, my friend. And what be yours?"

"I'm Jon," Bondurant said. "And I'm getting dizzy. If we go around this circle again, I'm going to ask you to pull over. We're in a hurry to get a car."

"Here's the problem, Mr. Jon," the cabbie said. "Sure as this tam on my head, we got company." He gestured with his thumb to their rear.

Bondurant jerked his head around to look behind them. Three satellite TV vans that bore logos representing the local affiliates were in a tight formation, right on their tail.

"Time to shake them loose, mon?" the cabbie asked. He'd finished careening through the traffic circle at high speed once more. All three vans were still close behind.

Bondurant looked back again. He reached for his wallet and pulled out a hundred-dollar bill. He placed it on the dashboard in front of him. "Start shaking," Bondurant said.

In an instant, the cabbie jumped the curb onto the wide pavement that fronted an entire block of jewelry and fashion stores. Soon they began to coast down the middle of the sidewalk at ten miles an hour. They rolled past the traffic snarled on the street beside them. A crowd of shoppers on the walkway farther ahead scattered on the pavement as the cab approached. The cabbie laid his hand on the horn and laughed loudly as he crept slowly forward. He split the remaining crowd in two. Parenti closed his eyes and placed a hand in front of Christopher's face to shield him from the sight. Bondurant's own face went pale.

"I take the alley to Twelfth," the cabbie said. He made a sharp right turn without touching the brakes and missed a cement wall by inches. "Give thanks, mon. They don't know Portland like Jamar know Portland," he boasted.

When they were halfway down the narrow alley between the walls of two buildings less than a foot away on either side, Bondurant turned around to see if they had lost their pursuers. For the moment, they had.

"If they smart, they catch up on Curry," Jamar said. Suddenly, the cab emerged from the deep shadows of the alleyway into the bright sunlight again. It tore past a crosswalk, barely missed a pedestrian, and then accelerated down the street again.

"How far is Curry?" Bondurant shouted out. The roar of the engine nearly drowned out his voice.

"Mon, we on it," the cabbie said.

Bondurant turned to look behind them again. Fifty yards to their rear, the TV trucks had begun to advance on them once more. Jamar seemed to pay them little mind. He adjusted his rearview mirror again to see Christopher and Parenti hunkered down in the backseat.

"Christopher, my mon," the cabbie shouted. "Tell us why you wants to be the Christ child. You better watch. You might get hurt."

Bondurant watched Christopher, who stared up at Jamar in earnest. Domenika froze at the driver's words.

"God wants us all to be like Jesus," the boy said. "Right?" He looked up at Parenti.

"He certainly does," the priest said.

"Hah!" the cabbie said. "This is righteous. I love God, mon. He loves me. Do you love God, Mr. Jon?"

The moment the cabbie posed the question, he took a hard right turn onto Marquam Hill Road and steered the cab across a break in the median strip. Then he accelerated down the wrong side of the street as if he owned it. Cars on the divided four-lane road honked their horns and steered wildly out of the way to avoid a head-on collision with the cab. Aldo let out a frightened yelp and receded deep into his knapsack home.

"Whoa! Whoa! Whoa!" Bondurant cried out. He wanted to escape the vans in pursuit, but not at the expense of their lives.

"I said, do you love God?" the cabbie shouted again.

Bondurant stared straight ahead as the scene unfolded. Then he heard a cacophony of car horns behind them. When he turned around, he saw that one of the pursuing vans now sat sideways, stalled in its lane. It had spun out to avoid oncoming cars. The remaining two vans still swerved in unison like the tail end of a snake behind the cab. Bondurant looked at the speedometer. It read forty-five mph. With the speed of the oncoming traffic, it felt like they were traveling at the speed of light.

"You get us to a rental-car place in one piece, and I'll love God all you want," Bondurant shouted.

"Hah!" the cabbie said as he pounded his palm on the steering wheel.

After another half mile of terror headed the wrong way down Marquam Hill Road, the cabbie hopped the median again and took a sharp right turn onto Jackson Park Road.

"Here's the thing, mon," the cabbie said. "God, he puts us here in this world. To live. To learn. To love. But the greatest of these things is love. Trust me. Am I righteous, Father?"

Before the priest could answer, they crossed over onto Terwilliger Boulevard and came upon a small bridge that arched over the Willamette River. Just before the bridge, Jamar hit the brakes hard, bringing the taxi to a full stop. As the TV van behind them swerved to avoid slamming into their rear, it quickly ran out of room. It veered into a construction zone at the edge of the bridge. Several workers in hard hats dashed to the side as the van skidded through a temporary guardrail and ground to a halt in a shallow ditch below. The cabbie hit the gas once more and looked at Parenti again.

"Unfortunate, but unhurt," the cabbie said, pointing to the now-stalled van. "Am I righteous, Father?"

"You are insane, son. And you are high," Parenti said as he continued to shelter Christopher in his arms. "But yes. Righteous, too."

"How far are we from Hertz?" Bondurant asked. "There's still a van behind us."

"You want to lose this van too, yes?" Jamar asked.

"As badly as the others," Bondurant said. He was intent on losing the last van, as it was beyond his imagination to try to explain the miraculous events of the day to the press.

"Then we take the scenic route," the cabbie said.

Jamar executed a daring hairpin turn and headed in the opposite direction on Route 26. The taxi jumped a sidewalk again at a narrow point right before a high cement curb. As its engine roared, the taxi bounced hard onto the surface and swerved to avoid a set of light poles that lined the street. The last remaining van on their tail, wider than the cab, followed but broadsided the tall curb. Its undercarriage slammed onto the sidewalk with a bang. Sparks flew from underneath the van. The van's driver, who'd made a safe escape from behind the wheel, looked on forlornly as his vehicle's drive shaft lay twenty yards behind.

"Hah!" the cabbie shouted out as he looked back and flashed the victory sign. "Scenic route. You'd better hold on."

Bondurant peered ahead and cringed. He saw only blue sky before them for a moment and knew it meant they approached a steep decline ahead. He was right. Within a second, the cab launched off all four wheels and careened down a steep concrete embankment in what felt like an uncontrolled dive. A flock of angry seagulls scattered in every direction. The car bounced and scraped its way noisily toward the freeway at the foot of the embankment below. When it finally cleared the freeway entrance and skidded onto the street, Jamar accelerated hard. As his tires smoked, he spun the cab into a four-wheel drift across the road toward a parking lot marked with a massive yellow-and-black Hertz sign. As he entered the lot at high speed, he missed the two parked cars at his front and rear by only a hair. The cab's tires lightly bounced against the curb and mercifully brought the car to a sudden halt.

"Yes!" the cabbie cried out as he turned the radio down. "We live. We learn. We love. But the greatest of these is what, my mon Christopher?"

"Love!" the boy shouted as he squeezed the cabbie's shoulder. He climbed from the backseat of the car as if he'd hopped off a carnival ride and raised both arms high into the air. "The greatest of these is love!"

Chapter 26

Dickerson, Maryland

ondurant had left a half-dozen urgent phone messages for Khan at WHO offices scattered around the world. He didn't know Khan personally but presumed she would at least take his call. None was returned, and he was livid at her lack of response.

Now that Christopher had clearly demonstrated the unbelievable power to heal others in need, Bondurant knew there was no time to waste. Many more people had died from the plague since his son was born. It was time to act. When he was finally able to confirm that Khan was in Washington, D.C., not far from their new home, he moved fast.

It was late in the evening when he arrived at WHO's offices on 23rd Street. He banged on the steel entrance door to the building in the faint hope that she might be there. A security guard at the front desk tracked down an assistant, who told Bondurant that Khan had already left for the evening. She had just departed for the subway, was headed out of the country, and would not return to the office for two weeks. With any luck, he might be able to catch her at the station if he stepped on it.

Bondurant sprinted to the Foggy Bottom station three blocks away. He was out of breath when he finally reached the dimly lit subway platform. The station was quiet, long past rush hour, and only a handful of late-night commuters waited for the next train to appear. Bondurant scanned the platform for any sign of Khan. He had never met her before, having only seen her face on TV. But he remembered her as a striking woman. He was confident he would recognize her if he could only get close.

As the next train arrived and slowly glided to a stop, a woman at the far end of the platform rose quickly from behind a post where she'd sat. She stepped into the first car of the train when its doors slid open before her. She was too distant to recognize, and Bondurant wasn't certain it was Khan. He knew the train would depart soon and that he might lose his only chance to catch her. He hopped into a car at the middle of the train just seconds before the sliding doors sounded their warning chime and closed behind him. He hoped he'd made the right decision. He began the long trek to the front car of the train as fast as he could.

After the train barreled through the tunnel deep beneath the Potomac River, it stopped at the Rosslyn, Virginia, station. Bondurant stuck his head out of the open car doors and looked left and right down the deserted platform. Not a single passenger got off the train. Now almost to the front car, where he might find Khan, he tore down the center aisle of the nearly empty train in a dead run, determined to reach her before the next stop.

As he burst through the last of the connecting doors that opened onto the lead car of the train, he caught his breath. Khan, absorbed in a book, sat twenty feet from him facing the rear of the train. Given that they were total strangers, Bondurant hastily tried to gather his thoughts about how best to introduce himself. But as he approached her in the aisle, the train slammed hard on the brakes in the middle of the subway tunnel with no warning and for no apparent reason. Everything in the car that wasn't sitting or was lying untethered—newspapers, a few empty bottles, a forgotten umbrella, and Bondurant himself—submitted to the law of inertia and flew forward until it found a solid object against which to come to rest. The heart-stopping incident was accompanied by a brief loss of power that left the car in total darkness.

This unfortunate combination of factors—no handhold, plenty of brake, and cruel physics—conspired to throw Bondurant into a trajectory where he tumbled forward, out of control. When he landed several feet from the point he'd been launched from, he found himself on all fours, his face planted squarely between Khan's shapely legs. When power was restored only a second later and the lights of the train car were lit again, Bondurant assumed the time was ripe for an introduction.

"And you are?" Khan asked.

He looked up from her lap. "Jon. Dr. Jon Bondurant," he said. "Nice to meet you, Dr. Khan."

"Do I know you?" she asked. "You're not the first man to kneel at my feet."

Bondurant was still crumpled on the floor where he'd fallen. Stunned and off balance, he watched helplessly as she grabbed him by his hair and tilted his head back to get a better look.

"I'm afraid you don't," Bondurant responded. He closed his eyes for a moment in embarrassment.

Khan, nonplussed, grabbed Bondurant by both ears and turned his head from side to side as if she were examining a puppy for sale.

"Just a moment," she said. "I do know you. You're the anthropologist-turned-author. The blood on the Shroud and all that?"

Bondurant frowned, grabbed her wrists, and pulled her hands from his ears in an effort to regain some composure. Freed from her thighs, he pushed himself off the floor and sat down directly across from her as the train lurched forward and started on its way down the tunnel again. He watched as she reluctantly set her book aside to deal with him.

"Yes, I'm afraid that's me," Bondurant responded. He wasn't going to argue with her. "I've been desperately trying to reach you for a while."

"I saw your messages. I don't take calls. I speak to others only when I wish to. Besides . . ." She let what she was about to say hang for a moment. She slowly crossed her legs to reveal them to mid-thigh in her leather skirt. Bondurant watched her follow his eyes to her bare legs.

"Besides?" Bondurant said.

"Besides, I wouldn't have taken your call anyway. I saw that ridiculous press conference you held. God is dead. God is not dead. You're a confused man.

"I'll tell you about God," Khan continued as she gave him too little time to respond. "He's not in a church. He's not in a temple. He's not in a mosque. He's here, Dr. Bondurant," she said. She jabbed a finger at his chest. "In you. In me. In all of us. In everyone and everything. That's where God lives."

"Dr. Khan, if this train were going all the way to California, I could talk theology with you until we reached L.A.," Bondurant said. "Right now, I need to talk to you about something that's critical for you to know."

"What do I call you?" she asked as she ignored his request. "Dr. Bondurant?"

"Yes, that's fine," he said. He began to grow impatient, and it showed.

"I will call you Jon."

"Fine. Call me Jon."

"You like my legs? Obviously, yes. You haven't stopped staring at them."

"That's not true," Bondurant said.

"Other men, they try to look me in the eye. Not you."

"I have difficulty with that at times," Bondurant said. He half considered getting off at the next stop, leaving his important busi- ness with her undone. Frustrated that he had gotten nowhere, Bon- durant could think of no other way to get her attention than to drop the bomb directly in her lap. He pulled a small glass vial from his pocket and held it within a few inches of her eyes.

"Dr. Khan, I think this blood might be the key to the antidote you've been seeking for years. I finally have some proof. I think it may have the power to stop the Devil's Sweat."

"When pigs fly," Khan said, not missing a beat. She grabbed the vial from Bondurant's hand. "Whose is it?" she asked.

"You wouldn't believe me," Bondurant said. "Suffice it to say it's a long-held hunch. But it's a good one. And if I'm right, the end of the plague you've been seeking is at hand."

Khan looked at Bondurant dismissively. She flipped the delicate vial high in the air the way she would toss a coin. It forced Bondu- rant to leap toward her. He barely caught it before it hit the ground. Khan grabbed him by his shirt collar with both hands as he leaned forward in his attempt to rescue the vial. She pulled him in close.

"I've been hunting for the source of this godforsaken plague forever, it seems," she said. "Just about every lab in the world has exhausted itself to find an antidote. Most have given up. I don't give up. I *never* give up. But there's no hope in sight. Fifty million now dead. My math says fifty million more if there's no antidote soon. And you, of all people, are going to lecture me about a hunch you have about some blood?"

Bondurant instantly realized how ridiculous the proposal sounded.

"I'm going to let you in on a secret," Khan continued. She stared directly into Bondurant's eyes, and it was clear to him that as tough as her exterior might be, there was a person inside who was clearly exhausted. "This monster, this Devil's Sweat, it's not of this world. Do you understand me? It's not derivative. It's not a strain of anything we've seen before."

The train stopped at the open-air station they'd reached in the Virginia suburbs. The exit doors opened and revealed only the black of night smothering a solitary lamp outside.

"This is my stop," Khan said as she got up to leave.

Bondurant could tell he'd lost her interest entirely. He grabbed her by the hand and pressed the vial into it. She squeezed his hand in return and paused before she let go.

"Just test it," Bondurant said, pointing to the vial now safely in her hands. "I trust the source. He has the power to heal. What have you got to lose?"

"Lose?" Khan asked. She turned and passed through the train's doorway into the night. She looked back only once. "Dr. Bondurant, it's the Devil's Sweat. We could lose where God lives. We could lose it all." She pointed again, this time to her own chest. "Everyone and everything."

Chapter 27

Dickerson, Maryland

Domenika was concerned that it was far too early to remove the training wheels from Christopher's tiny red bike, but Bondurant had assured her the right time had arrived.

"Chris, if you feel yourself falling over," Domenika told the boy, who was all of "almost six years old," "then you just put your feet down to stop. You hear?"

"I know, Mommy," Christopher responded as he stared down the street outside their home. He had a slight look of trepidation about him, not nearly matched by his mother's angst. "But when I stop, I use the brake."

"He'll be fine," Bondurant said.

They'd moved to a quiet street in Dickerson, a tiny hamlet on the banks of the Potomac River just off rural Maryland Route 28. The charming town of fewer than 2,500 inhabitants was home to White's Ferry, which operated daily near the small town as it had since the late 1700s. It was the only such outfit left on the river.

Its modest platform, topped by a tiny pilothouse, carried a handful of passengers, bicyclists, and cars back and forth at a point in the wide green stream where the muddy waters ran still. An idyllic village in which to raise a family, Dickerson had one other advantage that Bondurant and Domenika appreciated. Like Coos Bay in Oregon before it, Dickerson was a small haven where strangers stood out quickly and—also important—could be seen coming from far away.

Bondurant steadied Christopher on the bike and grasped the edge of the seat as he prepared to push the boy forward in a straight line down the middle of the street. Several vehicles were parked on the side of the road, but there wasn't a moving car in sight.

It was at moments like this when Domenika felt she could strangle her husband for his stubbornness. His confidence in Christopher's abilities wasn't unfounded. The boy had done well in kindergarten. Reading was his first love, particularly stories that involved animals. He was smart and athletic and had demonstrated excellent coordination in just about everything he tried. With some loving coaching from Bondurant, he'd caught his first fish and learned to tie his own shoes, and with a little supervision on the water temperature, could even draw his own bath. Domenika had gotten him over the challenge of zippers, buttons, and clasps and taught him how to fix himself cold cereal and juice before Bondurant dropped him off at school each day.

There were some spills and challenging moments when it came time to pick up his toys, make his bed, or tidy up his room. There was an occasional tantrum over not getting what he wanted. He wasn't perfect by any means. But in Domenika's eyes, with every such wonderful advance as riding a bike or brushing his teeth came a fear that her son, the precious child she'd given birth to what seemed like only days ago, had suddenly, truly begun to grow up. Christopher was doing "grown-up" things, and with such things came a mother's concern.

Domenika looked on as Bondurant leaned over Christopher and prepared to launch him down the peaceful lane.

"The secret is to keep pedaling, Chris. Keep going. Don't stop," Bondurant said. "If you stop pedaling, the bike will slow, and then you could fall. So keep pedaling. Keep going. No matter what."

"Oh, my Lord," Domenika said. "I can't watch this."

Christopher had a look of determination in his eyes. He placed his right foot on the high pedal and pushed down with all his might. When he did, the bike surged forward several feet. Christopher barely managed to hold on to the handlebars. As his father had instructed, he pedaled furiously away with both feet. The bike traveled twenty yards, wobbled left, right, and then left again. Christopher found his balance, straightened his trajectory, and soon was smoothly on his way. He yelped with delight.

"First try!" he cried out.

"Too much, too soon," Domenika said, nearly under her breath.

"What?" Bondurant said. He reached his arm around her shoulder. "Look at him. He's doing great."

"It's not just the bike, Jon," Domenika said. She knew it wasn't the right time to have the argument, but there never seemed to be a right time. "It's so much more."

"What do you mean?" Bondurant asked.

Domenika could feel that her husband's concern was genuine as he caressed the back of her neck. She watched as Christopher, out of earshot, continued to sail with confidence down the center of the road. "I know this is going to sound crazy. It will," Domenika said. "But I hope, with all my heart, that those precious drops of blood you took from Christopher and gave to Dr. Khan . . . Well, I—" She stopped herself short, certain her husband wouldn't understand.

"You what?"

"I hope they're worthless, Jon. I hope they don't help a single soul."

"What? What could you possibly mean?"

"I mean, maybe I've changed my mind. I don't know. I just—" Domenika stopped herself short again.

Bondurant's voice had begun to rise, and she was certain he wouldn't, or couldn't, understand. How could he? He wasn't a mother, and she hadn't fully reconciled how she felt herself.

Bondurant's arm left her shoulder. "I'm not getting it, Domenika. This is something we agreed to a long time ago."

"We did."

"And now that it's obvious Chris has some kind of incredible gift, the kind we'd hoped for, you want to put it away?"

"I want him with *us*. Not with the world. I'm afraid if he stands out—and he will—we'll lose him somehow."

"Domenika, I, for one, can't believe my own eyes. I don't understand this gift he has. But I know we have an obligation to use it for good."

"Use *it* or use *him*? You know where all this is going, just as I do," Domenika said. "This is about more than his blood. Special powers or not, he's just a child. He's my child. My son. And I can't—excuse me, I *won't*—let you or anyone else put him in danger from the devil."

"Right. Just look the other way?"

Domenika watched Christopher as he stopped at the end of the street. She could tell he was afraid to make a circle and turn himself around. He'd hopped off the bike and turned it the other way. He put his feet to the pedals again and headed directly toward them.

"Call it a mother's instinct," Domenika said. She looked her husband directly in the eyes. "Call it what you want. I care about what happens to this world. I do. And I know you have all the right intentions. But every feeling I have tells me to be careful with him, Jon, or we'll be sorry. I want to spare Christopher from Meyer, from the Watcher, and from anyone else."

As soon as Domenika had finished, she turned from Bondurant to look at her son down the lane. He took his hand from the bike's handlebars to give her a wave. Then, without warning, she heard a car's engine start. The roar was loud and distinct but far enough away that she couldn't tell exactly where to find the car. She looked toward Bondurant.

"Jon!" she said.

She watched as Bondurant bolted from his spot toward his son, who rode forward right down the center of the road. Christopher smiled and waved once more, this time to his dad, oblivious to the cars parked on both sides of the road.

Suddenly, a set of brake lights on the rear of a pickup truck only fifty feet from Christopher's path lit up. They glowed bright red. Domenika pictured the driver in a rush, unaware of the tiny bike of her child. She tried to scream but in her panic had lost her voice.

The engine revved loudly once more, as though the towering truck, a four-wheel-drive monster with enormous wheels, was preparing to leap from its spot on the side of the road.

It did.

And as it lurched into the roadway with a squeal of its giant tires, Domenika's heart jumped. She nearly fell to the road. Her son, his eyes now wide in total fear at the sight of the truck's massive grille before him, simply couldn't stop.

Domenika grimaced as the driver of the truck looked up without a second to spare and saw the little boy directly in his path. He hit his brakes and swerved as hard as he could.

When Domenika had the courage to open her eyes again, she could see that the truck had missed Christopher by less than a foot. She bit down on her lip hard. Of one thing she was sure. She would never let him be in harm's way again.

Chapter 28

Dickerson, Maryland

Domenika was proud of herself. She had never made such a perfect cake before. It was her husband's birthday, and she was excited to celebrate. Christopher had said his prayers and been put to bed. The kitchen was filled with warmth. She'd planned the perfect evening, one that would begin with two of her other favorite people coming to help celebrate.

Father Parenti would be there, of course. He was family. He'd taken a small above-garage apartment just down the lane. Her other guest for the small celebration that evening was Father De Santis, her college adviser and friend who had long held a special place in her heart. He'd made the long trek from Europe and gone out of his way to have dinner with them before moving on to attend to Vatican business in New York. He had been a father figure to Domenika during her studies, when she found herself lonely and far away from home at the Gregorian University in Rome.

She knew, of course, that the Vatican had once had a special interest in Christopher. Ever since the child's birth, which the pope himself had been present for, there had been a couple of visits by De Santis and a handful of others from the Vatican curious to track the child's progress and well-being. There had even been a secret conclave formed at the behest of the pope after the incident at the children's hospital in Portland had briefly been in the news. Led by De Santis, the group was charged "to consider the important theological questions on the possibility of divinity to reside in, and be transferred by, the DNA of man."

When the conclave's secret report on Christopher to the Curia, the pope's inner circle, was issued, it came as no surprise to Domenika. There was heaven, and there was earth. There was God, and there was man. But it was God who had created man, and as the pope had decreed, it was impossible for man to create the divine.

Beyond the Vatican's passing interest in documenting the appearance and intelligence of the child for curiosity's sake, the Church, through De Santis, had whispered to Domenika that Portland was a fluke. The Church was content to leave her family alone. Which was absolutely, positively fine by her.

Domenika also knew that Parenti was suspicious of De Santis. He'd confessed to Domenika that he was convinced De Santis's watchful eye over Christopher's well-being meant more than his brief visits implied. Bondurant had told Domenika that he was sure Parenti was simply jealous of the relationship she enjoyed with her former mentor and the attention De Santis showered on her when he came around. That explained everything, Bondurant said. Domenika would smile when reminded of Parenti's affection toward her. She adored the tiny priest all the more for his tender considerations.

Now, when Bondurant burst through the kitchen door with a bag full of groceries in one hand and a bottle of wine in the other, Parenti and De Santis were close behind. Bondurant gave Domenika a warm kiss, and the four soon sat down together for their meal. As they prepared to say grace, De Santis reached out for Domenika's hand, which drew a distinct roll of the eyes from Parenti. The little priest, on the opposite side of Domenika from De Santis, quickly took her other hand. Domenika watched Bondurant smile, take each of the two priests' free hands in his to complete the circle, and bow his head in silence. She knew Bondurant saw no value in prayer and might only mumble along with the blessing. He'd told her he had real trouble seeing the practical use for it, and she had accepted rather than argue with his point of view. At least there was real progress in his attitude of respect for others who saw the benefit of prayer in their lives, she thought.

When the meal was over and they had enjoyed another bottle of wine before dessert, De Santis set his empty glass on the table. He looked intent, as though he were ready to make a point.

"Jon, I know I'm among friends, so I'm sure you won't mind me raising this," he said. "But I couldn't help but notice that when we asked the Lord to bless us and thank him for our food, which Domenika so graciously prepared for us, you did not join us in prayer. Was there a reason for that?"

Domenika watched Parenti shift uncomfortably in his chair. It was Jon's birthday, and she too preferred to keep the conversation light for the evening. Aldo, who had been sitting beneath the table, made a hasty exit to the daybed in the room next door.

"Father," Bondurant said, "I—"

"I'm going to insist you call me Giancarlo," De Santis said.

"Giancarlo, while I don't pray, I'm also not the bona fide atheist I once was. I've come to believe there is some kind of higher energy, a higher source," Bondurant said.

"I see," De Santis said. Domenika detected the tone of studied skepticism she'd heard in the priest's theology courses years before.

"I'm still a doubting Thomas when it comes to the significance of all this ceremony surrounding faith. Not just your own, Father, but faith of any kind."

"If there is a higher energy, a higher source," De Santis said, "isn't the value of prayer obvious?" He looked toward Domenika.

She could tell Bondurant had hit a nerve. She interpreted De Santis's stare as though it were a signal for her to defend the practices of the faith, given Bondurant's opposition toward something as fundamentally important as prayer. She reached for the wine bottle in front of her and began to fill each glass again.

"I'm sure it's obvious to *you*, Giancarlo," Bondurant responded. "And when I find myself in need of help from this higher power, you can rest assured I might try it." His forced smile spelled some angst.

"I'm going to clear the table for the cake," Domenika interrupted as she rose and reached for their dinner plates. She hoped De Santis would interpret her movement as a sign that the conversation, if taken further, might spark an unpleasant debate she would prefer to avoid.

"Yes, we all have those times, don't we?" De Santis said. "When our higher power is the only place to turn for help."

Domenika watched Parenti stare at De Santis across the table with a studied look, one that portrayed a real wariness.

"I've had some close calls these last few years when I thought it was all over," Bondurant said in earnest. "I didn't find myself in prayer at the time. Perhaps I should have. In any event . . ."

"You knew how to pray as a child," De Santis said. "Of that I'm sure."

"How can you be so sure, Father?" Bondurant asked.

"You were an altar boy, Jon. It's in our records. The Vatican has quite an extensive library, does it not, Father Parenti?"

"Yes, it does," Parenti said. He tapped his spoon on the table as if he were impatiently waiting for the cake to arrive and the conversation to end.

"That's right; I was an altar boy," Bondurant said. "That was a long time ago. I was a child. It's what I was taught. I think I've experimented with prayer only once since then."

Domenika set her homemade cake, adorned with candles, on the table directly in front of Bondurant as the most obvious signal yet that it was time to change the subject.

"And of course, there are the *other* records that reference you as well as your brother in our vast archives, ones I've been made privy to and for which I cannot stress enough on behalf of the Church how terribly sorry we are."

Domenika could see that De Santis's glass was empty again. She watched as he reached over, took Parenti's glass of wine, and managed a large gulp.

She stopped in her tracks. She had been prepared to light the candles on Bondurant's cake but now stood in abject terror over what De Santis was up to and what he might say next.

"What do you mean by that?" Bondurant asked. He pushed the cake slightly aside as though it helped to hide a secret.

"Nothing. He means nothing," Parenti proclaimed, eager to stop the inquiry.

"Father Parenti, I know that both you and Domenika have been privy to the same documents I've seen regarding the Church's sordid history involving Jon and his younger brother as a child. Domenika herself told me of them long ago."

"Giancarlo, you mustn't," Domenika said. Her head began to spin slightly, and she suddenly felt ready to faint.

"Mustn't?" De Santis said. "But it was you, Domenika, who wrote the memo. It has your name on it."

"What memo is that?" Bondurant asked. He had turned toward Domenika and faced her directly.

"The Jozef Memo, Jon," De Santis said. "No doubt you're familiar with it. Why, your own wife wrote it. While she's not a psychologist, I thought she did a splendid job pointing out that your lifelong animosity toward faith stems from gross and personal injury."

Bondurant immediately pushed himself back in his chair as if a knife had been lunged across the table. Domenika watched his face instantly turn pale as though he were in shock.

"Just what are you saying, Father? Domenika, what the hell is he talking about?" Bondurant asked.

Domenika could hear the voice of the man she loved tremble with fear that someone might have discovered the terrible truth about his past.

De Santis had a look on his face she had never seen before, one determined to harm instead of heal. "The old priest, the one from Maryland, who preyed upon you and your little brother as a child. He's now long gone, but we have records of his deathbed confession."

Domenika could see Bondurant had turned red with rage or embarrassment, both of which spelled disaster.

"And we have the Jozef Memo," De Santis said. "Surely you've discussed it."

"Father, I'm afraid we haven't," Domenika said.

She collapsed into her chair and stared blankly at the wall, unable to look at Bondurant or to speak. Her knowledge of the incidents and the horror the Bondurant children had faced before Jon's brother's suicide was so terrible that unless he decided to raise the subject, it was a nightmare she planned to take to her grave. Now it was too late. She had long deceived the only man she had ever loved about what she'd learned of his past, and now he plainly knew it. Domenika gathered the courage to glance toward Bondurant for just a moment and saw only utter helplessness on his face.

Bondurant looked in shock. Then, in one great heave, as if to expunge a terrible secret, he vomited onto the table before them. Parenti stood, placed his arm gently around Bondurant, and held a napkin to his mouth. Bondurant quickly shrugged Parenti away. When he had gathered the strength to stand, he looked over at Domenika in complete disbelief.

"Jon, there is no shame," was all Domenika could bring herself to say. She urged him to sit back down.

"We were just boys, Father," Bondurant said to De Santis as he choked forth the words. He grabbed the jacket that hung on the wall behind him, ready to leave. "And you know something? I did pray to your God to stop the madness and bring my brother back. But he didn't."

With those words, Bondurant moved swiftly toward the front door. Domenika could only watch. She saw him hesitate for a moment, as if to stop before he did something he might later regret. Then he turned from the wife and the life she knew he loved and slowly walked away.

Chapter 29

Bethesda, Maryland

When Khan saw the huge crush of reporters, photographers, and television cameras staked out at the bottom of the front steps of the National Institutes of Health headquarters in Bethesda, she understood why her assistant, Juliet, had moved the announcement outdoors. The NIH's briefing room inside was too small to accommodate the throng of media gathered for the news she was about to convey. While being introduced by the Institutes' director standing at the lectern beside her, Khan took a moment to gaze out toward the heavens. In all her life, she had never seen the sky more blue or the sun more brilliant than on this day.

The string of events that had occurred over the previous weeks—which landed her in front of the most prestigious health research organization in the world with major findings to report—was improbable at best. When Bondurant had literally stumbled upon her in the subway several weeks before, Khan was on her way to pack in preparation for a trip overseas to investigate another supposedly promising lead in the fight against the Devil's Sweat.

While Khan had heard of Bondurant before and knew of his reputation as a skilled forensic anthropologist, she also knew he was clearly out of his league in the field of immunology and contagious disease. She'd taken the vial of blood he had begged her to examine as a source for a candidate vaccine and dismissively tossed it into her briefcase. She'd given it about as much attention as the pack of gum that lay beside the vial for several days.

When she'd arrived at the Department of Infectious and Tropical Diseases laboratories in London to hear of their latest thesis on the virus's propagation, she'd rested her briefcase against her chair and opened it to reach for some papers inside. When she did, Bondurant's vial had fallen onto the rug and rolled under the chair of her assistant. When she'd spied the blood-filled container, she'd reached down and picked it up.

"What's this?" the aide had asked.

"Oh, that. Have them spin it, Juliet," Khan had whispered, so as not to interrupt the presentation. "Test it against the Sweat. When it fails, just dispose of it."

Five days later, Khan had opened her door at three o'clock in the morning, bleary-eyed, to see Juliet with a set of charts that demonstrated the impossible. The tests conducted on the sample of blood Bondurant had passed to Khan had revealed properties that were impervious to the virus and that had been successfully replicated in a primitive serum. Several plague-stricken test patients injected with the first crude batch of vaccine derived from the sample had been cured. It was the first incident of patient survival the WHO had witnessed since the outbreak of the unknown disease several years before. Three of the largest pharmaceutical labs in the world were now on alert and set to manufacture a more refined vaccine at a breakneck pace to ready the drug for emergency trials in the field.

It was this news that Khan was prepared to bring to the world, absent the story of the source for the cure. Bondurant's phenomenal gift was still a complete mystery to Khan, and she had no credible way to explain it.

"I'm pleased to announce," Khan said, as she paused for a moment in front of the cameras, "that the long nightmare known as the Devil's Sweat is near an end."

Khan was completely drained and physically exhausted, but she knew the import of her words. She gave the press extra time to settle in as the camera crews pushed and shoved their way toward her. She knew it was the sound bite that would dominate the news cycle around the entire planet for days.

She continued. "In the past week, through the tireless work of hundreds of scientists, a vaccine that renders one immune to the virus has been developed. It has been tested with both active carriers of the disease who are now on their way to recovery and healthy individuals who have been successfully immunized. We have every reason to believe it will satisfy our need for a cure and widespread inoculation on a massive scale. We estimate that millions of lives will be spared."

The assembled media members broke into applause. It was a reaction Khan had not previously expected or seen from an often-skeptical press corps. She wanted to savor the rare moment. A few reporters began to shout questions as she paused.

"A moment, please," Khan said. "The international travel restrictions, onerous as they have been, will continue to be in effect until WHO announces they are no longer necessary. They have saved many millions. All quarantine procedures in place in those countries classified as high risk will continue as well. With the rapid vaccination regimen we have planned for the population in the regions affected, I believe we will see the complete eradication of the disease within a time frame of two months." Khan rested her hands on the podium. "Now I'd be happy to take a few questions."

A cacophony of questions shouted all at once quickly set Khan on edge. She was tired from the marathon work of the week behind her as well as her red-eye flight from London.

"One at a time!" Khan shouted. "You." She pointed to a correspondent from CNN who had followed the story of the plague for years.

"Only a week or two ago, the director of the World Health Organization suggested that the identification of an antidote to fight the virus was nowhere in sight. Some in the scientific community had actually given up hope entirely. How do you explain such a rapid and fortunate turnabout?"

"Between the diligence of our hardworking scientists and an unexpected discovery, a source carrying the effective antibodies was located. It was tested in short order. I realize this is good news, but perhaps you will feel obligated to report it."

"Carolyn Mason, CBS. Are you certain the vaccine you've described is absolutely effective? One is treated or vaccinated, and one lives?"

"In all my years, I have never seen immunity and, indeed, a complete cure develop as rapidly or effectively from the antibody discovered."

"Mark Jaffe, *Washington Post*. Can you elaborate on the 'unexpected discovery'?"

Khan knew the simple truth involved being handed a mystery vial by a stranger on a train. That would only raise a raft of questions for which she had no good response. "Suffice it to say," she said, "one scientist in particular had a remarkable hunch that deserved a closer look. Fortunately for millions, his hunch was correct."

A flood of questions, one piled on top of another, burst forth. She singled out a correspondent from NBC she knew well in an attempt to bring some order to the chaos.

"Dr. Khan, who is this scientist you've referred to who deserves the credit?"

Khan had no interest in converting Bondurant, whom she hadn't seen since the night on the train and whom she'd treated like a fool, into an instant worldwide media sensation before he was prepared. "I'm not at liberty to divulge that at present, but I assure you there are *many* who have worked diligently to bring us to this point. I've got time for just one or two more questions, and then I'll turn it over to Dr. Richardson."

"A name! A name!" one reporter shouted. "Give us a name."

"I've said it would be premature to release that," Khan said. The frustration rose in her voice.

"Come on," another reporter from the back of the pack yelled out. "How about a name?"

"You ask again," Khan said, "and I'll give you the finger."

"A name, please," another correspondent in front pleaded.

Khan raised her right hand, lifted her middle finger, and flipped off the entire swarm of press before her. Then she stepped back from the podium and left it to the NIH director to manage the melee as she headed for her waiting car. They got what they came for, Khan thought. Enough was enough.

She turned toward Juliet. "You remember that anthro I told you about?" Khan said as she opened the rear door and threw her briefcase onto the backseat.

"Yes, I think so," Armistice said. "The one who brought you the vial?"

"That's the one. Find him. Find him fast," Khan said. "I'm going to thank him like he's never been thanked before."

Chapter 30

The Vatican

Pope Augustine slowly closed the cover of his briefing book, which he'd avoided for days as though it were a snake half-asleep on his desk. He stared out toward St. Peter's Square. The famous basilica that towered behind his office lit the night sky of Rome. While the windows before him were closed, he could still hear the din of street vendors and a smattering of tourists enjoying the late-summer evening outside.

The pontiff had never felt more alone. His beloved Church, to which he had devoted his entire life, was in deep trouble. The material he'd finally forced himself to read after he'd stalled for a week was a summary report of questionnaires provided by parishes around the world. He'd ordered the surveys two months earlier and now wished he hadn't. The tale the documents told was a devastating mess.

The Vatican, the report bluntly stated, faced its biggest crisis in a millennium, perhaps its entire history. The church had lost faithful by the millions during his relatively brief reign as pope, and, worse yet, the trend had started to accelerate. For every person who converted to Catholicism today, the estimates were that four more would desert the Church in the decade to come. Thousands of parishes had closed their doors due to a lack of funds, and thousands more, while still nominally open, had no celebrant to call their own. Many priests had jumped ship. Ten thousand had deserted their calling in the last few years, which left a historic low of barely forty thousand to administer to all of the Church's faithful worldwide. At the present rate, the total number of Catholic priests was projected to fall to an astoundingly low thirteen thousand in twenty-five years. The situation in Europe alone was even worse. In Ireland, which had stood as one of the strongest bastions of Catholic faith for centuries, the churches were abandoned. Spain was now Catholic in name only, if that. Nearly three-fourths of its people reported rarely or never attending Mass.

There were other reasons for the Church's decline. The advent of the sexual revolution and the evolving role of women in society were key. The Church had been criticized for its prohibition on ordaining women as priests, its intolerance toward the gay community in its fold, and its opposition to same-sex marriage.

Augustine knew that while the Vatican's positions on these controversies had left the Church severely battered, their effect on the faith paled in comparison to a more sinister flaw. The revelations of widespread child sexual abuse committed by some within its priestly ranks had done the greatest harm. The well-publicized cases of pedophilia and abuse and, worse yet, the discovery of numerous cover-ups that could be traced all the way to the steps of the Vatican had left an indelible stain on the Church. More than fifty Roman Catholic bishops from around the world stood accused of sexually abusing children. The Church's moral authority, the one thing it could not afford to lose, had waned. The Vatican's own studies had revealed a direct correlation between the terrible scandal and a severe decline in both the numbers of faithful and contributions. Many felt there was no chance of recovery or absolution. While these self-inflicted wounds were bad enough, it was conceivable that those combined with Hans Meyer's efforts to destroy the Church might spell the end for the Catholic faith. Mankind, the pope felt, was in dire need of a miracle.

It was with these troubles in mind that Augustine stared out in silent gloom at the courtyard below, where thousands would gather the following morning to receive his papal blessing. He closed his eyes and rubbed his temples as he had countless times in recent years to relieve the debilitating, migraine-like pain that now seemed to routinely invade his days. He had been told by his doctors that it stemmed from stress, but at times the pain and the noise that accompanied it inside his head were so great that they felt otherworldly. Preoccupied with his mood and the suffering from his headache, he barely took notice of the papal secretary, his longtime aide, who had arrived and stood patiently at the entrance to his office, not saying a word.

"Father De Santis?" the pope finally asked.

"Yes, Your Holiness. He only just arrived. I know you've been waiting."

"Yes, thank you."

"Your Holiness, I presume you've heard the news?" the aide said before he turned to escort De Santis from the room next door.

"What news is this?"

"The announcement this morning, Holy Father. With God's blessing, the terrible plague has come to an end. It seems a cure has been found."

"I see. That is wonderful news," the pope said as he looked toward the heavens. He took the briefing book that sat on his desk, placed it in his secretary's hands, and grimaced once again at its sight. "One scourge ends, another awaits."

As his aide retreated, the pope took a seat in his red velvet reclining chair. De Santis had not communicated in days, and Augustine had anxiously awaited news from him all afternoon.

"Holy Father," De Santis said as he entered the pope's private office. It had the smell of leather, books, incense, and just a hint of cigar smoke, precisely to Augustine's liking. "I can only hope I find you in good spirits and good health in his name." De Santis knelt to kiss the ring on the pope's extended hand.

"Yes, thank you, Father De Santis," Augustine said. "I'm feeling fine, with the exception of the heartburn."

"Heartburn?" De Santis said. "I never had any idea that you—"

"Just a figure of speech," the pope said as he motioned for De Santis to sit across from him.

De Santis sat and sank deep into the soft red velvet cushion of the massive chair. The pope's own seat was as hard as the marble floor beneath him. He liked the substantial height difference he enjoyed while in his favorite chair. The seating either put his visitors at ease through comfort or at a distinct disadvantage due to their lower physical stature, both of which Augustine was pleased to accept.

"So," the pontiff said. "What do you have for me? What have you learned?"

"I must be uncharacteristically brief, Your Holiness, as I must leave for New York within the hour. From there, I'll return to Rome with perhaps more useful information. I can discuss this with you more fully next week. In the meantime, I have some exciting, even potentially miraculous, news."

The pope's eyes widened as he rubbed his aged hands together in anticipation of De Santis's report.

"I've confirmed the new location of the Watcher child," De Santis said. "He has been moved around a lot in the past few years, but my various reputable sources in Switzerland place him back at Meyer's compound, which, as you know, lies just a few miles outside of St. Moritz."

"You have seen this Watcher child?" the pope asked.

"I'm certain he can be found just outside St. Moritz," De Santis said.

"That's not what I asked, Father De Santis," the pope said. His voice carried a hint of irritation. It had been a few years since he'd first asked De Santis to learn everything he could about the Watcher child, but very little information on the demon had been found. "I asked whether you have *seen* the Watcher child."

Augustine could tell De Santis was exhausted as well. He watched as he slumped entirely into the cushion that now seemed to envelop him.

"I have not seen the Watcher child," De Santis said. "There is extraordinary security at the Meyer compound. But I have had it confirmed firsthand by housekeeping staff that a child resides there who matches the expected age. Meyer has no other children. It's a certainty the Watcher is there."

The pope could not help but look disappointed.

"Your Holiness," De Santis said, "all church officials in the area, of which there are many, have been alerted, and I'm certain we will soon be seeing reports of daily sightings of the child, his movements, his appearance, and the like."

"Very well, then," the pontiff said. He had heard identical updates from De Santis before. "When you said I would be excited by the news, I presumed—"

"I believe I informed you that my travel plans also involved a brief stay with our Domenika and her family on my way to New York for the meeting with Cardinal O'Brien," De Santis said.

"Yes, yes."

"Here I have most unexpected news. It has caused me to reconsider the conclusions reached by our conclave formed some time ago regarding the other child, the child of the Shroud," De Santis said.

"The child of Domenika," the pope said. "The boy whose birth we attended."

"Yes, Your Holiness," De Santis said. "You will recall that we agreed the Church could not sit in scientific judgment as to the efficacy of DNA passed from one source to another in the unethical practice of human cloning."

"Yes."

"You also know it was our steadfast belief that the transference of divinity in any sense through human cloning would, by its very nature, reach beyond the bounds of both reason and faith. In other words, it would be impossible."

"Of course," the pope said. The Church's 1987 magisterium had forbidden human cloning. Augustine began to wonder whether De Santis had brought with him well-worn history rather than any news at all.

"Your Holiness," De Santis said, "I must report that during my visit with Domenika, I became privy to something incredible worth pondering. Domenika and I did not part company on the best of terms, for reasons I can explain later. But when I first arrived and had the chance to spend time with her and the child alone for just a moment, she confirmed for me that Dr. Bondurant had a sample of the child's blood drawn at birth. I have been curious about this for years."

"Go on."

"His hypothesis was that the child's blood might contain some sort of divine healing qualities that would put this infamous plague to rest. I realize that, on its face, this theory might seem ridiculous, but you must know that Domenika also conveyed to me that the infant's blood sample was delivered by Bondurant to health authorities for testing just weeks ago."

The pope's eyes lit up again. "I just heard they believe they have found a cure for this Satan's Sweat," he said.

"Devil's Sweat, Your Holiness."

"Call it what you want. It has taken many millions of innocents in his evil name."

"Your Holiness," De Santis said, "I realize I might be speculating, but if there is truly a connection between the blood of the child of the Shroud and the cure for the terrible plague, we—"

"We now have *two* unique children we must mind," the pontiff said. He was perched on the very edge of his ornate chair. He sat in silence as he pondered the remarkable possibilities. His aged heart began to race. He knew De Santis had no definite proof, and there was a great deal more to be learned. But if the power of the child of the Shroud's blood was true, it was possible that the glorious miracle he so badly needed to rescue his beloved Church had finally arrived.

Chapter 31

New York City

alerkin closed his left eye and drew a bead on his target with his right through the high-powered scope. As he peered through the glass, he felt as though he could almost reach out and touch her. She reclined on a bright-blue lounge chair ten feet from the rooftop pool. She was leggy and tan and just seconds away from the end of her life.

He carefully rested his Barrett M107 sniper rifle against the rooftop railing and picked up his laser range finder to recheck the distance. She was eighteen hundred meters away, a bit more than a mile. It was a long distance but one he had killed quite capably from several times before.

Galerkin had watched her hard body glisten in the sun for nearly twenty minutes. Tanning alone on the rooftop of her boyfriend's magnificent townhome on Manhattan's Upper West Side, she wore an inviting bright-white bikini that contrasted well with her bronzed skin. He could see through the scope that she was pretty, even at a distance. Short blond hair, athletic frame. He could almost count the number of freckles on her shoulder.

But he'd grown impatient with her lack of cooperation. He'd made up his mind that he wasn't going to shoot her as she lazed in the lounge chair. There was just no sport in it. The proper way, Galerkin's way, would involve a bullet through the center of her chest as she dove into the pool. Preferably a swan dive or something similarly graceful to mark her last gesture in life. But there she sat, interminably, having shown interest in a *Vogue* magazine, her drink, and suntan lotion. Everything but the pool.

He wiped the perspiration from his brow with his shirtsleeve and turned to locate the position of the midday sun at his back. It had to be at least ninety-five degrees out. The small patch of blue water looked inviting to Galerkin from a great distance. He could find no reason why, given the heat and the tiny droplets of sweat that had collected on her stomach, the pool had not yet beckoned to her. Eventually, she would dive in. She had to. It was only a matter of time.

He pulled her dossier from his satchel to reexamine her particulars during the wait. Socialite. Argentinian. Spoke three languages. Into Pilates and martial arts. Raised at elite boarding schools. Her father had run a global manufacturing empire for years. When the business began to slide, so did his personal wealth. It was only then that the authorities discovered he'd raided the company's bank accounts to save his sinking empire. When he was found dead in the water near his yacht in the Caribbean, most believed it was suicide. Some claimed it was murder. Galerkin had been told the death was a hit by the Mossad, the Israeli intelligence service, an organization her father had blackmailed along the way. At least, that was who had paid him for the present job. His bronzed target had made the mistake of boasting to friends that she'd gathered evidence the Mossad had murdered her father. She had plans to go to the press.

Galerkin detected some movement on the roof and pressed his eye against the scope once more. Now she sat on the edge of the lounge chair as she tightened the string of her bikini across her back. It was a sure sign she was ready to move. He slowly pulled the bolt of his rifle backward and, careful not to remove his eye from the sight, felt around in his pocket for the single bullet that was about to earn him one hundred thousand dollars. He placed the large brass cartridge in the chamber of his gun, slammed the bolt forward into its firing position, and locked the long rifle barrel into the crook of his left arm.

His cell phone vibrated.

Galerkin hesitated to answer. The distance to his target, the bullet's time of flight, a slight breeze from the west, and some downward vertical velocity due to gravity meant that catching her in a dive mid-flight would require every bit of his concentration. He watched as she pulled her hair into a ponytail and stared at the shimmering water, still glued to her chair.

"I'm busy," Galerkin barked into his cell phone. The phone looked the size of a matchbook as he mashed it up against the ear of his massive head. "Who's this?" He scowled when he heard Meyer's voice on the other end of the line.

"He's in Washington again," Meyer said.

"Who? Who is in Washington? I am busy."

"Bondurant. Bondurant's there. And I'm sure he's with the girl, Jozef. He must be."

"No," Galerkin said. "Now I hear yesterday he lives in pissant town outside D.C. But very close."

"Check it out, Vitaly. Check both places."

"Yes, well, I am in New York City. I am on different job right now, you see? I get to him later."

Galerkin tried to angle his eye back toward the scope while he simultaneously used his shoulder to sandwich the cell phone against his ear. He could see that the target had risen from her lounger and started to walk toward the far end of the pool.

"Vitaly," Meyer said. "Your assignment on Bondurant has taken forever. I think you have difficulty managing priorities."

"Look," Galerkin said, preoccupied. He followed the woman with his crosshairs around the edge of the pool and smiled as she began to make her way to the diving board. "That's it, pretty one," he said.

"What did you say?" Meyer asked. "Are you talking to me?"

Galerkin placed his fat forefinger ever so lightly against the trigger. "No, I am talking to poor little rich girl," he said. He pressed the butt of this rifle hard against his right shoulder.

"Vitaly, I'm talking to you," Meyer said, obviously frustrated. "What does it take to get your attention? I need you in D.C. Bondurant's apparently assumed *my* name in order to hide."

"I go to D.C. for you," Galerkin said. He smiled as he watched his target step onto the diving board. "But first I finish here."

"My source says he's at the Four Seasons," Meyer said.

"Mine says pissant town. This place, they have nice pool?" Galerkin asked. He placed a small amount of pressure on the center of the trigger to prepare it.

"How would I know?" Meyer said. "It's a nice hotel. I'm sure they do."

"With diving board?"

Galerkin watched his target take three quick steps and plant her feet hard at the end of the board to soar high. As he squeezed the trigger to remove the slightest bit of slack remaining, it hit its break point. He aimed precisely where the bullet should capture her sternum in flight.

Galerkin gave the trigger a full squeeze and stiffened his shoulder to absorb the recoil of the massive rifle. He counted "one-two-three" and then watched the bullet tear into its target. It splayed her entire chest cavity in half before she had the chance to belly flop into the water.

"Okay," Galerkin said as he peered through the scope and then watched the entire pool turn blood-red in an instant. "I go to D.C."

Chapter 32

Rome

When De Santis arrived at the clinic across from Rome's Gemelli Hospital, he sat in the crowded waiting area and nervously tapped his foot. He vowed that no matter what prognosis they had in store for his aching lower back, it would be his last doctor's visit until his next annual physical exam. He was already late for his scheduled meeting with the pope at the Vatican, which was a full twenty-minute cab ride away. Time was of the essence. He vowed to say little to the doctor. He would simply nod his head quickly at the suggested remedy and be on his way with a prescription as quickly as he could.

At least, that was the plan. De Santis's previous efforts to put an end to the nagging pain he'd experienced over the past few months had already resulted in more visits to the clinic than he felt necessary. Today he was seeing a specialist again. He presumed, given his senior position at the Vatican, that they'd made more out of his chronic pain than was deserved. De Santis had simply gotten older, and he knew it.

Unlike several bishops whom he'd served who always flew first class, he'd traveled too often on long flights in cramped coach-class seats. He was always on the go. It wreaked havoc with his diet, the likely cause of his recent weight loss and lack of appetite. These were all contributing factors to his current lethargy, he was sure. But they certainly didn't warrant the number of medical tests he'd been put through during previous appointments when the medications and exercises he'd been prescribed hadn't worked. His frustration had grown. His last visit to the clinic had involved a CT scan and an endoscopic ultrasound of his abdominal area when his main complaint was the discomfort in his lower back.

A nurse finally came into the waiting area and waved for De Santis to enter. On previous visits, she'd normally taken the time to chat while De Santis waited for the doctor to arrive in the examination room. But on this occasion, she left him alone.

When the doctor finally entered the examination room ten minutes later, De Santis wanted to make it clear from the outset that he was in a hurry. "I have very little time, Doctor," he said.

The doctor arched his eyebrows at De Santis's declaration. He sat on a low stool next to the examination table and silently flipped through a set of medical charts on a clipboard.

He cleared his throat. "Father, I'm afraid that after all the tests we've bothered you with, your own prognosis is prescient," he said. "You do have very little time. And I'm very sorry I have to be the one to say it."

"What on earth do you mean by that?" De Santis asked. He assumed he was about to be forced through another examination and began to unbutton his shirt to speed the process along.

"I'm afraid that won't be necessary," the doctor said as he stared intently at the charts.

"Good, then," De Santis said as he buttoned up his shirt. "I'll take my medicine and be on my way."

"Father," the doctor said, "in your line of work, I'm sure you must be involved in counseling of one sort or another from time to time."

"That's often so," De Santis said. He was in a hurry, but the doctor's stoic tone bothered him.

"You are a man of the cloth," the doctor said. "Perhaps you might take the news I have for you better than most." The doctor removed his glasses, rubbed his eyes, and then stared down at the checkered green-and-white tile floor.

De Santis figured the doctor might have a strange sense of humor and decided to play along. "Give it to me straight, Doctor. How long have I got?"

"I want to say from the start that few of us are heroes in the face of the kind of news I have to give you. So before you leave today, I'm going to give you the names of several counselors I'd like you to consider if you're not familiar with one already."

De Santis gave the doctor a strange look, now certain the man was confused. He was obviously talking to the wrong patient. "This is too much, Doctor," he said. He'd grown testy. "I have a simple pain in my lower back."

"I know you do, Father," the doctor said. "Unfortunately, what I must tell you is that while the chronic pain you're feeling in your lower back is real, it's actually emanating from another area. It's radiating there from your abdominal region, and for good reason."

"What do you mean?" De Santis asked.

"Hold out your hands for me, please," the doctor said.

De Santis held forth both hands, palms down. When the priest looked down at them, he noticed he'd started to tremble.

"The yellow discoloration has intensified since I last saw you," the doctor said. "Stare straight ahead for me, if you would." He pulled an ophthalmoscope from his pocket to examine De Santis's eyes with a light. "This light jaundice in the whites of your eyes. How long has it been there?"

"I don't know. I never really noticed it much before," De Santis said. "I assumed it was from lack of sleep."

"No, it's characteristic for a patient in your condition," the doctor said. He examined the skin of De Santis's forearms and sat back down on his stool. "The jaundice you're experiencing stems from the obstruction of the bile duct that runs through your pancreas."

"My pancreas? Who needs one of those?" De Santis said. He was determined to try to lighten again what had too fast become a serious conversation.

"Everyone, I'm afraid," the doctor said. "You've lost more weight?"

"I couldn't say."

"Please step up on the scale for me, and let's take a look."

De Santis kicked off his shoes and stepped onto the rickety scale. The doctor pushed his glasses back onto the bridge of his nose to read the number. He stroked his beard. Then he looked down at De Santis's charts once more.

"Loss of another five pounds," the doctor said. "I see here from your most recent lab tests that your blood glucose level is elevated further as well."

"Yes, so?"

"Add to these signs the combination of CT scan and the ultra-sound recordings we have, and I'm afraid the conclusion is definitive, Father."

"Definitive?"

"Father De Santis, I'm sorry to tell you this, but you have pancreatic cancer. It's one of the tougher ones to beat."

De Santis had never fainted before in his life, but the dizzy feeling that instantly overwhelmed him buckled him to his knees. He saw what he thought were tiny white sparks and stars careening away from his eyes in a haze of purple for a few moments. Before he knew it, he was lying on his back on the examination table. He looked up helplessly at the doctor and the attending nurse.

"It's not an uncommon reaction," the doctor said. "You've fainted. Now I want you to breathe deeply for a few moments and try to relax."

De Santis stared up at the fuzzy U-shaped neon light above him. His arms felt lifeless at his side. He had only the strength to listen.

"I'm going to have you remain here for an hour, and when you've regained your strength, I'm going to perform a simple endoscopic needle biopsy on the affected region of your pancreatic tissue," the doctor said. "I'll need those results. But unfortunately, I have no doubt from the CT scan that the head of your pancreas is in great distress. You have an adenocarcinoma there. A large tumor. The chances of it being benign are, unfortunately, very small."

De Santis struggled for words. He fumbled for his rosary, a constant companion that always rested in his left pants pocket. "Oh, my God," he said. A wave of nausea overcame him, and he felt the urge to vomit. He tried to rise off the table under his own strength but couldn't.

"I want you to relax, Father," the doctor said. "The good news is that I believe we have discovered your cancer relatively early, which is unusual with pancreatic conditions. You are only at stage two."

De Santis reached for the nurse's hand, heartened by the news. Her smile brought some reassurance.

"But," the doctor continued, "while this means we can likely prolong your life for a few years through various treatments—radiation therapy, chemotherapy, and the like—I'm afraid recovery from pancreatic cancer is extremely rare."

"How rare?" De Santis asked as he ran the beads of his rosary through his fingers inside his pocket. Every dream he had ever had about rising through the priestly ranks to that of bishop and possibly beyond had come to a terrible halt.

"I've been practicing for forty-five years, Father, and in my entire career, I have never seen a patient survive into stage four beyond five years. As I've said, at least we caught it early. That's a gift. You have some time—something many of my patients do not."

The doctor and the nurse turned and left the room. De Santis rolled over onto his side on the examination table and stared blankly at the white cinder-block wall. He had never felt more alone. He gathered his strength, got down on his knees, and began to weep as he had never done before.

After nearly an hour, exhausted and late for his important appointment, he dried his tears and got ready to leave. As he reached for the door handle, an extraordinary thought suddenly came to his mind, powerful enough to send him to his knees again. Only this time, De Santis was not praying. Far from it. He'd determined that he might one day still have the chance to answer the bishop's call after all.

Chapter 33

Dickerson, Maryland

F ather Parenti adored the child.

Christopher and the priest had a bond. He took the time during his morning walks with the boy to reveal to him his innermost thoughts, particularly his dreams. Strangely, Parenti often felt Christopher somehow understood his every word.

Time stood still around them as they wandered about. The town of Dickerson seemed perfectly preserved from an era gone by, with large turn-of-the-century Victorian-style houses complete with long front porches and white picket fences framing lush green lawns. Aldo, faithful as ever and rarely jealous of the attention showered on the boy, had developed a habit of herding Christopher, circling excitedly around him as they poked along, or playing fetch with a tiny stick the boy might pick up along the way. It was a time all three relished as they meandered each day down the narrow lane from Domenika's home toward the ferry landing a mile away.

While the beautiful child was a few weeks away from turning six years old, Parenti could already tell the boy would grow to become a handsome man. He possessed a quiet temperament that involved little fuss, and Parenti could not have imagined a more perfect child for Bondurant and Domenika to raise as their own. But as adorable as the child was and as idyllic as the town might be, neither masked the sad truth that Bondurant had left.

They hadn't heard a word from him. Money—much more than enough—arrived each week in an envelope. It bore no return address. It allowed Domenika to temporarily manage the home alone. Bondurant had also found a way to take care of all their bills from afar. There was never a note to accompany the money, nor were there any calls. And there were no sightings of Bondurant by Parenti or Domenika during their many forays searching for him in hotels or restaurants nearby. He *had* to be near. The word "abandoned" had not yet crossed either of their lips. But day by day, particularly with only Domenika and the little priest at home to look after Christopher, they had begun to feel forsaken.

For their part, there was some guilt. Parenti found that Domenika was often inconsolable for the loneliness she felt. Parenti and Domenika had discussed the horrifying evening—Bondurant's birthday of all days—a thousand times since De Santis's thoughtless words had sent Bondurant out the front door, perhaps never to return.

Parenti knew too that Domenika had tortured herself endlessly since Bondurant had bolted because she'd spoken so openly with De Santis, her mentor, about Bondurant's ugly past. He was certain she'd never expected her trusted professor to reveal what she knew, most particularly not to Bondurant himself.

What distressed Parenti at the moment was that he had lost a true friend in Bondurant, maybe forever. The little priest had made few friends before. As they approached the bend in the road that overlooked the boat landing he'd journeyed to each day since Bondurant had left, he gazed across the silent river with a heavy heart and wondered if he might ever return. He watched the ferry slowly draw away from his side of the river on a cable strung to the bank on the other side. He often prayed he would one day see Bondurant bound off the ferry and greet him warmly with his familiar smile.

As Parenti turned and called for Christopher to join him, he caught a glimpse of something out of the corner of his eye. It was a tall man in the distance who had disembarked from the ferry. He carried a small satchel across his back. He was headed up the hill on the opposite lane that eventually wound its way to Domenika's home. For a moment, Parenti's heart raced. Then, when he realized it wasn't Bondurant, it just as quickly sank.

"*Porco diavolo*," the priest whispered to himself as he cursed the devil.

He looked down at Christopher, took his hand, and then looked up toward the stranger again. He didn't recognize the man who plodded his way up the hill. He could see only his back in the distance. But strangers were few in Dickerson. If only Bondurant were there. He squeezed Christopher's hand tightly and prayed that if trouble were to pay a visit, this time it would pass them by.

Chapter 34

Washington, D.C.

Bondurant lost his footing and nearly fell as he came out of the Four Seasons Hotel. He knew he was drunk. He caught the dismissive glance of the elegantly dressed couple who sidestepped him on their way into the hotel. But he still wasn't as wasted as he wanted to be. As usual, he'd been cut off at the hotel's upscale, ultramodern bar inside. They'd left him no choice but to follow what had become a nightly routine.

He would saunter up M Street in the hazy glow of antique street lamps all the way up to Wisconsin Avenue, three blocks up the hill. There Blues Alley awaited him. It was the secluded back-street jazz club he'd come to think of as his second home. The bartenders at the Alley, a dark but hip and lively musical hot spot in the city, knew Bondurant came and went by foot from the hotel. They would pour him a half bottle of Scotch if he wanted it. On several occasions over the past week, they'd done just that.

Bondurant had tried hard to pretend the time he'd spent in the city, only an hour away from Domenika, had been good for him. He'd set out to take measure of his life, and his time away had given him the chance he needed to think clearly and search his soul. But in truth, he knew he'd really just been on a binge. A big one. He'd made a big mistake when he left. That was clear. He'd learned little about himself during his self-exile and had never felt more miserable or alone. He had no defensible reason to wander the city and drink himself into a stupor day after day, but he also stubbornly resisted going home. He sorely missed his family—his remarkable little son and the only woman he'd ever loved—and knew they would take him back with open arms. But he also knew there was a terrible shame that waited for him there, one so great he just couldn't go home.

They know. It echoed in his mind. His abuse, like that of his little brother, was a nightmare he had always planned to take to his grave alone. But now the relentless questions haunted him. Exactly what had Domenika written? How could he possibly look her in the eyes again? How many others knew of his past, and what exactly did they know? What exactly had the priest revealed? Were the death-bed confessions explicit in their every detail?

Bondurant had thought about the concept of shame endlessly as he spent his days roaming aimlessly. When he would wake up hungover in his hotel bed in a cold sweat each afternoon, he would sometimes reach for one of the self-help books on his nightstand that assured him he was a victim without fault. But that was little consolation. The books were useless. The words on the pages stirred up memories and emotions that grabbed at his insides as if to disembowel him. Dishonored. Unworthy. Embarrassed. Disgraced. Shamed.

At times, he would drift into some church along the city's tree-lined side streets as he wandered. He found no comfort there. He'd even been tossed out of a few. He'd disrupted services when he shouted obscenities toward the altar in drunken anger at his plight. He didn't care which denomination was treated to his intoxicated wrath. His sole concern was to upset those who gathered in the foolish notion that it made sense to honor a distant, uncaring God. Somewhere in his haze, he'd lost his patented "timekeeper," the special watch he'd kept to measure his estimated time left on earth. He thought it might have fallen into a canal late one evening, but he wasn't sure. If he could only have it back, he knew it would reveal that his time was mercifully running short.

Now, as Bondurant stepped off the curb to make his way up the street, he heard the low rumble of a powerful engine approach. The sound was so loud that it reverberated off the hotel's walls and caused the ground beneath him to shake. As he looked up, he saw a large black motorcycle pull up beside him with two riders. The motorcyclists wore shiny full-face helmets with darkly tinted visors. Bondurant stared curiously at them as the driver gunned the throttle of the massive bike. It sent out a thunderous snarl that seemed to vibrate the entire city block around them. It was only when the figure casually flipped the visor up that Bondurant could see the woman's face inside.

"You're certainly not easy to find!" Khan shouted out with a laugh as she pulled the helmet off her head. Her silky black hair tumbled onto her shoulders and gave Bondurant his first chance to recognize her. Before he could realize what Khan was up to, Bondurant felt her hands slide mischievously deep into both front pockets of his jeans. When her right hand emerged, it held exactly what she'd set out to find. She casually tossed Bondurant's room key to her companion.

"See you inside, Juliet," she said to her passenger, who, with her long legs and auburn hair, looked like Domenika in more ways than one. Khan's rider smiled at Bondurant and threw her helmet toward him before she turned to go into the hotel.

"Get on," Khan said as she gunned the throttle once more.

"I'm uh—I'm uh—" Bondurant stammered.

"You're uh—you're uh what?" Khan asked.

"I'm a—"

"Drunk? Yes, I can see that," Khan said. "Finally tracked you down. I hear you've been living large, crashing church services. Making a nuisance of yourself and all that. I've got a friend. Works at the Alley. Said you were holed up here."

"What are you here for?" Bondurant asked.

"Hop on," Khan said. "Let's go for a ride."

By the time Bondurant had adjusted his helmet's chin strap, Khan had already rocketed down the steep entrance ramp to the Rock Creek Parkway into the black of night. Bondurant's head was abuzz, but the adrenaline that shot through his veins as they sped forward was enough to alert him to find the bike's rear foot pegs fast. He planted himself squarely on the seat behind Khan to stay on. He reached out his arms for something to grasp to keep his balance and felt his hands being pulled by Khan around her tiny waist.

"Hold on tight!" Khan shouted so Bondurant could hear her above the engine's roar. "You ever ridden a bike?"

"Of course," he said, trying to exude some drunken confidence.

"Maybe not one like this," she said.

When the motorcycle shot onto the parkway, Bondurant was

gripped with a sense of acceleration he'd rarely felt before. It was late in the evening as they flew headlong through the winding curves of Rock Creek Park. Mercifully, few cars were around late at night. But whenever Bondurant spotted the red taillights of a car up ahead, they were past them in a second. Khan dipped the bike hard back and forth through the dangerously narrow turns. He looked over her shoulder to get a fuzzy glimpse of their speed. The glowing speedometer read 105 mph, something he never thought possible on that stretch of road. He squeezed Khan tightly around the waist and followed her steep leans into every turn. He knew one wrong move or an accidental shift of his weight could throw the massive bike off balance and send them careening into the trees that passed by in a blur. At the speed they traveled, it would spell the end.

"Here's the fun part!" Khan shouted.

They came to a stretch of the parkway that ran straight into the darkness as far as the high beam of the bike's headlight could reach. Then, in an instant, their world went black, except for the dim light of the half-moon at their back. Khan had killed the headlight completely, which left the road ahead dangerously dark.

"Usually a speed trap here," Khan called out. "Can't stop what they can't see."

Bondurant strained to see the road in front of them as Khan seemed to double down on her speed. He squinted to read the speedometer. The gauge now read 110. When they flew by a patrol car parked behind a set of bushes near the side of the road, Khan let out a laugh as they hurtled forward, seemingly oblivious to any peril. As Bondurant carefully shifted his weight to turn and look behind them, he was amazed he didn't see the police car's lights begin to flash in pursuit.

"Told you!" Khan shouted. Bondurant grimaced until she switched the headlight back on.

After another ten minutes of dodging insanely through the city streets while they bobbed in and out of lanes to avoid the slower traffic ahead, Khan pulled up in front of the Four Seasons once more and shut the motor off. She leaned the bike on its kickstand, flipped her keys and helmet to the surprised valet, and motioned to Bondurant.

"Now I'm in the mood," Khan said.

"In the mood for what?" Bondurant said.

"To thank you. Buy you a drink. I owe you one," Khan said. She took him by the hand and pulled him through the hotel's tall brass revolving doors.

The next few hours in the bar at the Four Seasons passed by him in a confusing haze. He drank more Scotch, plenty more. Khan seemed to will it down his throat. Then he remembered only snippets of time. He remembered how she laughed softly as they twisted their feet together beneath their barstools. He remembered the fast, dizzy elevator ride to the fifth floor. He remembered Khan playfully shoving him from the elevator. She told him a surprise awaited him just down the hall. When he reached his suite, Bondurant found the door slightly ajar and his room hidden in total darkness. He half expected to find Juliet waiting for him, but no one was there.

As he fell onto the bed, Bondurant tried to recover his senses. He was in a deep, drunken fog, but knew that whatever might happen in the next few hours would be wrong. They had his room key, after all. Wracked with guilt, the same feeling he'd carried with him since he'd left home a few weeks before, he imagined Domenika's face before him. He started to retch.

He rose quickly to reach the bathroom while he tried to hold back one dry heave after the next. As he stumbled forward, he saw only a faint crack of light at the bottom of the bathroom door. It was barely enough to illuminate his path. Soon to be sick to his stomach, he had no choice. He hurriedly knocked on the door but heard nothing from inside. Then he tried the knob and found it unlocked. When he swung the door open wide to rush toward the toilet and find relief, he completely froze. It was a sight that would haunt him for the rest of his life.

Chapter 35

Dickerson, Maryland

When Domenika awoke from her afternoon nap to knocking at the front door, she was tempted to ignore the noise downstairs, return her head to the warmth of the pillow, and drift back into the grasp of her frightening, half-finished dream.

In her dream, she was with Jon. It was a brilliantly sunlit day. Both of them stood naked on a weathered wooden dock, their eyes focused on a distant swimming platform in the center of a placid lake. The lakeside was completely deserted except for the two of them, and she felt oddly comfortable being so exposed. They were to reach the platform together and spend the rest of the afternoon sunbathing, happily wasting the day away.

She squinted her eyes toward the floating dock, a tiny speck surrounded by shimmering water in the distance. The platform was far enough away that she feared she might not make it all the way there. She knew Bondurant was a powerful swimmer, able to cover the wide expanse with ease. He held her hand and urged her on. "Just jump," he said. "Jump."

When she did, she remembered being struck by how much colder the water was than she had expected. She gasped deeply as it took her breath away. Bondurant pierced the surface of the lake in a perfect dive beside her, and she watched as his long, effortless stroke pulled him ahead of her in seconds while they made their way toward the deeper water ahead.

When she recovered from the shock of the cold, she bore down. She carved through the water as quickly as she could and kicked her legs furiously to catch up to him. She grew worried. Every time she struggled to make up the distance between them, Bondurant seemed to pull farther away. The cold began to grip her, and when she stopped to catch her breath, Bondurant ignored her as he continued his pace out ahead. She looked up again and again toward their destination as she raised her head with each stroke. Hopelessly, it looked no closer than when she had begun her swim. As she turned to look behind her, the dock from which they'd leaped looked impossibly far away.

As she tired, she felt she had no choice. She cried out to Bondurant for help. Almost a hundred yards ahead, he turned. When he saw that she was dead in the water, he called back to her. But she couldn't make out a word he said. His voice became only noise that echoed off the water's frigid surface. Then she watched him turn from her and start out once again toward the swim platform on his own.

Amazed, and now angry, she summoned what strength she had left and turned in a desperate effort to swim her way back to the dock where they'd begun. After she'd made it nearly fifty yards, she became confused and turned around once more to head toward Bondurant. When she did, she could see that he now stood triumphantly atop the platform, a distant, faceless silhouette.

Bondurant waved his arms and beckoned for her to come. But he just stood there, a champion swimmer, and offered no help. Nearly frozen in the water and paralyzed with fear, she called out his name once more. His response was just another casual wave.

It was at precisely this moment that Domenika was awakened from her terrifying dream by the knock at the front door. The dream slipped away. She quickly reached for her robe, gathered it around her, and made her way downstairs toward the front door. Halfway across the living room, she stopped herself. She knew the pounding on the door wasn't "the knock," a certain one dreamed up by Bondurant, a code they'd used. It was three hard raps followed by four more. It meant it was safe to answer the door.

Domenika stood motionless with fear. She wondered whether to heed Bondurant's words: "If you value your life, never, ever answer the door to anyone without the knock," he had warned her repeatedly.

Domenika considered the warning, but the banging at the door only grew more intense. She thought once more about her dreadful dream and how Bondurant had left her all alone. Then she reached for the knob and slowly opened the door.

Chapter 36

St. Moritz, Switzerland

As Galerkin arrived unannounced at Meyer's residence at eight o'clock in the evening, the lights along the shore of Lake St. Moritz where the stone castle villa sat had just begun to flicker to life. It was the first time Galerkin had intruded on Meyer's private estate so unexpectedly. It signaled surprise news that couldn't wait. And Meyer despised surprises. As he made his way from the dining room on one side of the manor to meet Galerkin in his study on the opposite side, he trusted the surprise was a good one. Galerkin liked to deliver good news in person.

There was a noticeable bounce in Meyer's step as he made his way down the hallway toward the marble stairwell that led to the study below. He felt as if another five years of age had been lifted from his limbs since he'd seen Galerkin at his compound just a few months before. His private physician, who had treated him since his mid-thirties, had actually confirmed the miraculous transformation in Meyer's physiology through extensive tests. Meyer, at age

fifty-five, possessed the physique of a forty-year-old, and every aspect of his physical and mental health, from muscle tone to organ
performance to brain function, had dramatically improved. Meyer
knew his amazing makeover had nothing to do with diet or exer-
cise. He despised rigorous physical activity and had maintained the
poor nutritional habits of a bachelor that he'd followed for years.
He drank heavily, still chain-smoked, and spent many evenings
engaged in late-night affairs. It was the presence of the child—
presumably something about his aura—that had continued to reju-
venate Meyer, and he was glad of it.

The precocious child, now eight years old, was gifted far beyond
his years. He had mastered every imaginable intellectual and physical feat expected of a child twice his age, but also had more than his
share of purely strange faculties as well.

He was a voracious reader who digested books written for adults.
His several full-time tutors marveled at his comprehension level.
He also displayed an uncanny ability to learn new languages taught
to him by caretakers, including English, French, and German. He
adopted accents related to their dialects with little prompting. He
possessed extraordinary coordination in fine and gross motor skills
and seemed to excel at every game he played. He was thrilled to win
again and again at sophisticated diversions, from cards to checkers
and chess. Almost like a computer, he improved with every game.
When challenged by anyone in competition, he relished victory.
But when outmatched and beaten by an adult, he retreated into a
sullen mood and often vowed never to play again.

Among his more peculiar qualities was his diet. A finicky eater,
he ate very little. He was unable to keep in his stomach food that
was prepared with conventional oils, processed grains, and refined

sugar of any kind. His regimen was strictly limited to basic meals that included ingredients and preparation techniques seemingly from an ancient age. Pork, served extremely rare, proved to be his favorite dish. Dried fish, uncooked and salted duck and quail, a pemmican made of dry pounded meat mixed with melted fat, goat's milk, and coarse wheat bread made with beer were his staples. He eschewed candy or chocolate of any kind, but delighted in a crude mix of nuts and dried fruits coated with raw honey, a treat reminiscent of ancient Egyptian times.

Of all the gifts possessed by the child, it was the mystery of his command of an ancient tongue that amazed Meyer and his caretakers the most. Although he had never been exposed to Aramaic in any way, he had uncannily begun to speak it. Meyer was stupefied when the child broke into the primeval dialect without prompting one afternoon. He believed the boy had begun to speak in tongues. When he hired a language expert to sit with Hans Jr. and interpret the boy's words, he was stunned to learn the child was fluent in the ancestral dialect spoken well before the birth of Christ. It was a language that Jesus himself likely spoke.

There was also the child's other gift, which began with Adriana a few years before. An eight-year-old Swiss girl and the daughter of one of Meyer's most trusted household staff members, Adriana had been afflicted with a severe form of cystic fibrosis since her birth. A cruel disease that stemmed from a genetic disorder, it had wreaked havoc with the unfortunate girl's lungs her entire life. Not only did the child have great difficulty breathing, but her constant struggle with the disease, for which there was no cure, had left her sickly, chronically underweight, and pale. According to her doctors, it was unlikely she would see her tenth birthday. Her mother, in great distress, had hoped that some precious time spent between Adriana and Hans Jr., even if only a few minutes together, might provide her child the same kind of incredible benefit her employer had seen. Taking advantage of Meyer's absence from the home one day, she arranged for her husband to rush Adriana to Meyer's compound to visit with the boy. Hans Jr., delighted to have a rare young visitor inside the vast castle for an afternoon of play, spent several hours with Adriana and sat for several moments at her side.

Within a week, the young girl was totally, inexplicably cured. Her recovery was so dramatic, and the cure so unimaginable, that word of the miracle began to spread through the household staff and eventually the broader Demanian fold. When news reached Meyer that the likely source of the incredible cure was a few minutes spent alone with Hans Jr., he was furious at what his housekeeper had dared to do, but also fascinated to no end. His own doctors examined Adriana for several days and reported that there was no longer a trace of the disease to be found in her body.

This discovery led Meyer over time to execute a plan that would serve as the impetus for Hans Jr. to take his first critically important role in the Demanian Church. It would eventually mean untold riches and power for Meyer. But even more important, it would mean revenge against all Christians, and in particular the Catholic Church. It was the Catholics who had branded Meyer a "bastard," a sickening moniker that had stuck with him since childhood, one he would never forget.

Meyer's plan was bold. Over the course of two weeks, a dozen critically ill children from all over Europe, all afflicted with incurable diseases as hopeless as that of Adriana, arrived at Meyer's Swiss compound. While the sicknesses they carried were varied, the children had one thing in common: wealthy parents whom Meyer had contacted with a proposal. A cure for the cancers or genetic defects that gripped their priceless children was likely possible, he told them all. They needed to spend just a few days in treatment at his compound in Geneva. If the children recuperated from their terrible afflictions, something medical science dictated was impossible, a price would be paid. A donation to the Demanian Church of a million dollars would be required. If after one year's time their child was still in good health, enrollment in the Demanian Church and the irrevocable tithing of half their family's estate to the church's trust were mandatory.

While the price Meyer demanded of these families seemed absurdly steep, what was a child worth? he asked. Most of the families, wary of the offer but eager to attempt anything to save their beloved children where medicine had failed, deemed the fee worth paying. From these families alone, Meyer profited by more than ten million dollars in a matter of days. Over just a few years of healings by Hans Jr., the Demanian Church's riches were now in the billions.

Now, when Meyer entered his polished wood-paneled study, he found Galerkin at the far end of a long conference table. On the assassin's face was a look of immense satisfaction. The light in the room was dim, filtering down from a massive crystal chandelier that glowed faintly from above.

"I hope you brought checkbook," Galerkin said as he broke into a broad smile. In front of him on the table sat a black leather bag just large enough to hold something the size of a bowling ball.

"I hope you brought good news," Meyer said. He clasped his hands together in anticipation.

"I bring good news," Galerkin said.

Meyer watched as Galerkin looked about him. All around them were books and artifacts arranged neatly on the many shelves. Among them was a large porcelain plate that displayed an intricate seal. Galerkin walked from his end of the table toward the shelves and lifted the plate gingerly off its stand.

Meyer looked at him, bemused. "That's antique. Seventeenth century. Family crest," he warned.

Galerkin only smiled again as he set the large plate gently on the table before him. When he had adjusted its position to his liking, Galerkin turned to the black bag beside him and slowly unzipped it from one side to the other. Then, in one swift motion, he thrust his hand into the bag, grasped the contents firmly, and slammed his ten-pound prize onto the center of the plate.

"You said Domenika Jozef head on plate," Galerkin boasted. "Look here. Domenika Jozef, head on plate."

Galerkin then shoved the plate so that it slid with its horrid contents like a hockey puck all the way down the length of the twenty-foot table until it came to rest only inches from where Meyer stood at the other end.

Meyer looked down at the disgusting sight of a sickly, bluish human head cut clean off at the neck. He tried mightily to ignore the fact that it sat atop his family's sacred crest. The face oozed several thick trails of deep red blood onto the plate beneath it. Meyer's stomach turned slightly as he stared into the bulging eyes of the torso-less head before him. He couldn't believe he was finally staring into the rotting skull of Domenika Jozef, half of his exposure problem for years.

"It's almost unrecognizable," Meyer said. The blood caked on the woman's head and hair obscured a clean view of her face. He looked over at Galerkin, who had begun to stare at him impatiently.

Galerkin walked over to his trophy, pulled a handkerchief from his pocket, and swabbed as much of the dried blood from the eyes, nose, and cheeks of the lifeless face as he could.

"Domenika Jozef," Galerkin said proudly. "I do not find Bondurant. He's not there. I wait for hours. But I *did* get *her*."

Meyer leaned over again to within inches of the putrid head, which had begun to decay. He stared intently for almost a minute. Then he suddenly looked up in disgust.

"You damned fool," Meyer said. "I don't know what long-haired beauty lost her head to your knife over Dr. Bondurant, but I assure you, the wrong girl has lost her head."

Chapter 37

St. Bart's

K han knew the way to the beach from the trail they had followed for more than an hour. It was less than a hundred meters to the clearing ahead, where, for the first time, she could test both her stallion and Bondurant. He'd held his own from the mountaintop thus far, but the well-worn path they had ridden wasn't difficult. His horse had proved sure-footed, but she figured her companion would likely lose ground to her quickly when she led them out of the shaded woods and into wide, open space.

The moment they reached the trailhead and burst from the leafy forest into brilliant sunlight, she asked her stallion for speed when they hit the grass, and she got it. Her horse welcomed the challenge. He breathed deeply as they broke into a full gallop, and Khan urged him on. She could see their destination—a pristine beach—out in the distance ahead. She slapped her crop twice across her ride's right hindquarter and settled in. Her horse was running all out.

She had no interest in looking behind her to determine how long it might take for Bondurant to catch up. But when she could clearly see the white water of the breaking waves on the beach ahead, she turned briefly to steal a glimpse of him behind her. When she did, she felt an amazing rush beside her. Bondurant, who leaned into his horse's stride, blew past her in a blur so quickly that Khan was stunned. She couldn't believe it. Her heart raced at the sight. She laughed as she tried to catch him, but it was no use. He'd taken up the challenge and surprised her, again.

Did Bondurant remind her of her father? Not exactly. In fact, not at all. But he was every bit the "man's world" her father had warned her about. Successful. Handsome. Smart. Even sensitive. And talented in just about every way. She seemed to have lived her life to prove she could dominate his kind of manly prowess. Indeed, defeat it. But to her great dismay, Bondurant was ignorant of the contest. He seemed to pay her and her struggle no mind.

They tied up their horses beneath a few leafy palms at the beach's edge and settled down in front of a small sand dune. They'd spent three days in hiding, tucked deep in the Caribbean. It was as far as they could quickly get from the trouble and danger that had found them in D.C.

She'd marveled at the number of times he'd unexpectedly and unknowingly proved himself to her. His broad shoulders and long, lean body lent themselves to natural physical talents. He was a world-class swimmer in open water. On most days, only the best could make it out past the danger of the reef at Lorient Beach, where the famous waves rolled in. Some had died there. But he'd managed the surf with ease. And when they dove from the rocky cliffs near their secluded hut on the north side of the island, it was Bondurant who'd tested the highest points above the emerald-green waters below.

But there was something else about the man she'd escaped with that separated him from the many others she had known before. She was grateful to him, of course. She owed him dearly. The *world* owed him dearly. But now they shared something else, something tragic, in common as well.

Juliet's death was hideous, to be sure. It was a terrible mistake. But to Khan, it was, above all, tragically unnecessary. And for this, she harbored anger at herself for not sensing trouble and resentment toward Bondurant for not warning her of the danger being in his orbit could possibly invite. An innocent, a promising young girl, had lost her life because Khan had involved her in a stunt to sexually thank someone she barely knew.

"I want to finish what we started last night," Khan said.

The beach was French and topless, so she removed her white bikini top as casually as she would kick off her sandals. She slid beside Bondurant and put on her sunglasses. She stared into the distance and could see a boat that shimmered like a speck on the bright horizon where the ocean met the cloudless sky.

"We have just one more day on this island, so you might as well spill it," she said.

After Juliet's headless body had been found at the Four Seasons, they'd left a gruesome murder investigation and a lot of unanswered questions behind. "Don't leave town," they'd been told by the D.C. police, but within hours, Khan and Bondurant were on their way to the rugged island for safety from Meyer's thugs and a temporary getaway to sort things through.

"I haven't wanted to talk about it for two reasons," Bondurant said. "The first is because I'm sure you won't believe me." He cupped a hand around his match and cigarette to ensure that the slight breeze that blew off the ocean wouldn't stop him from lighting up. "Like everything else in my life, it seems, it involves the Shroud."

"So I figured," Khan said. She reached over and took the cigarette from Bondurant, enjoyed a short but satisfying drag, and handed it back. "I think you're going to tell me a vial of blood is somehow involved."

"That blood came from a newborn baby cloned from DNA found on the Shroud. There have actually been *two* children cloned to life from the Shroud. And they come from two different sources of DNA," Bondurant said. "One child was the source of the plague. The other was the source of the cure."

The boat Khan had first seen when they settled on the beach, about the size of a large yacht, had begun to turn and make headway toward them on shore. She admired the sleek white lines of the craft that towered at least five decks high and was now about a mile away.

"Domenika brought both cloned children to life through in vitro fertilization, the first time involuntarily, where the child stemmed from the DNA of a Watcher, the presumed source of the plague. The other child, cloned from—"

"What's a Watcher?"

"I was afraid you would ask that."

"It's getting interesting," Khan said.

"A Watcher is a fallen angel," Bondurant said. "Believe in angels?"

"I do. On earth? I don't know."

The yacht that held Khan's interest continued on its course toward them, only now at a faster clip. Bondurant seemed oblivious to it, his back turned halfway toward the water.

"You've called it an 'unearthly plague.' I'm convinced the Watcher brought us the Devil's Sweat. The plague's been put to rest, yes. But who knows what's next? At the moment, the Watcher is in the form of a young boy and is the ward of a very bad man."

"How bad?"

"Bad enough to want Domenika and me dead for what we know. Bad enough to chase us all over the world these past few years to quiet us forever."

"I think I see where this is going," Khan said. "What does your Domenika look like?"

"In the plain light of day? Like Juliet," Bondurant said. "And in the dark . . ."

"Like Juliet. I see," Khan said. "Speaking of chasing you all over the world, I'd ask you to put an eye on that yacht behind you. I don't know; maybe I'm imagining it, but I think it's had an eye on us since we rode in."

Khan watched as Bondurant turned and sat upright to get a good look at the boat, which now sat about a quarter mile offshore, no longer heading toward the beach. The boat's massive engines idled slowly as it drifted parallel to the shore. Bondurant appeared to be relaxed about the magnificent craft and its proximity, which set Khan at ease.

Khan hadn't been able to shake from her mind Juliet's last, horrifying moments of life. Juliet hadn't been her only love interest, but they'd grown close, and Khan had relished their companionship. They'd made some plans to spend more time with each other. Then, in an instant, she was gone. For Khan, the entire incident was surreal.

She had seen a lot of suffering in her career and dealt with death as an everyday occurrence, but the grotesque image of a lover she'd known for almost a year found dismembered at the neck was as sad and gruesome as anything she could imagine. Khan had tried hard not to reveal the slightest emotion to Bondurant over Juliet. But when she'd found herself alone on the beach for a few hours the previous day, she'd wept.

"I'm sure you were close," Bondurant said as he stared into the sand.

She couldn't help but watch the yacht again. This time, it had swung around to show its stern. From what Khan could tell, several crewmen looked to be frantically working away on a contraption on the rear deck. Khan stood up, reached for her beach bag, and quickly began to pack away their lunch.

"So what's the other reason?" she asked.

"What do you mean?" Bondurant said. "And where in the heck are you going?

"You said there were *two* reasons you didn't want to share the whole story with me," Khan said. The boat, now in reverse and closing on them fast, had sprouted a large tripod, which Khan was certain resembled a mount for a gun.

"The second reason? It's too late for that now," Bondurant said.

The colossal yacht was now close enough so that its engines sounded like thunder echoing off the sea. Khan watched as Bondurant turned toward the boat again, this time with his eyes wide. She reached down to grab him by the hand so they could try to make it quickly to the safety of the trees, where their swift horses stood ready.

"I think I have a good idea what the second reason might be," Khan said.

Chapter 38

Dickerson, Maryland

When Domenika slowly swung open the front door of her home and saw that it was Father De Santis who'd woken her from a deep sleep, she was completely surprised.

"You?" Domenika said. She held the door open only several inches, wide enough for her to see his face and no more.

"Yes, me," De Santis said. "May I please come in?"

"I have no doubt you've come a long way, Father, but I have no interest in talking to you now. Actually, not ever."

With her pronouncement, Domenika pushed the door shut and twisted the knob of the dead bolt to ensure that it remained locked.

De Santis was not deterred. He knocked on the door and resumed his plea. "Domenika, please," he said. "A moment. Just a moment of your time to seek forgiveness. That's all I'm asking for."

Domenika folded her arms and shook her head. She hadn't seen or spoken to Bondurant in weeks because of what De Santis had done. "If you want to apologize, you can do it through the door."

"Domenika, *please*! I told you I was wrong."

She watched as he tried to twist the doorknob several times to gain entry but had no luck.

"Domenika, I've done a lot of thinking," De Santis said. "I don't know what it was. Maybe jealousy. Can you believe that? Jealousy. I don't know what else to say."

Domenika was struck that De Santis had started to open up his heart to her from the other side of the door. And she knew she wasn't entirely guilt-free. She had never explicitly told De Santis not to raise the topic of Bondurant's boyhood troubles in front of him. But he should have known better than to spill it forth so clumsily. She unlocked the door and pulled it open several inches so that she could see De Santis again.

"I should never have taken you into my confidence," Domenika said. "That was my fault, I suppose. Never again, Father."

"I understand, Domenika. I do," De Santis said. "Please, may I come in? I have so much to say."

Domenika opened the door wide and gave De Santis a perfunctory hug. She turned toward the kitchen behind her. "I assume you'd like some coffee," she said.

"That would be wonderful," the priest replied.

De Santis carried with him only a small leather kit bag and no suitcase. She was pleased he hadn't come with any expectation of staying for long. He took a seat at the head of the kitchen table.

"It's not like you to surprise me, Giancarlo," she said as she reached into an upper cabinet for a coffee filter. "This must be important."

"I'm in the U.S. for just a few days this time, but we haven't talked in so long. A phone call didn't feel right. And the way we left things, I have to confess, I was worried that if I called ahead, you might just hang up," he said.

Domenika was sure he couldn't be more right. "I think it's best to put that behind us," she said. As the coffee began its slow drip into the glass pot, she set two cups on the table.

"How are you getting on, Domenika?" he asked.

She didn't want to revisit old ground. And in the event that De Santis was being the least bit disingenuous, she didn't want to give him the slightest satisfaction that his words that night had so badly rearranged their lives. She hadn't heard from Bondurant except for envelopes of cash since he'd left, but it was none of the priest's business.

"Jon is fine," Domenika said. She left it at that.

"Well, that's good to hear. And Christopher?"

"A gift, Giancarlo," Domenika said. Her eyes lit up. "I've told you before. I can honestly say I don't believe I've ever been more fulfilled."

De Santis looked about him with a curious expression on his face. "It's so quiet," he said. "He must be napping."

Domenika took her time responding as she slowly poured coffee into their cups. "Napping? Oh, yes," she said. She didn't have a clue why she'd lied and not simply told De Santis the truth, that Parenti had taken Christopher for a walk. It was such an inconsequential fact, but her instincts told her something was wrong. Suddenly, she felt a certain unease about the two of them being together in the house alone but didn't understand the reason for the feeling. She didn't know how long De Santis planned to visit over coffee, but she began to hope it wouldn't last longer than the cup before him.

"There is nothing more beautiful than the sight of a child at peace. Nothing," the priest said. "You must let me peek in to see him before he wakes."

Domenika panicked slightly at his insistence on seeing the boy and the prospect of being caught in a lie. She decided to quickly change the subject. "And you? How have you been?" she asked. Domenika thought De Santis looked frailer than she had ever seen him before. His face was drawn, and his skin had taken on a light yellowish pallor.

"I have to say I've been a bit out of sorts lately with all this travel, but it's nothing to be concerned about," De Santis said. She watched the priest gulp down his coffee as if he were in a hurry. He was already almost to the bottom of his cup.

"More?" she asked.

"No, thank you, I'm fine," he said. "So, is Jon off on an errand? I didn't see a car outside."

"Yes, he'll be back any minute."

"I see. And Father Parenti? Still nearby? Why have I not yet had the pleasure of seeing him? Don't tell me he's off on another of his adventures."

Domenika shifted uncomfortably in her chair. "I'm sure he'll be along shortly as well," she said. She grew more anxious by the second.

As they looked at each other across the table, there was a long, uncomfortable silence between them.

Then De Santis reached down for the leather kit bag he'd brought along. "Domenika, I don't have much time, and I'd really like to see the child," he declared.

Domenika caught her breath. The abrupt change in the priest's tone came out of thin air and felt like the stab of a knife. De Santis steadied his eyes on hers as he nervously unzipped the bag he'd brought and removed from it a small paper pouch.

"I told you, he's sound asleep, Giancarlo," Domenika insisted. She was suddenly frightened to be alone with a man she would once have trusted with her life. "I really don't want to wake him."

"The last time I was here, before we had our troubles, you passed along some very helpful information. It was about the child's blood. Do you remember that?" De Santis finished the last sip of his coffee and stared down into the cup.

"Yes, I told you that in confidence," Domenika replied. "Just like the information I shared with you about Jon." She hadn't a clue where De Santis was headed with his questions, but she'd grown as angry as she was frightened with his strange behavior.

"You said, if I recall correctly," the priest said, "that you believed it was the child's blood that had provided the antidote to end the terrible scourge, the Devil's Sweat; do you recall that?"

Domenika rose from the kitchen table, careful not to turn her back on her guest. She began to regret telling De Santis a lot of things. "Yes, I remember that," she said in a near whisper.

"As you know, our commission studied this issue at great length and found nothing. But you are the one in the best position to know. Has the child displayed any marvels, any wonders to speak of, since his birth? Anything at all in the way of special abilities that we haven't been aware of?"

"What do you mean? Like changing water into wine?" Domenika shot back. Her sarcasm was clear. She was certain De Santis knew more about Christopher's healing powers than he'd let on. All the media attention given to the "miracle boy" at Portland's children's hospital previously ignored by the Church ensured that. She was sure the priest was now just acting coy. "He's just a child, Giancarlo. You know full well that you and, for that matter, the whole Vatican have already reached the conclusion that Christopher is nothing but a normal boy. The answer's no."

De Santis got up from his chair and looked toward the door that led to the stairs to the second floor. Domenika was certain the priest knew where Christopher's room was from his brief previous visits. She began to edge toward the stairs as though prepared to block his path.

He held the paper pouch in both hands and tore the top from it. Then he poured the contents of the bag onto the table. A few packets of sterile alcohol wipes, a hypodermic needle affixed to a small tube, and a tiny glass vial for collecting fluids lay before him.

"I'm going to need a very small sample of the child's blood, Domenika," De Santis said. "I won't harm him, I promise you. He will feel just a prick as he sleeps. But I'm going to need a very small amount."

Domenika looked at De Santis as though he were the devil incarnate. Suddenly, she saw Parenti's head pop into view through the kitchen's side door. He had arrived home from his walk to the playground with Christopher. It was clear to Domenika that from Parenti's vantage point on the stairs, the tiny priest couldn't see De Santis, who stood, needle in hand, just a few feet away. As Parenti opened the door and entered the room, Christopher gleefully ran into Domenika's arms. Aldo was close behind. It was only then Parenti turned to see De Santis, who towered beside him.

"My word, you frightened me," Parenti said, startled. He looked as if he had seen a ghost.

"Napping upstairs?" De Santis said.

Domenika, with Christopher in her arms, immediately began to backpedal away from De Santis but ran out of room when she backed into the refrigerator behind her. She was cornered and had nowhere else to move.

"If you so much as touch this child, Giancarlo, I swear I will—"

"What's this all about?" Parenti shouted. He took a step backward when he saw the needle in De Santis's hand.

"Domenika, all I need is a drop or two, I'm sure," De Santis said. "I need you to work with me." He began to slowly inch toward her and paused for a moment as Christopher, frightened by the commotion, clung to his mother and began to cry.

When De Santis resumed his march, Domenika stood helpless, trapped with the child and unable to move. She pulled Christopher in tight and shielded his head with the palm of her hand while he sobbed. As De Santis pressed toward her, she watched Parenti step bravely in front of the priest and try his best to shove him away. Aldo, who'd instantly leaped as high as he could in defense of his master, had De Santis by the shirtsleeve with his teeth. De Santis reached down and with one arm flung the little priest aside. Parenti stumbled and struck his head hard against the marble edge of the countertop. De Santis, now only inches from Domenika and the boy, reached out the hand not tethered to the dog, ready to grab for the frightened child.

"Domenika, don't make me do it this way," he said.

"Get away from him!" Domenika cried out. She turned her shoulder toward De Santis to further shield the child from the needle held by the oncoming priest.

"Domenika, for God's sake, I'm dying. Can't you see that?"

"Stop!" Domenika cried out. She could feel that De Santis had Christopher by the leg and had started to tug on him hard.

"I said I'm dying!" De Santis shouted.

The gunshot was so loud it echoed throughout the house and deafened Domenika. For a moment, she could hear only ringing as she crouched in the corner with the boy. She watched as shards of plaster fell from the ceiling directly above where Parenti had fired the gun. The top of Parenti's head was completely covered in white plaster dust that had fallen from the gaping hole left in the ceiling.

"You don't understand me. I said I think I'm going to die!" De Santis screamed as he reached again for the terrified child. He now held Aldo by the scruff of the neck in his hand.

"You touch a hair on that child or my dog, and you'll die for sure," Parenti said. He now aimed the .44 Magnum pistol, with a barrel nearly as long as his arm, directly at De Santis's head.

"You wear the collar, Father," De Santis said as he turned around. He saw the gun pointed directly at him. "You can't threaten me."

"So do *you*, you devil," Parenti said. He used both his thumbs to cock the gun's hammer while he slid his forefinger to the trigger. Then, with his free hand, Parenti reached up, grabbed De Santis by the hair, and squared the barrel of the gun against the priest's temple.

De Santis, mindful of the barrel, cautiously stood. Tears had begun to stream down his face. He looked at Domenika in desperation but said nothing. She watched as he carefully set Aldo on the floor, struggled to free his hair from Parenti's grip, and bolted through the kitchen door to escape outside.

Where her once-trusted friend and teacher was headed next, Domenika didn't know. But as he ran for his life as fast as he could, she thought it might be hell.

Chapter 39

Potomac, Maryland

Father Parenti sat in the alcove next to the bar inside the rustic Old Angler's Inn and waited for Bondurant. It was twilight outside and dark inside, with only the light of a warm fire to set the room aglow. Several worn armchairs were gathered near the hearth. Bondurant was late. Parenti propped his feet up near the fireplace to warm them during the wait.

The little priest was nervous. He'd promised Bondurant he would come alone. He'd lied. A white lie, Parenti reasoned. He *had* come alone. He'd just not bothered to tell Bondurant that Domenika would join them at the restaurant as well. But it was the other white lie Parenti had told that had the little priest doubly concerned. Domenika thought she was meeting Parenti alone for dinner, too. It would be a complete surprise to her that Parenti had tracked Bondurant down. But he knew it would be even more shocking for her to see Bondurant in the flesh without warning after their time apart. Parenti was beside himself with excitement over the prospect of the surprise reunion.

Domenika showed up early. When she came through the front door, Bondurant had not yet arrived. Parenti rushed to greet her and asked the maître d' to seat the two of them immediately. She took them through the rustic main dining area to a smaller, quaint room that held just a few tables. It had a lovely view of the inn's outdoor courtyard, where the glow of tiny lanterns in the trees swayed and twinkled in the early-evening light. When Domenika was settled, she turned to Parenti and looked at him as though there was something she needed to get off her mind.

"I'm moving back to Rome," she declared. "I've found an apartment. And I've sent a deposit of three months' rent."

Parenti cringed. How could she so overreact? Then he craned his neck as best he could around the corner. He had his eye on the larger dining room in search of Bondurant.

"Moving to *where*?"

"Rome. You've heard of it," she said. "I believe it was your home for many years."

"You can't do that!" the priest exclaimed. "It's no place for a single mother. It isn't. And besides—"

"He isn't coming back. He isn't. I dreamed about it," Domenika said. Parenti hadn't heard her this upset over their situation in days. "And honestly," she continued, "I don't want him back now. I'm sorry for what I did. But all this waiting. Waiting for what?"

"Domenika—"

"It's strange. I love him. I do. But he's not here for us. I also think I've started to resent him too—really resent him, you know, for what his plans are for Chris."

Parenti stood abruptly at their table. "I'm sorry, but I have to use the restroom. Will you excuse me?"

"Of course," Domenika said. She looked disappointed. "But I want you to know I'm quite serious. Jon's acting like a child, and our goals for Christopher are entirely different."

Parenti rolled his eyes as he turned away from the table. He hoped her mood was just a temporary lapse. He presumed that by now Bondurant would have found his way inside. As the priest scurried his way through the main dining room toward the inn's entrance, he couldn't believe his eyes. There sat Bondurant, already seated at his own table for two near the front. He looked worn, even several years older. Bondurant stood up at the sight of the priest, and Parenti, who had sorely missed his dear friend, embraced him in a warm hug. Tears began to well in Parenti's eyes. After they exchanged pleasantries, it was clear Bondurant wanted to get right to the point.

"I knew somehow I would have no trouble eventually seeing you again, Father," Bondurant said. "It's so good to see you. I just want you to know right off that I've thought a lot about it, and I can't say the same is true of my feelings for Domenika."

"What do you mean?" Parenti asked.

"I love her. Absolutely. But I don't think it can work between us," Bondurant said.

"May I just say—"

"I miss her so much. But she lied to me."

"Would you excuse me for just a moment?" Parenti asked. "I think I'm in need of the restroom."

"Of course, Father. I'll just look over the menu."

Parenti turned on his heels and rushed as quickly as he could back toward the room where Domenika sat. When he reached their table, he sat down, slightly short of breath.

"Is everything all right?" Domenika asked. It had been more than ten minutes. "Are you ill, Father?"

"I'm fine, I'm fine," he said. She handed him a menu, but Parenti, exasperated, tossed it aside.

"What's wrong? Aren't you hungry?" Domenika asked. "I thought we were having dinner."

"Of course we are," Parenti said. He tapped his foot and stared out the window.

"As I was saying," Domenika said, "deep down inside, it's really abandonment I feel. Abandonment of me, Christopher, you, his family. I've searched my soul for how someone could be so cold that he's able to walk away and abandon those he once professed to love. And I hate to say this, but it's only someone like Jon who's capable of desertion."

"Desertion?" Parenti said. "Don't you think you're being a bit hard on him?" He tapped his fork on his water glass loudly enough to summon the waitress, who he hoped could help change the subject.

"He knows where to find us," Domenika said. "He could have come back if he wanted to, and he hasn't. So I'm moving on."

Domenika had a helpless look on her face, and Parenti could tell she was as upset as he'd ever seen her.

"If you'll excuse me for just one more moment, I think I have to return to the restroom," Parenti said.

"But you've only just been there," Domenika said. "Are you not feeling well? Let's just call it a night. We'll find another time." She reached for her purse, prepared to leave.

"No, no," Parenti said. "This will be quick."

"Fine, then," Domenika said.

As soon as Parenti turned the corner and was out of her sight, he dashed all the way toward the other end of the dining room to Bondurant. Parenti's tiny legs had carried him so fast that he gasped for breath when he sat.

"I hope you're all right, Father," Bondurant said.

"I'm fine, I'm fine," the priest replied as he panted for air. "Now, where were we?"

"I've thought about it, and I can't love someone I can't trust," Bondurant said. "How would you feel if Domenika had lied to you from the first day you met, and that her every kindness toward you was probably driven out of pity rather than respect? How would that make you feel?"

"Pity?"

"It's obvious," Bondurant said. "She spent the better part of her career at the Vatican having to deal with the Church's sins against children, and then I turn up as what? One of her victims, that's what. She felt sorry for me ever since. True love is not born from pity. She felt sorry for me, that's all."

At this point, Parenti had completely lost any appetite he'd brought with him. He felt as though his task of reuniting his two dear friends was as useless as trying to mate a cat and a dog. He sat quietly for a moment and stared at his old friend.

"What is it, Father?" Bondurant asked.

Parenti had heard enough. "I'm sorry, but you're going to have to excuse me again for just another moment."

"The bathroom? Again?" Bondurant said.

"Yes, the bathroom. Before I return, I just want you to think on this, you stubborn mule." Parenti raised his voice loud enough for those at the tables nearby to hear. "Every night that's gone by since you walked out has left Domenika terribly alone. She pines for you. Nearly every waking hour has found her in tears that you might never return. She loves you with every fiber of her being and has vowed to search the world for you. Every breath she takes is just another sigh calling out your name."

Parenti looked down at Bondurant before he turned to flee to the other side of the restaurant again. He could see he had stunned his friend into silence. As he turned and ran as fast as he could back to Domenika's table, he cringed at how he'd embellished a bit, particularly the part about the sighs. It was a ridiculous exaggeration, to be sure. For the sake of the couple he loved, he hoped his words had their intended effect.

Parenti silently sat back down. He had never felt more forlorn, and he knew he looked it.

"Why the sad face?" Domenika said.

"*Porco diavolo!*" Parenti said. He threw his napkin onto the table in disgust. His plans had completely fallen apart. Then he got up from his seat and wagged his finger at her. "I've thought this over too. Bondurant hasn't abandoned you. *He's* the one all alone. You're abandoning *him*. He's hurt, he's ashamed, and he's hiding. Now he needs your help. You're the only woman he's ever loved, and the only one who can ever bring him back to love. He's saved your life more than once, and now you need to save his. I know you'll never find a more decent man as long as you live."

Parenti, his speech complete, turned to march out of the room.

Domenika, dumbfounded, posed a simple question as he walked away. "Where are you going?" she asked. "Back to the restroom again?"

"I don't know," Parenti said. He felt helpless. "I don't know."

And he didn't. He'd said all he needed to say. But he was convinced, given the distance that had grown between the couple he loved, that his words were not nearly enough to save them.

When Parenti reached the middle of the dining room with his head hung low, he heard a commotion toward the front of the restaurant and looked up. Bondurant had left his table and made his way deliberately toward him. The little priest cowered as if he were about to be tackled to the ground, presumably for the tongue-lashing he'd given his friend. Then he heard the voice of a woman right behind him. He turned to see Domenika rush toward him from the opposite direction with equal and deliberate intent.

Parenti looked briefly toward the ceiling with thanks, as though the heavens above were prepared to smile after all on the once-doomed reunion of those he loved most. Then he stepped aside in anticipation of the long-awaited hug between his dearest friends.

Unfortunately, both Bondurant and Domenika stopped short of the hoped-for embrace. They were engaged in more of a shoving match in the center of the aisle.

"You're acting like a child, Jon," Domenika said. "Adults talk these things out. They don't run away from home. It's just like you to abuse Father Parenti with a stunt like this."

"Abusing Father Parenti?" Bondurant said. "Talk about abuse—what kind of home is it when it's a house full of secrets and there's no one to trust?"

"Trust? Who are you to talk about trust?" Domenika cried out. "One day we're a family, with a child and responsibilities, rent and report cards, and the next day we're nothing? Abandoned! Deserted! And why? Because of *hurt feelings*? This is a sick joke, right?"

"Tell me, Domenika," Bondurant shouted, "how many more in

your damned Church hold records on me? How many others can recite my past from memos you wrote? Is it common practice to publish the sexual exploits of priests when children are involved? Is that what the whole Shroud project was about? A way to deflect attention from what's really going on inside the Church? That's the joke. It's just disgusting."

Before Parenti knew it, both Bondurant and Domenika had ended their shouting match and made their way out through separate exits. Every dinner guest within earshot sat stunned. Parenti lost any notion that he might ever reconcile the two. What a disaster, he thought. He'd had another premonition, one he'd confided to no one. Reuniting the couple to prepare their son was now an emergency, as the world was about to be threatened once more.

Chapter 40

Geneva

Meyer stared at the note in his hand, which bore the red wax of the distinct papal seal. The message stated that a Father Giancarlo De Santis was number 2,327 in line. His request was to move to the front of the queue for a private meeting with the supreme elder. Meyer quickly snapped his fingers and waved to get the attention of Galerkin, who stood at the other end of the cavernous room.

Galerkin at least made a decent bodyguard. Meyer's only expectation of the Russian oaf was that he take a bullet for him or Hans Jr. if ever the need arose. He was paid a monthly retainer and attached to Meyer's growing personal security unit. It had been years since Galerkin had developed a lead worth pursuing on the couple. Meyer, preoccupied with his gigantic and still-growing church but still supportive of their elimination, was resigned to finding another way.

Once Galerkin ambled over, Meyer leaned in to whisper instructions. Then he handed Galerkin the note he'd received. After

Galerkin read it slowly several times, the Russian made his way out of the room.

Meyer assumed De Santis was ill. Unless the priest was on some sort of highly unusual mission for Meyer's archenemy, Pope Augustine, there was no other reason for him to join a line of thousands that stretched around the block. They formed a large ring that surrounded the modern, newly christened Demanian Convention Center just outside Geneva. All those in the queue who'd camped outside for days to reserve their places in line were younger than eighty, deathly ill, and planning to convert. These were the criteria for their admittance. Each was prepared to pay the steep price of conversion for a miraculous healing of some kind.

Today the cutoff for the end of the line was two thousand. Those farther back were out of luck. It was a sizable number of people, enough that it would force Hans Jr. to stand or sit in one place for ten hours to heal the afflicted who desired to be saved by his extraordinary gift. All the converts would, as required by Demanian Church law, first renounce their present faith in front of two familiar witnesses, sign contracts to tithe away a negotiated percentage of their earnings and estates, and submit to cheek swabs to produce the requisite DNA sample for church storage. Every convert was required to bring along a female of childbearing age who had to secure an appointment for a future egg donation.

Once processed, the ill could receive the child's healing touch and be cured, usually within a few weeks' time. Five worldwide healing tours had been conducted, and to date, more than fifty thousand people had been cured of chronic ailments, mental illnesses, or terminal diseases through the boy's miraculous touch. Almost fifty million more people had converted to Demanianism from other faiths in the past few years. Most of them were in good health but in want of an insurance policy of sorts in the event they ever required Hans Jr.'s touch. Most had been lured to the prospect of everlasting life the "Demanian Way."

The Demanian Way. Meyer relished the sound of it. The promise of protection against diseases for some, but, just as important, the prospect of eternal life through his church had been heavily promoted around the world. There were so many converts that it had been difficult for the church to manage its growing rolls. It required massive new and expensive data centers and DNA storage facilities, which the church rushed to establish on every continent. The faith's coffers could afford them. The church's funds now totaled more than two hundred billion dollars, and if its finance department's projections held true, the Demanian faith would sit atop one trillion dollars in assets before the decade was through. Such massive amounts of money would be necessary to build the kind and number of facilities needed to accommodate the influx of worshippers. And the funds would also be necessary to lobby governments worldwide, buying off officials where necessary, in favor of the practice the church desperately needed to legalize in order to ensure its future existence: human cloning.

But of all the accomplishments Meyer had counted since he was blessed with the gift of Hans Jr. eight years before, it was the slow but sure strangulation of competing faiths in which he took the greatest pleasure. There would be one, and only one, worldwide faith of any consequence when he was done, and it would be Demanian. Given Meyer's predilection, driven by the death of his mother at the hands of a faith as a child, Hans Jr. had taken a particularly strong interest in converting those of one religion in particular. He insisted that Meyer focus the church's efforts on conversion in those areas of the world with the greatest concentrations of Christians, in particular Catholics. As the father and son had agreed, it was critical to eliminate organized religious opposition to Demanian plans while simultaneously disassembling Christianity at every possible turn.

One pious voice in particular stood publicly against Demanianism and resurrection cloning, the church's most basic precept. Pope Augustine had steadfastly labeled the Demanians' quest for human cloning "an affront to human dignity." By inference, then, there could be no pope. No pope, no Catholic Church.

Meyer wondered whether it was this last pronouncement, one he had openly discussed in recent press interviews, that had finally gotten the Vatican's attention and sent De Santis his way. As Meyer waited for Galerkin to bring De Santis to the sky suite from which he overlooked the healing ceremony under way on the convention center floor below, he stared out across the large table before him. Spread over its length was a set of blueprints the Demanian Church's Capital Projects and Construction Committee had prepared for his review. The drawings revealed a massive complex—indeed, a church stadium—that would accommodate worshippers more than one hundred thousand strong. The coliseum was planned for construction in Mexico City, but four identical structures would soon rise on the outskirts of Boston, Brasilia, Manila, and Rome, the present capitals of Catholicism in the modern world. Each was designed to conduct Demanian Church services for the huge and growing number of faithful as well as to efficiently process masses of converts through conversion and other rituals Meyer had in mind. A massive, shallow pond the size of four Olympic swimming pools sat at the center of each stadium to accommodate thousands undergoing baptism at once.

Meyer glanced up from the blueprints and watched Galerkin escort a priest into the suite by the arm. The man didn't look well. His skin, a pale yellow, hung from a frame that looked emaciated and frail.

"If you're here with a communiqué from your pope that involves anything but unconditional surrender, I won't accept it," Meyer said. It was the first and only time he had come within inches of a priest who had the pontiff's ear. He leaned uncomfortably close to De Santis as he spoke and stood nose to nose with him to be sure he was understood.

De Santis looked Meyer directly in the eyes. "I'm not here on behalf of Pope Augustine," he said. "I want to be clear about that. I've come of my own accord." His voice was hoarse.

"Then I have no use for you. This bastard's busy," Meyer said. He turned from De Santis and looked down on the drawings of his future church stadium. He smiled broadly, knowing he had begun to open Demanian churches faster than the Vatican could shutter its own.

"I'm dying, and I want to live," De Santis said.

Meyer glanced at him but immediately went back to the blueprints as if to pay De Santis no mind. "Is that so?" Meyer said, disinterested. "You look fine to me."

"I'm not well," De Santis whispered. "I have pancreatic cancer, stage four."

Meyer looked over as the priest stared down at his shoes, unable to look up, as if in shame.

"Is contagious?" Galerkin asked.

"Of course not," De Santis said.

"You want him back in the line?" Galerkin looked toward Meyer for a signal. He reached for De Santis's arm, ready to yank him away.

"Not yet," Meyer said. "Is that all you've brought me? A simple illness?"

Suddenly, De Santis dropped to his knees at Meyer's feet, in tears. Meyer, surprised, took a step back. He could see the broken priest had lost whatever courage he'd brought with him.

"I have six months, maybe less," De Santis said as he crept forward and bowed his head low. He was within an inch of Meyer's feet.

"I thought you might bear a message from your convalescent master in Rome. But given that's not the case, why should I take an interest in saving the life of a sworn enemy, a common priest?" Meyer asked.

"Perhaps I can give something in trade," De Santis said. His voice had become a whimper.

Meyer watched as the priest began to tremble terribly before him. "And what is that?" He placed his hand on the priest's shoulder as though he were dealing with an errant child. If the priest had valuable information, he wanted to hear it.

"I can lead you to Bondurant, the Jozef girl, and the child as well," De Santis said. "I have no doubt that's who you're after."

Galerkin shifted uncomfortably on his feet.

"Is that right?" Meyer asked.

"It is," De Santis said in a whisper.

"Any idiot can find me Bondurant and the girl," Meyer said. He looked at Galerkin as if to burn a hole straight through him with his eyes. "Tell me about this child."

"It is the other child of the Shroud," De Santis said.

"The what?" Meyer asked. He thought he'd misheard the priest.

"The other child of the Shroud. Surely you must know this," De Santis said.

Meyer instantly felt as if a bolt of lightning had struck him. He hadn't a clue what the priest was talking about, but he also had no interest in letting him know that. In an instant, his world had changed. If there was another child born of the Shroud, one who possessed powers anywhere near those of Hans Jr., it was a problem. His *biggest* problem.

"Of course I do," Meyer said.

He wondered what to believe. Another child cloned from the Shroud? He clenched his teeth. Extinguishing Bondurant and Jozef had been relegated to a nicety, something Meyer personally desired. But if what De Santis had claimed was indeed true, the mere sparing of the cowardly priest who knelt before him was scant pocket change for the fee.

Meyer looked through the suite's giant glass panels at Hans Jr., who sat on a massive thronelike chair in the center of the auditorium floor below. A line of people, many confined to wheelchairs or strapped to gurneys, snaked from the throne all the way out the exit door a hundred meters away. Each person in line anxiously awaited the child's gentle touch to be cured.

"You want to live?" Meyer asked as he looked down on the priest.

"I want to live."

"Then I want them dead," Meyer said as he pulled the priest up by the collar. "All three. Can you do that for me?"

De Santis only nodded.

Meyer snapped his fingers, and with the wave of his hand sent

Galerkin away. He'd learned his lesson. It was no longer a job he could leave to the once-trusted assassin. He placed his arm around De Santis's shoulders, then led him to a corner of the room where they could talk quietly alone. After nearly ten minutes, Meyer signaled for Galerkin to come over once more.

"Place our newfound friend at the head of the line," Meyer said as he looked once more toward the auditorium floor.

De Santis, whose face had begun to glow, was led by the arm out of the suite toward the healing ceremony below. After a minute, he and Galerkin emerged onto the auditorium floor. Meyer looked down. When they reached the front of the serpentine line, Galerkin grabbed the priest by his shoulders, lifted him several inches off the ground, and set him down before the child.

Meyer looked on as the boy reared back on his red velvet throne, surprised that he suddenly faced a priest. It was obvious Hans Jr. was reluctant to touch De Santis in any way. Somewhat stunned, the child quickly glanced up at Meyer in the sky suite and looked for a sign. Meyer slowly nodded. Hans Jr. paused. Then he tapped the priest on the shoulder as he had done to so many others who'd been healed by his touch. In an unusual gesture, he held out his hand as though to proffer a deal. De Santis extended his own hand in return.

"This is my beloved son," Meyer whispered to himself as he watched the pair clasp their hands together as one, "with whom I am well pleased."

Chapter 41

The Vatican

Pope Augustine stood with his arms outstretched in the center of the sacristy that adjoined St. Peter's Basilica. He shrugged his shoulders. The weight of the papal regalia with which the half dozen priests and attendants had adorned him felt like an unusually heavy burden.

It was a clear and bright Easter Sunday morning at the Vatican. The famous basilica was framed by a welcome cloudless azure sky. The pontiff was about to commence the most celebrated annual Mass in all of Christendom. A standing-room-only crowd of fifteen thousand worshippers packed the basilica. Nearly two hundred thousand more faithful crammed into St. Peter's Square outside in anticipation of Mass and the pope's traditional apostolic blessing. Incense that burned from a half dozen giant thuribles filled the solemn air around him, some escaping from the ancient sacristy windows above and wafting toward the massive crowd gathered outdoors.

The pontiff motioned toward one end of the ornate marbled room and signaled for Father De Santis to approach him. Before De Santis could reach the pope, two attendants, identical in height and ceremonial dress, delicately tilted Augustine's head forward to slip the pallium over his chasuble. Worn only by the pope, the sovereign of Vatican City, it was a two-inch-wide strip of cloth that displayed six red crosses along its length. The red crosses symbolized the blood of Christ, and the three golden pins that affixed the pallium to the pope's vestments represented the nails with which Christ was crucified. Another attendant stood several feet away and minded the papal cross in preparation for its procession. When the pope's official regalia was in place, he would be handed a staff topped by a golden crucifix, the same one carried into such solemn services since the thirteenth century.

"God bless you, Giancarlo," the pontiff whispered once De Santis reached his side. The attendants retreated several steps away. "You look magnificent. Is it true? I'm told the sudden cure for your cancer is nothing short of a miracle."

Augustine had kept tabs on De Santis's sad and slowly declining health, and he had never seen him look so good. The pope's own physician had examined De Santis recently and assured the pontiff that he had never witnessed such an amazing recovery, a retreat from the brink of certain death. De Santis's pancreas was not only intact but had been restored to perfect health, cancer-free. The pope reasoned he might know why.

"A miracle, Holy Father. A miracle indeed," De Santis replied as his face broke into a broad grin.

"Now, tell me," the pope said. "We have just a few minutes. Tell

me this means you have somehow located the child of the Shroud.
Tell me this is the source of your extraordinary recovery."

A surprised look spread across De Santis's face. "Holy Father,
I—I—"

"The child, Giancarlo. The child! This child of the Shroud with
our Domenika. Tell me you've finally located him. Tell me he's the
source of your cure. There is no other way!"

Augustine had hoped against hope that De Santis would find
the child and confirm the impossible. He had prayed that he might
learn one day that the same child who had stemmed the tide of the
horrid plague had other gifts to offer that might be the salvation of
the Church in its time of dire need.

"Oh, yes, yes, Holy Father. I now understand what you're asking," De Santis said. "At long last, I have been in contact with this
child of the Shroud, and I have no doubt benefited from his healing
powers. They are indeed miraculous!"

To the pope, it was news befitting such a glorious Easter Sunday morning. The Church's authority and the size of its flock had
been in steep decline for years, but its recent slide into near despair
alongside the amazing emergence of the Demanian Church had
made life almost unbearable for the pontiff. He never imagined
that he or any other pope might preside over the dissolution of
the Catholic faith. At the center of the Demanian ascendancy was
the famed child, Hans Jr., reported worldwide to offer healing and
salvation akin to the biblical miracles of Jesus Christ.

Christians worldwide had converted to the Demanian Church
in growing numbers, and the Vatican could do little to prevent their
migration other than offer the centuries-old tenets of its tired faith.
The pope, weak from the struggle between the two near-warring

religions as well as the scandals that had rocked his Church, had actually considered resignation from the papacy. It would be an act not unprecedented in modern times but still extremely rare.

Of particular concern to the pontiff was the degree to which those who'd converted to the Demanian faith refused to see the deception all around them. The pope felt that forgiveness might be forthcoming to the sick and dying, those who had converted with the assurance of healing by the Demanian Church's Watcher child. After all, the promise of rescue from terrible afflictions and certain death, akin to a serpent's temptation fit for Adam and Eve, was understandable for the desperate. Their rapture over cheating death was consistent with mankind's very nature. But acceptance of the idea that salvation could be had for the price of tithing or that eternal life could be purchased with scientific cloning was beyond the pale. Mass conversions to the Demanian Church, which had acquired untold riches, had brought with them mass hysteria and a desertion of God that only an agent of the devil could sow. Of this the pope was unalterably convinced.

Augustine watched as the two attendants who carried the triregnum began their journey across the sacristy toward him. The traditional triple tiara headdress worn by popes for centuries on such occasions had been readied. It would be the last adornment placed on the pope before he entered the basilica to celebrate Mass. It was the signal that the Mass was about to begin.

"Giancarlo, we have but another moment," the pontiff said. "Come close."

De Santis leaned in. "Yes, Holy Father?"

"We are at war with the devil, to be sure," the pope said. "You know this."

De Santis merely nodded.

"You have heard recently that this man Meyer, the puppet master of the Watcher child, has called me out, as it were?"

"I have, Your Holiness," De Santis said.

"The 'impostor of Christ' is what he's called me," the pope whispered. "It's in the newspapers. I have seen it on TV."

"Simple name-calling," De Santis said. "I would pay it no mind."

"He says that he acts as the ward of the true Christ. Have you heard this?"

"I have, Holy Father. But—"

"Giancarlo, the devil is throwing down the gauntlet. Turning the faithful against the Church in an effort to destroy us. Extracting promises of payment for eternal life instead of the Lord's ways."

"I've heard these statements, Holy Father," De Santis said. He stared at the marble floor as he spoke.

"Giancarlo, you are well now," the pope said. "I have for you the most important assignment of your life. The Church is in your hands."

"What is it, Holy Father?"

"We must have that child, the child of the Shroud. I'm afraid this is a struggle in which we must fight evil with eternal good."

"But, Your Holiness—"

Augustine leaned over toward De Santis as close as he could and kissed him on the cheek. "A swift success and a special seat await you, Giancarlo," he said. "A bishop's seat at the Vatican, no less."

De Santis's eyes grew wide with astonishment.

"But we *must* have that child," the pontiff said. "The one who has saved you. He can save us. He is our hope. Dr. Bondurant is a lost cause. But you can bring me Domenika. Bring her to me. We must reason with her to give us the child."

The two attendants who carried the triregnum stepped in unison onto the small platform behind the pope and slowly placed the bejeweled silver tiara topped with a golden cross on his head. De Santis looked anxious to slip from the pontiff's side to let him proceed.

The pope pulled him in close by the sleeve. "This crown—it is worn only by the Vicar of Christ. You know this, don't you?" he said.

"I do, Your Holiness," De Santis said, still unable to look the pontiff in the eyes.

"It represents the triumphant Church."

"It does, Your Holiness."

"We must have that boy, Giancarlo. I will crown him myself as the true Vicar of Christ if that is what it takes to rescue the faith and save my Church. But first you must bring him to me."

Chapter 42

London

Bondurant set his cup of coffee down on the front page of the tabloid and, for the first time since he'd seen the newspaper the day before, allowed himself to laugh at the photo that nearly jumped off its cover.

The picture, a large black-and-white photo that splashed over the front of London's *Daily Mirror*, was of Bondurant and a topless Khan on the beach at St. Bart's. For readers of the *Mirror*, the image it captured was of two famous star-crossed lovers caught on camera in a romantic moment as they gazed toward the sea. For Bondurant and Khan, the photo stirred very different meanings and memories.

The *Mirror* headline that accompanied the photograph said it all: "Scientists Take a Holiday: Bare Breasted in St. Bart's." The prized photo of the world-famous Khan alongside her new scientist boyfriend had been taken by enterprising paparazzi. Both Bondurant and Khan had turned off their cell phones since the paper was published the day before to avoid the dozens of calls from supposed "well-wishers" who'd now left voice messages about the attractive but nonexistent couple's plight.

Bondurant looked up from the pages of the tabloid to the view outside; it was a scene designed to impress. Khan's apartment had a magnificent view of downtown London that encompassed the old and the new—the London Eye, Big Ben, the Houses of Parliament, and the muddy River Thames—as far as he could see. Khan's home was a secluded and trendy two-floor flat with a grand outdoor balcony that overhung the Thames.

Reading the story over again, Bondurant knew a single word in the article used to describe his relationship with Khan was loaded with all the wrong implications. The story, in describing the two, read: "Khan, bisexual and not normally known for long-term affairs, has carried on with seldom seen dashing anthropologist and author boyfriend Bondurant, leading some to believe there's some 'there' there. Khan has been known to devour her male mates, much like the female praying mantis known for decapitating and often eating her loves alive."

Khan, barefoot, freshly showered, and dressed for the day, brought to the table a tray with more hot coffee and cream, jam, some croissants, and a pack of Gitanes to smoke.

"It's good to see you've regained your sense of humor," she said. She'd overheard him laughing at the article. Bondurant had been in no mood to chuckle when he first saw the story the night before, but he'd lightened up. He'd reminded himself of what he'd often heard about the British tabloid press, that today's news wraps tomorrow's fish and chips.

Bondurant watched Khan as she set down the breakfast tray and poured him more hot coffee with a splash of cream. She stared at the view from the window, and Bondurant took the opportunity to take in Khan as well—her smell, her grace, her movements, her stunning features. But "boyfriend" was wrong. She'd remained a friend, not a lover, since they met. He figured it would be impossible for anyone, including Domenika, to believe, given how he'd treated—even mistreated—women before. But Domenika, even though they were now far apart, had changed him in deep and important ways. While they'd had their troubles, Domenika was still his only love, and to Bondurant, his integrity was everything.

"There's something in that story that requires some real reflection and perhaps just a bit of conversation. I'd like to see if you agree," Khan said. She finished buttering a croissant and, after applying a light coat of jam, slid it onto Bondurant's plate. "It says here that you're my 'boyfriend.'"

Bondurant shook his head and reached for his coffee to take a long sip in order to stall as he searched for a good response.

She always found a way to get straight to the point of what mattered. Sometimes he liked it. Sometimes he didn't. But it always sped things along.

"It also says you decapitate and eat your mates. Does that go for friends as well?"

"Not all of them," Khan said with a smile. She leaned over the breakfast table and playfully dabbed a small amount of butter and jam from the croissant she'd prepared onto Bondurant's lips. "But this is your chance. Now or never. Would you like to be my boyfriend, Jon?" She placed one bare foot on the chair beside him, and in the process revealed one of her shapely tan legs to the top of her thigh.

"I think I—I think I—" Bondurant said. He'd never lost the shyness that took him at the age of twelve.

"You think, you think. You think about your Domenika, right?" Khan said. She moved around the table and sat next to him. She stroked the back of his hand. "Jon, you haven't seen her for weeks. You've survived. And I've left you alone. But," she said as she tapped on the newspaper spread before them, "inquiring minds want to know. Would you *like* to be my boyfriend?" She licked her forefinger and used it to wipe away a speck of jam at the corner of his mouth.

Just then, her home phone rang, almost as if on cue.

"That's odd," Khan said. "That phone never rings."

"Ignore it?" Bondurant asked, although he fully welcomed the interruption.

"I've got my hands full," she said. She'd already left his side and carried a breakfast tray toward the kitchen. "Can you get it? Whoever it is, as you can see, I'm not at home."

Bondurant made his way to the pantry, where the cordless phone sat on a counter. He picked it up.

"Hello? Khan residence," Bondurant said. He felt odd.

"This is the Khan residence? Shakira Khan residence?"

"May I ask who's calling?"

"Actually, this is a bit of a long shot, but I'm trying to reach Dr. Jon Bondurant. Would Dr. Bondurant happen to be there?"

"You've reached him. That's me," Bondurant said. He knew immediately that something was wrong. "Who am I speaking to?"

"Oh, thank God we've found you. This is Dr. Jon Bondurant?"

"It is," he said.

"Dr. Bondurant, I'll be brief. This is Dr. Kenneth Hepps. I'm with the Pediatric Neurosurgery Division at Johns Hopkins Hospital in Baltimore."

"Yes, yes, I know the hospital," Bondurant said. He watched as Khan slowed her steps through the kitchen and set down the breakfast tray.

"I'm afraid your son, Christopher, has had to be admitted to the hospital, Dr. Bondurant," Dr. Hepps said. Bondurant's face went pale. He pressed the receiver hard against his ear to make sure he caught every word.

"What exactly is the problem, Doctor? Is Christopher all right?"

"We're investigating that right now," Hepps said. "Christopher was admitted to the hospital last night, and we're running several tests. He's been in and out of consciousness several times since he was admitted."

"All right, then, I'm on my way," Bondurant said. He looked at Khan, who had wrapped her arm around him reassuringly. "We're on our way."

"I think that might be best," Hepps said. "He's asked for you several times, and I'm certain the family would appreciate having you here."

"The family?" Bondurant said. "I'm the family. His mother, Domenika, is she there? Is she there with Chris?"

"Yes, she is," Hepps said. "She asked if I might help track you down. You are her husband, is that correct? She said that you were. Is that the familial relationship?"

Khan had left the room. Bondurant figured she was already upstairs packing their bags.

"I'm Christopher's father," Bondurant said. "I'm Domenika's husband. I'm family. Do you hear? And I'll be there right away."

Chapter 43

Geneva

Meyer looked down the imposingly long table in the sleekly appointed, high-tech conference room of the new Demanian Church headquarters toward Hans Jr., who sat at the other end. He shook his head.

The size of Meyer's council had become unwieldy. Thirty-eight church elders who had gathered in Geneva sat in high, red leather chairs on either side of the polished ebony table. A dozen decanters of ice water and an assortment of expensive crystal glassware dotted the table. Legal pads and pens, all adorned with the Demanian Church logo, sat like place settings in front of the trustees.

Each of them represented a region of the faith, which now reached every corner of the globe. Meyer had visions of an eventual territorial consolidation and a smaller ruling council, but that was a topic for another day. There were more important issues to cover before the daylong meeting concluded, one in particular that Meyer knew he could no longer avoid. As he watched the boy take his place for the first time at the opposite end of the long table—Hans Jr.'s first outward sign of challenge to his rule—Meyer knew the game was on.

The room was dark except for the glow of the massive projection screen high on the wall behind Meyer. It showed a colorfully illustrated map of the world. Every one of the tiny red spots scattered across the atlas on all seven continents represented a Demanian Church facility. Given that there were thousands dotting the globe, it was impossible to count them all. The title of the slide revealed the newest estimates of the church's total congregation: "One Billion and Counting." The number of Demanian faithful worldwide had grown to rival the size of the Catholic Church. The council had reason to celebrate.

But Meyer knew that most of the elders gathered were also aware that the impressive numbers of Demanian converts disguised a particularly vexing problem for the future of their faith. On a cash-flow basis, the church was nearly broke. While its physical assets rivaled those of any organized religion on earth, the number of new church and stadium construction sites required to accommodate the dramatic influx of converts had exceeded the church's projections twofold.

Capital requirements to fund the cost of these new facilities, in addition to the recently launched television studios, an international university, five more critically needed DNA repositories, and three church-related resorts, were enormous. The Demanians' banks knew that nearly every project under way was over budget. The new headquarters in Geneva, a magnificent cathedral with offices like no other building in the world, would take another two years to complete. Its cost alone topped ten billion dollars. Contributions tithed from the earnings of the faithful—ten percent of their gross income—had grown substantially but not quickly enough to keep up with building needs. The elders needed to make a decision: increase the percentage of mandatory tithing from its members, or resort to Plan B.

Meyer felt secure that he knew which way the council would vote. Surveys conducted in the past few months had revealed vehement opposition among the faithful to an increased tithe from ten percent to fifteen percent. The question for the council came down to whether it had the stomach to proceed with the alternative plan Meyer had secretly devised. Meyer knew there was no choice but to test the council's resolve.

"Elder Yeung," Meyer called out to his chief financial officer, who sat halfway down the table from him. Yeung was also the church's regional chairman for eastern Asia. "If you would, present the particulars of the alternative plan."

"Certainly," the man answered. The moment he stood, a fresh slide appeared on the screen before the group. It contained a list in three columns that included the names of almost one hundred people. "This is the list of the proposed deceased we have previously circulated. I presume you've read it before. It's in the packets of confidential material provided to all of you."

Several of the elders nodded. All of them, including Hans Jr., had their eyes fixed on the screen.

"As you are all obviously aware, the alternative method by which we propose to more quickly accumulate the funds required to meet our cash shortfall involves triggering the estate-gift mechanism of a select number of our wealthiest faithful," Yeung said. "Those with net worth in excess of one hundred million dollars."

"'Proposed deceased'? You mean to kill them to get their money," the elder from Australia interrupted.

"If you want to put it so bluntly," Yeung said. He removed his glasses, and his eyes scanned the assemblage for dissenters. Meyer had told him he thought there would be little opposition to Plan B.

"How else would it be possible to access the church's half portion of their estates upon their passing? There must first be a passing," another elder at the far end of the table said.

"Before we move to a vote," another elder near Hans Jr. said, "may I ask how the church plans to eliminate these faithful? I presume we're planning to take care of their immediate families upon their deaths."

"The majority of these people are over the age of sixty," Meyer said. He could tell it was time to steer the conversation in the right direction. "We will ask for volunteers from among all those on the list. For those who courageously come forward, we will guarantee them a space near the front of the line for resurrection."

"How much of an advantage is this for the average volunteer?" an elder asked.

"Given the billion Demanian faithful accumulated thus far," Yeung said as he pointed to a bar graph that appeared on the screen, "volunteering will ensure their chance for cloning, and rebirth will be accelerated by approximately five years. For many, particularly the elderly on the list who come forward, it will be well worth the price to recapture their youth and live again so soon."

"And for those who don't volunteer?" another asked.

Meyer shook his head over the consternation. He was anxious for a vote and the end of discussion. As for how those on the list who refused to volunteer would be treated, he would reluctantly leave that up to Galerkin. The Russian stood right outside the conference room, prepared for his orders should the vote to approve Plan B succeed. Meyer estimated that the number of those on the list who might resist volunteering would provide enough work to keep Galerkin busy, incompetent though he may be, for quite a while.

"As for their demise," Meyer said, "we have those plans in hand. The council need not concern itself with the details. Depending on how many refuse to volunteer, we foresee the process taking several months. As much as a year."

"A year?" an elder asked, sounding startled.

Meyer ignored him. "And as for the families of those who go unwillingly," he continued, "I would make a motion before this group that those unfortunately sacrificed for this important cause be second behind the volunteers to be cloned when the laws of their countries of origin allow. The church will count them as true martyrs. Once they're cloned, they will be repatriated to their families with the full honors they deserve."

"I second the motion," one of the elders called out. "Let's vote."

"The motion being seconded," Meyer said, "I move that—"

"Excuse me," Hans Jr. called out. "I want to talk."

The entire group of elders turned toward the eight-year-old at the end of the table. As he leaned back in his chair, his face was barely visible above the tabletop, even with the pillow he sat on. He rarely spoke up during such sessions, but when he did, every ear leaned in. Meyer hadn't a clue what the precocious boy had on his mind now, but as of late, the child had been difficult to manage.

"I don't like it that only the richest must die for the church to succeed," the boy said. "They are of use to us."

"What do you mean?" another elder asked.

"I mean they have lots of money. They tithe each year. It's a lot," Hans Jr. said.

"He has a point," an elder said.

"Is there a list of all the converts I've saved?" the boy asked.

"Of course," Yeung said. "As you know, it numbers more than a hundred thousand people now."

"We should start with a list of those I've helped who were once Christian," the boy said. "Give me their photos."

"Just their photos?" Yeung asked.

"Yes. I need to recognize them," the boy said.

"And then?" Yeung asked. "We need thirty billion dollars of net worth immediately. That's a lot of people."

"Get me their photos. Whatever number it takes. They will be gone tomorrow," the boy said with finality.

The room went perfectly still, as quiet as a church. Meyer watched as Hans Jr. rose and stood at his place. The boy scanned the room full of elders as if searching for a sign of weakness among them.

"Listen: If they didn't expect something like this to happen someday, then they shouldn't have made a deal in the first place," Hans Jr. said.

Meyer looked intently into the boy's eyes as if to discern what darkness lay behind them.

"I like that better than a year's wait to get all the funds we need," one elder chimed in. "It seems such a torturous amount of time to wait."

"I want three things in return," Hans Jr. said. He returned Meyer's glassy stare from the other end of the table.

Meyer braced himself for the demands that might come next from the boy. He'd long ago determined that this clone-child of the Shroud was by no means descended from Jesus Christ—and the boy's newfound scheme was only the most recent proof.

"First, I want the monster man fired," the boy said.

While many of the elders looked around them, clueless about the meaning of the demand, Meyer knew exactly what Hans Jr. meant. It was clear the boy had despised Galerkin for years, and it was a cheap price to pay for the boy's helpful intervention. Meyer would place all the blame on the child anyway once he met with his Russian assassin to break the news outside the room.

"Fine," Meyer said without hesitation. If Galerkin would not be needed to eliminate those identified as part of Plan B, he had little use for the assassin anyway. "Consider him gone. What else?"

"I want to convert more Christians," Hans Jr. said. "Only Christians now."

Meyer had no problem at all with targeting Christians, and the Catholic Church in particular. As of late, the Church in Rome had debilitated itself through its own actions, so much so that its faithful were already leaving in droves.

"Can we see the map again?" the boy asked. As the map of the world reappeared before them, Hans Jr. began to recite a list of countries. "Brazil, Mexico, the Philippines—this is where I must go next," he said. "There are too many Catholics there."

Meyer didn't like the prospect of Hans Jr. dictating the Demanian Church's conversion strategy in front of the other elders and on the fly, but this request was at the heart of his own interest.

"Fine, Hans," Meyer said. "You choose the cities where you'll appear. You said three things. What's the third?"

"רוכבה תויהל הצור ינא!" the boy responded as he raised his voice in anger.

Hans Jr., as though speaking in tongues, had recited ancient Aramaic many times before. Meyer recognized the sound of the biblical Hebrew-like tongue. He didn't speak a word of the ancient language. Neither did any of the other elders in the room.

"I'm afraid you're going to have to translate that for us, Hans," Meyer said. His exasperation with the boy was at its peak.

"I said I want to be the supreme elder," the boy stated flatly.

Meyer couldn't help but burst into laughter. The sheer absurdity of the demand to replace him as the supreme elder of the Demanian Church was a childish overreach, and Meyer knew the council would see it that way. But as he looked about him, he saw only solemn faces. Most were not spoiling for a fight.

"Hans," Meyer said as he tried to keep his temper in check, "there can be only *one* supreme elder."

"I know that," the boy replied.

"Then how do you propose to succeed to the post?" Meyer asked. "I am the supreme elder." Even from the distance down the long table, Meyer could see the boy clench his jaw in disgust at his words.

"When you're dead," Hans Jr. replied. "When you're dead and the church needs a new leader."

"I see," Meyer said as he looked to the group assembled around him for supportive faces. Most averted their eyes. "My son, that could be quite a long time."

"I can wait," the boy said as he sat back down in his seat. Meyer watched Hans Jr. look toward his lap. The boy had already turned his attention to a game he had just launched on his smartphone.

"And like you, Hans Jr., I shall live again," Meyer said as if to reassure himself. Several elders nodded their heads.

Meyer could see the boy was ignoring his words and only looking over toward Yeung.

"Now, if you would, get me the photos of those who will die tonight," Hans Jr. said.

Meyer watched as the boy preoccupied himself with his game again and began to laugh.

"What's so funny?" Meyer asked. Every head turned again toward the boy.

"I was just thinking; those who perish tonight," Hans Jr. said. "They've been promised eternal life through cloning like every other Demanian, correct?"

"Of course," Meyer said.

"What will we do when they return, grow up, and find their wealth in our hands?" Hans Jr. asked. "Just like all of you, they will someday live again too."

Chapter 44

Baltimore

Bondurant carefully closed the door behind him so as not to awaken Christopher, who had just fallen back to sleep. He had spent the last twenty minutes with his son at the hospital and was relieved to see him doing so well. When he stepped into the hallway just outside the boy's private room, he was met by Khan in mid-conversation with Christopher's physician, Dr. Hepps.

"He fell back to sleep as we talked, and I thought it best to let him rest," Bondurant said.

"That's fine," Hepps said. "The more rest, the better. He's going to be in and out of deep sleep like that for another day."

"So you believe the worst is over, Doctor?" Khan asked.

"I do. Between the fluid we were able to drain last night to relieve the pressure on his brain and the IV antibiotics he's receiving to address the infection we found, we should see him return to normal in the next few days."

With Hepps's positive prognosis, Bondurant felt he could finally relax for the first time since he'd heard the news of Christopher's illness only twelve hours before. What started out as a low-grade fever that had bothered Christopher for a few days had suddenly elevated into the range of 103 to 104. At first, it showed no sign of abating. After running several tests, including an MRI, an infection was discovered that had created excess fluid at the base of Christopher's skull. In turn, the fluid had caused a dangerous pressure buildup around his brain, a life-threatening condition if not addressed right away.

Bondurant had tried desperately to reach Domenika from his cell phone on the overseas flight to Baltimore but had had no luck. A nurse had told him that Domenika had slept by Chris each night and stayed with him 24-7 since he'd first been admitted. She'd gone home for the first time in three days to shower and freshen up when she heard the same good news from Dr. Hepps. The nurse expected that Domenika would return to the hospital soon.

Bondurant stared out the window across the maze of buildings—old brick structures and new, modern glass ones—that made up the sprawling hospital complex. He was tired, and couldn't help but wonder what emotion might overtake him next. He'd spent the previous sleepless night worried sick over Chris and guilty that he hadn't seen him in weeks. More than anything, now that Chris was out of danger, he was concerned about Domenika. It was troubles like this that they'd once faced together as a family. Only now, since Bondurant had walked out, it had been up to Domenika to face them alone. That wasn't right, and he knew it.

No doubt, she'd betrayed him with her secrets and for the moment destroyed their trust. But now it was impossible for Bondurant to feel anything but a profound sense of selfishness for having left his wife and son alone. He'd supported their every need. He'd watched over them from afar. But their separation was over. It had to come to an end.

A bank of busy elevators was just steps from Chris's room. The doors of one car opened wide, and Bondurant watched Domenika, whom he hadn't seen for weeks, step out. Without hesitation, she walked directly toward Khan and held out her hand in an invitation to shake it. Khan gladly did. Bondurant, the very definition of uncomfortable, was certain his entire face either was on fire or had turned beet-red.

"I guess you must be Shakira Khan," Domenika said. "It's a pleasure to meet you."

"And you must be Domenika," Khan said. "I'm so sorry to be intruding on your family and that we have to meet in circumstances such as this. But I'm thrilled that your son seems to be improving nicely, and I just want to offer any assistance I can."

"Yes, yes. Thank you so much," Domenika said. She turned toward Bondurant, embraced him, and held him close. "Jon, I'm so glad you came. He's been asking for you a lot, and I thought—"

"You thought right," Bondurant said as he tried to gain some composure. "I'm so glad you reached me. Christopher seems to be doing fine."

"Oh, Jon," Domenika said.

It was as though their words and the sound of each other's voice had instantly melted the fortresses they'd both developed in order to cope. Domenika's eyes began to well with tears. Khan quietly slipped away from the two to give them privacy and took a seat in a chair down the hall.

"It was such a scary few days," Domenika said. "And when I couldn't reach you right away, well, I—I—"

As Bondurant watched Domenika quietly break into tears, he pulled her in close to comfort her. Their embrace was deeply familiar to him, and, with every sense he had, Domenika was instantly recognizable as the soul mate she'd always been. As Bondurant looked over her shoulder, he could see Khan smile.

"Domenika, I feel like a fool. But I've been afraid to come home. It's just that—"

"No, Jon," Domenika said. She pulled his arm toward her and wiped her tears with his shirtsleeve, as she'd often done before. "I'm the fool. I should have told you about everything I knew about when you were a boy. I should have. But it was none of my business in the first place. I was afraid you wouldn't understand."

At her words, Bondurant burst into tears of his own. Then he lost control. It was as though the container that had held his deepest fears and saddest feelings for more than forty years had suddenly cracked open inside him. It spilled forth its ugly contents but had no place to go. He didn't know what else to do as he searched desperately for a way to keep the feelings inside him but also to hold on tight to Domenika, the one he loved. He buried his head in her shoulder and, for the first time in his life, wept out loud. His breathing was labored. He moaned quietly with every heave of his chest. His entire body shook in Domenika's arms.

After several minutes of Domenika consoling him, Bondurant had reached a calm but felt he barely had the strength to stand. He felt Domenika crane her head over his shoulder.

"Oh, not again," she said.

"What? What is it?" Bondurant asked. He was exhausted.

"I need to move my car, and right away," Domenika said. They peered out the nearby window toward the parking lot below. A tow truck had arrived. "I think I parked in the red zone at the emergency entrance again. I'm losing my mind. The last time this happened, it took half a day to get it back."

Bondurant reached for the keys in Domenika's hand. He was ready to move the car himself.

"No," Khan said. She'd left her seat and approached them. "The two of you need to spend more time alone before Christopher wakes up. Give me the keys. Which is your car?"

"I can't let you do that," Bondurant said. "It'll just take me a minute. I'll be right back."

"No, *I'll* be right back," Khan said, and she snatched Domenika's keys from her hand. "Which one is it?"

"All right, all right," Domenika said. "Do you see the Land Rover?"

"I'll be right back," Khan said.

"I'm glad you brought her along, Jon," Domenika said. "At first, I thought of how insecure it might make me feel to see her here. But now that I've had a chance to meet your 'girlfriend,' I'm all right. I haven't made a fool of myself quite yet, have I?"

"Domenika, first, she's not my—well, she's certainly not—"

"Certainly not what, Jon?"

"Certainly not, you know, my whatever," Bondurant said.

"There's 'whatever,'" Domenika said as she pointed to Khan, who had made it to the car and spoken to the driver of the tow truck. "Let me say this. She's certainly charming. And kind too."

Bondurant waved to Khan, who waved back at them and smiled. She reached for the door handle of the car, released it, and took a step backward. She paused for a moment as though to think twice about the gesture she'd made. She looked up at the couple once more, hesitated, and then smiled and waved again. Then she slowly slipped into the front seat of Domenika's car. The tow truck went on its way.

"Domenika, I want you to know that—"

Before Bondurant could finish his thought, a thunderous explosion sounded, accompanied by a brilliant flash of light from inside the rear compartment of Domenika's car. It shot a plume of fire one hundred feet into the air. As the mushroom cloud of smoke from the blast lifted, it revealed a crater in the parking lot the size of a bus. Not a trace of Domenika's car survived. The explosion set fire to everything within fifty meters. It shattered or damaged scores of windows on the lower floors of every building within a city block.

Shakira Khan was dead.

Chapter 45

I-95, Baltimore

Father Parenti sat with Christopher on the hood of Bondurant's Audi and gazed out at the vast truck-stop complex on Interstate 95 outside Baltimore. The lampposts stretching toward the horizon lit an empty parking lot that seemed endless under the stars at that early morning hour. The car's hood was warm to the touch. They were two hundred miles from JFK Airport in New York, and would make it there by daylight. There they would catch an international flight, destination unknown.

Parenti was not overly philosophical about their situation. Once again, they were a united family. But they found themselves in real danger and on the run once more. The little priest's heart had sunk when they passed from Baltimore through Dickerson a few hours earlier. It was a certainty now that they couldn't go home again, as there simply was no house to call a home. A small crowd had gathered on the lawn outside Domenika and Bondurant's residence, accompanied by a swarm of fire trucks from Leesburg and TV satellite vans from nearby Baltimore and Washington, D.C. The chaotic scene that invaded their tiny rural neighborhood had forced them to drive right past the spectacle of their house after they left the hospital, with Christopher now well. An arsonist—likely another of Meyer's men—had completely burned it to the ground. Within the stone foundation that remained was all that they owned, now ruined; a treasure trove of memories turned to ash.

Bondurant and Domenika, arm in arm, were inside the truck stop in search of supplies for their journey. Parenti, Christopher, and Aldo were left to commiserate on their plight in the parking lot outside. Aldo skittered from one lamppost to the other and marked his outsized new territory as best he could.

Parenti looked at the boy's face. He knew Christopher had done his best to form a tough resolve over what he'd seen and what he'd been told on the car ride so far. The boy had clenched his tiny fists when they broke the news to him about the need for the family to move again. But the priest could see that Christopher, now six years old, had begun to suffer the sadness of leaving a happy life behind. Parenti could tell the boy was still worried that their plight was somehow his fault. Tears had begun to stream down Christopher's face, and the priest, heartbroken himself about their inability to go home again, placed his arm around the boy to console him as best he could.

"Why do we have to go?" Christopher asked. "Why are we in trouble again?"

"We're in trouble because there are people who want to stop your mother and father from . . . well, from ridding the world of a very bad thing," Parenti said as he gently rubbed the boy's shoulder. He stopped to ponder what he should say next.

"You mean the Watcher, Father?"

Parenti was stunned that the boy had any real knowledge of their predicament. "How is it you know that, Christopher?" he asked.

"I've heard of this Watcher many times, and in my dreams too," Christopher said.

"My boy, you have a gift possessed by no other," the priest said. He watched the red taillights of several cars trail off into the lonely stretch of freeway beside them. "It's a gift that many will want from you but few will understand. Your parents and I will have to help you decide how best to use it until you're older."

"If we can't go home, then I don't want to use it. I *won't* use it anymore."

Parenti shook his head. He started to tear up himself as he looked at the boy he loved who felt so distraught. He placed Christopher's hand in his own.

"What you have is a gift from God," the priest said. "As you get older, you'll have to decide how best to use it to serve him. You'll have to choose when and where to use your gift wisely, I'm sure."

"Only for good," the boy said.

"Yes, for good people," Parenti said. "And how did you decide that?"

"I was told by my father," Christopher said.

"He's raised you well."

"I mean my *other* father," the boy said. "My father in heaven. The one we pray to at night."

"I see."

"'Use your gift for the good,' he said. And I did," Christopher said. "And look what happened. I don't know why."

Parenti watched the boy wipe his tears and his runny nose with the sleeve of his jacket. The priest reached into his pocket for his handkerchief but by mistake pulled out the plastic bag that carried the Veil of Veronica. He had accidentally discovered it years before in the Vatican's secret archives and faithfully carried it with him since then. It was sacred. He hadn't made use of it for several years. He began to push the bag back into his pocket, but, given the day's events, he thought twice and pulled it out for Christopher to see.

"Christopher, I have something here that I've held on to for a very long time," Parenti said. "I guess you could say I've held on to it for you. It's yours."

"What is it, Father?"

"Well, it's a piece of material. A very special cloth," Parenti said. "And believe it or not, it has proved to have a special power. A gift. Much like the gift you have." Parenti pulled the Veil from the bag and gently spread it out on Christopher's lap.

The boy looked down at the cloth. "It's dirty, I think," he said.

Parenti smiled. "It is. It's very old. It's a long story, but let me just say it once belonged to a wonderful woman who lived a long time ago, and it's something I'm sure she would feel you should have."

Christopher picked up the cloth and examined it. He turned toward Parenti and gently dabbed a stray tear from the side of the priest's face.

"You keep it," Christopher said. "Then there will be two with the gift. I would like that." Christopher shoved the Veil back into Parenti's plastic bag and handed it to him.

"All right, then. For now, I'll hold on to it for you," Parenti said. He slid the bag deep into his pocket.

"Does the cloth always work?" Christopher asked.

"I can't say for sure," Parenti said. "I've used it only twice, and it's worked both times. It works only as a gift of healing from one to another. Once it saved Aldo's life."

Aldo, hearing his name, ran to Parenti's feet and scuffed his paws against the priest's trousers, a sign that he wanted to be held. Parenti bent over and picked him up. As he did, Christopher scratched the backs of Aldo's ears.

"It's a good cloth," Christopher said.

They both stared into the night, quiet save for the low whine of car wheels that ran along the freeway toward the vast expanse ahead.

Christopher broke the silence. "Sometimes my gift doesn't work. Like when I get headaches," he said.

"I see," Parenti said. "They didn't find your headaches at the hospital, did they?"

"No. Maybe they won't find them. They only come with the noise," the boy said.

"The noise?"

"Yes. When my head hurts, it's from the noise. A big noise. Like when the radio or TV is on too loud. My head hurts then, and the gift goes away for a while."

"I see," Parenti said again. "Does your head hurt very often, Christopher?"

"Sometimes. I don't know. I think someone tries to hurt me," the boy said.

Parenti handed Aldo to Christopher for him to pet. Aldo always seemed to comfort him.

"What do you mean?" the priest asked.

"There's someone I don't know who wants to hurt me," Christopher said. "That's all I know."

"Do your mother and father know that—"

Suddenly, Christopher gripped Parenti's hand as tight as he could and stopped him in mid-sentence. The boy looked at him with genuine panic on his face. "I think someone wants to come for me right now!" Christopher said. The boy slipped off the hood of the car and quickly hid behind Parenti's legs.

The priest felt the boy put one arm around his leg and squeeze Aldo close for comfort with the other arm. Mystified, Parenti looked out into the darkness that surrounded them, but saw and heard nothing strange. The night air was still. As he looked toward the inside of the truck stop, he saw Bondurant and Domenika at the cashier as they paid for their things. What had frightened the boy Parenti wasn't sure. But he was reassured that they would soon be on their way down the road again.

Then, as if from nowhere, he heard a faint, strange sound off in the distance, one he didn't immediately recognize. It wasn't a car or a truck that approached, as the noise seemed to come from out of the black of night far overhead. Aldo began to turn his head from side to side as if aware something was headed their way from above. Parenti held his breath and listened as intently as he could to determine the source of the sound. He positioned himself in front of Christopher to defend him against whatever invisible threat might be headed their way.

As the noise came closer and grew louder, the sound began to envelop them from above. At first, Parenti thought it could only be thunder, but the night sky, filled with stars, was nothing but clear as far as his eyes could see. Eventually, from out of the black and at a great height, the priest detected a small red light. It seemed to float above them in a wide circle and then slowly started to descend. Then, in an instant, a brilliant flash of light blinded the little priest. A funnel of intense luminescence as bright as the sun enveloped everything around them in a circle almost fifty yards wide. Parenti strained his eyes to determine what had beset them, but it was useless. He simply couldn't see. Then a tunnel of wind that seemed to blow from all directions began to circle about them, a surge so intense it made it difficult for Parenti to stand. As it buffeted them and rocked the car violently, Parenti thought they might next be lifted into the night by the invisible source's tornado-like grasp.

Aldo jumped from Christopher's arms and cowered beneath the car.

"Helicopter," Christopher said as he pointed into the beam of light above them.

Parenti, his vision still blurred by the light, watched in amazement to see that the boy was right. Less than thirty yards from where they stood, a large helicopter as black as the night quickly set down before them. Its rotor wash was so intense that it shook the ground beneath them and sent dust and dirt from the pavement flying in every direction as it singed his skin and stung his eyes.

Events moved so quickly that Parenti barely had time to react. He saw several figures dash toward them, heavily armed and shrouded in black as they ducked their heads beneath the massive rotors that chopped the night air. Men were on top of them before the priest could cry for help. He felt a terrific blow to his head, so hard he lost whatever strength he had to hold on to the boy. Parenti was knocked to the pavement, and his head hit the ground, his body unable to move. From his strange vantage point as he lay on his side, he saw a surreal sight. He looked on helplessly as Christopher struggled furiously to free himself from a man who carried him like a small sack across his back. Christopher kicked and screamed as his captors made their way purposefully back to the helicopter they'd leaped from only seconds before. Then, as swiftly as the masked strangers had descended upon them, they lifted off in their machine into the void of the night.

One of the last things Parenti knew before he fell unconscious was the sight of Bondurant and Domenika as they rushed toward him. Unable to lift himself from the pavement, he remembered Christopher's last words of warning. He knew it was time to pray for the boy.

Chapter 46

New York City

When Father Parenti walked into the Rose Club, the storied bar inside Manhattan's Plaza Hotel, he was nervous. He found himself so uneasy that he decided to head straight to the bar. He hadn't a clue what a "stiff drink" meant, but he'd heard Bondurant complain often enough about needing one when life deserved complaint, and these were difficult times. A few minutes early for the extraordinary rendezvous he'd hastily planned, he climbed up onto a tall stool at the end of the bar, one that afforded a nice view out the large window toward Central Park South. That way, he might see him coming.

"Telephone book, Father?" the bartender asked as he leaned over to get a glimpse of the little priest.

Parenti thought it was an unusual offer. He gave the bartender a strange look. "For what?" he asked.

"To sit on," the bartender said. "You're so short I can barely make you out from behind the bar."

Parenti rolled his eyes. The meeting he was about to have portended nothing but danger, and he was in no mood for a comedian. "I'll take a stiff drink," the priest said. He pointed to the dozens of brands of liquor arrayed before him on the wall. "And make it snappy." Parenti dangled his feet from the tall stool like a child and wondered what concoction he would be served.

The bartender smiled. "I'll make it stiff, but maybe you should tell me what you're having first," he said. He swept his hand across scores of brightly lit bottles that rested on mirrored shelves behind him.

Parenti scanned the wide assortment of elixirs on display without a clue what to choose. "I'll take the Macallan," he said. He recognized the name of Bondurant's favorite Scotch on a bottle at the end of the bottom row.

"A man who knows his drink," the bartender said. "You want it straight up? On the rocks?"

"I'll have a bottle of the twenty-five," Parenti said with authority. "Bring it over."

"Father, I can't sell you the whole bottle."

"All right, then, just pour some in a glass," Parenti said. He began to grow testy. "Is getting a drink in this town always this complicated?"

The bartender reached for the bottle and gave the priest an odd look. Then he poured Parenti a tumbler half full, neat, and slid the glass in front of him. "Bottoms up," he said.

"Bottoms up," Parenti replied.

The bartender looked on in amazement as the tiny priest chugged the entire glass of some of the world's most expensive Scotch down his throat in an instant. Before Parenti could slam his empty glass back down on the bar, a loud wheeze of air spewed forth from his lungs. His throat was on fire, and his eyes, seemingly floating in Scotch, sent a small trail of tears down the priest's face.

The bartender tried not to laugh. "Have another?" he asked.

Parenti attempted to recover from the burning sensation that quickly drove its way toward his stomach. His could tell his face was as red as the pope's shoes, and, uncharacteristically, he was momentarily speechless. He couldn't believe Bondurant would ever let the awful, poisonous liquid anywhere near his lips.

"Double or nothing," Parenti croaked as he shoved his empty glass toward the bartender. He was positive he'd heard Bondurant use the expression before when he drank.

"You mean double it?"

"Yes, yes, that's what I mean," the priest said as he stared out the window to avoid the bartender's odd gaze while he wiped away his tears and attempted to recover.

"No dogs allowed in here," the bartender said. He pointed to Aldo, whose head had popped out of Parenti's shoulder sack.

"I'll have you know he's a therapy dog, sir," Parenti said.

"What's that supposed to mean?"

"He's been in and out of therapy his entire life. He stays right here with me."

Once Parenti's second drink was poured, the bartender mercifully left him to tend to another customer who'd arrived at the other end of the bar. Parenti nursed his Scotch in tiny sips and prayed that several more ounces of the liquid courage would do the trick.

He was on a mission. He'd been with Bondurant and Domenika at the St. Regis Hotel in New York, where they'd been holed up for days, desperate for news about the boy. Domenika had become hysterical. Parenti could take the tension no more. He'd secretly phoned one of the few trusted researchers remaining at the Vatican library who would talk to him. After a series of several surprisingly productive calls with contacts in Tel Aviv, Geneva, and Rome, the priest found himself bound for the Plaza. He'd departed his room without a word to Bondurant or Domenika about where he was headed. Now he sat ready to negotiate a life-and-death deal with someone who was five minutes late.

As he looked out at the lush green of Central Park and counted his troubles, Parenti felt a tap on his shoulder. It soon grew into a painful thump. When he turned around to see the massive hand that now covered nearly half his back, he stared at a Goliath of a man who towered above him.

"You are Father Plenty?" the man grunted.

"Parenti, Father Parenti," the priest said. He looked the giant up and down from head to toe. He'd never seen such a man before. "You are Galerkin?"

"Yes. You look like Father Tiny," the assassin said. "You have the money? We don't talk without the money."

Parenti reached into his coat pocket and, his hand visibly shaking, turned over to the behemoth an envelope stuffed with cash. Galerkin shoved the money into his coat pocket. He didn't bother to count it.

"First, you tell me how you find me," Galerkin said. "Then we talk."

"Through the Vatican," the priest whispered. "Papal Intelligence. Swiss Guard."

"Doesn't fit," Galerkin said.

"It works like the CIA."

"I don't see connection."

"They were aware of some work you did for the Mossad, apparently right here in this city. They say you also work for Hans Meyer."

"Yes, I did job for the Jews. But you," Galerkin said as he stopped and inserted his massive forefinger between Parenti's white collar and his neck. He yanked him in close. "You are fish eater. No connection."

Parenti could feel the breath being choked from him as his collar tightened. He tried to twist his neck away from Galerkin's grasp, but it was no use.

"Jesus was a Jew," Parenti croaked. "We get along fine with them."

Galerkin plucked his finger away from the priest's throat and sat down on the stool beside him. He reached over and gently scratched the top of Aldo's head.

"I am just playing. Okay, little mouse," Galerkin said. He reached over for Parenti's Scotch and downed it quickly, like a shot of water. "What you want?"

"The child of the Shroud," Parenti said. "We only want the child. We will pay whatever it takes."

"You can have the little bastard," the assassin said. "He lives in Geneva. You don't need me."

"He's in Geneva?"

"Since he's a baby. He's the devil. Got me fired."

"Are we talking about the same child?" Parenti said. "I'm talking about young Christopher. He's six years old. Meyer's men stole away with him by helicopter just a few nights ago."

"No, Meyer has just one child, no more," Galerkin said. "But he's no child. He's the devil."

Parenti was dumbfounded. He couldn't believe someone other than Meyer had nabbed Christopher. Then he made the connection.

"You're referring to the boy they call Hans Jr., is that right?" Parenti asked.

"Hans Devil," Galerkin said. "I had year of work lined up. Not now. He's the competition. He works on his own."

"I see."

"But Mr. Meyer, he knows of this boy, this one you mention. The other boy. He's with the doctor and this lady, Jozef."

"Yes, that's him!"

"Impossible to find. Impossible to kill," Galerkin said.

"What do you mean?" Parenti pushed back on his stool but knew he would have been dead by now if the assassin had wanted it so.

"I mean I search for years. Maybe you are the priest they travel with all this time? I think is you." Galerkin looked at him with contempt. "You are too clever. But doesn't matter now."

"What do you mean?"

"I try many times to find all of you. No luck. I chop head off wrong woman. I get final chance. I blow up wrong girl. Nice car. Now the contract to kill the boy, the doctor, the girl, maybe you, I don't know. Not the dog. It goes to someone else, I guess." Galerkin reached for the silver container full of nuts that sat on the bar between them and emptied the entire bowl into his mouth.

"Someone else?" Parenti said. He was relieved to hear that Galerkin had lost any interest in ending his life. It was the risk he'd taken when he arranged the meeting in the first place. But now the priest looked all around him and wondered who else might be a threat. "Who? Are you able to tell me who?"

"I don't know him. Seen him only once," Galerkin said. "Fish eater like you."

"A Catholic?"

"A priest."

"A priest?" Parenti's mind began to reel with the preposterous thought. It was impossible. He immediately wondered if Galerkin had reason to lie. It didn't matter. Christopher was not in Meyer's hands after all, and Parenti began to question whether his heroic mission was a colossal waste of time.

Then, like an epiphany, it came to him. Parenti was certain he knew who held Christopher captive. And with his revelation came another inspiration, one that could possibly halt his seemingly endless time on the run with Bondurant and Domenika forever.

"Mr. Galerkin?" Parenti said. This time, it was the priest who grabbed the assassin by his collar and pulled the giant in close, nose to nose.

"Yes, little mouse," Galerkin said.

A broad smile grew across Parenti's face for the first time in days. He reached for his pocket and pulled out his life savings, another thick envelope stuffed with more cash.

"I, my friend," Parenti said, "have another proposition."

Chapter 47

Castel Gandolfo, Italy

■f all the places to have a breakfast meeting, Bondurant sat in
the one spot in the world where he never expected to dine: the
Pontifical Villas that overlooked the magnificent shoreline of Lake
Albano and the idyllic town of Castel Gandolfo below. The pope
would soon arrive.

The agreement to meet with Pope Augustine at his grand and
guarded summer residence had resulted from an accord reached between Parenti and a special emissary of the pope who'd traveled
from Rome to New York to arrange their meeting. It came with a
single condition: secrecy. His audience with the pope high above
the crystal-clear lake and every word they uttered were to remain
strictly confidential. Given what Parenti had discovered involving
the whereabouts of Christopher and who had kidnapped him, Bondurant immediately accepted the terms. Twenty-four hours later, he
found himself in the pleasant, rolling hills just outside Rome.

It was still morning, but the temperature outside Villa del

Moro had already reached ninety degrees. Bondurant sat at a small table complete with a colorful assortment of fruit, breads, juice, and coffee. He watched as the pope slowly emerged from his living quarters onto the balcony, dressed as though ready for a day at the beach. They were at the pope's vacation home, and Augustine's casual appearance and approach seemed designed to take some of the edge off Bondurant's angry mood. Bondurant got up from his chair, quickly loosened his tie, and shook the pope's hand. In doing so, he was certain he had likely violated every protocol established over the centuries for greeting the Holy Father, but the pontiff waved off formalities and asked Bondurant to take his seat once more.

"We are speaking in utmost candor and in complete confidentiality. Our meeting this morning is a secret. Is that your understanding, Dr. Bondurant?" the pope asked.

"By your choosing. You have my word."

"That's excellent."

"Your Holiness," Bondurant said. He blanched at the term he had never used before, but he was in the pope's home, and he knew no less formal title to address him by. "I've come a long way. You know I'm here for Christopher. It's plain you've taken him. I want to discuss the terms for getting him back." There was sternness in Bondurant's voice that he had no intent to disguise. Previous popes during the early history of the Church had been murdered, and Bondurant was angry enough to consider it.

The pope averted his eyes, looked down, and slowly buttered his toast. Bondurant could see that the pontiff's hands trembled and wondered whether it was a sign of age or a tremor caused by the tone with which he had started their conversation.

"First things first," Augustine said. "How is my Domenika? Please tell me she's well."

"She's not," Bondurant said. "She's lost all her spirit and maybe even some of her faith in the Church. She's lost a son. And, like me, she wants him back."

"But she hasn't lost a son, has she?" the pope said as he reached for a jar of jam in the center of the table. "At least, not one that's her own."

Bondurant pushed aside the bowl of fruit he'd begun to pick at and looked up in disdain. "Your Holiness, forgive me, but you were there at the moment of the child's birth."

"Jon. May I call you Jon?"

"Yes, fine. I'm not interested in formalities."

"It's a good name, you know. I'm sure Domenika must like it."

"She does. What's your point?"

"Saint John was martyred, you know?" The pope stirred the cream he had poured into his coffee and looked up at his guest. "They placed a rope around his neck and dragged his body through the streets before he was beheaded."

"I have no doubt that there are those in the Church, including yourself, who wish the same fate for me," Bondurant said.

The pope raised his eyebrows and gave Bondurant a wry smile. He gently set down his spoon. "Well, to your point: While it was indeed Domenika who gave birth to the child, the one you call Christopher, surely you must know that the child belongs to the Church."

"How could you possibly say that?" Bondurant said. He wondered if he'd heard the pontiff correctly. "She gave birth to the boy. We've raised him. Until now, the Church has shown only a passing interest in his well-being."

"I want to assure you that your stewardship of the boy to this point has been greatly appreciated by the Vatican," the pope said. "In fact, although I understand you are already a man of great means, we are prepared to pay you handsomely for your paternal efforts to date."

"We have no interest in money," Bondurant said. "We want Christopher back. It's beyond me that the Church, any church, would swoop down and kidnap him with armed commandos in the dead of night."

"It was an unusual act, I must admit," the pope said. "That particular theater was Father De Santis's doing."

"'Thou shalt not steal.' Does that ring a bell?" Knowing that De Santis was involved only further angered Bondurant. He tried to keep his rage in check, but the pope's self-righteousness mixed with such a calm demeanor didn't help.

"One cannot steal what one rightfully owns," Augustine said.

"What do you mean by that?"

"I mean that the child was born of material extracted from the burial cloth of our Lord and Savior, Jesus Christ," the pope said. "The Shroud is the property of the Church. The material that resides on it—you call it DNA—is owned by the Church. And most certainly, if there is even a semblance of Christ our savior who walks this earth derived from that DNA, as a clone or otherwise, he belongs to the Church as well. He *is* the Church."

"I came here to reason with you as a father," Bondurant said. "Someone who has raised the boy from an infant. I expected more from the Church than legal mumbo jumbo."

"Indeed, our lawyers have reviewed the matter. But that is beside the point."

Bondurant tried to process what the pope had said, but he was so stunned at what he'd heard thus far that he was at a loss for words. Then he found them. "You're a criminal," he said.

"Good. Just the kind of candor I asked for," the pope said.

"No, truly. That's legal thievery. I would expect reasoning like that to come from a lawyer, but please don't tell me that you, the supposed voice of your Christ on this earth, believe it's acceptable to steal a child from his parents."

The pope looked away. Bondurant could tell he didn't want their eyes to meet. "I've searched my soul over this," the pope said. "I suppose you might say my councilors and I are living proof that desperate faiths sometimes do desperate things." For the first time, there was a sense of regret rather than righteous indignation in the pontiff's voice.

"I see," Bondurant said. "As long as the child was like any other, the Church had no use for him. The moment he begins to demonstrate some magic, he's branded Church property. Is that it?"

The pope only shook his head. Bondurant continued to try to meet his eyes with his own but had no luck. He knew he had no choice but to burrow in.

"You know yourself, Holy Father, that the child is a clone. A *clone.* What could possibly drive your interest in him? The Church's own doctrine—your own declaration—specifically forbids the existence of life by cloning."

"It does. It's the same as playing with stem cells. And if I were asked today to support the cloning of any other man or woman who has walked this earth, I would not."

"Then what are you saying?"

The pope paused and stared out across the picturesque lake, as smooth as glass in the morning sun.

"It's no secret to you, is it, that my Church, our faith, is in the gravest of trouble? You've written about it yourself."

"Entire books."

"Bestsellers. I've read them, as have many others, apparently. You've written that less than half the people in your own country accept a faith of any kind. For every person who converts to Catholicism today in this world, many more will leave. Things are not what they used to be."

"And abducting children from their legitimate parents will help?" Bondurant shouted as he banged his fist on the breakfast table, rattling everything on top of it. A tall, plain-clothed member of the Swiss Guard, the force that customarily provided protection for the pope, swiftly emerged from a side room off the balcony, seemingly ready to draw his gun.

Augustine casually waved him away, but his face quickly grew red with rage. "Surely you will not sit here and tell me I have a choice?" the pope insisted. "A Watcher walks this planet. You know that. He lives and breathes in the form of this Demanian child. He steals our faithful by the millions for his evil purposes, and I am to ignore it?" He rushed his hands to his temples and began to massage them as if he were in tremendous pain.

"Funny," Bondurant said.

"What's funny?" the pope asked.

"Do you have headaches? Spells that happen often?"

"In fact, I do. I have for several years." The pope closed his eyes, still in deep distress.

"Christopher has begun to have them too," Bondurant said. "It's why we had him seen by doctors."

"It's not something a doctor can cure, I'm afraid. It's an attack by the Watcher, of that I'm sure," the pope said. "I've been convinced of it for some time. That and the incessant noise in my ears."

After a few more moments of anguished silence, the pope raised his eyes from the table to speak. His voice was so soft that Bondurant had to lean forward to hear.

"I won't deny our complicity in all this," Augustine said. "Believe me, I've worn my knees to shreds in penance for what the sinful among our ranks have done over the years. Even you were a victim years ago."

Bondurant could only grit his teeth.

"It was our vanity that led us to you in our quest to prove the divinity of the Shroud to the world," the pope said. "It was only meant to serve as a distraction from our troubles. But from that prideful sin, the devil himself has been reborn. I know that my God is a forgiving one, but my atonement for our sins may be too little, too late. Now we need a miracle to stop this beast Hans Meyer has raised, and I believe the so-called resurrection of this boy, the one you call Christopher, might be it."

"Our little Christopher is only six years old, sir," Bondurant said. "Right or wrong, Domenika and I conceived of the very idea of him to stop a plague. We'd hoped to prepare him for this inevitable moment as well. Even now, I count myself as likely insane for believing a small and innocent child might help stop this descendant of the devil. But you? You've upped the ante. You're counting on him to save your Church."

"The Church is facing the greatest crisis in its history under my guardianship. I took a vow to fulfill my obligation to promote Christ's work on this earth by every means. *Every* means, Dr. Bondurant."

Bondurant threw his napkin on the table. He'd heard enough. He got ready to leave, with no intention to extend his hand.

The pope stopped him, reached forward, and grasped Bondurant's hand in his own. He gripped it uncomfortably tightly. "The Church can give this child a home, a home where he belongs. A place to heal countless others," the pope said. "Join with us."

"You mean a way to heal your ailing Church," Bondurant said.

"Help us with our cause, Dr. Bondurant. Join us at St. Peter's Square for the celebration of the child this Sunday. Please bring our Domenika. These are exciting times. There is a world to be cured, a devil to be fought, and a Church to be saved and reborn."

"It sounds as if you have a coming-out party planned for Christopher," Bondurant said.

"We do. It will be a grand one," the pontiff said as he nodded his head and smiled. "And you are invited!"

"We accept," Bondurant said. "We accept."

Chapter 48

The Vatican

Bondurant had never seen a crowd so large.

He hopped up onto his folding chair and stood for a moment to get a view above the colorful throng, then turned to look behind him at the sea of faces gathered in St. Peter's Square. A multitude of people looked toward the papal basilica. Centered in the middle of the piazza was the famous Egyptian obelisk that towered above the crowd. It was the same monument that stood in observance of the crucifixion of Saint Peter nearly two thousand years before.

As far as Bondurant's eyes could see, the ellipse around him was awash with banners and flags of red and gold. The faithful who'd gathered had been asked to dress in festive colors of green and white, worn to symbolize the renewal—the rebirth—of the Holy Roman Catholic Church. Flanking Bondurant and Domenika for nearly a hundred yards on both sides and extending twenty rows to their rear was a specially prepared section of seating filled with the infirm. They were cordoned off from the rest of the crowd but still subject to the heat of the sweltering sun. The sick, many in wheelchairs and carts, had been positioned close to the stage.

The procession was led by a dozen altar boys dressed in black cassocks and white lace surplices. They were followed by the most senior members of the Vatican's Curia as they marched before the crowd. They ascended onto a specially built platform that rested atop the entrance stairs to St. Peter's Basilica. At the rear of the stage was the Vatican's impressive orchestra, encompassed right and left by a chorus of fanfare trumpeters. Their brass instruments reflected brilliantly in the light of the sun. In line behind the Curia was an assemblage of cardinals dressed entirely in bright red. They represented more than two dozen countries around the world, from Latin America to Africa to Asia, the last remaining strongholds of the Catholic Church.

Behind them proceeded the Holy Father himself, dressed in simple white and gold. He waved to the crowd and proudly held young Christopher by the hand as he shuffled forward. Taking up the rear was an assortment of other Vatican officials, including one whom Bondurant and Domenika easily recognized from their seats close to the stage: the newly minted Bishop De Santis. His bright red vestments and cap took on a radiant sheen. Finally, by invitation from Christopher and granted special permission to attend by the pope himself, none other than Father Parenti was there. He held a more marginal seat onstage at the end of his row toward the rear.

Separating the Vatican assemblage from the crowd was a tall, temporary chain-link fence designed to provide security for the pope. Bondurant figured it was also there to keep the worshippers at bay once it became clear what the boy's miraculous healing powers could do.

Two gates were positioned for access to the stage through the fence that separated the ceremony's officials from the sick. Most were ill enough that they couldn't reach the platform without the assistance of the caregivers beside them. Cancer patients, the deaf, and more than two thousand suffering from one serious illness or another pressed desperately toward the fence to get a good look at the child who sat next to the pope. Bondurant and Domenika stood on their chairs and waved to Christopher to get his attention, but the crowd was so huge he could not see them.

After the orchestra had completed its movement and the trumpeters finished their flourish, Pope Augustine came forward to speak from a gilded lectern at the center of the stage. Bondurant sat and listened as Domenika simultaneously translated. The pope delivered his remarks in Italian. Bondurant sat transfixed as the huge mass of people bowed their heads while the pope gave them his blessing. A woman who sat next to Bondurant with an arm shriveled by disease hung on the pontiff's every word.

As Bondurant listened to Domenika's translation, he fixed his eyes on Christopher. The boy, who looked unusually worn, had his eyes shut tight. His hands were cupped to his ears as if he was in pain. It was a worrisome sign. Bondurant couldn't tell if Christopher was frightened by the commotion around him or if his head truly ached. While he hadn't a clue how he would reach Christopher, given the tight security that surrounded the platform, he had every intention of rushing the gate to his right when it opened to allow some of the sick to access the stage. His hope was that between the sea of humanity that made its way past the fence and the confusion created by his bold move to snatch the child once he made it onstage, he might somehow run, evade his pursuers, and make it to a side street in the chaos that would ensue. It was a long shot at best, but given that he would likely never get this close to Christopher again, it was the only way.

A tremendous roar erupted from the crowd.

"He has introduced Christopher as 'the child of God' and asked the first of the sick to come forward," Domenika said.

Bondurant felt her squeeze his hand in anticipation, tighter than she had ever done before. Christopher stared straight ahead into the crowd and continued to hold and shake his head. As Bondurant freed himself from Domenika's grip and began to slowly make his way through the crowd toward the stage, he watched as a middle-aged man in a wheelchair was shoved through the entry gate. Several assistants lifted him onto the platform. Bondurant tried to press in behind them to gain access to the stage area, but two Swiss Guards, both armed, shoved him backward. He knew the only other gate to the stage sat a hundred yards away. Given the mass of people who stood along the fence, it was likely a full ten minutes away. He made his way back to Domenika, stood beside her, and eyed the height of the fence. He could easily scale it, but would just as readily be seen. He watched as the man in the wheelchair was rolled into place at center stage, just in front of where Christopher sat. A line of other invalids began to form behind the disabled man.

The pope took Christopher by the hand and stepped forward toward the crippled figure. As he spoke into the microphone, the pontiff's voice was clear for all assembled in the square to hear. "My son," he said as he leaned in toward the man in the wheelchair, "when was the last time you left that chair and walked?"

"Forty years, Holy Father," the man replied. "I've been bound to it since I was a child."

"Take his hand," the pope instructed the man as he pointed to Christopher beside him. "Take his hand. Stand and behold."

As the assistants helped bring the invalid to his feet, the man reached his hand out for Christopher to hold. The boy, his hands still pressed to his ears, hesitated for a moment. Then he extended one hand to touch the man before him. When they touched, the man stood suddenly erect. Amazed, the assistants at his side stepped back from the once-crooked figure and quickly swept his wheelchair to the side. As the dumbfounded man took his first step forward, the crowd let forth a roar that seemed to shake the very foundations of the ancient square.

Then, as quickly as the man had risen, he stumbled on his second step and fell flat on his face onto the floor. A moan of disappointment from the huge throng rolled across the piazza like a wave. The pope, who looked completely confused, stared down at Christopher in total disbelief. The man's assistants peeled him from the carpet and sat him with a bloody, broken nose back in his chair. Following him was a woman who had a swollen red goiter the size of a golf ball protruding from her neck. She bent down toward the child, got on her knees, and began to beg for his touch. Christopher, obviously aghast at the sight of the ugly sore before him, hesitantly reached out his hand and stroked the woman's cheek. Feeling his touch, she leaped to her feet. As she pressed her hand to the goiter, it was clear to both her and those in the first several rows of the stage that the boy's touch had done nothing to help.

A third, a fourth, and then a fifth afflicted person came forward for the child's healing touch. But each left disappointed, unable to stand or walk or breathe easier as they had been led to believe they would. Not a single cure appeared. Bondurant watched as Christopher began to shake his head. He sat back in his chair as if to protest against a continuation of the event. As he did, the din of the crowd began to grow. It was then that the once-joyous affair began to take an ugly turn. A shoe flung from far back in the crowd landed on the stage, followed by a nasty roar. A plastic folding chair, and then another, crashed into the protective fence against the stage, followed by another half dozen shoes that arced their way across the platform toward the child.

"*Vergogna!*" several in the crowd shouted. "*Imbroglione!*"

Hundreds more took up the chant.

"What are they saying?" Bondurant called out to Domenika through the growing howl of the crowd.

"They're saying he's a fraud," she said.

As the pope slowly backed away from the child, De Santis rose from his chair and took Augustine's arm as if to lead him to safety. A vicious glare, one like Bondurant had never seen before, appeared on De Santis's face as he looked down at the helpless boy. Bondurant knew immediately that Christopher was in real danger. He leaped across two rows of chairs and shoved several people out of his way as he pressed toward the fence. When he reached the barrier, almost ten feet high, he quickly began to scale it. Almost to the top, he felt a sharp stabbing at his knees. It was the barrel of a guard's rifle aimed directly at him. As Bondurant tried to ignore the pain and continued his climb, he looked down to see another rifle, now aimed at his face.

"*Fermo o sparo!*" the guard shouted.

"Jon!" Domenika cried out. "He's going to shoot!"

Bondurant, his head now barely above the top of the fence, stopped his ascent. As he stared out across the growing commotion on the stage, he couldn't believe his eyes. Twenty feet from him but impossible to reach, De Santis stood only a few feet from the boy. The new bishop's face was now the visage of a madman. What looked at first to be a small, shiny object De Santis had pulled from his vestments quickly took shape as a knife a foot long. It glinted in the light of the sun. Gasps of astonishment flew forth from people at the front of the crowd who were close enough to see the thick blade held high. It was clear to Bondurant that if he didn't reach his son in seconds, Christopher would die.

Bondurant flung himself headlong over the top of the fence, hit the ground with both feet, and landed on the platform in full stride. But as he dashed toward De Santis, he was broadsided by two huge uniformed guards, who tackled him to the ground. Desperate, Bondurant called out for Christopher and wrested himself free from the grasp of the guards. From there, he made a diving leap and bounced hard onto the stage only ten feet from the deranged bishop. De Santis, his eyes filled with rage, stood over Christopher. But before Bondurant could spring toward De Santis, who held the menacing blade aloft, he saw something incredible out of the corner of his eye.

It was Parenti. The tiny priest soared across the blue sky in front of him like a bird of prey in flight. Having bounded from his chair onstage, the priest hurtled with all his might toward the child to shield him from De Santis's blow. Parenti's timing was amazing. The instant his body cloaked the child like a blanket to protect him, it was met with the sharp downward thrust of De Santis's deadly blade. The knife was planted deep into Parenti's chest.

The razor-sharp blade, eight inches long with a tip as sharp as any stone could hone, drove like a tooth from the devil directly into the tiny priest's heart. In just seconds, Parenti lay dead, cradled in Christopher's arms.

Chapter 49

Over Italy

The flight time from Geneva to Rome's Fiumicino Airport aboard the private Boeing 737 was just more than one hour. The plane Meyer and the elders of the council were aboard, replete with a full bar, TV lounge, conference room, and private cabins, was one of two sleek jets the Demanian Church had purchased from a Saudi sheikh only days before. The recent overnight passing of so many of the wealthy faithful had set loose an army of lawyers headquartered in Geneva. They'd begun to secure the Demanians' rightful share of the deceased's estates. The sect's projected balance sheet had dramatically improved. These fortunate developments, among others, had Meyer in an unusually good mood.

In his lap was a copy of the *International Herald Tribune*. The headline that screamed across the top of the fold said it all: "Vatican in Disarray Following Child Healer Disaster—State Investigation Launched."

Meyer smiled as he dug into the story on the front page.

"It seems," he said, looking up from the newspaper in Hans Jr.'s private cabin, "the pope has not been seen for days."

"Hiding, I suppose," the boy casually replied.

Meyer listened intently as Hans Jr. spoke. The boy's voice dropped about two octaves from his normal range. The dramatic shift in tone had become a more regular occurrence. It was eerie when the deep sound of a grown-man's voice came from a child of no more than eight years old. Hans Jr. was engrossed in another of his handheld games. This one blared the noise of bombs that exploded as they hit their targets.

"It says here that he's secluded, holed up in his apartment and seeing no one," Meyer said. "The good news is he's obviously defeated. The bad news is the police have forced a return of the child to Bondurant. Now the boy will be tougher to find."

Hans Jr. smirked at Meyer's mention of the boy. "I can find him," Hans Jr. said. "I just need to be in the same city. The rest will take care of itself."

"De Santis was a disappointment," Meyer said as he tossed his newspaper onto the seat next to him in disgust. "It says they're charging him with two counts, manslaughter for the priest and attempted murder of the boy. I don't know what jail they've thrown him into, but let the incompetent rot there forever, as far as I'm concerned."

"I told you before," Hans Jr. replied, "I will find the boy."

"People are difficult to predict," Meyer said. "De Santis is a bishop. Close to the pope. He had access to the boy. What better way to get at him than from the inside?"

Hans Jr. shook his head and turned off his game. He looked

angry at Meyer's incessant interruptions. "When I healed him, you claimed this priest, De Santis, would be our messenger of death. Some messenger. Some death," he said.

The boy's sarcasm wasn't lost on Meyer. While Meyer wasn't happy being chided by an eight-year-old, he was glad to see Hans Jr. stewing over the problem at hand. The other supposed child of the Shroud, the one called Christopher, unfortunately still walked the earth. But once they reached Rome, Meyer hoped it would be just days before the child was located and disposed of so that the rest of his plan could succeed.

Meyer wasn't seeking an unconditional surrender from the forlorn pope. Rather, he figured a slow and gradual capitulation to his terms that spared the pontiff further embarrassment would better serve the Demanian Church's interests over time. Augustine had resisted several overtures from Meyer for a friendly merging of the two faiths. A secret pact he'd suggested would quietly place the Church in Rome in subservience to the Demanian faith. Meyer knew there was talk of rebellion among the worried Curia that surrounded the weakened pope. It was time to act. He was determined not to leave Rome without an agreement in hand from the pontiff that would, over a period of years, transition the Church in Rome to his care. How could the pope possibly decline? In Meyer's mind, it was a match made in heaven.

Later, Meyer was awoken by the flight attendant, who gently reached toward his lap to fasten his seat belt. He'd catnapped during the last few minutes of their flight.

"We'll be landing any minute," the attendant said.

Meyer looked over at Hans Jr., who'd been staring at him from across the aisle as he slept. The boy held a large knife with his name engraved across the handle, a gift from Meyer when he'd turned eight. It rested inside its scabbard. An intent look was on the boy's face.

"This boy they call Christopher," Hans Jr. said. "He is not without powers, you know."

"If he has them, he certainly doesn't show them. Not like you," Meyer said.

The boy pulled the knife from its slender case and practiced slicing it through the air. "He has them, and more," he said. "I've been disrupting them when I can. Just as I've been giving hell to the pope as well."

"What are you saying, Hans?" Meyer asked.

"I'm saying the child was weak because I made him so. But the effort makes me weak too. We have to be quick."

"First him, and then I approach the pope, as agreed," Meyer said. "We'll be as quick as we can."

"I cannot be near him for too long, or he will win," Hans Jr. said.

The boy looked to have a sense of trepidation, one Meyer had never seen in him before. Then Meyer felt the aircraft's wheels touch down on the runway beneath them. He looked at his watch. "We're early," he said, and smiled.

"Good," Hans Jr. replied. He raised his knife high and with uncanny force slammed the blade deep into the wooden coffee table between them. "I was late for his rising once," he said. "That was almost two thousand years ago. I won't be late again."

Chapter 50

The Vatican

F ather Parenti had lain dead inside the Vatican's ancient basement morgue for two days before Bondurant was able to receive
permission from the pope to see him. Bondurant wanted to say
good-bye before the little priest was buried in the Vatican's small
cemetery set in a corner of a courtyard beneath the long shadows
of St. Peter's Basilica. The leafy graveyard surrounded by olive trees
was a place of honor reserved for very few, and the pope had specifically chosen one of the last remaining plots for Parenti to lie at
rest. The priest's grave would sit beside a modest wooden bench, a
place for contemplation often frequented by dignitaries who visited
the Vatican. Parenti would be remembered by many.

Chastened by the disaster two days earlier in St. Peter's Square,
the pope had isolated himself in prayer in his private chapel within
the papal apartments. After many hours of penance, as well as meet-
ings with the commander of the Pontifical Swiss Guard, the State
Polizia, and his advisers from the Congregation of the Doctrine

of Faith, plus a private audience with Bondurant and Domenika, Augustine had decided to release Christopher from Vatican hands. Upon reflection, it was only right, he said.

He knew he had no choice. One of his most trusted confidants, for reasons no one understood, had obviously gone mad and nearly taken the child's life. In the process, he'd stolen the life of another, one of the Vatican's own. The pope had turned De Santis over to the authorities. He sat in a Roman jail awaiting judgment for his crimes. The child's purported healing powers had proved, at least in the hands of the Church, to be nonexistent. And Bondurant and Domenika, who the pontiff knew had raised the boy as their own, were the only rightful parents.

Domenika was inconsolable over Parenti's death. She had no interest in joining Bondurant to see the little priest lying lifeless and so terribly alone. She remained at the hotel to pack the family's things for their journey, while Bondurant, with Christopher by the hand, made the forlorn trek through the Vatican's vast underground to bid farewell to their friend. They'd been provided a guide by the pope, a necessity given the arcane and twisting path of underground tunnels that wound their way to the isolated morgue. The mortuary had existed in the damp and lonely caverns beneath the city-state for centuries.

Bondurant found their attendant a fitting escort for the excursion. He was a decrepit soul with bulging eyes who crept ahead of them in the dank and narrow underground corridors, hunched over in pain. Bondurant was vexed by the mystery of where he had seen the man before. It wasn't until they passed briefly by a solitary bright light as they rounded a bend in the tunnels that Bondurant recognized him: Father Barsanti, the former prefect of the Vatican archives and longtime nemesis of Parenti. Christopher held his father's hand tightly along the way. Bondurant could tell it was fear of their guide as much as the dark that troubled the boy.

Finally, they came to a small, nondescript hallway lit by a single naked bulb. A heavy steel-gray door stood between them and their friend.

"Christopher," Bondurant said as he took a deep breath to lessen his own anxiety, "you can wait here if you want. You don't have to go in."

"I want to," the boy said. He pulled at the pouch slung over his shoulder and lifted the flap. Aldo's head peered from within. "We want to say good-bye."

The moment Christopher revealed the tiny pup, Barsanti reared back. Bondurant remembered the late-night pursuit Barsanti had given him and Parenti through the Vatican archives years ago. Aldo had bitten the priest as he chased them and sent him tumbling toward injury and disfigurement down a steep flight of marble stairs.

"He does not deserve this honor," Barsanti said as he turned away and twisted the key to unlock the door to the morgue. "Very few have rested here before, and most of them were popes or saints."

Aldo let out a slight growl from his pouch. Bondurant grabbed Barsanti by the collar with both hands and moved him to the side as the door swung open. "Mind yourself, old man," he said. "A martyr lies in here, and he'll have your respect—if not in life, then in death."

A pale yellow light hung from overhead, dimly exposing the small room, a space barely bigger than a closet. At the far end sat four large drawers encased in the wall. Above them rested a wooden crucifix. Chiseled into the granite above the cross were three simple words: *Sileo in Pacis*, "Rest in Peace."

"Which one is he in?" Bondurant said as he turned toward Barsanti.

"The lowest one, of course," the priest said.

Aldo gave out another sharp growl.

Bondurant pulled Christopher in close to him and leaned slightly over to grasp the handle of the wooden drawer. As he pulled on the drawer and the narrow table glided open before them, a slight whoosh of cold air blew forth from the dark cavity in the wall. Bondurant was familiar with the stale, sweet odor. He knew it as the smell of death. A simple gray linen shroud rested atop Parenti, covering his body from head to toe. Bondurant paused for a moment and pressed Christopher's face away from the sight before he pulled the fabric from the dead priest's face. But the boy, at eye level with the body, resisted the gesture and stared stubbornly straight ahead. Bondurant could feel Christopher squeeze his hand hard once again.

As Bondurant gently lifted the cloth from Parenti and drew it away from his body to his waist, he was relieved. The tiny priest's face, while gray as slate, looked completely at peace. Rather than resting flat on his back, the priest lay tilted slightly toward them as they stared down. Bondurant wondered why. He reached his arm over Parenti's body and searched behind him to determine why the priest leaned over to one side. As he moved his hand up and down Parenti's back to determine the cause, Bondurant was suddenly filled with rage. In one powerful pull, he removed a ten-inch-long knife from the center of the poor priest's back.

He held it in his outstretched hand for a moment and then stared at Barsanti. "What's the meaning of this?" he cried out. Bondurant yelled so loudly that his voice echoed off the walls. It forced Christopher to cover both his ears.

"I don't know where that came from," Barsanti murmured.

The sight of Parenti's blood on the knife made him gag. When Bondurant recovered, he was so angry that he had the idea of plunging the knife he held deep into Barsanti's chest. Instead, he tossed it to the floor, turned toward Parenti once more, and slowly pressed the poor priest's shoulders flat against the table to place him more comfortably at rest.

"Christopher," Bondurant said, "there is—"

"I know what you want," the boy said. Bondurant could see tears had begun to flow down his cheeks. "I don't know if I can."

"If you can what?" Bondurant asked. He was mystified at Christopher's words.

"Use my gift. To bring him back from the dead." The boy started to reach out to touch Parenti but then cautiously pulled his hand away.

Bondurant's heart sank. "That's not what I was going to say at all, Christopher. That's not what we're here for. Our dear friend is dead. We're here to say good-bye. It's not up to you to try to bring him back." Bondurant had never felt more heartbroken. He knelt and used his sleeve to wipe away the boy's tears.

"Sometimes it works. Sometimes it doesn't," Christopher said. "When my head hurts, it stops working. I'm sorry."

"Does your head hurt now?" Bondurant asked.

"Yes, very much," the boy said.

Bondurant watched as Christopher quickly reached out his hand again toward the dead priest. This time, he slowly stroked the side of Parenti's face. He then placed his hand on Parenti's forehead and then on his chest. Nothing happened.

"Then we're here to say good-bye," Bondurant said. He reached over and gently pulled Christopher's hand away from Parenti's lifeless body. He was saddened by the prospect of the boy's feeling so helpless, unable to save his best friend from the cruel finality of death when he'd been able to help so many others. Then Bondurant did something that surprised even himself. He clasped his son's hands together. "Would you like to say a prayer? One that Mommy taught you?"

"Yes," Christopher said.

But as soon as Bondurant removed his hands from his son's, he watched the boy's eyes suddenly grow wide. Christopher reached out his hand again, but this time shoved it into Parenti's vestment pockets, one after the other, as if in a frantic search. He reached his arm all the way down into the pocket of Parenti's pants and, breaking into a wide smile, proudly produced a small plastic bag.

"What's that?" Barsanti said.

"It's his!" Christopher exclaimed.

"This is the morgue. You're not to take anything from here." Barsanti stepped forward to approach the child and take the bag from him.

As Christopher fumbled for the contents in the bag, Bondurant elbowed Barsanti hard to keep him at bay. He instantly recognized the bag Parenti had long had and was certain he knew what was inside.

Christopher produced the ragged cloth, an ancient veil, and held it in front of his eyes for a moment. "He told me," he said as he looked up at Bondurant. "He told me it can heal."

As Christopher pressed the veil on Parenti's chest, directly above the spot that marked his torn heart, Aldo stuck his head out of the boy's satchel and began to bark. Then the dog leaped from the sack onto the table where Parenti lay. He began to lightly lick the side of the dead priest's face as though to wake him. Bondurant watched as Christopher closed his eyes and silently prayed. After a minute of quiet entreaty from all in the room but Barsanti, who wheezed with every breath, Parenti still lay cold and lifeless, perfectly at rest. Bondurant grew anxious as he watched his son begin to tear up again.

"Time's up," Barsanti called out, breaking the silence. "You've made your peace."

He grabbed Bondurant by the sleeve and motioned for him to collect the boy. The dog, recognizing a retreat when he saw one, had nuzzled his way beneath the shroud. He sat motionless on top of Parenti's chest, as he used to do when the tiny priest read books to him aloud. Christopher reached for the pup and motioned for Aldo to jump back into his traveling sack, but the dog would have none of it. Bondurant bit his lip to try to stop tears of his own. He had never seen a dog as faithful to his master and friend than the one that sat before them. Aldo's expression wasn't difficult for Bondurant to read. He was going nowhere. Bondurant knew the dog would rather lie with Parenti in the morgue and join the priest in the hereafter than leave his master so alone.

Bondurant was prepared to allow the dog his wish, but he could see that Christopher, who knew the dog's personality as well as Parenti, had no intention of losing a second friend as well. He reached over, snatched Aldo in his arms, shoved him into his satchel, closed its flap, and backed away from the table that held the priest.

In the commotion, Christopher's movements had caused the veil to slip from Parenti's chest and glide lightly to the floor. Barsanti bent slowly over to pick it up, yet the moment he touched the ancient cloth, the fabric spontaneously combusted in his hand. It ignited and consumed itself, momentarily lighting up the room in a brilliant blue hue. Barsanti shook his hand and howled from the swift burn he'd received.

The boy, visibly upset at the loss of Parenti's most prized possession, a gift to him, turned and kicked Barsanti hard on the shin. As he scowled, Barsanti pulled the shroud back over Parenti's face and unceremoniously shoved the table back into the wall. Then he limped toward the doorway and prepared to turn out the light. As he did, he signaled again that it was time to go.

Bondurant was the last to exit the room as the large steel door closed with finality behind them. When he turned to walk away, Bondurant paused. He thought his ears had fooled him, but he couldn't be sure. Just a split second before the door slammed shut, he thought he'd heard the faintest of sounds escape from inside the ancient morgue. As Barsanti sauntered forward ahead of them, Bondurant grabbed Christopher's hand. The boy looked up at him.

"Daddy, why—"

"Shhhh," Bondurant said. He held his forefinger to his lips and listened to the quiet around them more intently than he'd ever listened to silence before. Then his eyes shot open wide.

"Barsanti, the key," Bondurant said.

The priest turned around. "I said you've said your peace, sir," Barsanti said. "We'll be on our way."

"Open the door again, or you'll eat this," Bondurant said. He held in his hand the bloodstained knife that he'd pulled from Parenti's back just minutes before.

Barsanti limped back to the door of the morgue. As soon as he'd turned the key and opened the door a crack, Bondurant shoved it open with his shoulder and turned on the light. Christopher was only a half step behind.

Bondurant rushed over to the drawer that contained Parenti and held his breath. Then he tugged hard on the handle and quickly slid the table out once again. Parenti immediately bolted upright from the table and sat erect before them. He turned his head from side to side and looked about him wide-eyed, as though he'd suddenly awoken from a terrible dream.

"Whatever you do," Parenti cried out when he saw Bondurant and Christopher standing before him, "for God's sake, please don't leave me in here!"

Chapter 51

Rome

Domenika!" Bondurant shouted as he entered their hotel suite. Father Parenti and Christopher were right behind him. He hoped she'd gotten a good head start on packing their things so they could be on their way to the airport quickly. Bondurant was worried that once Barsanti relayed the story of Parenti's resurrection in the Vatican morgue, any deals involving Christopher's custody might be off. He could see that two of their suitcases had been packed and sat ready near the front door, but he knew there was more packing to be done when he spied several of Christopher's toys still strewn about the living-room floor.

"Mommy, we have a visitor for you!" Christopher cried out as he tugged at Parenti's hand.

"Domenika, where is Christopher's backpack?" Bondurant called out. She must have been in the shower, he thought, unable to hear him at all. Bondurant entered the master bedroom and glanced at two more of their suitcases on the bed. Both were empty. He turned to look in the bathroom but found the lights off with no one there.

"Domenika!" Bondurant yelled out.

He watched as Parenti entered the room with a worried look on his face. "There's no trace of her here," the priest said.

Other than the balcony, there was no place left to consider. Bondurant ran into the living room and hurriedly yanked open the drapes that had been drawn to block the morning light. Domenika wasn't there either. The realization that something might be terribly wrong hit Bondurant hard. His eyes began to dart about the room to find even the smallest clues.

"Look everywhere for something, anything, that might let us know," Bondurant said. He went back into the master suite and for the first time realized it had been ransacked. A lamp from the nightstand beside the bed was broken into several pieces. It was then that he found the note. He'd missed it before in his hurry, but it sat in plain sight on top of one of the suitcases on the bed. It wasn't just the contents of the note but the manner in which the writer had obviously been forced to pen it that turned Bondurant's stomach. Every painful word had been spelled out in blood, written by what appeared to be a bloody fingertip:

Meet 9:00 p.m.

Castle Bridge

Child, no police

or

she's dead.

"What time is it, Father?" Bondurant shouted out.

"Eight thirty-five," Parenti called back. He was already headed for the door.

Bondurant stuffed the note into his pocket and passed Parenti and Christopher as he leaped down five flights of stairs and back onto the street in search of a cab.

As soon as he'd hailed one, Bondurant jumped into the back of the taxi and reached for the door to pull it shut. Before he could grab the door handle, Parenti had wedged himself halfway into the cab.

"What do you think you're doing?" Bondurant cried out as Christopher scrambled to get into the car right behind the priest. He knew he hadn't a minute to lose.

"What do you think *you're* doing?" Parenti asked frantically. "You read the note. You need the boy." The little priest strained hard to keep the cab door open for himself and the child.

Bondurant paused and closed his eyes for a moment as if to summon every bit of his genius that he could. He didn't have a plan, and he knew it. And it was his fault. He'd never thought that Christopher would have to confront Meyer or his Watcher like this. He'd thought it might be years before the boy was asked to encounter such evil and perform a miracle powerful enough to bring the beast's life to an end. As Bondurant sat and focused on their predicament, Christopher jumped squarely into his lap and looked his father straight in the eye. The boy possessed an amazing sense of calm.

"I must go with you," the boy said. "There is a plan."

Bondurant sat stunned for a moment at the child's words, certain the boy had somehow read his mind.

"Christopher, I can't risk—"

"*Andiamo! Andiamo!*" the cab driver said, anxious to get his fare into motion.

"This is how it must be," Christopher said.

"You don't understand, Christopher," Bondurant said. "You need to stay here with Father Parenti. I'll be back—"

"I know the plans of my father, and *this is how it must be,*" Christopher said again, this time with so much conviction that Bondurant suddenly felt his words were more of a command than a request.

He found himself yanking Parenti the rest of the way into the cab. He pulled the taxi's door shut. The cab shot forward as Parenti called out their destination.

"Castel Sant'Angelo, *signore!*" the priest said.

Their destination was an ancient brick fortress just minutes from St. Peter's Square. Bondurant cursed himself as he pulled the note from his pocket and read it over and over. He shouldn't have left Domenika alone when they were within inches of escaping Rome with Christopher in hand. He wrapped his arm around the boy as their taxi sped across the Ponte Cavour toward the glow of Vatican City ahead.

After years of successfully evading Meyer, the clock had finally run out. He would gladly give his own life to spare Domenika's or Christopher's, but given Meyer's demands, perhaps now they were all in jeopardy. Christopher's words echoed over and over in Bondurant's mind: "There is a plan . . . This is how it must be . . . There is a plan." Bondurant would try to negotiate. He would offer whatever fortune he had left, every penny they owned. State any demand, and he would meet it. If either of his loved ones was harmed, he would have no reason to live.

As they rounded the corner of Via della Conciliazione and came to within a hundred meters of the dimly lit bridge, the cab came to a sudden stop. The driver would go no further. He said nothing, but the dread on his face as he pointed toward the scene down the road explained his halt. It was the moon that hung over the bridge, as large as any Bondurant had ever seen. But it had turned blood-red and cast a crimson light over everything it touched.

Once they'd been deposited by the cab in the center of the deserted street, all three of them stood at the edge of the ancient marble pedestrian passage known as the Bridge of St. Peter. It spanned the Tiber River, which now lashed about in waves so high that the froth they created had begun to form a blanket of foam on top of the bridge.

Bondurant lifted Christopher in his arms and held him close to his chest. Then he looked toward the bridge. Not a soul was on it. A clock on a tall tower behind them showed the time was 8:55.

"Father," Bondurant said as they warily approached the bridge, "this is where you leave. If there's any trouble, you know what to do. Call the police." He looked all around, certain Domenika's captors were eyeing them in wait from some shadow nearby.

"I know what to do, all right," Parenti said. "I'm going with you and Christopher onto that bridge."

"Father, I beg you—" Bondurant said.

"Beg all you want," Parenti said as he took over the lead and marched toward the marble span. "Besides, I've returned from the dead once before."

Bondurant could only shake his head.

As they made their way under the last of the lengthy shadows that lined the cobblestone street in front of the bridge, Bondurant slowed and looked around. The castle in the foreground, also aglow in the blood-red light of the night sky, towered above him. Bondurant could feel Christopher's tiny heart pounding away inside his chest. He was wary with every beat of his own heart that his next step might be his last. He listened carefully to detect the sound of footsteps but heard only the river sloshing noisily beneath the bridge ahead. He looked behind at the clock tower again. The hands showed exactly nine o'clock.

As he stepped onto the bridge, he turned toward Parenti beside him. He could hear the priest nervously mumbling away.

"What are you saying?" Bondurant whispered.

"I'm not saying, I'm praying," Parenti whispered. "You should try it sometime."

"Just whom do you pray to at a time like this?" Bondurant asked.

"We all have our favorites," the priest said. "Tonight it's Saint Peter and Saint Paul. It's their bridge. Or choose an angel, if you wish. See, they all rise before you! May they protect us as well."

Bondurant looked down the length of the span to the other end. There stood sentries on either side of the ornate bridge, a dozen exquisitely carved marble statues of winged angels in a line that flanked the two famed apostles. Bondurant peered into their faces, hoping they would inspire strength. He found none. He knew they might be walking into a trap, and his knees felt weak beneath him.

When they had nearly reached the center of the bridge, Bondurant saw several figures emerge from the darkness at the opposite end. He counted four, then five, then six as they began to make their way onto the bridge. One looked smaller than the others. Another appeared to be hooded and was being dragged blindly along beside them. *Domenika.* He breathed a sigh of relief; if it was her, she was still alive. Three large men dressed all in black brought up the rear.

As the group moved forward, it was clear to Bondurant that the men standing behind the smaller figure, the child, meant business.

They were heavily armed. Each held an Uzi-style machine gun at the ready, their barrels pointed menacingly straight ahead. When the group had come within twenty yards of Bondurant, the leader held up his hand and motioned for his entourage to stop.

"I am Hans Meyer," the man called out. "Nice to meet you after all this time, Dr. Bondurant."

Bondurant watched the man look nervously about him as if searching for protection Bondurant might have stationed nearby. The child, just a step behind Meyer, had his arms crossed. He ignored the world around him and stared only at Christopher. He seemed almost twice Christopher's size, and Bondurant could swear his eyes actually glowed a faint red.

"Domenika!" Bondurant called out, ignoring Meyer. "Is that you?"

"It's me, Jon!" Domenika shouted from under the black hood. "Jon, I'm so sorry. I—"

"Let's dispense with the apologies, shall we?" Meyer interrupted. He reached over and yanked the hood off Domenika's head. Bondurant could see from a distance that she was all right. Both of her hands were bandaged.

The moment Christopher heard his mother's voice, he turned his head and called out. "Mommy!" he shouted. He struggled to free himself from Bondurant and run toward his mother. Bondurant set Christopher down gently, turned him from the gaze of the Watcher, and placed the boy's hand in Parenti's.

"Christopher, I promise you will be with your mommy soon," Bondurant said. He knelt and stroked the boy's hair. He looked at Parenti and whispered, "I need my arms free. Whatever you do, don't let go of him."

Parenti nodded.

"I'll be quick about this," Meyer called out. "It's a trade. Ms. Jozef for the boy."

Domenika tried her best to swing her fist at Meyer, who stood just a few feet away. She missed by inches and was quickly restrained by one of the armed men behind her.

"Jon, you shouldn't have come!" Domenika cried out as she fought to set herself free from the man's grip. It was no use. "Take Christopher and run. Do it now, or I swear I'll kill you."

"I'm afraid you have it all wrong," Meyer said. "You send the boy over in exchange for Ms. Jozef, or *I* swear I'll kill *her!*"

"Mommy!" Christopher called out. Parenti had to restrain him hard.

Bondurant's heart raced. His entire body broke into a cold sweat. "What could you possibly want with our boy?" he called out. "You have a boy of your own."

"I do, if that's what you'd call him," Meyer said. "But I know where your boy's from. He's from the same place as mine. And I can't afford to have another one like him around. Not unless he's on my side." Bondurant watched as Meyer grabbed his child by the back of his collar as though holding a vicious dog on a leash.

"Take me," Bondurant said. "Christopher's just a harmless boy, you know that. There's no magic in him."

"Let me be the judge of that," Meyer said.

"I said, take me," Bondurant pleaded again. He had no doubt that Meyer had no intention of letting anyone live.

Bondurant began to walk forward to force the deal. If he could reach Domenika alive, no doubt he could sweep her over the side of the bridge and submerge her beneath the surface until the current carried them safely away. But that left Parenti and Christopher to make a dash of it on their own, something nearly impossible to do. Bondurant held his arms high in the air as if to surrender while he stepped even closer. As soon as he did, all three armed men raised their guns and pointed them straight at him. One lowered his weapon and fired off several rounds at Bondurant's feet to keep him at bay.

Meyer raised his hand to stop the gunfire. "Simple as this, Dr. Bondurant," he said as anger grew in his voice. "Hand over the child, or she takes a bullet in the head. I'll count to three."

"You can't be serious!" Parenti cried out.

"Dead serious. One," Meyer said. The man behind Domenika pulled a pistol from his jacket and held it to her head.

"Mommy!" Christopher shouted as he began to cry. He struggled to free himself from Parenti's grip.

"Two," Meyer said.

"Don't do this!" Bondurant called out, ready to charge forward to end his life with hers.

Before Meyer could get to "three," Christopher kicked Parenti hard in the shin, which caused the priest to fall backward in pain. As he did, the boy broke free from his grasp and charged toward his mother.

Bondurant leaped forward to grab Christopher, but at the sound of another gunshot, he stopped in his tracks. He looked toward Domenika and saw that she continued to struggle against the force of the gun still pressed to her head. Then a deep, searing pain burst from Bondurant's right side. When he looked down, he knew for sure he'd been shot. Warm blood trickled down his leg. Hobbled and in agonizing pain, he stumbled to the ground and watched helplessly as Christopher, just inches from his reach, dashed toward

Domenika. The only two loves of his life were now within Meyer's grasp.

"Stop, Christopher!" Bondurant shouted. It was all he could do. "Stop!"

Christopher ran the last few yards toward his mother, and Bondurant looked on helplessly as Meyer moved aside. When he did, the Watcher stepped directly into Christopher's path. He then hurriedly drew forth a knife. Bondurant tried desperately to get up to reach his son, but it was useless. He fell to the ground again and called out once more for Christopher to stop.

It was too late. In an instant, the Watcher child lunged toward Christopher and buried a knife deep into the center of the boy's tiny chest. Christopher collapsed to the ground at Domenika's feet. The Watcher stooped over, withdrew his bloody blade, and held it victoriously aloft like a sword. Then, his eyes aglow in red, he shouted triumphantly, "Your God has forsaken you!" He then let out a primeval scream.

Domenika, now hysterical, finally wrestled free from her captor and collapsed on top of Christopher to protect him from another blow. She called out to her son over and over, but he only lay motionless beneath her.

Bondurant knew it was his time to die. He rose painfully, this time using Parenti as a crutch. He paused for his last breath of life as he readied himself to pounce on the devil that still held his triumphal weapon high. But as Bondurant stumbled forward toward the evil force, ready to take another bullet, he watched a tiny spot of light appear on the forehead of the Watcher. Soon that beam of light became a red laserlike dot. It glowed bright as a fire and then fixed itself right between the eyes of the beast.

The Watcher child's head instantly exploded before him, followed immediately by the sound of a high-powered rifle. Before Bondurant could turn to find where the shot had come from, the torso of the beast remained standing for a split second and then dropped like a lifeless sack to the blood-splattered ground. A pool of blood began to surround the body of the Watcher. It grew into a giant puddle and spread across the bridge until the Watcher's entire body had seemingly melted away. Meanwhile, the red veil that had covered the moon was lifted to reveal a bright evening, crystal-clear as far as the eye could see. Meyer and all three of the armed men, obviously worried that they were next in line to die, turned and ran from the gruesome scene.

When Bondurant reached Domenika and the lifeless body of his boy, he collapsed to the ground beside them. It was only then that he could hear the whispers between the two.

Christopher, his eyes half shut, took Bondurant's hand. "Faith, hope, and love," Christopher said to them. Bondurant could already feel the boy's grip go limp. With his other hand, he reached for Domenika's hand and held it tight. "And the greatest of these?" Christopher said.

"Is love," Bondurant said with all the conviction he had inside him. "Love."

With those words, Bondurant and Domenika watched Christopher summon a last smile for them both and quietly pass away.

Bondurant, not knowing whether the hidden sniper was preparing to set his sights on any of them, looked about him for the origin of the deadly shot. With Parenti's help, he rose and stood. He stared out into the shadows. He searched for any sign of movement he might find. As Christopher lay dead on the ground behind him, Bondurant half hoped he might be next.

Chapter 52

Chesapeake Bay

Twilight approached. It was Bondurant's favorite time on the water, but he was ready to turn for home. Given that it was late summer, he knew the dark would descend quickly once the sun had fully set. It had been almost a year since Christopher's death, and their quiet respite on the bay was, like so many other days before it, an attempt to move on.

As he spun the wheel of his vintage pilot cutter hard to the left, the sleek wooden boat turned windward. It made its way past the picturesque Thomas Point lighthouse that guarded the mouth of the South River where it flowed into the bay. Domenika emerged from the cabin below with two glasses in her hands. One was filled with Scotch for Bondurant, the other with Parenti's beer. Bondurant smiled appreciatively as she handed him his drink.

"Home now?" she asked as she looked about them. The water around them took on an inviting glow as the last vestiges of sunlight played across the horizon ahead.

"Home," Bondurant said as he pointed toward shore.

Aldo lay beside Bondurant, sound asleep. Parenti sat ahead of them near the bow and dangled his feet over the side of the antique boat.

"Have you thought about it?" Domenika asked.

"A little," Bondurant replied. He'd received a letter the week before, and it now sat in the pocket of his jacket on the seat beside him. It was addressed to him from the pope.

Parenti, having seen his beer arrive, made his way to the stern to join them.

"Hasn't given you an answer yet either, I see," the priest said as he looked toward Domenika and reached for his drink.

"Still thinking," Bondurant said.

"I brought something along with me that might help you make up your mind," Parenti said.

Bondurant watched as the priest left them to duck below. He pulled Domenika toward the helm and placed her hand on the wheel. Then he put his hand on hers and leaned in close behind her.

They'd returned to Maryland's eastern shore. They'd started out together there years earlier, before there was Christopher and before they'd been on the run for so long. Bondurant liked the bay. It helped to recapture moments and a place in time with Domenika when life was simpler and safe.

With Meyer in jail in Switzerland for a long list of fraud-related crimes, they could breathe easier. Meyer might languish in prison for years. The Demanian Church was in a state of collapse worldwide. The promise of eternal life through cloning had never materialized for a single one of its converts, and once the miraculous healing events that involved the boy had ceased, so did the conversions and contributions. The church's stadiums had fast become the weed-infested monuments of a dying cult, converted to public soccer stadiums once they'd gone into neglect.

For his part, Bondurant had returned to the Enlightenment Institute he'd founded years before. He was anxious to occupy his mind with projects that would pass the time and help him overcome the immense sadness of losing his son.

He also knew that no matter how far his life's adventures took him in the future and no matter what fantastic tales might unfold, one of the greatest mysteries for him to consider would involve an exploration of faith from within.

For Parenti's part, Bondurant could tell the little priest had never been more content. Assigned by the pope himself, Parenti had become the pastor of St. James Catholic Church in nearby Crofton, Maryland. While he could be found there three times a week preaching the Lord's word or regaling his congregation with stories of his recent adventures, his heart was in exploration. He often made time to visit with the young graduate students Bondurant employed at the Enlightenment Institute. There he could trade tales and dream of discovery for hours on end.

When Parenti emerged from the cabin to rejoin Bondurant and Domenika, he had a small duffel bag in hand. He took a seat on the bench across from where Bondurant stood near the helm and reached for the papal letter he'd shoved into Bondurant's jacket to ensure that he would discuss the subject on their sail. Until now, Bondurant had done all he could to avoid it.

"It says here 'unfettered access to *all* church records'!" Parenti called out so as to be heard above the sound of the mainsail flapping noisily in the wind.

"So I've read," Bondurant said.

"You realize that's unprecedented," Parenti replied.

"I know."

"Where is the explorer I once knew?" Parenti said, obviously frustrated. "The pontiff himself promises all the Church's resources to find the Sudarium and seek proof it's genuine. That's all you can say? 'I know'?"

"It's a bone," Bondurant said. "He wants to make amends. A few years ago, I'd have given my right eye for this chance. Now I don't know."

The letter Parenti held was an extraordinary request from the pope for Bondurant to locate and return to the Church the famous Sudarium of Oviedo. It was the celebrated cloth mentioned in the Gospel of John said to have covered the face of Jesus Christ before he was wrapped in the Shroud and laid to rest in his tomb. Unbeknownst to the world, the bloodstained Sudarium had recently been stolen from the Church. It had sat for centuries inside the Arca Santa, the reliquary chest kept within the Cathedral of San Salvador in Oviedo, Spain, displayed only three times a year. The pope's visit to Oviedo to view the sacred artifact on Good Friday the previous Easter season had been secretly canceled when it was discovered the cloth had mysteriously vanished.

"Stolen or not, recoverable or not," Bondurant continued, "it's a fake. Others have claimed to possess versions of it over time. That's a telltale sign."

"I seem to recall you saying something similar about the Shroud," Domenika chimed in. She elbowed Bondurant lightly in his ribs.

"Well, as the pope has decreed, 'unfettered access,'" Parenti said. "Let the access begin." He yanked the drawstring of his duffel bag loose and pulled from within it a large book. He began to thumb through it quietly.

"What's that?" Bondurant asked.

"Nothing. You've seen it before," Parenti responded. "It held your interest at the time. But obviously you have no interest in it anymore."

Bondurant looked down at Parenti to see what he was missing. He instantly recognized the ancient cover. "Is that the same—"

"It is," Parenti said, and smiled. "The same book I took—I mean, I borrowed—from the Vatican's shelves the night you and I were chased from the library by Barsanti long ago."

The little priest now had Bondurant's full attention. Bondurant placed both of Domenika's hands on the boat's steering wheel. He pointed to a buoy off in the distance. "Steer us that way," he said. He took a seat next to Parenti, who now had his full attention.

"You'll recall," Parenti said, "that this book is a truth teller of sorts. It contains more than a thousand years of documentation by the Church on which of our venerated relics are real and which are not." Parenti reached down and grabbed Aldo so that he could see the ancient text. He too was now wide awake.

Bondurant leaned in close to examine the worn, yellowed pages.

"You see here, as I told you before," the priest continued, "this section contains the relics that have been proved false. There are too many to count." He then opened the book to a spot near the middle. "Now, these, my friend, are counted as real."

The stories of the magnificent artifacts, a veritable treasure trove of historical information, had never been made available to scholars, scientists, or the public over the centuries. Bondurant had a photographic memory and did his best to retain every word he saw as

Parenti flipped casually through the pages that documented some of the Church's best-kept secrets.

"Here, you see," Parenti said. "Veronica's Veil. Authentic, but, as we know, now sadly lost to the world."

"And here, look," Bondurant said. "The holy blood in Bruges!"

"Now, that was an adventure, was it not?" Parenti said with a smile. "Here we are!" he cried out as he pointed his finger at the center of a page. He read from the book beside the entry for the Sudarium.

"'While blood tests have yet to be conducted to compare the source found on the Sudarium with that of the Shroud of Turin, the likeness of the facial image and the stains captured on the cloth at Oviedo and those that appear on the Shroud are identical. Further tests to compare the two should prove conclusively that the cloth bears the facial image of Christ Jesus, one even more vivid than that found on the sacred Sindon.' There, you see?" Parenti said as he turned excitedly toward Bondurant. "We need only track down the thief of the Sudarium, retrieve the relic, authenticate it, and return it to the Church where it belongs. What could be more rewarding? What could be more fun?"

As they passed by the red buoy on their starboard side, Bondurant got up from his seat, leaned in toward Domenika, and pointed out the next buoy for her reference, closer to shore and another mile away. They were nearly home, and would barely beat the dark.

"It's tempting, Father, to be sure," Bondurant said.

And it was. But *fun*? There were other important adventures to be considered much closer to home—one in particular that Bondurant and Domenika had decided to pursue after Christopher was gone. Bondurant wrapped his arms around Domenika as she angled the boat toward the point, where nightfall lay around the next bend. He looked at his new "life watch," the one Domenika detested but that he still wore. It was generous. It gave him twenty more years, much more than it had granted before. Then he slid his hands toward Domenika's waist and gently pulled her in close to him. The slight bump protruding from her belly seemed to grow more pronounced by the day. He smiled. Soon another child would be born who was sure to change their world forever again.

Acknowledgments

First and foremost, my thanks to Beth Adams, my editor at Howard Books. I would say "words cannot express," but she has proven time and time again that they can. Praise to my agent, W. Scott Lamb, as well. He helped me earn my start. A tribute is owed to Dorothea Halliday too. She skillfully guided my very first words onto page after page in the early going.

I won't ever forget the encouragement of Carolyn Magner-Mason, whom I've known for many years and was so fortunate to rediscover as a wonderful writer and friend. I owe much to my pal Gary Sinise. He was at my side for the launch of my first novel and has been a motivational force ever since. I'm also grateful to my longtime friend Ted Waitt. We shared some wonderful adventures over the years, some that served as inspiration for my storytelling here.

There are good friends and colleagues whom I want to thank for their kindness, interest, and advice along the way. They include

Craig Engle, Craig Shirley, Fred Ryan, Mark Jaffe, Tom Kelso, Al Frink, John Barger, Norma Zimdahl, Sean McCabe, Margeaux Appel, Giovanni Navarria, and the indomitable James R. Wilkinson.

About halfway through the writing of this book, I was diagnosed with a rare form of cancer and given just six months to live. From the bottom of my heart, and the other vital organs that remain, I want to thank Linda Bond, Dr. Gary Dosik, Dr. Jaffer Ajani, Dr. Ken Hepps, and Dr. Jeffry Glaser for saving my life and, indeed, making this book and more possible in the years ahead.

When it comes to family, I spent some time away from mine while writing this book. I hope that my incredible wife, Marcella, my talented sons, Brock and Max, and my fearless, darling daughter, Jordana, know that all my efforts in life, including this book, are dedicated to them.

About the Author

In a career that has spanned philanthropy, politics, public service, and the Fortune 500, John Heubusch served as the first president of the Waitt Institute, a nonprofit research organization dedicated to historic discovery and scientific exploration.

In 2007, working with a team of scientists and underwater-exploration experts, he spearheaded the organization's first deep-sea expedition to solve one of the last great American mysteries: the disappearance of pilot Amelia Earhart during her famed attempt to circumnavigate the globe in 1937. Since then, successive efforts to locate Earhart and her airplane have failed, and the mystery remains.

In partnership with the National Geographic Society, John's efforts at the Institute also helped lead to the discovery, authentication, and preservation of the famed lost Gospel of Judas, the ancient text deemed heretical and ordered destroyed by the early Christian Church. The Gospel purports to document the last conversations between Judas Iscariot and Jesus Christ, as well as the true rationale for history's most famous betrayal.

His involvement at the Waitt Institute also helped lead to National Geographic's launching of the Genographic Project, the largest-ever effort of its kind to chart the migratory history of mankind using DNA donated by hundreds of thousands of people worldwide. The project is informing the world about our ancient migratory history.

Cited often by the *New York Times*, the *Washington Post*, and the *Los Angeles Times*, John has also been a contributing writer for the *New York Times*, the *Wall Street Journal, Investor's Business Daily, Forbes*, the *San Diego Union Tribune*, and other leading national publications.

Currently the executive director of the Ronald Reagan Presidential Foundation and Institute, he oversees the activities of the largest and most visited of the nation's presidential libraries. He resides with his wife and children in Los Angeles, California.